"YOU ARE JUST IN TIME!"

Yrilla went on, "There is a monster in the mountains. A shape-changer, skulking in the shadows. According to some, it is the size of a man, upright and covered with feathers. Others say it runs on all fours and has scales. It has killed our best hunter. He went after it."

"I can't help you," said Esperance. "I'm a housewife from south Minneapolis. I have no idea how to get rid of a monster."

"You have no idea who you are," said Yrilla. "Or what you are capable of."

Other Avon Books by
Eleanor Arnason

TO THE RESURRECTION STATION

DAUGHTER OF THE BEAR KING

ELEANOR ARNASON

AVON
PUBLISHERS OF BARD, CAMELOT, DISCUS AND FLARE BOOKS

DAUGHTER OF THE BEAR KING is an original publication of Avon Books. This work has never before appeared in book form. This work is a novel. Any similarity to actual persons or events is purely coincidental.

AVON BOOKS
A division of
The Hearst Corporation
105 Madison Avenue
New York, New York 10016

Copyright © 1987 by Eleanor Arnason
Published by arrangement with the author
Maps by P. C. Hodgell
Library of Congress Catalog Card Number: 87-91154
ISBN: 0-380-75109-7

First Avon Printing: August 1987

AVON TRADEMARK REG. U.S. PAT. OFF. AND IN OTHER COUNTRIES, MARCA REGISTRADA, HECHO EN U.S.A.

Printed in the U.S.A.

K–R 10 9 8 7 6 5 4 3 2 1

For
Susan,
Craig,
Zolia Jane
& Shoshona

TABLE OF CONTENTS

IN

WASTE · OF · ICE

BEAR PASS

NORTH FORK RIVER

GREY PROMONTORY

THE GREAT BAY

·YMHOLD

THE · GORE · OF · THE · YM

YM · RIVER

YM MOUTH

THE · PLAIN OF · SURR

THE · HOOK · OF · EIBE

←
TO · THE
BARRIER
MOUNTAINS

THE DRY PLAIN

·EMBLAR TOWN

BASHOO

AM · I · BASHOO

THE · GREAT · SALT
MARSHES · AT · THE
MOUTH · OF · THE
AM · I · BASHOO

PENDI

ISLAND
of IRON

THE · EASTERN · COAST · OF ·
THE · GREAT · CONTINENT · OF

GILLIM

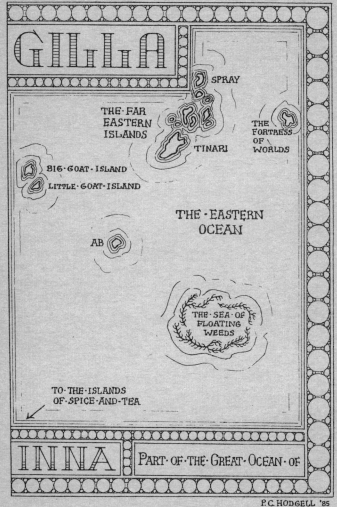

GILLA

SPRAY

THE FAR
EASTERN
ISLANDS

THE
FORTRESS
OF
WORLDS

TINARI

BIG·GOAT·ISLAND
LITTLE·GOAT·ISLAND

THE·EASTERN
OCEAN

AB

THE·SEA·OF
FLOATING
WEEDS

TO·THE·ISLANDS
OF·SPICE·AND·TEA

INNA · PART·OF·THE·GREAT·OCEAN·OF

P.C. HODGELL '85

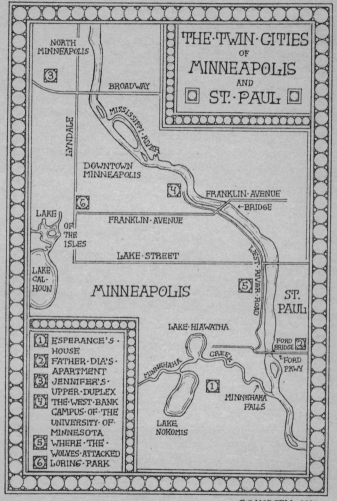

THE·TWIN·CITIES
OF
MINNEAPOLIS
AND
ST·PAUL

NORTH MINNEAPOLIS

[3]

BROADWAY

MISSISSIPPI·RIVER

LYNDALE

DOWNTOWN MINNEAPOLIS

[6]

[4]

FRANKLIN·AVENUE
←BRIDGE

LAKE OF THE ISLES

FRANKLIN·AVENUE

LAKE·STREET

LAKE CAL-HOUN

MINNEAPOLIS

WEST·RIVER·ROAD

[5]

ST. PAUL

LAKE·HIAWATHA

FORD BRIDGE [2]
↑ FORD PKWY

MINNEHAHA CREEK

[1]

MINNEHAHA FALLS

LAKE NOKOMIS

1. ESPERANCE'S· HOUSE
2. FATHER·DIA'S· APARTMENT
3. JENNIFER'S· UPPER·DUPLEX
4. THE·WEST·BANK CAMPUS·OF·THE UNIVERSITY·OF· MINNESOTA
5. WHERE·THE· WOLVES·ATTACKED
6. LORING·PARK

P.C.HODGELL·1986

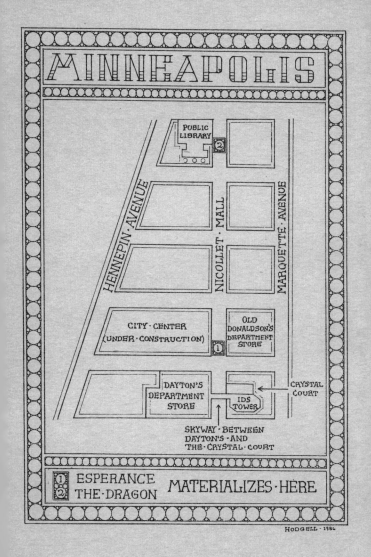

MINNEAPOLIS

PUBLIC LIBRARY

HENNEPIN·AVENUE

NICOLLET·MALL

MARQUETTE·AVENUE

CITY·CENTER
(UNDER·CONSTRUCTION)

OLD
DONALDSON'S
DEPARTMENT
STORE

DAYTON'S
DEPARTMENT
STORE

IDS
TOWER

CRYSTAL
COURT

SKYWAY·BETWEEN
DAYTON'S·AND
THE·CRYSTAL·COURT

ESPERANCE
THE·DRAGON   MATERIALIZES·HERE

HODGELL · 1986

The sailor on the ocean,
The archer with a bow,
The potter at the turning wheel—
What do they know?

Respect for the water,
Respect for the wind,
Respect for the lump of clay,
Respect for mind and hand.

PART ONE:
THE BEAR CHILD

All her life she had been troubled by dreams: the same dreams, repeating over and over. There was the gray land, flat and empty. Fog hid the distances. She heard—or thought she heard—the roar of the ocean, a faint dull sound. It was not near. Something else was. What, she did not know. A presence in the fog. She was afraid to move. A movement might bring her closer to the thing. She waited, her heart pounding, fear in her throat and mouth like a bad taste. Nothing happened. The presence did not appear. She woke.

Another dream was of a city, high in the mountains, built of black stone. Water ran through channels in the streets. There were fountains in the squares. Water shot up and was blown to one side by the cold mountain wind. On the fronts of the houses were faces, carved out of black stone. The sad faces dripped water from their eyes, and the merry faces pursed their lips and spat out water: thin jets that glittered in the sunlight.

A woman greeted her, tall and gracious, wearing a crown of silver, enameled black. The crown was set with moonstones and diamonds. The woman took it off and held it out.

Me? asked our heroine. For me?

1

For you, answered the queen, oh daughter of my spirit.

There were other dreams: the forest at night, the dance of ghosts, the shipwreck, the burning dirigible. She had names for all of them, descriptions written down and the explanations of a good therapist.

In the real world—the world of sunlight and waking and ordinary obligation—she married at twenty, bore two children, and raised them in a house in south Minneapolis.

By the time she was forty, the children were gone. One was at school in the East on a scholarship. The other washed dishes in a restaurant in Santa Fe and sent home postcards about Georgia O'Keefe, Indian art, and photography.

Her husband—a tall grave professor of English—busied himself with the novels of George Eliot and local party politics. She loved him and respected him, but she had never cared for George Eliot (the other woman in his life, he liked to say). The internal struggles of the Democratic Farmer Labor Party seemed less interesting with every year that passed.

So there she was at forty, a bit plump but in good condition. (She walked a lot and worked out at the YWCA.) Her hair was half gray. Her face had a few wrinkles; and if she looked closely, she could detect imperfections in her complexion: spots, broken blood vessels, all the subtle horrors of early middle age.

Who am I? she thought, staring into the bathroom mirror. What am I? Is that maturity I see and strength of character? Or merely an old bat with no idea of what to do next?

She began to read catalogs: classes at the Y, classes at the U, seeds for the garden, new clothes, new furniture, digital watches and computer clock-radios. Nothing seemed worth doing or buying. Maybe she ought to return to therapy. There were, after all, signs that she was going around the bend. Her dreams had gotten worse, more frequent and more vivid. Now, when she woke, she could taste the salt of the ocean that washed along the edge of the gray land. Or she could hear the water running through the city of black stone. The words of the queen echoed in her mind, as she stared at the ceiling of her bedroom.

Daughter, daughter, why have you waited this long? We need you. We have needed you for twenty years.

Balderdash, she told herself. Garbage. Gibberish. The wish-fulfillment fantasy of a fat old lady.

Then, one Monday morning, the washing machine made a funny noise and stopped working. She fiddled with all the dials, not noticing that water had crept out from under the machine and surrounded her feet. She was standing in a pool of water.

Maybe there was something wrong with the cord or the plug. She reached for the plug. She touched it.

Zap!

She was standing naked on a beach of gray stone. On one side of her was the ocean: white waves rushing in, curling over and crashing on the shingle. On the other side was fog.

She shivered. (Her name, by the way, was Esperance. It was the one touch of imagination her parents had ever shown.)

"About time," a voice said—a harsh male voice.

She turned. Out of the fog came a man, tall, with silver hair. He wore a black robe embroidered with moons.

"What?" she cried.

"I am an old man with rheumatism, and I have waited here for twenty years. Time and time again, I saw you—but only as a phantasm or illusion. I called out. You did not hear me. I tried to weave a binding spell. But who can bind the creatures who dwell in dreams? Always, you eluded me. I remained, though every year the pain in my bones was more severe. You were our only hope. The others—" He spread his hands wide. "Lost, utterly lost.

"And you"—he glared—"wasted your time looking at the Burpee Seed Catalog. Who do you think you are, anyway?"

"Esperance Olson," she replied.

"Wrong. You are the bear child, the hope of the mountain." He beckoned. "Come with me."

She followed, too confused to argue. He led her into the fog. After a minute or two or three, they came to a hut built of stone, conical, with a low door and no windows. They went in. There wasn't much room. She had to keep her head bent to avoid hitting the ceiling. She looked around. The hut was bare, save for a fire burning in the middle of the floor. The air was full of smoke. Her eyes watered. The man crouched down, groaning softly. He opened a bag. Why hadn't she seen it before?

"Here." He pulled out clothes. "Get dressed."

Was this another dream? A new one? It had to be. The clothes were unfamiliar, but they fit perfectly, as if made for her. She put on the underwear: knickers and a shirt, made of a soft white

fabric. Was it silk? Then a tunic of fine wool, as black as mid-
night. The pants were leather, thin and supple and as black as the
tunic. She must look absurd. She was far too hippy for clothes
like these. Why hadn't she gone on a diet, as she had planned?

She pulled on the boots: high and handsome, made of stiff
black leather. The heels were inlaid with silver, and the tops were
trimmed with white fur. Last of all, she put on the belt. It was
linked silver, with a big silver buckle in the shape of a bear. The
eye of the bear was a moonstone.

She fastened the buckle. The man stood up. His bag was gone,
she noticed. "Who are you?" she asked.

"Gerringarr the Wise." He smiled briefly. "Or maybe I ought
to say, Gerringarr the Rheumatic. I am chief wizard to the queen
of the mountain."

"And who did you say I am?"

"That is a story I will save for the queen. We have to hurry.
Much has been lost in the years when you dallied in—What is the
name of that place?"

"Minnesota."

"What a name! Absurd! Unreal!" He led her outside.

Two animals stood in front of the hut, saddled and bridled.
They were shaped like deer, the ordinary deer of northern Minnesota. But they were much larger, and they were white. Their
heads bore—each one—a pair of long straight horns, pale yellow, the color of ivory. They had black eyes and black noses.
Their breath came out in clouds.

It was cold, she realized for the first time. Really cold.

The animals turned their heads. They looked at her, and then
they bent their necks, bowing gravely.

"They recognize you," the wizard said. "Mount up."

She had ridden a lot as a teenager and even some as an adult,
going on trips with her children up into the western mountains
and down into the Grand Canyon. But she had never ridden anything like this. As soon as she was in the saddle, she felt the
animal's power. The great muscles tightened; the wide back quiv-
ered. The creature snorted, impatient to go.

The wizard mounted. The animals sprang forward. What
speed! What smoothness! It was like riding a rushing stream. (She
had done that too. Her daughter was into white water canoeing.)

The land flowed past here, gray and featureless. The fog grew
thick. She couldn't see at all. The fog grew thin. She looked to

one side. The ocean was there, white with foam. There was no sign of life: no vegetation on the rocky ground, no gulls on the wind, not even a dead fish or a piece of seaweed washed up on the beach. What kind of place was this? They traveled on and on. The animals seemed tireless.

All at once, the fog was gone. The sky above was blue. Sunlight made her blink. Startled, she reined her animal.

The wizard did the same. "What is it?" he cried.

Esperance looked back. There it was: the fog, a gray wall that stretched across the land and out over the ocean.

"Oh." She took a second look at the water. It was smooth and blue, rolling gently and showing not a single trace of white. "What is that?" She pointed at the fog.

"The Gray Promontory. The fog never lifts, the ocean is always wild, the air is always cold. Animals avoid the place, though it isn't usually dangerous. Not to them. Human folk fear it and quite rightly. It is a Place of Power."

"A what?"

The wizard frowned. "You have so much to learn, and we have so little time.

"Very well! There are many ways to view the world. One is as follows: A pattern exists, a pattern of power. It underlies our everyday reality. It is the skeleton that gives our world its shape. In most places, this pattern—this skeleton of power—is well below the surface. Only a wizard or a sorceress can perceive it and reach down to it."

He frowned again. "Maybe skeleton is the wrong metaphor. Maybe the power is like an underground river—like a network of rivers, all underground. The world we see draws nourishment from them. A wizard can dig down and tap the source." He rubbed his forehead. "I'm still not saying the right thing. I can feel what the power is like. But the words do not come.

"In any case, in a few places the power is close to the surface. Even ordinary people can feel it, like a bone under the skin or like an artery pulsing. There"—he pointed to the fog—"on the Gray Promontory, the power is right at the surface. I knew it would draw you, for you are a creature of power. Now let's get going."

It was late morning when they left the promontory. They rode all day, over dunes covered with yellow grass and then through a forest of scrub pine. At twilight, they made camp.

Esperance unsaddled the animals. "What are they?" she asked, stroking a pale neck.

"Ushaia. Don't bother to tie them. They are magical. They will return in the morning."

She let them go. They vanished into the forest like ghosts. The wizard built a fire, then opened his bag. Where had that come from? she wondered. It hadn't been with him on the ride. He pulled out bread, still warm from the oven, and a jug of hot soup. Beef vegetable, she decided after taking a sip. They ate and drank. She was too tired to ask any questions. He groaned from time to time—his rheumatism. Esperance lay down and slept.

She dreamt of her children: Jennifer, the photographer, and Mark—dark, thin, and intense, who worried about the environment. The dream was ordinary, so ordinary that it didn't seem to be a dream. She was walking with her children by the ocean. The day was hot and bright. They took off their shoes and splashed in the shallows. They gathered shells. They talked.

When she woke, Esperance was crying. She wiped her eyes, then sat up. It was morning. The sky was cloudless. At the edge of the forest, the ushaia waited, gleaming like snow in the shadows.

They ate breakfast: croissants with butter and jam and a jug of café au lait. Esperance saddled the animals. They mounted and rode west, away from the rising sun, away from the ocean.

All that day they traveled through the forest. Their speed was incredible. No horse could move as quickly as the ushaia, especially on trails such as these: narrow winding tracks for deer and foxes, not human folk. Once they crossed a road.

"Why don't we take that?" asked Esperance.

"I prefer to be secret."

They camped by a stream. Esperance dreamed of her husband —at home, in his easy chair, reading *Middlemarch*. Or was it a biography of Hubert H. Humphrey? Once again, she woke with tears in her eyes. It was still dark. A full moon hung above the trees. An owl hooted. What am I doing here? she asked. She had no answer. After a while, she went back to sleep.

The next day, they followed a trail that wound up among boulders and outcroppings of rock. Trees grew everywhere, ancient and twisted, leaning at odd angles. There were lichens on the boulders. Mosses grew around the roots of the trees. What amazing colors! The lichens, most of them, were royal blue. The mosses were dark brown or burgundy red.

They camped in a hollow near the crest of a hill. At sunrise, the wizard woke her. "Come quickly. I will show you what we are up against."

She followed him to the top of the hill.

"There." He pointed to the next hill over.

A dirigible floated above the trees. It was huge and gray, lit by the rising sun. And it was surrounded by black dots that swooped and darted. What were they? They reminded her of bees around a hive.

"Dragons," said the wizard. "They aren't big. Three feet long at the most, with a wingspread of six feet. But they breathe fire, and the gas in the airship is explosive."

"Hydrogen," said Esperance.

"We call it phlogiston."

A dragon swooped in toward the airship, stopped in midair, then plummeted.

"Ah!" said the wizard. "The archers got that one. All the ships have carried them, since the dragons appeared."

"Are they new?"

"Yes." The wizard frowned. "Something is wrong with the web of power. Something—some*one* is twisting it and changing the shape of the world. Not in good ways. Oh no!"

Another dragon swooped in. It reached the ship and clung to the side: a black dot, just barely visible. There was a roar—an amazing noise. The vast bag of hydrogen ripped apart. The dirigible listed, ablaze—it seemed to Esperance—from one end to the other. It was sinking. Tiny figures dropped from it: crew members jumping.

"They are too far up," the wizard said. "The fall will kill them."

There was another explosion. Bits of the ship fell burning into the forest.

"We'd better get out of here," the wizard said. "That may start a forest fire."

They ran back to camp, saddled, and mounted. Their animals, aware of the danger, sprang into motion as soon as they were astride. Up they went, into the mountains.

Around noon, they descended into a valley full of trees. There

was a river in the bottom of the valley. The water was swift and
clear. A road went along the river: narrow and stony, a caravan
trail.

"We will have to take it," the wizard said. "It leads to Bear
Pass. There is no other way through."

As they followed the road, the valley grew narrow, the trees
disappeared. Looking up, Esperance saw bare cliffs, rising and
rising. Hawks sailed on the high wind. A streak of white went
down one huge gray slab of stone. Snow? No. It was a waterfall.
The air, thin and clear, absolutely clear, acted like a tonic. For the
first time in years, she felt really alive. Too bad this was only a
dream. Or maybe an elaborate hallucination. The madness of a
housewife.

Evening came suddenly. Light faded off the cliffs. They
camped in a shallow cave. There was no vegetation anywhere
nearby. The wizard pulled wood out of his bag. They made a fire
and ate hot sausages wrapped in bread. Delicious, thought Esperance. The sausages reminded her of hot dogs. She had always
liked junk food.

When they were done eating, the wizard got out a knife and a
bowl made of silver. There was a liquid in the bowl, as clear as
water, but thicker. It moved sluggishly.

"What is that?" asked Esperance.

"The blood of the earth. You can draw it out of the well at
Kol, if you are brave enough." He held his arm above the bowl
and cut the skin. Blood dripped down: human blood, thin and red.
When it touched the liquid in the bowl, smoke rose.

"What are you doing?"

"We are in the country of the bear king. You are his daughter,
but you may not be safe. I confess, I do not understand him. He is
ancient and terrible and very strange." The wizard touched the cut
on his arm. It stopped bleeding. He tilted the bowl. The two
liquids intermingled. "There. Now I will take a silver pen and
draw a circle around us, a circle of blood. He will respect that, I
hope."

He drew his circle. The camp fire burned low. Esperance went
to sleep. She dreamed that she woke in the middle of the night.
She sat up. All around the camp, a fire burned. It rose from the
bare ground, from stone. The flames wre pink, the color of the
two liquids after they combined. Beyond the fire two eyes shone

deep red. She tried to shout a warning. No sound came out of her mouth.

Two more eyes appeared, dimmer than the first pair, less fiercely red. Now she saw the bodies, huge and shaggy. Two enormous bears. They shuffled along the line of fire. One of them batted at the flames. She saw the glint of claws. The other bear sat up on his haunches and moaned. A human sound. Esperance was terrified. No, she thought. I want no part of this. I want to be back in south Minneapolis.

The bigger bear, the one who had taken a swipe at the flames, stopped and turned his head. He stared at her. Laughter filled her mind. The sound was harsh and growling, not at all human. But she recognized the mirth.

Then the bears were gone. The fire died down.

She woke, lying on her back, shaking, staring at a roof of gray stone.

"He came," the wizard said. "I can feel his presence in the air and hear the echo of his laughter."

"There were two of them," said Esperance. She sat up and looked at the wizard. He was rebuilding the fire: the little fire, made of ordinary wood.

"Ah." He glanced up. "That was his son, your half brother. Arden Everett. In your world, he is a miner of coal. At night, he dreams that he is a bear, roaming in the mountains. We see him, of course. The great ghost bear. One of my colleagues has hunted him for years, calling him, trying to get him to come into this world entirely, as you have come. Hopeless. He thinks"—the wizard waved at the gray cliffs and the high peaks, already in sunlight—"he thinks this is only a dream."

Three days later, they arrived at the city of black stone. It went up a mountain side, like Lhasa in Tibet: terrace after terrace, wall after wall. Bright pennants flew from the towers. White birds fluttered over the houses.

"Messenger doves," the wizard said. "This is a city of merchants and wizards, curious people, always eager for news."

They entered through a gate of stone and rode up a wide street. Everything was the way she had seen it in her dreams. A stream of clear water ran down the street, and faces on the house-fronts wept or spat out water.

At the top of the city was the palace: black stone and white stone and gates of silver. The gates were open. Guards bowed to them: tall women dressed in black and silver, who carried spears.

In the courtyard, they dismounted. Servants took their animals. Like the guards, the servants were tall and handsome and courteous. Unlike the guards, they were men.

The door to the palace was white jade, bound with silver. What opulence. thought Esperance. She had never understood where she had gotten her imagination. The things that she dreamed up were constantly surprising her.

They walked to the door of white jade and silver. The wizard raised a hand. For a moment, nothing happened. Then the door swung open. A woman came out.

Who was she? Not the queen. Short and plump, her face the color of ebony—she was nothing like the queen. She wore her hair in a multitude of braids, decorated with beads of gold and silver. Her robe was yellow. Her belt was gold.

"Welcome," she cried. "You must be weary."

"I am," said the wizard. "I can barely walk. But this one"—he waved at Esperance—"shows no sign of fatigue."

"I don't tire easily," said Esperance. "And exercise has never bothered me. It must be my heritage. I come from a long line of Norwegian farmers. Good strong peasant stock."

"You come from the bear," said the woman. "And that is one of his signs. Strength and endurance. You, Gerringarr, go take a hot bath and put on a clean robe. Something made of wool. Wool against the skin is good for rheumatism."

He laughed briefly, then nodded.

"And you, bear child," the woman said, "come with me."

They left the wizard there. Esperance followed the woman through dim corridors. The floors were marble: black and white and gray. The walls were covered with tapestries: the Hunt of the Unicorn, the Hunt of the Bear, the Signs of the Zodiac, the Seasons of the Year. The colors were dark and rich.

"I am Yrilla, the High Speaker. The Tongue of the Queen, I am called."

"Oh yes?" said Esperance.

"She has a stutter, you know. Most of the time, it's barely noticeable. But when she is tired or uneasy—and speaking in public always makes her uneasy—then it comes back."

"But you have magic, don't you? Can't the wizard do something? Weave a spell or brew a potion and cure the stuttering?"

Yrilla stopped and looked at her. "You have so much to learn! Her stutter is one of the prices. She has wisdom, yet can barely utter it. Gerringarr has power. The mountains themselves will stir and shift, when he commands it. But in the winter, when it is cold and damp, he can't get out of bed without assistance." Yrilla paused for a moment. "And as for me, I have quickness of wit, eloquence, and insight. But I never dream. For everything there is a price."

They continued through the hallways, then up a winding stair. Up and up and up, into a room with walls of crystal. The room was full of sunlight. Esperance stopped and blinked. A white floor. A roof of silver. A view of the city and the mountains, the high peaks streaked with snow.

A woman stood looking out. She turned.

Was this the lady of her dreams? The woman was tall and had an air of dignity, a certain gravity, a certain grace. But she was thin, her face was worn. There were streaks of gray in her long, straight black hair.

The crown was the same one that Esperance remembered. It was in place, atop the salt-and-pepper hair. The diamonds glittered. The moonstones glowed.

The woman held out her hands. "W-w-wel- . . ."

"The queen bids you welcome," said Yrilla. "Beloved daughter of her spirit! Hope of the mountain!"

The queen gestured.

Yrilla said, "Why don't you sit down?"

Esperance looked around. There were three chairs, made of silver and ivory. She took the smallest one. The other two women sat down. Servants brought wine. Esperance took a sip. Was it Chablis? She couldn't tell. It was light and dry and a bit too harsh. A young wine, not yet mature.

"You are just in time," said Yrilla. "There is a monster in the mountains."

"The bear king?" asked Esperance.

The queen shook her head.

"No, no," said Yrilla. "The bear king is a manifestation of the old power, the real power that rises out of the bones of the earth. We respect him and avoid him. He causes us very little trouble.

"This monster I speak of is something new, and it is in no way as impressive as the king of the bears. It skulks in the shadows. It eats sheep, and it terrifies farmers. According to some people, it is the size of a man, upright and covered with feathers. Other people say it runs on all fours and has scales or a patchy unhealthy-looking coat of fur."

The queen leaned forward. "Sha-sha-sha- . . ."

"It is a shape changer," Yrilla said. "It has killed one man that we know of. Our best hunter. He went after it."

"I can't help you," said Esperance. "I'm a housewife from south Minneapolis. I have no idea of how to get rid of a monster."

The queen frowned.

"You have no idea of who you are," Yrilla said. "Or what you are capable of."

"All right. Tell me."

The queen shook her head.

"Not today. Tomorrow, after you have rested. It is a long story. It goes back fifty years."

A servant came and led her out of the tower, down to a bedroom on one of the lower levels. The windows overlooked a garden, brown and dry. It was autumn here, as it had been in Minneapolis. Esperance felt a mild surprise. The servant kindled a fire in the fireplace.

"There are clothes in the wardrobe," he said. "And that door leads to the bathroom." He pointed. "I will bring your dinner here. The queen believes you ought to have a quiet evening and time to accustom yourself to your new role in life. It is never easy to become a hero." He bowed and left.

Esperance went into the bathroom. The plumbing, she was relieved to discover, was completely modern. She took a shower to get rid of her dirt, then washed out the tub and filled it with hot water. A long soaking bath would relax her. Maybe she would fall asleep in the tub—she had done that before—and wake up in Minneapolis.

There was a bottle of bath oil on the edge of the tub. Thick soft towels lay folded on the toilet. On the back of the door was a robe of dark red velvet. Simple pleasures, domestic pleasures were always the best. She tested the water in the tub.

An hour later, she got out and dried herself. She put on the robe and went into the bedroom. Dinner waited on a table: spaghetti with clam sauce, a salad, warm bread; for dessert a cannoli, followed by espresso coffee and a glass of brandy.

As she sipped the brandy and looked at the fire, she realized this wasn't a dream. The meal had been too specific, too concrete, and too ordinary. She made better clam sauce and the brandy tasted as if it came from California. She much preferred French brandy. Surely—if this were a dream—she would have given herself Courvoisier or Remy Martin. And she knew with absolute certainty that she would never have imagined a flush toilet in a magical castle. Though of course she was happy to find it there.

What exactly had happened? She had been in her basement, fooling around with the washing machine. She had touched the plug. She must have gotten a shock. And the shock had transported her into a world where magic worked, where she was a hero or—more correctly—a heroine. She took another sip of brandy. She wasn't going to wake up and hear Walter snoring beside her. The children were gone, maybe forever. Strange, to think of no more postcards from Jennifer, telling her about the light in the desert and the colors of New Mexico. Mark never wrote, but he called. Most of the time, the calls were short and cryptic. He was fine, his grades were okay. He was going on a demonstration at a power station. His parents were not to worry, he would call if he got arrested.

All at once, her eyes were full of tears. She blinked them away, then refilled her glass with brandy.

The next day at noon she was taken to the queen. This time, they met in a room of black marble. There were tall windows along one wall. They opened onto a terrace of gray stone. On the terrace were pine trees in pots. Some of the trees were twisted like bonsai. Others were trimmed into cones and spheres. Beyond the terrace was the city—going down, level after level, like a flight of black stairs. Beyond the city were the mountains and the sky.

The queen sat on a throne. On one side of her was Yrilla. On the other side was Gerringarr.

"F-forgive me," the queen said. "Y-yesterday I was overcome with emotion. Today I can speak." She gazed at Esperance. "There is more fat on you than I thought there would be. Well, that is the way of the bear. He eats when he can. He knows winter will come. G-Gerringarr?"

He raised a hand. A chair appeared in front of the throne.

"Sit down," the queen said.

Esperance obeyed.

The queen glanced at Yrilla. "You begin."

The short woman nodded. "About fifty years ago, we noticed a change in this world of ours, subtle but definite. There was a deterioration in those qualities that make life worth living; and—at the same time—an increase in aggravations. Cockroaches became more difficult to kill. Men who went—as common men will do—to taverns to enjoy themselves by having a few quiet beers, began to argue and then to fight. As you might expect, this took all the pleasure out of going to taverns.

"What else did we notice? Our craft people lost some of their skill. Our poets became too elaborate. Our merchants, always known for their honesty, began to cheat their customers.

"All these changes were small at first. We noticed them and worried, but we did not suspect that a human mind was at work. Rather, we thought they were some kind of natural fluctuation. The moral equivalent of a bad winter or a locust plague."

Gerringarr spoke, his voice deep and harsh. "Then my old master came to the city, leaving his home by the well at Kol. The well is a Place of Power. A wise man can learn much in such a place. He told us, 'Beware. The pattern is changing. I can feel it shift and twist. And I can sense a mind that moves among the currents and eddies of power. That mind, cold and strong, is doing all this.'

"'Who is it?' we asked.

"He answered, 'I do not know. The mind, for all its power, is curiously flat and empty of personality.'

"He left to return to Kol. He never got there. The dirigible he rode in was attacked by dragons."

The queen leaned forward. Her face was flushed, and she looked angry. "These were not the great dragons out of legend, the first children of the earth. They—the original dragons—were enormous. They shone like jewels. They were as wise as sages. When they fought a hero or one another, it was like a ballet.

"No! The great wizard of Kol was done in by dingy little flying lizards with no wit at all, only malice. They spit out their gobs of fire and blew him to—I don't know where."

Yrilla smiled. "Well said."

The queen looked surprised. "Th-thank you."

Gerringarr continued. "We—the wizards of the city—began to search for the cause of our troubles. But my old master was right. The mind in the pattern was ungraspable. We could sense the changes, the distortions and perversions of the pattern. And we could sense an odd attenuation of reality: the world was becoming dimmer and grayer and shabbier."

Esperance looked around. "But this is splendid."

"It is less than it was," said the queen.

Gerringarr nodded. "We could sense, as well, a presence in the pattern: cold and flat and empty. But who it was, where it was—" He shook his head. "That was beyond us.

"In the meantime, the dragons increased in number and made air travel very difficult. Monsters appeared. Like the dragons, they were second-rate: creatures that looked like chickens or snails or a combination of the two. We sent out heroes to kill them. Usually, the heroes won the fight and came back with the head of the monster, which turned into slush after a day or two. Now and then, a monster killed a hero."

"There were so many monsters," the queen said. "And we had never had more than a few heroes."

Yrilla said, "We began to run out of heroes. We decided to breed more."

"Now," Gerringarr said, "the story turns to the king of the bears. As you know, his home is three days east of here, on the great mountain above Bear Pass. In ordinary times, only fools go up there. He has a number of tricks which he plays on people who enter his domain.

"But when the pattern began to change, we began to watch him. Would he be affected? Could the mind in the pattern reach him?"

The queen smiled. "He lost none of his power. He remained as awful as ever. And the farmers in the valley below his mountain were not troubled by monsters."

Gerringarr nodded. "When the dirigibles reach Bear Pass, the captains know they are safe for a while. No dragon will fly near his mountain."

Yrilla said, "We decided to use one of the bear king's tricks to our advantage. There is a warning which every mother gives her daughter. 'Don't go up on the bear king's mountain.' For if a girl does go, and if it is the right time of the month, she will become pregnant. The father is the bear king. The child is human in most ways, except that it has sharper teeth than most people do, and it has claws."

Esperance glanced at her hands. Her nails looked ordinary, but they were not. They were strong and thick and almost impossible to cut. They never broke. If she didn't trim them, they grew long and narrow and sharp. She glanced at Yrilla.

"You have the teeth too," Yrilla said. "The pointed canines, the sharp incisors, the molars that will crush anything."

"And not a single cavity," said Esperance, more in fear than pride.

"The bear children are not born in the usual way. You see"— Yrilla leaned forward—"they develop their teeth and claws while they are still in the womb."

Oh-oh, thought Esperance.

"When labor begins, when the mother's womb contracts, then the child panics. It begins to claw and bite. If nothing is done, it will tear its mother apart."

The queen shuddered. "I s-saw that once. A woman who went into labor unexpectedly, alone. We found her dead, her belly torn open, and the child alive—covered with blood—crawling away from its m-m-m—"

"Murdered mother," Yrilla said.

"Therefore," said Gerringarr, "our midwives have an ancient custom. If they know—or suspect—that a woman carries a child of the bear, they abort the creature."

"I killed my mother?" asked Esperance. She looked at her hands. She ran her tongue over her teeth. There was no question about it. Her canines were unusually long and pointed. Her boyfriend in high school had made jokes about Dracula and drinking blood. What an idiot! Why had she ever gone out with him?

"We thought we had a solution," said Yrilla gently. "We would deliver the children by caesarean section. It was not entirely safe, of course. But our wizards had magic. Our surgeons had skill.

"And we knew the old legends. Bear children were not evil. They were powerful and wise, though always a little strange. They would make good heroes. And maybe they, helped by their father, could find a way to defeat the mind in the pattern."

"I asked for volunteers," the queen said. "Twelve young women came forward. Six were from my own guard, and one was my cousin, Yfara. She was the captain of the guard: strong, proud, willful, and lovely." The queen closed her eyes for a moment. She was remembering, thought Esperance. She opened her eyes, which were pale gray, and made a gesture, waving away the past. "They went into the country of the bear king, up onto his mountain and camped for a month. When they returned, all were pregnant. Eleven were safely delivered as planned. The children were freed before they could do any harm.

"But Yfara grew restless. This was months before her time. She could not endure the confinement. She took a horse and rode out of the city." The queen frowned. "She did not go into the farmland below the city in the wide valley of the river Ym. Farmers might have come upon her, after she fell, and sent for us. She might have lived. And she did not go into the high meadows, where the shepherds are. She had to enter the forest.

"Something must have frightened her horse—what, we do not know. We found the place where her horse began to run. And then we found her. She had been thrown. The fall had induced labor. By the time we reached Yfara, the child had been born. She—my cousin—was dead." The queen paused. Her face was white, and her gray eyes were unfocused. She was looking at something not present in the room. "The child was so early and yet so strong!"

"Whose child am I?" asked Esperance.

"Yfara's." The queen looked at her steadily. "Heroes are often born with portents, out of horror and terrible pain."

"I am not a hero!" shouted Esperance.

"There is one more thing to tell," said Yrilla. "How you ended up in south Minneapolis."

Gerringarr said, "As soon as the children were born, our troubles increased. The palace swarmed with rats, all trying to get into the nursery. And dragons flapped outside the nursery windows, breathing fire against the panes. We found a monster in the cellar of the palace: a huge black slimy thing. It broke every bottle of wine and then began to ooze upstairs, moving toward the children.

"The mind in the pattern knew what we were doing. The children were not safe."

The queen rested an elbow on the high arm of her throne. She put her head in her hand. The wizard looked at her anxiously.

"She is tired," Yrilla said. "This story wears on her."

"To be brief, then. As you must have realized by now, there is more than one world."

Esperance nodded. "Earth and here."

"And many more. All derive from the pattern of power." Gerringarr rubbed his nose and frowned. "How to explain? Maybe I can use a geometric analogy. Relationships differ. Each world exists at a different distance from the pattern and at a different angle. Thus the variety of kinds of reality. For a thousand years, we have investigated the other worlds. And long ago, we found a world so far from the pattern and at such an oblique angle, that magic does not work there."

"Earth," said Esperance.

Gerringarr nodded. "The mind in the pattern could not reach there. The children would be safe. When the children were grown, we would call them back." He smiled. "Alas for our well-made plans. We had underestimated the power of the children. Even there, in a world without magic, they were able to draw on the same ancient sources of strength their father knew. But, growing up on Earth, they did not believe in occult powers. They used their strength to reinforce the reality they knew. They built a gray wall around themselves: a wall of magic which magic could not pierce. And they called that wall *reality, practicality, the world of ordinary people.*

"We called for twenty years. The children hear us, but only in their dreams." The wizard laughed without pleasure. "One digs coal in West Virginia. One drives a tractor in the Ukraine. One is a writer in Senegal, and one is a guerrilla in El Salvador. The others—I forget what they do. But they all dream strange dreams; and waking up, each one forgets his or her true heritage."

"You are the only one who has answered the call," said Yrilla. "We don't know why."

"My washing machine. It gave me a shock, and that sent me here."

"Electricity," said the wizard, musing. "We have not investigated the magical effects of electricity." He glanced at her, smiling. "Maybe we can find a way to shock some of your siblings out of their false reality."

"Enough," said the queen. She rose. "Think of what we have told you, Esperance. We will meet again at dinner, and you will meet the rest of my court. The mayor of the city. The illustrious First Artisan. My cousin Ana, who is the head of the Royal Council of Witches, Midwives, and Hags." The queen smiled. "The council is ancient and has an ancient name. Nowadays, most practitioners p-prefer to be c-called—"

"Wizardess or sorceress," put in Yrilla. "Or obstetrician,

though that is a very modern term. And not easy to pronounce. It isn't only the queen who stumbles over that one."

The queen glanced at her, raising her eyebrows.

Yrilla went on. "And you will meet our last hero, the great warrior, Umon Hu."

"All right," said Esperance. She stood up and bowed to the queen, feeling a bit self-conscious.

The three left. Esperance was alone. She found a door out onto the terrace. She walked all afternoon, up and down the stairs that led from one terrace to another. Gray clouds moved above her. The wind was cold, and she could smell snow. Fortunately, her clothes were warm.

She ended up at the top of the palace, on a wide windy roof. There was nothing there except chimneys. A red light shone on top of the tallest stack; and a few leaves skittered—windblown—over the stone.

Crazy, thought Esperance. The story was crazy. She was the only child of Hank and Inga Johnson of Minneapolis. She had a birth certificate at home in the desk in the second-floor study, the one she never studied in, though she had promised herself she was going back to school.

She paced around the chimneys. It was beginning to get dark. She remembered her father's story: how the hospital lost her, when she was only a week old.

"We were all ready to leave," her father had said. "And they couldn't find you. 'Damn it,' I said. "I came in with a fat wife, and now she's thin. Either you give me back Inga the way she was, or I want something extra. I want a kid.' Well, I got kinda noisy, and they took to running around. And in the end, they brought you. And I think I got the best of the bargain. I never had liked the way Inga looked when she was fat. And I've gotten kinda fond of you."

Changeling? Was she a changeling? She turned the corner of a chimney.

Something stood in front of her in the shadows. Esperance paused. "Yes?"

The figure seemed to blur, to grow vague for a moment. Then it was solid. "Esperance?"

It was Walter's voice.

"You? Here?"

"Esperance, we've been trying to get through to you for days. Your mother and I and Dr. Ferris."

Her therapist. A good man, though a bit literal-minded.

"But how did you get here?" She waved around at the chimneys and the dark cloudy sky.

"You are in a ward at the University Hospital. I did not find it especially difficult to get in. Esperance"—he spoke calmly and gently—"you have had a breakdown. According to Dr. Ferris, you are in a fugue state. You are fleeing from reality." Walter took a step toward her, holding out his hands.

"No!" cried Esperance. She stepped backward.

Walter kept coming. "Esperance, my dear, you cannot stay this way. You have to confront—"

She tried to push him away. His suit felt like feathers; and his mouth—coming down toward her—was full of long sharp teeth.

She clawed at his face and left four lines. Walter howled. She pulled away and ran. Damn it! Why hadn't she let her nails grow? She could have taken out an eye.

She reached the stairs that led off the roof. He was right behind her. She spun around. He had a muzzle now, and his hair had become feathers that stuck out in all directions, like a crazy breed of chicken she had seen at the State Fair. She kneed him in the groin. He bent double, and she kneed him in the face.

He fell. She started down the stairs. Lights came on, dim lanterns that gleamed all along the stairway. At the first landing, she glanced back. A thing bounded toward her, four-legged and spotty with a huge open maw.

Now she was terrified. She began to growl. The thing reached her, and she slapped it away with a single paw. The thing tumbled down the stairs and hit the next landing. It lay there for a moment. Then its body flowed. It rose up. It was a girl. Her daughter, Jennifer.

"Mother," she cried.

Esperance went down on all fours. She stared at the girl, growling.

"Mother! No! It's me!"

Esperance lumbered down the stairs. Her claws made clicking noises on the stone treads. She kept growling.

The girl turned and ran. Down and down. Esperance followed. She was having trouble with the stairs. Jennifer was getting away.

She paused on a landing and went up on her hind legs. A moment or two later, her old body was back. She was naked now. Her clothes must have torn when she changed into a bear. She ran after Jennifer.

There were no more landings. The stairs went down—endlessly, it seemed—along the face of a cliff. On one side of her was rough stone, lit by lanterns. On the other side was a balustrade, ornately carved. Beyond the balustrade was darkness and cold and, way below, the lights of the city. Where was the palace? Who cared? She was gaining. The girl was getting tired. She stumbled once and almost fell, but recovered. Esperance gained some more.

Down they went. The stairway ended at a wall: part of the palace, emerging—apparently—from the cliff. There was a door. The girl tugged at it. It did not open. She turned and flowed and became Mark.

Esperance reached him. He was crying, shaking with fear.

"Mother, I love you. We all love you."

"No." The word was a rumble, deep in her chest. "It will not work."

Mark stretched up and up. He was eight feet tall and covered with fur. He reached down and grabbed Esperance, flinging her over the balustrade.

She caught at the carved stone and hung there for a moment, looking down. There was a terrace below her. Lanterns gleamed among the branches of trees.

She glanced up. The Mark thing was above her, bending and reaching. His hands had claws. She let go. She dropped, changing in midair, becoming heavy and furry. She crashed through a tree, then hit the pavement. Stunned, she lay motionless.

Up, she thought. She had to get up. She lifted her head. The air stank of monster. A creature with wings flapped down among the trees.

She pushed herself up on her front paws. Walter—he landed. His body was covered with feathers, and his feet were claws. He looked at her through his favorite reading glasses: horn-rimmed bifocals.

She was up on all fours. Her entire body hurt, and she felt confused, uncertain. "Walter?" she growled.

His wings became arms. He held out a hand. "You have got to

accept treatment, Esperance. We can't help you, if you keep fighting like this."

She went up on her hind legs. "Walter, I'm so tired."

His face became gentle. His hair, she noticed, was still feathery. "I know you are. Relax."

"Please help me."

"I will."

She went to him. He folded her in his arms. Her bear mouth bit deep in his throat. There was a choked scream. She tore. Blood poured out over her. Walter collapsed.

Esperance dropped onto her front paws. She stood on all fours, looking at the body. It was bleeding and flowing, dissolving into blood. She snuffled at the edge of the dark pool, then touched the liquid with a paw. She licked the paw. The liquid burned. She sneezed and panted. The burning sensation went away. Too bad, she thought. She had been hoping the monster was edible.

A voice spoke in her mind. It was deep and harsh, inhuman: *You have done well, my daughter.*

The bear king. She lifted her head and sniffed the wind. It smelled of pine forests and coming snow.

Come to me, the voice said. *Learn who you are.*

She looked at the pool of blood. It was seeping in between the stones of the terrace, vanishing. She ached. She was tired. She needed time to think. She sniffed again. The wind had changed. Now she smelled the city: wood smoke and garbage and human beings. She didn't mind the garbage, but the human beings disgusted her.

She shuffled to the edge of the terrace. Below the balustrade, a slope went down, covered with bushes without leaves. A trail went through the bushes. Maybe it led to the mountains. She climbed onto the balustrade. It was narrow. She teetered for a moment, then jumped and hit and rolled. Down the slope she went, through bushes, frightening the birds that had roosted for the night. They flew up, cheeping. She came to a stop, then climbed to her feet and shook herself. The trail? Where was it? Ah! There it was. She sniffed the ground. People had passed along it and a fox. That was hopeful. She followed the scent of the fox.

By dawn of the next day, she was well out of the city, at the edge of the forest. She paused for a moment and looked back. Being nearsighted, she saw nothing much: a misty slope, a dim gray sky.

"Wurf," she said. She continued along the trail: a huge sow bear, shambling toward home.

PART TWO:
A SAILOR IN
THE MOUNTAINS

Her partner said, "Enough is enough. I'm an old man. My bones hurt. I'm tired of bad weather and cargoes that just barely make a profit. I'm going to quit."

She argued with him, to no avail. He was the senior partner: by custom and law, he got the final say. Their ship was sold at auction. At thirty-eight, Ayra was prosperous and unemployed.

She got drunk with her partner one final time. They ended up in bed together, something that had happened only twice before. It was never wise to mix business and pleasure.

In the morning, her partner got up. He groaned and rubbed his face. Then he began to dress. He was right, she thought as she looked at him. He *was* getting old. His hair was still black, but his beard was as gray as iron. And the hair on his chest—a thick curly mat—was almost white. He had scars all over him and a truly impressive gut. He fastened his pants. The gut hung over his belt.

"You ought to drink less beer," said Ayra.

"No." He shook his head. "You don't understand. I am going home. I plan to buy a house. Then I will look for a wife. I know what I want: a decent comfortable woman who knows how to cook. In time, with her help, I will be the fattest man on Little Goat Island."

"What an ambition!"

"To each his own." He sat down and pulled on his boots, grunting each time he had to bend over. Then he stood and reached for his jacket. "I have given you a gift, though you didn't want it. Freedom, while you are still young enough to put it to some use." He looked at her, frowning with bushy brows. "Think about what you are doing! Don't sign on with the first merchant bound out to Emblar or the Far Eastern Islands."

He put on his new jacket, covered with embroidery and lined with the fur of the great hairy serpent of the ocean. He bent and kissed her. His breath stank of alcohol. "Consider! Do you want to end up like me? A rheumatic old salt, with nothing ahead of him except eating and drinking and telling lies about 'the good old days when I was a-sailing on the *Golden Porpentine.*'" His voice rose and wavered. He sounded twenty years older.

"But you expect to enjoy all that."

"Aye, and so I will, matey. But I am not you." He fastened the jacket. "Good-bye. Good luck. If you ever land on Little Goat Island, ask for the fat man. You'll have a place to stay."

The door slammed behind him. Ayra lay back, her hands clasped behind her head. What did she want to do?

Travel, she decided an hour or two later—and not on the ocean.

She took passage on a sailing barge, going up the Ym River. For two weeks, she watched the plain of Surr go by. Then the land rose into hills covered with forest. The river ran faster. The captain of the barge hired a team of horses: enormous animals with furry feet. They pulled the barge upriver, plodding along a trail on the bank.

Now, for the first time, Ayra saw locks and dams, high cliffs and mountains. She got a strange feeling in her gut: a twisting. Her back was tense. There was a sour taste in her mouth. Why? What was going on? Was she coming down with a new kind of influenza?

After several days, she realized the sensation was longing. The mountains called to her. She had to visit them.

The barge reached the last port on the river. She bought a horse and supplies, a crossbow and a map.

The man who made the map explained it to her. "It's an easy trip," he said in conclusion. "Except for one thing."

"Yes?"

"Bear Pass." He tapped the paper. "Make camp before you reach the pass and cross over in the day."

"Why?"

"The pass is at the edge of the country of the bear king. He does not like intruders. If you are in the pass at night—" The mapper paused.

"Yes? What will happen?"

"He has tricks. A lot of them. Most famous is the one he plays on women who are young enough to have children."

Ayra looked at the mapper. His face grew red. She waited. At last, he said, "He makes them pregnant. Not the usual way, through intercourse. But through magic." He paused again. "The children are terrible. They are born with claws."

Ayra grinned. "Well, I am safe. He can't do anything like that to me."

"Why not? Do you have magic of your own? An amulet or a spell?"

"No. I had a tumor years ago, when I was barely a woman. I had to have an operation. I will never have any children, whether ordinary or magical."

"Nonetheless, be careful," the mapper said.

The road led north and west. It wound through hills. On the high slopes were pine trees, huge and dark. Farther down were other lesser trees: birches and aspens, beginning to turn yellow. It was early fall by now. The weather was cool and bright. Birds sang. Butterflies fluttered over flowers at the edge of the road. Ahead of her a mountain rose, dim and blue, just barely visible. The peak was white. It floated in the sky like a cloud.

Ayra felt happy. This was the right thing to do. But why? she wondered. She had lived her whole life by the sea. Why did the mountains call to her?

Her mother, of course, had come from a village in the valley of the Ym, high up, where the river was nothing more than a creek, shallow and narrow and full of rapids. Was there something in her heritage that made her respond to these great heaps of stone, rising into the sky?

That evening, she camped by the trail. She woke toward dawn. The fire was ashes. The air was cold and still. Her horse nickered and stamped a foot. Ayra sat up. Something moved in the underbrush. She reached for her bow.

There was another rustle. She waited, her bow in her hands. Silence. The thing was gone. She rebuilt the fire. At sunrise, she went on. She was a little stiff, and the saddle was a little less comfortable than it had been the day before. Nothing serious. Her trip was going well.

The trail went between cliffs, high and bare except for lichens. The lichens were orange and yellow. The sky was blue: a deep pure color. A river ran next to her. The water tumbled over rocks, then glided through pools. There ought to be fish, thought Ayra. Too bad she had no equipment. And no experience. All her fishing had been done with lines trailed off moving boats. Ocean fishing. This would be different. She didn't even know what lived in those pools. Not cod or haddock, redfin or spiny hrul.

Late in the morning, she began to feel pain. Her back ached from right above her hips to between her shoulder blades. And it seemed as if the skin on the insides of her thighs had gotten rubbed off. This was impossible. She could not go on. She stopped and made camp in a shallow cave. There was no wood and only a little grass. She tethered the horse where it could eat. Then she got out her lunch: bread and a sharp red cheese. She ate and did exercises. After that, she walked along the river. There were fish all right. Minnows darted in the shallows, and a dim shape moved at the bottom of a deep green pool. The shape was as long as her arm. Oh well, she thought. Maybe it wasn't edible. The next time she went on a trip, she would know to bring a line.

Toward evening, Ayra went back to the cave. She ate more cheese. The sun went behind a mountain. The canyon grew dim. No wood, she thought. That meant no fire. An unpleasant idea. Fortunately, she was well below Bear Pass. She checked the map. Satisfied, she unrolled her bedding. She lay down and watched the light fade off the cliffs on the far side of the river. When the light was completely gone, Ayra went to sleep.

She woke to a scream, scrambled upright, and heard hoofbeats. Her animal! It must have broken free! She grabbed her crossbow and ran out of the cave.

The moon was up. It hung above the cliffs, almost full and

very bright. Her horse was gone. On the bank of the river was a bear.

Enormous! Did they really get that big? She checked the bow. It was loaded. She could feel the bolt, and the bowstring was cranked tight.

The bear looked at her, then growled. Ayra waited. The bear shambled toward her. Why? Weren't they supposed to be timid, like all wild things? She remembered her bag of supplies. Maybe it could smell the food. Did bears like sharp red cheese? She had one bolt in her bow. The bear was huge. Maybe she ought to let it have whatever it wanted. She moved away from the entrance to the cave, keeping her bow ready and her eyes on the bear.

The bear shambled past her, giving her a glance and a growl. Ayra kept still. The bear disappeared. Now she could hear it in the cave, scuffling and growling. It re-emerged. It had the strap between her saddlebags in its mouth. It was dragging the bags, jerking them and growling.

She knew what the noise meant. The animal was having trouble getting into the bags. And it was getting angry. Everyone knew that bears had short tempers. She took a step back.

The animal let go of the bags. It swung its head up and glared at her. Her heart was going twice as fast as usual. She felt sweat in her armpits and on the palms of her hands. The growling became a roar. She lifted the bow and settled the butt in the hollow of her shoulder. Careful, she told herself. Don't shake. Don't fire too soon.

The bear charged. She pulled the trigger and heard the whine of the bowstring. The bolt was gone. Where to? The bear was still coming. That was it. She was dead. The bear stumbled. Ayra turned and ran.

Sometime later, a distance down the road, she tripped and fell headlong. She lay in the dust, gasping for breath. Her lungs burned, and her heart beat like a drum: *thum-thum* in her chest.

She rolled over. The moon was above her. She listened and heard only the river and her heart. No bear.

She sat up, still breathing heavily. The crossbow was gone. She had a big tear in her pants, and one knee was badly scraped. There were cuts on the palms of her hands. She got onto her feet. The road was empty. What next? She wiped her nose, then went to the river and washed off her injuries. After that, she drank water. It was cold and fresh. She sat down on a rock and waited for dawn.

The sky turned gray and then blue. The sun rose from behind a mountain. Ayra limped back toward the cave.

She found her crossbow lying in the road and picked it up. She limped on.

Her saddlebags were where she had last seen them, lying in front of the cave. The bear was gone. It had left a trail of blood, leading west along the road.

She thought for a while, then went through the saddlebags, taking out everything that wasn't essential. She would have to leave her bedroll and the saddle. She had no idea where the horse had gone, maybe all the way back to its stable in the little river town. In any case, the animal was not available to her. She would have to travel light.

There! She was done. Money. Food. A good knife. The map. Her bow and a dozen bolts. What else did a woman need? The next question was, where would she go? East to the Ym Valley or west, along the track of the wounded bear? She looked at the sun. She had plenty of time. She would be through the pass by evening, and there was a farm marked on the map. *Hargastead*, the writing said. *The farmer is a friend to travelers*. As for the bear, in all likelihood it would leave the road. It was a wild animal, after all. It would feel safer in the forest or up on the cliffs.

She hoisted the bags onto her shoulder and picked up her bow. She began to walk—going west, toward the pass.

Hour after hour went by. Her knee swelled up, and she had trouble bending it. Her back ached. The strap on the saddlebags cut into her shoulder. Now and then, she saw splotches of blood on the dusty stony road. The bear, still ahead of her.

A little past noon, she saw a shape ahead in the road. Not the bear. It was too small and pale. She limped onward.

It was a woman: naked, on her back. She looked to be forty or so. Her body was heavy and sleek. Her skin was fair. Her tangled hair was black. She had a crossbow bolt in her shoulder.

"Now, what is the meaning of this?" said Ayra. She dropped her bag.

The woman's arms lay along her sides. They looked relaxed, as if she were only resting. Her hands were broad with thick fingers. Powerful hands, not lovely. Her nails were long and narrow and curved. The nails had sharp points.

"You are a bear."

The woman opened her eyes. The irises were yellow. "Help me," she whispered.

"What can I do? I can barely walk. I can't carry you."

The woman frowned. "Cut out your arrow. Bind up the wound."

Ayra did as she was told. The woman cried as she did the cutting. The bolt head was deep, and there was a lot of blood. It got on Ayra's jacket and on her torn pants. She pulled out her one spare shirt: the blue one with the silver embroidery. She had not been able to throw it away, back at the cave. Now she tore it into pieces and used it to bind the wound. "There," she told the woman. "That's the best I can do."

"I will recover," the woman said. "I heal well. But I have to get to shelter."

"And I have to get through the pass before nightfall."

The woman smiled. "You think you can?" She closed her eyes for a moment, frowning. Evidently she was in pain. "Anyway"— she opened her eyes again—"what are you afraid of? I will protect you. My father will do you no harm."

Ayra looked around. They were in a canyon. Steep cliffs rose on either side. There was little vegetation: brush willow along the river, dry grass by the road, and a grove of silverleaf—four little trees with slender trunks and lacy white foliage. "There." She helped the woman get up. Together, they staggered into the grove. Ayra eased the woman down. "I'll get water."

"Yes," the woman said.

She had a jug. She filled it in the river. The woman drank.

"Who are you?" Ayra asked. "Why did you attack me?"

"The cheese. I could smell it. I haven't had cheese since I left the city of black stone."

Ymhold, the great fortress, home of the sorceress queen. Ayra knew it by reputation.

"It was a year ago," the woman said. "The aspens had already lost their leaves. He called me out of the city."

"Who?"

"My father. The bear king. I went to his cave, high in the mountains. I slept all winter— That isn't right." The woman frowned again, trying to concentrate. "I woke from time to time. But I was always sluggish. There was no way I could think. I didn't want to. Only sleep and dream." She paused for a moment. "I can't remember any of the dreams. Food, maybe. Fish and berries. And those big fat grubs that you find in rotting logs."

"Oh," said Ayra.

The woman smiled faintly. "Anyway, spring came, and I woke entirely. But I had forgotten that I was human."

Ayra said nothing.

The woman shivered. "I'm cold. I wonder if I can change back into a bear. No. I won't try." She touched the bandage. "I would tear this off."

Ayra took off her jacket and laid it over the woman. It wasn't long enough. The woman's legs—thick and muscular and hairy —were uncovered. "You don't know if you can change?"

"No," the woman said. "I've done it only once. There was a monster in the city—"

"Within the walls? In spite of all the magic? And the famous guard of warrior women?"

"Yes."

"I knew these were bad times—though not for me, especially. But things must be worse than I had imagined."

"In any case," the woman said, "the monster attacked me. I became a bear in self-defense. And I remained a bear until you shot me. You frightened me, you know. The arrow hurt. I was bleeding. I ran until I wasn't able to run any longer. And then I kept moving, as best I could, away from you. And then I fell down. And when I woke, I was a woman. I'm not sure that I could do it—change my shape—just by wanting to. I may need terror and pain."

"Well, don't try now," said Ayra. "I don't want a bear on my hands." The woman was still shivering. "I'll build a fire."

Ayra gathered wood along the river. The willows had a lot of dead branches. She built a fire and lit it. "What next?" she asked, once the flames were shooting up and warmth was spreading out, filling the little clearing in the middle of the grove. "I ought to get help. But I can't leave you. And where would I find it? Help, I mean."

"Wait till dark," the woman said. "I think I'll be able to reach my father or my brother."

"Is your brother another bear?"

"Don't worry." The woman smiled. "Arden can't hurt you. He is an illusion. Visible and audible. You can even smell him. But if you tried to touch him, you would feel only air. His spirit roams the mountains with me and my father. His body remains in another world. A place called Earth. I am from there."

"Ah," said Ayra.

"Do you know about the other worlds?"

"Yes, of course. I used to be a sailor. I have been to the Fortress of Worlds."

The woman frowned. "The what?"

"You don't know about it?"

"No. I was here—in this world—only a few days, before the monster attacked. I haven't learned much of anything, except how to be a bear."

Ayra put another branch on the fire. "It is a castle on an island way out in the ocean, three days beyond the Far Eastern Islands. Magic built it, and magic guards it. The water around it is full of dolphins and whales. They guard the fortress, too. Wizards live there and devote their lives to exploring other worlds.

"As you may or may not know, nothing inanimate can move —or be moved—from one world to another. But the wizards bring ideas from the other worlds. Ideas have a kind of life. And they bring plants and animals. Anything interesting or useful goes to Ymmouth and then overland to Ymhold in the mountains. It used to go by airship, but since the dragons appeared, air travel has been dangerous."

The woman frowned again. "I remember. You have dirigibles, and they are full of hydrogen."

"Phlogiston," said Ayra.

"It's the same difference," the woman said.

Ayra continued. "The dragons are small. They wouldn't be dangerous, except they breathe fire."

"And hydrogen burns."

Ayra nodded.

"Why don't you use helium?"

"What?" asked Ayra.

"It's another gas. One that doesn't burn."

"I've never heard of it."

The woman frowned. "Maybe you don't have it on this world. I wonder if it could be made?"

"I have no idea," Ayra said. She scratched her nose. "What was I talking about?"

"The Fortress of Worlds."

"Oh yes. Nowadays, everything that leaves the fortress travels by sea. I have carried animals you wouldn't believe, mewling and chittering and moaning in my hold. And some pretty strange kinds of vegetation. Plants that move of their own volition. Green leapers, for example. They were hard to keep track of. But we managed. We lost only one. It went overboard and got eaten, before we could rescue it. A lot of sailors won't go to the fortress. It's too far out, and the cargoes make them nervous. But the money was always good." Ayra looked at the woman. Her eyes were closed, and her face was pale. "That's enough talking. You rest."

"All right," the woman said.

Evening came. Light faded out of the canyon and then out of the sky. Ayra put wood onto the fire, until the fire roared and snapped. Sparks floated up—almost as high as the white foliage. She was frightened, she realized. Green leapers might not bother her. Ghost bears did.

Something growled. She looked up. There he was: black and shaggy, standing on four feet at the edge of the firelight. He was as big as his sister had been, maybe bigger. His head had a high dome. His eyes were yellow.

"Arden," the woman said.

Ayra glanced around. The woman was sitting up, holding the jacket in place over her front.

The bear groaned. He was coming closer, shuffling into the firelight. There were highlights in his fur. It wasn't pure black. It had a reddish purple sheen. A band of white fur went across his chest and shoulders: a half-collar or a crescent with the two horns pointing up. He groaned a second time. The noise had a rising inflection. Was he asking a question?

"Go to our father. Tell him I need help. I've been wounded, and I'm too weak to travel on my own."

The bear growled some more, then he turned and lumbered into the darkness.

The woman lay down.

"Do you want anything to eat?" Ayra asked. "I have bread and dried fruit and a little bit of that cheese you wanted to try so badly."

"No. I'm thirsty. I think I have a fever."

Ayra brought her water. She was right. She did have a fever. Her face was flushed, and her forehead was hot. "I hope the bear comes back soon," Ayra told her. "We have to get you to a farm. And find a witch or hag. Someone who knows medicine."

"He can travel quickly," the woman replied.

The bear returned a little before dawn. He sat down on his haunches. His shoulders were hunched. He looked unhappy. He growled and moaned. The woman listened.

"He won't come," she said at last. "According to Arden, he has found a hillside covered with ripe berries. He plans to stay there till he has eaten all of them. 'Take care of your own business,' my father says." She glanced at Ayra. "He is a true bear. Not human at all. He taught me a song, when I first came to him:

> "Fish in the spring,
>   flipped out of the river.
> Honey in summer,
>   high in a tree.
> Berries in autumn,
>   hanging on bushes.
> A cave in the winter,
>   snow falling and sleep.

"Those are the things that interest him. I will have to find my help in another place." The woman sat up and looked at the bear. "Arden, if I can travel between the worlds, so can you. Come over. Bring your body here. You can help me, even if Father won't."

The bear swung his head from side to side and growled.

"He refuses," the woman said. "'This is only a dream,' he says. He sleeps—his body sleeps back on Earth—and in his dreams, he imagines he is a bear. But none of this is real."

The bear climbed to his feet and lifted his head, staring to the east. He growled again.

"He is saying good-bye. His alarm clock will go off in a minute."

Ayra looked east. The sky was gray. One cloud hung there, little and round. The lower edge began to brighten. She glanced at the bear. His dark shape began to spread and blur. It was growing less dark, growing less solid. Now he was a huge dim shape, no longer bearlike. He filled one side of the clearing, billowing like a cloud. She could see the foliage beyond him. Parts of him began to separate. He turned into a dozen wisps of grayness, which drifted through the grove, gradually dissipating.

A ray of sunlight hit the canyon wall above them. The sky was blue, and Arden was gone.

Ayra let her breath out. It was a loud exhalation. After a moment, she said, "And I thought that I had seen marvels!"

"But what a fool!" said the woman. "Do you know what he is on Earth? A coal miner in West Virginia. He's waking now. Do you know where he is? In a tract house at the edge of a miserable little mining town. He's told me about it. Verna Mae and the kids and the pickup truck with the transmission that's going, but the damn thing isn't paid off, and he doesn't know where he's going to get the money to fix it." The woman's face was red, and her eyes were bright.

"Lie down," said Ayra. "Rest. I'll figure out what to do next."

The woman dozed. Ayra tried to think of a plan. The sun moved toward the middle of the sky. The air grew warm. In the grass, the hummers roused themselves. *"Mmmmmmmmmm."* Their sound filled the canyon. Once she saw one. It was a dull brown bug, until it unfolded its wings. They were the color of gold or new bronze. *Wizz!* The hummer flew away. Ayra went back to thinking.

Toward noon, a man came into sight. He was riding one horse and leading another. Ayra shaded her eyes. He wore no armor. He wasn't a bandit. And he was definitely human. She had heard about the monsters that appeared from time to time in the mountains. Horrible creatures, feathered like chickens or patchy-furred like a dog with mange. They ate sheep and an occasional traveler. For the most part, they went on foot. But a few rode what appeared to be horses, until one got close.

She took another look. There was nothing abnormal about these horses. No claw-feet, no long sinuous tails covered with scales like a serpent.

Clop. Clop. Clop. They came slowly down the road. Their gait was entirely ordinary.

She ran out and waved. The man came up to her and reined his horse.

"Well now," he said. "It seems that my dream was right."

He was middle-aged with a ruddy, friendly face. His clothes were plain and well made, though not well cared for. The green jacket had a hole in one elbow. The leather leggings were stained. A prosperous farmer, thought Ayra, or a merchant who did not believe in display. A man without a wife.

"What dream?" she asked.

"A voice spoke to me and said, 'There are travelers in the pass who need your help.' I saddled up Brownie and Star and came."

What luck! But who had sent the message? The bear king? Had he relented?

The man looked around. "Are you alone? The voice said 'travelers.'"

"My companion is in the grove. She has no clothes."

"What? Were you set upon by robbers?"

Ayra thought for a moment. She couldn't tell the truth. The man might not want to help someone who was half bear. But she didn't want to make up an entire story. Her partner had always said, "Keep your lies short and simple and close to the truth. They'll be easier to remember."

"We were attacked by a bear. It came after us at night. We scrambled away as best we could and left almost everything behind. My companion likes to sleep in the nude. She didn't have time to dress."

The man nodded. "I have a cloak. She can wear that."

"Thank you. I am Ayra of Ymmouth." She held out her hand. He shook it. "I am Hargi."

They went to the grove together. Ayra roused the woman and wrapped her in the cloak. They got her on her feet and helped her to the horse. It took both of them to heave her up into the saddle. Ayra mounted behind.

"This is Brownie," the man said, patting the horse's neck. "She is gentle and surefooted and knows the way home. You worry about your friend. Leave the rest to Brownie."

The horse nickered. Hargi mounted the other animal: a black gelding with a star between his eyes. They went west along the road. The bear woman slumped against Ayra; unconscious.

Hours passed. They traveled down out of the high mountains into a valley. It was little and narrow. The upper slopes were covered with a forest. Dark pine, for the most part. Farther down were meadows and little groves of aspen. At the bottom of the valley were the fields: all stubble now, yellow and tan. There was a river and a small farmstead: a house, a barn, a couple of pens made of fences that sagged and leaned, a flock of chickens and a dog.

The dog ran up, barking.

"Quiet!" shouted Hargi.

The dog leaped and yipped. Hargi dismounted and rubbed the dog's ears. "Silky, I call him. My wife gave him the name. She said she'd felt silk only once in her life. A fine lady stopped here, caught in the snow and afraid of the pass. The clothes that she had on! All silk! Every piece! My wife always said this fellow had fur just as soft and fine."

Ayra looked around. The house was stone. One shutter hung halfway off. The barn was wood. It needed painting. The chickens were Bridge Island Blues: large and blue-gray with combs as pink as coral. They looked scruffy. "Uk-uk-uk," they cried and ran under the barn.

"It was better when Gerra was alive. What a housekeeper she was! What a gardener! When she died, I lost heart." Hargi glanced around at the house and then at the barn. He smiled. "I was a good farmer in my time. Ah well! Come in."

Ayra dismounted. Together, the two of them carried the bear woman into the house. They laid her on a bed. Hargi lit a lantern. They were in a large room—the hearth room. This was the center of the house. Ayra saw dusty furniture and rugs that needed washing. A chicken roosted on a rocking chair. Something rustled in the fireplace. Ayra turned her head and saw a black lizard among the ashes.

"A salamander," said Hargi. "It can't live in fire. That's a children's story. But it likes to be near fire. And as long as I have it in my chimney, I don't have bats coming in." He scratched his nose. "My father told me there were no salamanders when he was young. They must be like the dragons. Something new. Another aggravation. Everyone says we live in a bad time, full of decay and decline, of strange signs and portents."

"The dragons cause harm," said Ayra. "Does this creature do anything?"

"No." Hargi smiled briefly. "Well, maybe yes. It hisses at me, and sometimes I think that I can understand it. The folly of an old man, who is getting lonely enough to clutch at any kind of company." He leaned over the bear woman and feit her forehead. "She is running a fever. What happened to her? Why does she have a bandage around her shoulder?"

"The bear," said Ayra. "It almost got her."

"Do you want me to look at the wound?" asked Hargi.

If he did, he would know at once that it hadn't been caused by a bear. Ah, the trouble that came from lying! Ayra shook her head.

Hargi straightened up. "I don't know much about medicine, in any case. If your friend is no better in the morning, I'll go for a witch. There is one a short distance from here, on the edge of Heron Lake. For now"—he glanced around—"you build a fire. I'll take care of the horses. And then we'll see about dinner."

"All right," said Ayra.

As soon as he was gone, she undid the bandage. The bear woman groaned, but did not wake. The wound looked fine. It was no longer bleeding; and there was very little swelling. The skin around the wound was white. She touched the skin. It felt warm, but not hot. And the woman *was* running a fever. She ought to feel warm.

Ayra retied the bandage. There was no point in running a risk. Tomorrow, she would ask the man to go for the witch at Heron Lake. And while he was gone, she would work on a new lie.

The woman groaned again.

"Peace," said Ayra. "You can rest now. I am done."

She left the woman and went to the fireplace. She knelt and began to clean it out. The lizard scurried up the chimney. She heard it, up in the darkness, hissing. She tried to make out words. There were none. Hargi was right: he was getting old and foolish. She built a fire and lit it. Flames shot up. The lizard began to make a purring sound. She rocked back on her heels and watched. The lizard crept down the chimney into sight. It was on the back wall of the fireplace, head down, holding on to the stone like a gecko. As the fire brightened, its dark body began to shine like oil: iridescent.

How lovely! It lifted its head and looked at her. Its eyes shone like opals. The skin on its throat had a reddish glimmer. It reminded Ayra of coals, shining out of the darkness on a night without light.

Her mind filled with images of fire: a dirigible aflame from end to end, tipping and falling out of the sky; the house across the street from her mother's house—burning, as it actually had one night in the winter when Ayra was nine or ten. She remembered falling snow and the fire, glowing red through the whiteness. She reached for another piece of wood.

"Take care," said Hargi behind her. "The fire is big enough already. I don't want flames roaring up my chimney and sparks landing on the roof of my house."

Ayra shivered, then put the wood back on the pile. She stood up. "What does the lizard say to you?"

"Only a few words. It isn't much for conversation. 'Lovely,' it says. 'Hot. Bright. Make it bigger.' The words appear in my mind, and I see the bonfires we used to make when I was a boy, to celebrate the Long Day and the Heart of Winter."

Ayra glanced at the fireplace. The lizard was still on the back wall, basking and shining. "You ought to get rid of that thing."

"No. It frightens the bats, and I ignore what it says. And as I told you before, it is a kind of company. Now about dinner—I have bread and cheese and the ale my neighbor makes. Does that sound good to you?"

"Yes," said Ayra.

The main table was covered with dirty dishes. They cleared it off and set out the food. The bread was stale. She knew that the moment she took hold of the loaf. But the cheese was the kind with a mold in it, that couldn't go bad. And the ale looked wonderful: thick and dark. All at once, she realized that she was famished.

They ate. Ayra had four cups of ale. She felt herself relax and grow comfortable. In the fireplace, the lizard purred; and the chicken on the rocking chair clucked from time to time, a soft noise. Ayra leaned back and dozed.

"Your friend is awake," said Hargi gently.

"What?" She blinked and tried to rouse herself.

"Don't worry. I'll get food for her. You rest. You've had a hard journey."

"Un-huh," said Ayra. She closed her eyes.

When she woke, she was aching. A hangover, she thought. And something else. After a moment, she figured it out. She was freezing; she ached from cold. Ayra opened her eyes. Nothing. Darkness. Not a glimmer of light. She pushed herself into a sitting position. The floor she was on was dirt: hard-packed, damp, and cold. A basement, she thought. She sneezed.

Somewhere nearby, something growled.

Oh no!

"Is that you?" she asked. "The daughter of the bear?"

She heard a noise, a movement, and smelled fur and halitosis. She reached out, touching fur. It was long and coarse. Something touched her face. It was wet. The bear sneezed. Ayra felt warm air on her cheek, along with a few drops of moisture. The wet thing was the nose of the bear. The head of the animal was right next to her. She remembered what it looked like: high forehead, long muzzle, sharp teeth, and a heavy crushing jaw.

"Do you know who I am?" she asked.

Words formed in her mind. *Yes. The woman who shot me.*

"And helped you," Ayra said quickly. "You might have died in the road, if I hadn't come along."

Maybe. The animal moved away. The bear stink diminished. Ayra heard scuffling. The animal must be pacing around the room. *Who did this? Why are we here?*

Curious, thought Ayra. Even in her mind, the bear had a bear voice: low and rough.

"Do you remember the man who came to help us? The farmer? Hargi?"

Yes.

"He brought us to his farm and fed us dinner. Do you remember that?"

Yes. A little. The fire and the ale.

"Un-huh. I think he doctored the ale. I don't usually pass out, after a few drinks. Once we were asleep, he brought us here. I think it's a basement or a root cellar."

A root cellar. I found a potato in one corner and ate it. It was rotten. The bear was still pacing. Ayra could hear it going 'round and 'round.

"He must be a robber. Although the mapper said nothing about it. Maybe they work together. Hargi knew we were coming. He said a voice in a dream told him about us." Ayra laughed. "More likely, the mapper sent word."

No. He could have gotten a message in a dream. There are people—no, things—after me.

"The monster in the city of black stone."

Yes. For a moment, the bear was silent. Then Ayra heard a crunching.

"What?"

Another potato. This one isn't bad. The crunching ended. *The queen of the city told me there is something evil loose in the world. It twists the pattern of power that underlies reality. It is behind—or below—the monsters and the dragons.*

"Why is it after you?"

It knows what I am.

"Oh," said Ayra. "What are you?"

She heard laughter in her mind, low and growling. After a moment, the bear woman spoke. *I am a heroine. I was bred to defend the city of black stone and to fight the mind in the pattern. That's what they call it, the queen and her wizards. They can sense it, they told me. A cold, flat, empty presence. A mind with no true personality. It moves through the pattern. It lurks around the roots of the world. But they don't know who it is. They have not been able to track it down.*

Ayra made a listening noise. The bear woman continued. *As you might expect, this puts them at a disadvantage. The mind attacks and then withdraws. They cannot follow. It is safe. It waits until it is ready and then attacks again. Bit by bit, it is chipping away at their defenses. In time, they told me, their charms will fail. The pattern will be twisted into a new shape. This world will be destroyed.*

This was terrifying, thought Ayra, but also unreal. She couldn't imagine the end of the world. She tried to think of a comment. There was a crunching sound.

"Another potato?" asked Ayra.

A turnip.

Above her, in the dark, something creaked. Ayra looked up and saw a line of light that widened and widened, until it was a square. A trapdoor, fifteen feet up.

The bear reared on her hind legs, growling. She was ten feet tall, maybe more. It wasn't enough. She tried to stretch, to extend her neck and go up on tiptoes. After a moment, she lost her balance and went down on all fours.

"The voices were right," said Hargi. "The woman can change her shape." He stood looking down at them, holding a lantern.

Ayra got up and moved back against the wall. From this

angle, she could see him clearly. A tired man—there were dark patches under his eyes and deep lines around his mouth. Why hadn't she noticed those before? "Why are you doing this?" she asked.

"The voices." He rubbed his face. "I was so lonely after Gerra died. We had no children. Well, only one. We quarreled long ago, and he left home. I thought I'd go crazy, living all alone. Then the voices began. Every night, they talked to me. They said they needed my help. They said I could have anything I wanted. All I had to do was watch the travelers that came by. Watch for a woman, the voices said. Heavy set with claws like a bear and long sharp canines. Or else, they told me, watch for a bear. A sow bear, huge, with purple shining in her fur. Find either one and send for us. We will come. We will bring you whatever you want."

He rubbed his face again. "At first, I refused. I am a friend to travelers. Did you know that? They write it on all the maps, even those made in Ymhold, the city of the queen. My Gerra used to say, 'Good comes of good. We've been hospitable, and now we're famous. Everyone who travels knows about us.'

"I began to dream of Gerra. She looked the same as ever. She sat and talked to me, explaining that it would be to my advantage to listen to the voices. 'You are a simple farmer, dear, and you'll never amount to much. A name on a map, that's all you are. Five letters in black ink. That's all you have to show for fifty years of life. Well, here is your chance to get anything you want—riches, power. Surely you have a secret wish, something hidden in your heart, that even I don't know about.'

"'I want you,' I said. 'And that is impossible.'

"Gerra laughed merrily, the way she always used to when I did something she thought was foolish. 'Nothing is easier,' she said. 'The voices are great wizards. It's nothing for them to bring people back from the dead. If you want me back, then help them.' And I did. When they told me to go into the pass and get you—get both of you—I saddled up Brownie and Star and went."

Ayra asked, "Couldn't they get her for themselves?"

Hargi frowned. "I don't understand."

"Couldn't the voices get the daughter of the bear without your help?"

A voice spoke in her mind. *Not on the mountain. Not in my father's domain.*

Hargi shook his head. "They told me no. I don't know why. They didn't explain very clearly. There was a rule they could not break. Not yet, anyway. Or else it was a technical problem. It was something minor, they told me. It would be easy to repair. There was something wrong with the basic plan. A few adjustments and power would flow smoothly. The system would work without impediment."

"What system?" asked Ayra.

"I don't know. I don't even care. I wanted to tell you, I'm sorry. I wouldn't have done this, except for Gerra. I have never harmed anyone before." He lifted his head. "They are coming. I can hear them." He turned and raised his lantern.

A door swung open. Ayra heard it creak. It closed with a thump.

"Gerra!" he cried. He took a step away from the trapdoor.

A voice spoke, warm and maternal. "You stay where you are, dear. I want to see what you have."

Hargi waited. A woman joined him. She was short and plump with gray hair and a pink face. Her gown was blue-gray. She wore a coral pink apron. She looked into the cellar. The bear stood up and growled. "Yes. Yes," the woman said. She folded her pink hands across her pink apron. "That is the bear child." She smiled. "We made a mistake the last time. Didn't we, my dear? That miserable little monster! How could we have imagined that it would be able to do in a child of the bear? But we didn't give up. We never do. 'When you start something, finish it.' That is one of our rules. We have a multitude, even though our enemies say we are the forces of chaos." She laughed. "What an idea! We are very well organized. We have diagrams of the chain of command and books full of rules and regulations. And moral precepts. We have them too. 'Winning is the only thing. Never back down. Do unto others, but do it first. And never give a sucker an even break.'"

Hargi frowned. "You don't sound like Gerra." He sniffed. "And what's more, you smell like a chicken house."

"What?" the woman cried. She stretched up, until she was eight or nine feet tall. She towered over Hargi. He stared, his mouth open. Her body expanded, becoming round and fat. Her legs narrowed and turned pink. Her arms were wings now, and her head had a beak. She was an enormous chicken. A Bridge Island Blue. "Uk-uk-uk!" she cried.

The man dropped his lantern. It fell through the trapdoor and broke on the basement floor. Oil spread out in a pool. It was burning. Now Ayra could see her prison: a large room with stone walls and a wooden ceiling. In one corner, in the shadows, was a huge shaggy shape. The bear. Her eyes reflected the light of the burning oil. The eyes shone red.

The man screamed. Ayra looked. He had his arms up, trying to protect himself. The chicken was pecking at him. Blood ran down his face, and there was blood on his shirt.

"Gerra! No!"

"Uk-uk!" The chicken ducked its head and drove its sharp beak into his belly. Hargi screamed again. The chicken raised its head, lifting the farmer up. For a moment, Hargi remained on the beak, impaled, hanging in midair, thrashing like an insect caught by a bird. Then he fell, hitting the side of the trapdoor and tumbling into the basement.

"UK!" It was a cry of triumph.

He landed in the pool of burning oil. Blood came out of his mouth and out of the wound in his gut. He made choking noises. His clothes began to burn. He made a new sound, in between a gargle and a moan. The bear lumbered over to him. She bent her head and bit his throat open. He shuddered. Then he died.

"Why?" asked Ayra.

To spare him pain.

"Generous," said the chicken.

Ayra looked up. It had become a man in a suit made of dark blue feathers. He wore glasses with heavy rims and held a book. What else did she notice? Short hair and gray sideburns and a grave pale face.

"Walter," the bear said. But she wasn't a bear any longer. Her body shrank. Her fur disappeared. She was a woman of average height, heavyset, and naked, with a wound in her shoulder that had begun to bleed.

"Who?" said Ayra.

"My husband on Earth. He is a professor of English at the University. The monster has taken his form. I guess, to demoralize me."

The man said, "You have never been good at analysis. Remember how much trouble you had with papers in college? Your memory is good, and you were wise to choose art history for a major. You always did well on the slide tests. But as for real thinking—analysis and logical argument—" He laughed.

"Come down here," the woman said.

"No." He closed the book and put it in a pocket. "I won't fight with you, Esperance. Not after what you did to poor Urbit."

Urbit, thought Ayra. That sounded like the name of a monster. Esperance must be the bear woman, and Urbit was the monster that she killed in the city of black stone.

The woman looked up. "What, then?"

He smiled down at them. His hair was moving, Ayra noticed, rising off his head and twisting like snakes. His grin widened. She saw pointed teeth. "Fire," he said, hissing the word. Ayra could not believe it. How could anyone hiss a word that didn't have a single *s?* His tongue flickered out: long, black, and forked. He extended a hand.

The pool of oil, which had almost burnt out, burst into flames. A moment later, Hargi was gone, consumed. Ayra crouched against the wall. Heat beat against her. Light dazzled her. She raised one arm to protect her eyes. The whole center of the room was ablaze. Orange fire went from floor to ceiling. Ayra smelled wood smoke. The ceiling beams! They were catching fire!

Through the roar of the burning, she heard a voice. Walter. The monster. He was chanting. "Don't you understand the danger? This is no time for weakness. We must be determined! We must be strong! Tighten your belt. Put your shoulder to the grindstone. We have to stop the cancer. The wound must be cauterized. First the struggle, then the reward. Only the strong survive! Don't you understand? There is a price for everything." His voice rose. He shouted. *"There is no such thing as a free lunch!"*

Gibberish, thought Ayra. She was being done in by a monster whose speech was made up of fragmented platitudes. It was another sign of the times. Even evil wasn't what it used to be.

The air was full of smoke. She was choking. She went down on her knees, then flat on her stomach. The air was better close to the floor. Wasn't there anything she could do? She tried to think of a charm that worked against fire. But she had never been especially interested in magic. It was hard slow work, learning the true nature of reality. And one could do nothing worth doing without understanding. All the witches said that.

She remembered a spell her old auntie had taught her. Her

father's sister, a sea witch with a good reputation in the villages south of Ymmouth. It was a song against monsters.

Ayra sang it. The tune was odd and wavering. It took her three tries to get it right:

"Dog-muzzled,
chicken-feathered,
creature who leaves a trail
like a slug across a fresh leaf of lettuce:

This song is to drive you off.
This song is to untie
the strong knot of your power."

She waited a moment. The fire kept burning. It was dimmer now, but that was because of the smoke. Her eyes watered, and her lungs hurt. Oh well. She hadn't really expected the song to work.

A hand grabbed her hand. She looked around, raising her head a little and blinking. It was the bear woman, on her stomach. She must have crawled over from wherever she had been, when the fire began.

"Good-bye," said Ayra.

The woman said, "Hold tight. I'm going to try something." She laid her head on the ground, then closed her eyes, frowning.

They'd be found this way, thought Ayra, lying side by side.

She was cold. She was falling. She twisted, trying to land on her feet. Then she was standing in a room. A new room with no fire. The bear woman was next to her. They were still holding hands, and both of them were naked.

Startled, Ayra looked around. The room had a floor of gray cement. The walls were stone, painted white; and there were a few small windows, high up. Light came in through them: the dim pale light of an overcast day. In the middle of the room was a huge gray cylinder. Pipes came out of the top of it. There were at least a dozen. Each one was a foot or more across. Ayra looked up. The pipes went into the ceiling, which was wood. There were other pipes—these ones narrow—running across the ceiling. One of the pipes was dripping. There was a bucket under the pipe, almost full of water. *Plop!* Another drop went in.

"Damn Walter," said the woman. "I told him about that leak a long time ago. Before I turned into a bear. Can't he do anything for himself?"

"Do you know this place?" asked Ayra.

The woman nodded, looking around. "Cobwebs all over!"

"Then tell me. Where are we?"

"Earth. Minnesota. This is the basement of my house in Minneapolis." The woman grinned angrily. "And they say you can't go home again."

PART THREE:
PURSUED BY
MONSTERS THROUGH
MINNEAPOLIS

She had been happy in Santa Fe, living with her boyfriend in a small and hideously expensive apartment. Kevin was apprenticed to a frame maker. She washed dishes in a restaurant. On weekends, they hiked in the mountains. She took photographs, landscape studies for her first portfolio: *Homage à Georgia O'Keeffe*. At last, at twenty-one, she was beginning to find herself.

Then her father called her from Minneapolis, calm—as usual —but with strain evident in his voice. Her mother had disappeared. Daddy had come home from his seminar on George Eliot and found the house empty.

"But her clothes were there, Jen. On the floor, right in front of the washing machine. I can't find anything missing, and she can't have gone out stark naked."

Her throat tightened. She knew what he wasn't saying. Unless Mother had been carried out by some kind of a pervert. Her hand was shaking. She could barely hold the phone.

"The police say there's no sign of a break-in and no sign of a struggle. They told me she probably left voluntarily, and she'll probably turn up in good condition. Women do the craziest things, they told me."

For a moment, Jennifer felt angry. But this was no time to argue about sexual stereotypes. Daddy needed her.

"I'll catch the first plane I can," she said.

"Thank you, Jennifer." She could hear his voice breaking.

When Kevin got home, she was packed. She told him what had happened and asked for a ride to the airport. "I'll be back as soon as possible."

"Un-uh."

"What?"

"You won't be back. I can tell. I always know when something is over."

She looked at him, considering. Kevin was blond and blue-eyed. He looked Scandinavian, but he was Greek, and his prophecies were usually true. "Are you sure?"

He nodded. "Daddy will need someone to lean on, and you'll volunteer. And then you'll remember that you can study photography at the U. and that the Art Institute has a terrific photography collection. And me, I'll get a new roommate. No problem. No hard feelings. Just give me a call when you want your stuff shipped north."

After that, they had dinner in a restaurant. Not the place she worked. Another place, much better and much more expensive. They had gone there once before, to celebrate their first six months together. Kevin drove her to Albuquerque to catch her plane. They kissed and parted. A month later, she called him and asked him to send her belongings back to Minneapolis.

"What did I tell you?" Kevin said.

"They haven't found any sign of Mother. And Daddy is so depressed. Mark was here for a couple of weeks, but he had to go back to school. And there's a big demonstration at a power plant. He said he couldn't miss it."

Mark was her brother, who was nineteen and into the environment. He was the family scholar, the pride of his father; though Daddy thought his grades would be better if he studied more and sat in less. She (Jennifer) took after her mother, who had been an art history major until she dropped out of college to marry Daddy and have babies and help Daddy get his Ph.D.

"Okay," said Kevin. "I'll make some crates at work. Your stuff will arrive in good condition. But you watch out, Jen. Don't get sucked into your parents' problems. You've got only one life to live. Make it the one you want."

She stayed in her parents' house for half a year, then moved in with a couple of friends who had an upper duplex in north Minneapolis. Daddy worried about the neighborhood, but the rent was cheap. She had another restaurant job, this time doing counter work at a pizzeria near the U. And she was taking two courses: Nonsilver Photography and the History of Feminism.

For a while, she wrote to Kevin and sent him copies of her recent work, photographs of grain elevators and railroad bridges. She was thinking of calling the series *Mill City* or *Homage à James J. Hill*. Then, after eight or nine months, Kevin sent a note saying he was taking off for Greece with a lady he had met who was into archeology. Jennifer cried most of an evening. But it was, after all, her decision to leave Santa Fe. She settled down to work. Daddy gradually recovered from his depression. Everything was going well, till the winter afternoon when her phone rang.

She picked it up. "Yes?"

"Jen! Thank God you're home. And thank God Walter wrote something down for once. I found your new number in the address book. What happened to Sante Fe?"

"Mother!" Once again, her hand was shaking. "Where are you?"

"At the house. When does your father get home?"

"Four o'clock, I think. I haven't talked to him lately. Mother, where have you been?"

"It's a long story. Come over here and bring some jeans. I have someone about your size who needs something to wear. My shirts will fit her, but my pants are too wide and too short. And stop on the way and buy some groceries. There's nothing in the icebox, and I'm as hungry as a bear." Her mother chuckled and hung up.

Jennifer sat staring at the phone. What was she going to do? She thought of calling Daddy. No, Mother sounded all right, so it wasn't an emergency. But it might turn into a fight. Kevin always said to stay out of fights between parents. 'That's a tough generation,' he said. 'The sixties and Vietnam. They can get mean. So when they get going, duck and run.'

She got up and put on her coat. She was almost out the door, before she remembered the jeans. She put them in a paper bag from one of the bookstores near the U. She caught a bus south, changing downtown to another bus: the Number 22. Her parents lived south of the parkway, between Lake Nokomis and the river. (It was the mighty Mississippi, running dark brown between high wooded limestone and sandstone cliffs.)

She got off at the supermarket and bought food, then walked the rest of the way. There had been two big storms in the past two weeks. The snow was thick and already gray. The walks were icy. She moved carefully, her arms full of groceries.

Home. A big frame house with a big front porch. There was a fire going inside. Smoke poured out of the chimney. She smelled burning wood. She paused at the front walk. A man sat in a car across the street. Strange. People never sat in cars in this neighborhood. Well, if he stayed there, Mr. Potter would come out and ask him what he was doing. Mr. Potter had short hair and aviator glasses and believed in community self-defense. He also believed that Daddy was a communist.

The front door opened a little. Somebody peeked out. Jennifer went up the walk and into the porch.

"Lock the porch door," her mother said softly.

Jennifer did as she was told. The front door opened all the way. She walked in. Her mother closed the door, and they looked at one another. Jennifer saw a woman of average height, not fat but not thin. Her face was wide and pale. Her hair was dark—at least, here in the hallway. In sunlight, the gray would be visible. There were lines around her mouth and at the corners of her eyes. Her irises were hazel, so light that they were almost yellow. She wore faded jeans and a buffalo plaid shirt and good sensible oxfords.

"I can't hug you, Jen. I've hurt my shoulder."

"How?"

Her mother smiled. "I got a crossbow bolt in it."

"A what?"

"It's a kind of arrow. Don't worry. The bolt head is out, and I cleaned the wound as soon as I got here. I put on every antiseptic and antibiotic in the medicine cabinet. Ayra helped me bandage it. It doesn't feel too bad, and you know I never have any trouble healing. What kind of food did you get?"

"Soup. Hamburger. Everything for sandwiches. Who is Ayra?"

"Come on in the kitchen." Her mother led the way. "What has your father been eating? I found moldy bread, a six-pack of beer, and a half-empty can of anchovies."

"He's been eating out a lot."

They went through the living room: dark woodwork, oak floors, modern furniture. Mother had bought all the art. It was all by local people, and there were a lot of pots. Mother loved pottery. A fire burned in the fireplace. Karl Marx, who was an orange tomcat, sat and stared at the flames.

There was a woman in the kitchen, sitting at the big table, a can of beer in her hand. She was tall and lean with short blond hair. Her face was weather-beaten. She wore underpants and one of Mother's flannel shirts.

A lesbian, thought Jennifer with horror. Mother had run away to San Francisco, and now she was back, expecting us to be reasonable about it.

"Did you bring the jeans?" asked her mother.

"Yes." The bag was in with the groceries. She pulled it out.

"Good." Mother handed the jeans to the woman. "This is Ayra, the daughter of Pela. She's a sailor from another world."

"What?" said Jennifer.

"You aren't going to believe this," her mother said. "But I've spent the last year in another world. I guess in another dimension. You read more science fiction than I do, Jen. You could probably explain what happened better than I can."

The tall woman put on the jeans. She had trouble with the zipper. "It's true," she said when she finally got it pulled up. "I'm not from this place." She glanced at Jennifer, smiling just a little. Her lips were thin, Jennifer noticed, and her eyes were pale gray. "I am from Ymmouth on the estuary of the great Ym River. And until I met your mother, I had never heard of Minneapolis. Or Minnesota. Or—what do you call this place? Soil?"

"Earth," said her mother.

The woman nodded. "Oh yes." Her smile widened. She was mocking Jennifer or maybe the situation she found herself in. "When I met your mother, she was a bear in the mountains where the Ym has its origin. A great sow bear with the mark of the moon on her chest and a purple glimmer in her fur."

Crazy, thought Jennifer, they were both crazy. This was worse than San Francisco.

Mother unpacked the grocery bag. "What do you say to soup and sandwiches?"

"Fine," said Ayra.

"Jen, you heat the soup. I'll make the sandwiches. Ayra, you go take a look out front. See if the man in the car is still there."

Ayra nodded and went out of the kitchen.

"Mother, I can't believe you," Jennifer said.

"I know. I told you that you wouldn't. I guess I should have made up something plausible. An attack of amnesia—that sounds good, doesn't it?" She laid out slices of bread in a row on the table, then got out a knife and opened the mustard. "Salami and cheese okay with you?"

"Yes," said Jennifer.

"And vegetable soup. Here." Mother handed her a red and white can. "Get the soup going. And could you get me a beer from the icebox?"

Feeling stunned, Jennifer opened the can of soup. She poured it into a pot and added water, put the pot on the stove, and turned on the gas. After that, she got her mother a beer.

Mother had finished the sandwiches and was eating a slice of cheese. "I'm still the fastest sandwich maker in the West," she said, sounding muffled. Her mouth was full of cheese.

Ayra came back. "The man is still there. A man in the house across the street is watching him."

"Mr. Potter," Jennifer said.

Her mother nodded. "I've decided that I've been suffering from amnesia."

"What is that?" asked Ayra.

"Loss of memory. I woke up— Oh, two or three days ago. Somewhere out West. Portland or San Francisco. I knew who I was, but I had no idea what I'd been doing for the past year. Walter will believe that. Although—" Mother frowned. "I'm not sure I ought to stick around till Walter gets home. He's likely to insist that I see a therapist. And I have more important things to do."

"What?" asked Jennifer.

"Ayra and I have to figure out how to get back into her world. Everyone take a sandwich." Mother popped the top on her can of beer.

Ayra took a sandwich. Jennifer stared at both of them, feeling horrified. Who was this crazy woman who talked calmly about going into an alternative universe? Not the mother she remembered!

"Jen, eat. You can't handle a situation like this on an empty stomach."

"No," said Jennifer. "I feel queasy."

"That's tension. Have a beer." The soup began to boil. Mother turned off the burner, then got out three mugs. She filled them with soup, then added three spoons. "There's a struggle going on in that world. It seems to be between good and evil or order and chaos."

"No," said Ayra. "It is between integrity and shoddiness."

Her mother looked at the woman, frowning.

Ayra said, "One of my aunts is a sea witch. Once in a while, she talks about her work." Ayra grinned. "Usually, it's at the gathering my family has to celebrate the Heart of Winter. We meet at my father's house. There's a big fire in the fireplace and food on the table and a bowl of hot punch. Auntie has a couple of drinks and begins to tell us about magic. Most of the time, I listen. She is an interesting woman. And a sailor can never tell what information is going to prove useful.

"According to Auntie, a witch does not create magic. She knows how to find magic. She is not powerful—that is to say, she is not full of power. It's the other way around. Magic surrounds her. She lives in it, like a fish living in water. She understands the ebb and flow of power, the currents and the eddies. And she can use her knowledge the way a good swimmer uses his knowledge of the sea—to go beyond his own strength and to outlast his limitations. That is integrity. Knowing yourself and being self-consistent. Understanding the true nature of power. Acting in harmony with the forces that shape the world." Ayra frowned. "Is this making any sense at all?"

"Yes," said her mother. "I never realized that you could be so articulate."

"I have a good memory. I know what Auntie said. Now, as to the shoddy people. My aunt used to list them for us. Beware the carpenter who doesn't care how the grain of the wood goes. Beware the potter who makes mugs with comic faces. Beware all writers and thinkers who fall in love with their own cleverness. And beware witches who think they own the magic they use. They are the ones, my auntie told us, who think they have the right to turn the whole world inside out to suit their petty needs. And they always make a mess of whatever they do."

Ayra stopped. Jennifer realized she had been listening seriously, as if the conversation were about something real. She had even imagined Ayra's auntie: a little fat woman, sitting in a more or less medieval room, a glass of punch in her hand, talking while the fire roared and the mantelpiece gargoyles stared down at her. No! It was a delusion or a lie. There was no aunt and no medieval room, no gathering at the Heart of Winter.

"Anyway," said her mother, "I'm mixed up in this struggle between good and evil or integrity and schlock. Ayra and I came here because a monster had us trapped. It looked—the monster, I mean—like a combination of your father and a giant chicken. Can you imagine that?"

"No," said Jennifer.

"It was a shoddy monster," said Ayra. "They all are."

"It set fire to the house we were in," said Mother. "There was no way out, except to come here. And I'm not even sure how I did it."

Ayra got another beer out of the icebox. "I told you, it is possible to move between worlds. Most people do it after years of study, with the help of powerful spells. You can do it naturally. I suppose because you are the child of the bear."

"Wait a minute," said Jennifer. "What bear?"

"Don't worry about that now," her mother said. "The point is, we made it, and I think we're safe. The wizard Gerringarr told me magic doesn't work on Earth. And the monsters are magical, which ought to mean they cannot exist in a place where magic doesn't work."

Ayra nodded. "That ought to be right."

"Good." Her mother bit into a sandwich and chewed and swallowed. "I'm ready for a rest. But after that, we are going to have to return to Ayra's world. The wizard told me I have abilities his people can use. If I can do anything to stop the monsters, I will. I don't care for them at all." She glanced at the tall woman. "Would you take another look out front? That man worries me. See if Potter has gone out to ask him what he's doing."

The woman left the kitchen.

"Mother," said Jennifer, "I think you need help."

"All I can get. But not from Dr. Ferris or any other therapist. I don't know a lot about magic, but I'm positive that you don't solve magical problems with modern psychology."

"This is all crazy!"

"Come here!" shouted Ayra in the front room.

Her mother ran. Jennifer followed.

Ayra was at the window. Outside, across the street, a man dressed in gray was kneeling on Mr. Potter, who lay on his back in a bank of snow. There was something peculiar about the man's costume. The coat. It was close fitting to the waist, then it flared out like something from the nineteenth century. The fabric had a dull sheen. The man's hair was long and gray and feathery.

"A monster!" her mother cried. She grabbed the poker from the fireplace and ran out. Ayra followed.

Jennifer got as far as the door onto the porch, then stopped. What should she do? Call the police? That seemed like a good idea. Her mother might be crazy, but that man—whatever he might be—was doing harm to Mr. Potter. The man bent. He seemed to be trying to bite Mr. Potter in the throat.

Halfway across the street, her mother slipped on the ice. She fell. The man jumped up and dove off the bank of snow. It was a remarkable dive, all the way from the boulevard to the middle of the street. He wasn't going quickly. Arms out and fingers spread, he floated down on Mother. She was almost up by the time he reached her. He hit. Mother tumbled. He was on top of her, his hands reaching for her neck or face. A moment later, Ayra jumped on him.

Jennifer ran for the phone. Stay calm, she told herself, as she looked for the number and dialed. When she spoke, her voice shook only a little. There was a fight, she said, on Gitche Gumee Avenue—a block south of the parkway.

The police said they'd be there as soon as possible.

She hung up the phone and ran out of the house. The gray man was running away with long, loping strides. He seemed to be half floating, like someone running on the moon. Something funny was definitely going on. Her mother and Ayra stood in the middle of the street, watching the man run. Mother had a poker. It dripped a brown liquid.

"Definitely a monster," her mother said. "That isn't human blood. We've been followed. I don't know how."

Jennifer said, "I called the police."

"We have to get out of here." Mother glanced at Mr. Potter, who was sitting in the bank of snow, looking dazed. "Hang on, Wayne. The cops are coming. We're going to chase that creep." Mother opened the door of the gray man's car. "The keys are here. Climb in."

Ayra got in the front and Jennifer in back. Mother slid behind the wheel. The engine coughed, then roared. They were off, following the gray man as he loped down the street toward Minnehaha Parkway. He was moving more quickly now and rising farther off the ground, flapping his long gray arms with every stride. At first, Jennifer thought he was escaping, getting smaller as he moved into the distance. No. That wasn't right. He wasn't receding. He was shrinking and darkening. He bounded higher and higher, almost into the branches of the few surviving elm trees.

"Dammit!" said Mother. "He is turning into a crow."

By this time, he was black and about the size of a two-year-old child. He flapped heavily, rising past the last elm on the block. Then he was over the parkway, high above the lilac bushes, which were bare of leaves and almost bare of snow. The wind had shaken it off. "Caw!" the gray man cried. He turned east, toward the falls and the river.

They followed, turning onto the parkway. By the time they reached Hiawatha Avenue, the crow was almost a normal size for a crow. He kept flapping east. Not quickly. They had no trouble keeping up with him.

Past Minnehaha Park they went. The snow was gray and marked with many footprints. The waterfall—beyond the picnic grounds and the pavilion—was entirely out of sight. But Jennifer got a brief glimpse of Hiawatha and Minnehaha. Cast in ageless bronze, the Indian brave carried his true love across Minnehaha Creek, which was about six inches deep at that point and frozen.

The crow took a left and then a right, leading them onto the Ford Parkway Bridge.

"He isn't trying to escape," said Ayra. "He could have done it easily by now." She leaned forward, glancing out the windshield. "And I see why."

Jennifer looked out one of the side windows. The sky above the bridge was full of crows, flapping and wheeling, gliding short distances with their wing feathers spread. The feathers looked like fingers. All the crows were too big; and they were, Jennifer realized after a moment, increasing in size. "Oh no!" she cried.

A crow swooped down over the hood of the car. Another one flapped across the road in front of them.

"Get moving," said Ayra.

Mother stepped on the accelerator. All at once, they were

going an illegal speed. *Splat!* Something hit the windshield. Mother swore. The glass was webbed with fracture lines. Beyond the lines, on the outside of the glass, were black feathers and dark brown streaks of blood.

"A kamikaze crow," said Mother.

Splat! Another one hit. The windshield shattered. The car veered across two lanes and hit the metal railing. It broke through. Jennifer screamed. The car stopped and hung halfway off the bridge. It was tilting down just a little. Before them and below them was the river.

Something hit the roof above Jennifer. *Ka-thunk!* Something else hit the back window. She glanced around and saw blood and feathers. The car was moving, she realized. Sliding forward. Not much. The motion was barely perceptible.

"Out! Fast!" shouted Ayra.

Jennifer opened the door and scrambled out. A wing brushed her head. She flailed with her arms. The crow flapped away. She turned.

Mother and Ayra were safe, standing on the pavement on either side of the car. The car was still moving. It was easy to see the motion now. The car was almost through the break in the railing. Jennifer stepped back. The rear wheels caught on the concrete base of the railing: a low parapet. It hung for a moment, suspended. Then it tipped. The front went out of sight. The back rose. The car flipped over. It was gone.

"Caw! Caw!" The crows swooped down. Feathery bodies hit Jennifer. Claws tore at her. Beaks bit. She ducked her head, trying to protect her eyes. Somewhere close by, her mother and Ayra shouted and cursed.

"In the name of God, begone," a voice said. It was male, deep and resonant, with a foreign accent. The man began to chant in a language Jennifer did not understand.

"Caw?" a crow asked.

Another one answered. "Caw! Caw!"

Then there was silence, except for one person who groaned and sobbed. It was Jennifer.

"Are you all right?" the man asked. "Have those devils done any serious harm?"

Jennifer wiped her eyes, then looked up. The man was tall and thin and black. Entirely black—his face, his hands, and his suit, except for the collar, which was a narrow band of white. He was a priest. In one hand, he held a crucifix. Behind him was a gray Honda Civic, the engine still running.

"It is fortunate that I came along," he said. "There cannot be many people in Minneapolis able to recognize a flock of evil spirits when they see one."

"You knew they were monsters?" her mother asked.

Jennifer looked at the two women. Their hands and faces were bleeding from many small wounds. There was bird shit on their clothes. Mother's hair was a mess. Ayra, who wore only sandals, had bloody feet.

"Yes, of course," the man said in answer. "The birds were an unnatural size, and they were behaving in an unnatural fashion. I looked around. I saw no cameramen. This was not a movie or a television show. Well, then, what was going on? I could see only one explanation. You were being attacked by devils. I stopped my car, leaped out, and held up my crucifix." He paused for a moment. "They continued their attack. I do not know the rite of exorcism. In spite of all the movies, demonic possession is rare, at least in Europe and America; and the average priest does not have to know how to get rid of demons. But I remembered a song which my maternal uncle had taught me. He is a follower of the old religion and famous for his ability to drive off evil spirits. I thought, anything is worth a try. I sang my uncle's song. A dubious action, I realize. But it worked.

"I often think spiritual forces must be all the same. Or at least, of only two kinds: good and bad. I do not believe God would have ignored Africa for almost two thousand years. Surely, He must appear in different guises to different people." The priest smiled gently and sadly. "I realize my ideas are close to heretical." He glanced around. "I suggest we leave before the devils regroup and return. Is there anywhere I can take you?"

"I don't know," said Mother.

"You must be in shock. Why don't I take you—all of you—to my apartment? It is just across the river, a little beyond the Ford plant. You can clean up and rest for a while. Then I will take you home."

"Or wherever," Mother said.

They went with the priest. He drove across the river to St. Paul, talking all the while. His name was Lucien Dia. D-I-A. Most likely, it was a corruption of Diaz. A Portuguese name. There had been plenty of Portuguese along the west coast of

Africa. He was from Senegal, from a little town near the ocean. He remembered palm trees and sandy beaches and his maternal uncle, a grave wise man. A pagan, of course. But no one is perfect. He (Lucien Dia) had been educated first by his father and then at a secondary school run by missionaries. The good Fathers of the Holy Ghost. It was then that he became interested in becoming a priest. He had gone to college in France. He had been ordained. What else was there to say? He was a poet and a student of literature, teaching in the French Department at the College of St. Bonaventura in St. Paul.

They parked in front of a brick apartment building, two or three blocks from the Ford plant. Father Dia led them upstairs to a small apartment full of books. They washed. Father Dia poured out wine: a very nice California chablis. Jennifer looked at the books. Most were in French: the poems of Léopold Senghor and Aimé Césaire, the novels of Sembene Ousmane, Marx in a French translation, several large coffee table books on African art. What else? Franz Fanon and Jean-Paul Sartre, Teilhard de Chardin, Claude Levi-Strauss. This was the library of a civilized man, thought Jennifer. She recognized all the authors. She had read none of the books.

"Senegal," said her mother. "What do I remember about Senegal?" Jennifer looked around. Mother was frowning. "I have it! Gerringarr! He said one of the bear children was a writer in Senegal."

"What?" said Father Dia. "What do you mean when you say 'one of the bear children'?"

Mother looked at him. "Do you dream?"

"Ma foi!" He set down his glass. "How do you know that?"

"What do you dream of? Places you have never seen? Do you dream of bears?"

"Who are you? How do you know these things?"

"I dream, too," said Mother. She picked up her glass and took a big swallow.

Ayra looked at the priest, then at Jennifer's mother. "Who is this man? Is he a relative of yours? I must say, I cannot make out much of a resemblance."

"Tell me about your dreams," Mother said to the priest.

He frowned, then stood up and paced around his living room. "It is in my book, *Rêves Noirs*. I do not write about the great bear. Only about the city of white stone."

"What do you mean?" asked Mother.

"One dream is about a bear. A huge animal with purple fur. It calls to me. I hear the voice in my mind, deep and growling. It says, 'Come to me, my child. I will teach you who you are.'" Father Dia stopped pacing. He looked puzzled. "Why should an African, a man of the tropics, dream about a bear? I asked my uncle. He said maybe it was an ancestor of mine. One of the Portuguese. He knew nothing about Europe. He thought, why couldn't there be bears in Portugal? And why couldn't one of my ancestors—one of my white ancestors—assume the form of a bear?"

Mother let out her breath in a sigh.

"The bear king," said Ayra.

Mother said, "Yes."

The priest stared at her. "What do you mean?"

"I'll tell you in a minute. What are the other dreams?"

"A city. I call it the city of white stone. But the stone is actually pale yellow, the color of ivory. It rises on either side of a wide brown river. There are bridges over the river and boats on the water. The boats are lateen-rigged, with brightly colored sails. Farther down—I have seen this in my dreams—trees line the banks of the river. Coconut palms and other trees I do not recognize. Their bark is deep blue, and they have orange flowers. There are fields of yams and peanuts. In the distance are mountains with terraces on their sides. Rice grows on the terraces. The people are black, tall and noble, like the citizens of the ancient kingdoms of Africa. Not everyone is black. I have seen white people and light brown people and even two or three people who are as red as copper. All of them—the ones who are not black—are visitors. I can see that. They are respected, but not feared and not hated. They have no power over the city.

"In my dreams, I see the king of the city. He is black and tall. He wears a long robe of brightly colored cotton and a shawl made from a leopard skin. Around his neck are necklaces of gold. There are gold bracelets on his arms. He looks to be my age, but his hair and his beard are gray. There are scars on his face. He says, 'My brother, you were bred to be our salvation. And you waste your time, fooling around with a strange religion that makes no sense to me. Return to us. Help us. We cannot last much longer.' And then I wake, wondering what all of this means."

"You know," said her mother, "I don't want to tell my story again. It's crazy. No one will believe me. I'm tired. My shoulder hurts. The weather is cold. I want to lie down and hibernate. But I guess I have to keep going." She looked at Father Dia. "I don't know anything about the city in your dreams or about the king. But if he says he is your brother, he probably is. Your half brother, anyway. Your mother—your real mother—must have come from there. But she met your father elsewhere. On the mountain above Bear Pass."

"My father is René Dia, a schoolteacher in Dakar."

"No." Mother drank more wine. "He is a spirit who lives in another world. Not Earth and not any of the planets we know about. A world where magic works. There is a struggle going on; and the good guys—the wizard Gerringarr and the queen of the city of black stone and I don't know who else, they were—they are—losing. They decided to breed heroes and heroines to fight for them. Twelve women volunteered to be the mothers. There was one father. The bear king. I don't know what he really is. But he appears to people as a huge bear, whose fur has a purple sheen. He is a magical being, ancient and powerful. Do you have strange fingernails?"

"What!" shouted Father Dia.

"Thick nails. Strong nails. Nails that never break. If you leave them alone, they grow out long and narrow. They begin to curve."

The priest looked at his hands. The nails were very short, Jennifer observed. "How did you know that?" he asked.

"Mine are the same. I let them go, when I was in the other world. And I had a terrible time cutting them when I got back here. What about your teeth? Are the canines long? The incisors sharp and cutting? Do you have exceptionally large molars? and no cavities?"

"Yes! Yes! That is right!"

"Those are the signs of the bear. You are not human, Father Dia. You are a changeling, as am I. We were put here—in this world—to grow up, safe from monsters. Then, when we were full grown, we were supposed to go back home and begin the fight against evil. Or shoddiness, if Ayra is right. But something went wrong. When the wizards called us, we did not come."

"This is ridiculous." The priest began to pace again. "My

uncle told me I have the signs of power. He said it was my Christianity that kept me from achieving anything. That and my European education. I refused, he told me, to believe in myself. Or anything else. I am not wholehearted. I doubt. I equivocate. I shift back and forth between the foolish ideas of the white folk and the ancient, time-honored, time-proven ways of my own people. No!" He stopped and turned. "Your story leads to madness! I refuse to admit that it might be true."

"Very well." Her mother stood up. "Thank you for your help, Father Dia. We'd better get going."

The priest drew a breath, then exhaled. He was forcing himself to be calm. "Let us agree to disagree about this question, madame. We need not become angry or upset. Let me drive you home."

Mother nodded. "All right. We'd better go to your place, Jen. Maybe Ayra can fit into a pair of your moccasins. There was nothing at our house she could wear, except for the sandals. And maybe I can figure out what to do next."

The priest drove them to north Minneapolis. After they got out of the Honda, her mother said, "Watch out for monsters. Supposedly, they can't survive on Earth. They depend on magic, and magic isn't supposed to work here. But you saw them. They are here. And if they find out who you are, they'll come after you."

"I hope not," said Father Dia. He smiled faintly. "If they do, I can always flee back to Senegal. My uncle will know how to handle them. At least, I hope he will."

Jennifer trudged upstairs. She heard her mother and Ayra following, stumbling now and then. They were all exhausted. What a day! She would never feel the same about crows. Or about reality. She unlocked the door to her duplex. "Hello?" No answer. Her roommates were not home. "Come in," she told her mother.

The two women entered. Her mother looked around. All at once, Jennifer was aware that the floor was dusty and the furniture was shabby and one of her roommates—Michelle, most likely—had left orange peels on the coffee table. The walls were okay, she told herself. White and freshly painted. In the front, a row of windows looked out on the snow-covered street. The back wall was decorated with photographs, blown up and framed— Jennifer's work. A close up of a cactus. The pueblo at Taos. The old stone railway bridge across the Mississippi at Minneapolis.

Mother looked at the photographs. "You are getting good, aren't you?" She slumped into the big armchair and stretched out her legs. "My God, I could sleep for six months."

"I need something to drink," said Ayra.

Jennifer went into the kitchen and got a beer. She gave it to Ayra.

"I wish I knew how the monsters were getting here," said Mother.

Ayra opened the beer can. "I think the wizards are wrong. Magic does work here. Look at Father Dia. He drove away a whole flock of monsters with an amulet and a song. As far as I'm concerned, that is magic."

Mother frowned. "What was it that Gerringarr told me? Something about the bear children and magic."

The phone rang. Jennifer picked it up.

"Jen?" It was Daddy.

"Yes."

"I just got home. Somebody's been here. And Wayne Potter came over with a crazy story. He said he saw your mother and you and some other woman come out of the house. But he couldn't stop you, because a man tried to kill him. A complete stranger. He thinks it has something to do with the Mafia or else with a religious group. One of the ones that brainwash people. He says your mother must have escaped and now they're coming after her. He said the man who tried to kill him looked foreign. Italian or maybe from India. I don't have any idea what he's talking about. Have you seen your mother, Jen?"

She covered the receiver. "It's Daddy."

Her mother groaned. "Wayne Potter! Damn him! Tell your father you don't know what's going on. You haven't seen me."

Jennifer shook her head. "I can't lie to Daddy."

Mother held out her hand. Jennifer gave her the phone. "Walter? This is Esperance."

Jennifer heard squawking.

"Walter, I have things to work out. I can't see you yet."

More squawking.

"Stop that," her mother said. "You sound like a chicken. I've had enough trouble with birds today. I'm perfectly all right. Stay away. I'll get in touch when everything is sorted out." She hung up. "Okay. Ayra, finish that beer. And Jen, find something for

Ayra to put on her feet. And if you have any money at all, get it. We're going to have to run. I know Walter. He'll be here in half an hour. And I wouldn't be surprised if he brought the police with him."

Jennifer found wool socks and a pair of boots that belonged to her roommate Beverly, who had very big feet. Ayra put on the socks and boots and a spare goosedown vest.

"I'm all right," said Mother. "This is a heavy shirt. Hurry!"

They took a bus to the university. The west bank area. It was an old student area, about to fall victim to urban renewal. There were bookstores and bars, a free store, a co-op restaurant, a coffee house where radical folk singers sang. All left over, of course, from the sixties and early seventies, when people had believed in the future. Nowadays, people took life one month at a time. If, after thirty days, they still had a job and they weren't radioactive, that was an accomplishment. According to Kevin, the tragedy of the eighties was the contraction of vision and the loss of hope.

They went to the co-op restaurant and had coffee and completely organic muffins. Night was falling, along with a fine granular snow. Looking out the window, Jennifer saw students hurrying by, their heads bent against the rising wind.

"Five-thirty and it's dark already," her mother said. "I hate this time of year." She broke her muffin in half and buttered it. "Where was I when Walter interrupted?"

Ayra said, "You were trying to remember something about the bear children and magic."

Mother ate the muffin, frowning. "Of course," she said at last. Her voice was indistinct. She swallowed and went on, speaking more clearly. "I haven't told you—either of you—why the bear children stayed on Earth."

Ayra nodded. "That is so."

"Apparently, though magic doesn't work here, the wizards can reach Earth with their magic. They got the bear children here, and they figured they'd be able to bring the children home. But when the time came, they found out that they couldn't get through. The children had shut them out." Mother paused for a moment. "Somehow, the children were able to draw on their father's power, even here on Earth. And because the children were raised to believe there was no such thing as magic, they used the power of the bear to create a defense against magic. They didn't realize they were doing it, of course. Unconsciously, they reinforced the reality they believed in. And they used their magic to build a wall that kept all magic out."

"I think I understand," said Jennifer.

"Don't you see? I have been to a world where magic works, and now I am back on Earth. I believe in magic now. I am using my power—the power of the bear—to make magic possible on Earth. The monsters are real and powerful because of me. And the terrible thing is, I don't believe I can beat them."

"What will we do?" asked Ayra. She took a sip of coffee. "I don't know what this stuff is, but it tastes terrible."

"It takes getting used to," her mother said. "We have to get back to Father Dia. He believes in his uncle's magic. Maybe not wholeheartedly, but at least a little bit. And that is more belief than I have at the moment. Maybe he can defend us until I can figure out how to get back to the other world. The monsters will follow me, I think. Unless I have managed to convince my brother that I am telling the truth."

"Who?" asked Jennifer.

"Father Dia. He's my half brother. Surely you realize that? We share a father."

Jennifer thought about it for a moment. An uncle who was a Catholic priest from Africa. How did she feel about it? Not too bad, she decided. Though she had a little trouble with the Catholicism. She had never much liked any of the western religions. Native American religions were much more interesting, and so were the religions of the Orient.

Her mother went on: "If Father Dia believes me, then his power will permit the monsters to survive on Earth. Unless his belief in his uncle's magic exceeds his belief in the power of the monsters. If that's so, he ought to be able to use his uncle's songs to drive the monsters away. This is getting complicated. Jen, call a cab, will you?"

The cab came. They climbed in. Mother gave Father Dia's address. By this time, the snow was falling thickly. It whirled in the wind. The cab moved slowly over icy streets. Jennifer looked out a window. She could see very little. Lights shone dimly through the whiteness. Dark shapes clustered at the bus stops. Now and then, headlights appeared, came close, then vanished. After a while, she noticed they were alone. There were no more headlights and no more people waiting at bus stops. Only the empty street and snow.

Her mother said, "Haven't you taken a wrong turn? We ought to be on the freeway by now."

"No," said the driver. He had Daddy's voice. He glanced back, just for a moment. He had Daddy's face.

"Walter!" cried her mother.

"It is impossible to get away," he said. "Don't you understand that by now? You understand nothing about the reality of the situation. You have never been the least bit practical, Esperance."

"I have heard this kind of thing before," said Ayra. "In the house where we were trapped, before we came to this world. The monster who tried to burn us spoke this way, using words like *practical* and *realistic.*"

All at once, Daddy seemed to divide. He still had two arms that held on to the steering wheel and a face that looked forward, out at the snow. But a second pair of arms appeared and reached back toward Mother. A second face stared out of the back of his head. The face opened its mouth, showing long sharp teeth.

"No!" shouted Mother.

Daddy—the Daddy monster—took hold of Mother's shoulders, pulling her toward his mouth, which was getting wider and more full of teeth. Jennifer screamed. Mother began to growl. What was happening? Jennifer cringed away. Ayra laughed out loud. Mother was gone. Where she had been, in the middle of the cab's backseat, was an enormous bear. The monster was holding on to it, one arm on each hairy shoulder.

"Oh no!" the monster cried. "Esperance! Don't do it!"

A paw with long claws slashed forward. The monster's face was gone. There was nothing except dark blood, pouring down the back of Daddy's head. The other face, the one in front, began to scream. The bear lunged forward and bit into the neck of the monster. The cab spun, going sideways down the street. Then it crashed.

A minute or two or three later, Jennifer crawled out. Her knees wouldn't lock. She wasn't able to stand. She sat down in the snow. Inside the cab, the bear was worrying what was left of the monster, growling all the while. Jennifer began to cry.

"We don't have time for that," said Ayra. Jennifer looked up. The tall woman was standing above her. She had gotten cut in the

crash. Blood ran down her forehead. "Your mother is right. We
have to get to Father Dia—and on foot, I'm afraid. Get up.
You'll freeze here, or the monsters will come and tear you into
pieces." She held out her hand. Jennifer took hold. The woman
pulled her up. "Esperance!"

"Wurf?" said the bear.

"You've finished off the monster. Come on. We have to get
away from here."

The bear lumbered out of the cab. It—or rather, she—was huge
and dark with a patch of white fur on her chest. The mark of the
moon, thought Jennifer, remembering. A crescent with its horns
pointing upward. The bear bent her head and sniffed Jennifer's
shoes. The broad head lifted. The bear sniffed Jennifer's crotch.
Finally, she looked up, staring at Jennifer with yellow eyes.

"Mother?"

"Rrrr," the bear said.

"Can you find Father Dia?" asked Ayra. "Do you know the
way?"

The bear turned and lumbered down the street. Ayra and Jennifer followed.

It must be a blizzard, Jennifer thought after a while. The snow
was so thick, and the wind was blowing so strongly. There was
almost no traffic. And she wasn't able to see more than a block, if
that far. Streetlights shone distantly, like stars. She was getting
numb and tired.

Where were they? South of the University, she was almost
positive, and still west of the river. She stopped at the next street
sign and looked up. Snow covered the name of the street.

"Keep moving," called Ayra.

She trudged after the bear.

At last, they came to River Road. She was able to recognize it:
winding and tree-lined, with houses on only one side. On the
other side was a dark wood. This was the top of the river bluff.
The river, of course, was invisible. It ran far below them, hidden
by the trees and the darkness.

They turned right, walking south along a sidewalk that had
almost disappeared under drifts of snow. Jennifer could no longer
feel her feet. She stumbled and almost fell. Behind her in the
distance something howled.

"A wolf!" said Ayra. "Is that possible?"

"No."

The bear growled.

There was another howl.

"Well then," said Ayra, "it must be monsters. I wish I had my crossbow. Or any weapon. I did not expect to die like this."

She looked around at the house lights and streetlights and the snow.

Nor did she, thought Jennifer. Torn apart by wolves on River Road. What a way to go!

They kept walking. The wolves—or monsters or whatever—stayed behind them. Jennifer heard more howling and looked back. She saw nothing. But what would she see in this kind of weather?

A car went slowly past, then stopped ahead of them. A cop car. A man got out. "Are you okay? Do you need a ride? You shouldn't be out in this. It's dangerous—That has got to be the biggest dog I have ever seen."

"Yes. We need a ride," said Ayra. "And that isn't a dog. It's a bear."

"In Minneapolis? Lady, you can't walk a bear in the city of Minneapolis. And I'm not going to have it in my car. I'll have to call Animal Control."

He turned back toward the cop car.

"Arooooo!" Out of the dark and snow came a huge gray body, then another. The wolves! Her mother turned at bay. One wolf went for Mother's throat. The other nipped at her shaggy flank.

"My God! My God!" the policeman said. He pulled his gun and fired.

The first wolf tumbled and lay still. Mother hit the second one. Her paw lifted the animal off the ground. It screamed—a human sound. Mother tossed the wolf away.

More wolves came out of the darkness. The policeman kept firing, hitting nothing now. The first shot must have been lucky. Mother roared. Jennifer dropped and rolled under the car, coming up on the other side. The front door was unlocked. She climbed in and slid over to the driver's seat. Keys in the ignition. Engine on. Good. She stepped on the accelerator. The car moved forward. She tried to turn. The car slid and spun all the way around. She saw the group in the glare of the headlights: two humans hunched down and the great bear in front of them, surrounded by leaping bodies. The cop was no longer firing. He must be out of ammunition. Jennifer drove forward, aiming at the wolves. It wasn't easy.

She had so little control. She slid by her mother and smashed into the pack. They screamed. She heard human voices. "No! Help! Don't. Have pity!" The voices stopped. She braked and looked back.

Half a dozen bodies lay in the street. Mother was chewing up one last monster. A couple more loped away. Jennifer opened the car door. "Is everyone okay?"

"Crazy," the cop said. "I've gone crazy. Or maybe it's the new ice age. The animals are coming south. Is that it?"

Ayra said, "Come on, Esperance." She walked to the car. The bear followed. Jennifer unlocked the back door. Ayra climbed in. The bear crammed herself through the door and took up most of the backseat. She had blood on her muzzle and on her chest and paws.

"Hey," said the cop.

Jennifer closed the back door, reaching across her mother. Then she closed the front door and drove away.

They were going in the wrong direction, of course: north, toward the University. But she didn't want to go back past the cop.

Mother growled.

"I'm taking the long way around," said Jennifer. "North to Franklin Avenue and across the river there, south along East River Road till we get to Ford Parkway, and east along the parkway to Father Dia."

"Wurf," said the bear. Jennifer took that to mean approval. She leaned forward, concentrating on her driving.

It was a terrible trip. Visibility was low. Wind blew the snow into lines that wriggled across the road like snakes. There were gusts that pulled snow up into the air, forming tiny white tornadoes—that didn't sound right. Snow devils? Was that what they were called?

A car pulled out of a side street. It slid into her lane. She pumped the brake. Her car began to slide and turn. The two vehicles went past one another with two or three inches to spare.

Ayra said, "I don't much care for this method of transportation. A horse would be safer, and an ushaia is almost as fast."

Several blocks later, Jennifer asked, "What is an ushaia?"

"A quadruped with white fur and horns. They are intelligent and magical. They travel extremely quickly."

"I see."

They went under the Lake Street Bridge. Later—Jennifer wasn't sure how much later—they passed a car that had gone off the road. It was on the right side of the road, the river side. The car had hit a tree and stopped before reaching the edge of the bluff. It was tilted up, and its headlights illuminated the low branches of the tree. Not well, of course. Mostly, she saw snow and a dim glow. Something large and black was perched on one of the branches. A bird? It couldn't be! It was far too big. There was a man next to the car. He waved, trying to flag them down. Jennifer kept going. She was, she realized, giving the Minneapolis Police Department a bad reputation. And maybe earning herself some bad karma.

Mother growled softly.

"Did you see it too?" asked Jennifer.

"What?" asked Ayra.

"The crow in the tree that car had hit."

"I have got to find some kind of weapon," Ayra said.

They reached Ford Parkway and turned onto it. Now she could see nothing except white flakes of snow, whirling in the beams of her headlights. She kept going, extremely slowly. She ought to be able to stay on the road. If the car hit the curb, she would feel it. She decided not to worry about traffic on the cross streets. Only a total maniac would be out in weather like this. She had one worry left. How could she possibly find Father Dia's apartment?

Mother kept growling. The noise got louder and louder.

"What is it?" asked Jennifer.

"Stop," said Ayra. "I think I see something."

Jennifer braked the car. When it had stopped moving, she looked around. Off to the left, something was shining through the snow. A dim purple light.

"What on earth?" said Jennifer.

Mother pawed at the door.

"Open it," said Ayra.

Jennifer reached back and opened the door. Mother squeezed out, then shook herself and roared. She leaped forward, disappearing into the storm.

"Come on," said Ayra.

The two of them followed. The wind was icy. Hard grains of snow hit Jennifer's face, and she got a stabbing sensation in her forehead, right above her eyes. That was the cold. She didn't have her gloves. She put her hands in her pockets and trudged across the street.

There was a building. She could just barely make it out. Reddish purple light poured from one of the front windows.

"What is that?" she asked.

"Some kind of magic," said Ayra.

Mother pushed in through the front door of the building. A moment later, Jennifer heard a roar of anger. Something went crash. There was an inner door, she decided. It was locked. Mother was breaking it down. She walked toward the building. Ayra was at her side.

"Don't go in there!" a man shouted.

Jennifer looked around. He was coming from the next building, his back hunched against the wind and his coat already white. "It's on fire. Can't you see? We got everyone out. I called the fire department—if only it doesn't spread!"

Inside the foyer, Mother made a sound between a roar and a bellow.

"My God," said the man.

"That's our bear," said Ayra. "We have to go after her." She hurried into the building. Jennifer followed.

"No!" cried the man.

The inner door was smashed to pieces, and Mother was going up the stairs. The wall at the landing shone with reflected light that flickered and changed from purple to red to purple. Up they went, turning at the landing. Now Jennifer could see Father Dia's apartment. It was on the second floor, at the head of the stairs. The door was wide open. The room beyond shone purple.

"Rrrrr," said Mother.

"Gently," said Ayra. "Let's see what we're up against."

They crept to the door and looked in. The room was full of monsters: men with heads of wolves or crows. There were other strange combinations. Jennifer saw a crow about three feet tall, covered with gray fur. Nearby was a wolf with black feathers. At the back of the room was a table. On top of the table was the strangest combination of all, upright, eight or nine feet tall. It brushed the ceiling. What was it? Jennifer made out a head with a big nose and a bare torso. The creature had two huge breasts. Below the breasts was a grass skirt that went most of the way to the table. Below the skirt was a pair of feet. The feet were large and bare and black. They were human feet.

Two arms emerged from the grass skirt. They were covered with a plaid material. It was the kind of material used in pajamas. The hands were human, large and black. Each hand held a cross.

Of course, thought Jennifer. It was an African mask, the kind that rested on a dancer's shoulders and rose well above his head. The skirt concealed Father Dia's body. He was in there somewhere, human and more or less ordinary. She heard his voice. He was singing in an African language. The purple light shone out of him.

A monster—a wolf with the head of a crow—leapt at the table. There was something there, surrounding Father Dia. An invisible barrier. The monster hit the barrier and fell.

"They figured out he was one of the children," said Ayra. "They came after him. And he discovered that he is capable of magic."

A monster heard her voice. It turned and shouted. Mother charged. A moment later, Jennifer was inside the room. She had a floor lamp in her hands. She was swinging it, smashing the metal pole into something that had feathers and fur all mixed together. The creature had a human face that blurred and shifted and became the face of Kevin.

"Jen! Don't do it!" he cried.

She smashed the face in. A crow flew at her head. She brought the pole up and beat it off. Something coiled around her leg. Glancing down, she saw a snake covered with feathers. It was as thick as her arm. Oh no! She hated snakes. Mother appeared. She bent her head and bit the snake, which opened its mouth, showing human teeth. It screamed like a child and thrashed, letting go of Jennifer. Jennifer took on the next thing, whatever it was. It had black human skin and the face of Father Dia. But the arms were wings.

Ayra was in the middle of the room, beating down a crow-man with a Marcel Breuer chair. Father Dia was still on the table, singing more and more loudly. The purple light was getting brighter. And Mother was getting larger. She was now twice her previous size. She bit and clawed, roaring and growling.

Jennifer was having trouble with the man with wings. He wouldn't die, and she was getting tired. Her adrenaline rush was over. What was she doing in St. Paul, in a room full of monsters, carrying on like Jirel of Joiry? It was the wrong role for her.

The room grew brighter. She couldn't look at the priest. He blazed like the sun. Or like *a* sun: one darker than Sol, deep reddish purple. But still too bright to look at.

Then he was gone, and the only illumination was the ceiling fixture. She blinked and looked around. The monsters had vanished. So had Mother. Only one other person remained: Ayra, still holding on to the Marcel Breuer chair.

"Ahhhh." It was a long sigh. Ayra put the chair down. Her clothes were torn, and she was bleeding.

Jennifer noticed that she hurt all over. She dropped the floor lamp. Her hands were bloody. "What happened?"

"They have gone to another world," said Ayra. "Your mother and Father Dia, I mean. Once they were gone, the monsters could not survive. Remember? They depend on magic. And there is only one source of magic here. The bear children, who are gone." Ayra looked around. "Leaving us with a terrible mess. I don't want to have to explain to anyone what happened in this room. Let's get out, while we can."

They found the back stairs and took them down, leaving by the door into the alley. As they went out into the storm, Jennifer heard sirens. The fire department, coming to put out Father Dia's fire.

They walked through the alley and then took a side street north, away from Ford Parkway. Snow was still falling thickly, and the wind still cut.

"What next?" asked Ayra.

How calm she was, thought Jennifer. She glanced at the tall woman, who was striding through the snow, looking almost cheerful.

"I have a friend not far from here. Janie. She lives in a big house in Merriam Park. I don't think it's more than a mile. Or two, on the outside. We'll tell her we were in an accident. She'll put us up for the night, and I'll think of some kind of lie to tell Daddy."

Ayra glanced at her. "You're willing to lie to him now?"

"How could I tell the truth? For one thing, he'd never believe a word of it. For another, we're criminals. We stole a police car. There's no way he'd ever understand—Oh my God!" Jennifer stopped under a streetlight. Snow whirled around her. "Fingerprints."

"What?" asked Ayra.

"My fingerprints are all over that car. Why can't I ever remember to take my gloves?" She started walking again. "Maybe it'll be okay. I'm not like Mark. I haven't been in any demonstrations. They don't have my fingerprints."

"Take one thing at a time," said Ayra. "If any serious problems arise, I think I know how to get out of this world."

"What?" said Jennifer. She stopped again. "How?"

"I know the name of one of the other bear children. Arden Everett. He lives in a place called West Virginia, and he mines coal. It ought to be possible to find him, and he ought to have your mother's ability to go from one world to another. And to take other people along. You know, Jennifer, I think we ought to keep walking. We could freeze, standing here."

"Oh. Okay," said Jennifer.

They continued north through the empty streets. After a while, Ayra said, "But that is a last resort, if we run into real trouble here. I don't think my world is going to be peaceful in the near future. I'd rather stay where I don't have to worry about monsters and dragons."

PART FOUR:
ESPERANCE IN
THE OCEAN

Something warned her not to breathe. What was it? The coolness that covered her body? Or the sensation of weightlessness? She opened her eyes. Green. The world was green, without feature and without distance. She couldn't tell far from near.

Her lungs hurt. Carefully, she exhaled, forcing the air out between closed lips. Silver bubbles floated up. She was underwater.

For a moment, she was terrified. She spread her arms, thrashing, trying to beat her way to the surface. No. That would waste oxygen. The water was full of light. She couldn't be far down. She looked up and saw dark shapes. There were streamers and tangled knots. Between them, the water was silvery. A ceiling. Whatever those things were, they were floating on the surface. She swam up. She was naked, which was all to the good. Clothing would have weighed her down and hampered her movement.

Vegetation. That's what the dark shapes were. She moved between the strands or fronds. What was the right word for these things? In any case, they were brown and feathery. Tiny fish darted among them; and there were shells—barnacles—growing on the stems.

She broke through to air, gasped and inhaled. Above her was

the sky, bright and cloudless. Around her was the ocean, empty except for mats of vegetation. There were plenty of these, but no sign of land. She drifted up onto her back and floated, resting and breathing. Thank God for her fat. She was fifteen pounds overweight, and she floated like a cork.

What had happened? She had been in St. Paul, Minnesota, in a room full of monsters. Creatures from another world, that had been drawn to Earth by her magic and the magic of her brother, Father Lucien Dia. She and Father Dia had been fighting the monsters and losing. There was only one thing to do. Flee! She had sent Father Dia a telepathic message, showing him how to move between worlds.

Strange, thought Esperance. She could never draw on her power until she was in a desperate situation. Then—always, so far—she knew what to do and how to do it.

In any case, she had fled Earth and ended up here, in the middle of the ocean. A place off the map, as far as she was concerned. She wasn't even sure that she was in the right world. And she had no idea what had happened to Father Dia.

"Urk."

What was that sound? Esperance lifted her head. She was near a mat of floating vegetation. An animal floated next to the mat, holding on with two front paws. Was it resting? Or gathering food? She didn't know. The animal was twice as big as a good-sized tomcat, brown, with a round head and little ears. It had thick fur and a cheerful expression. An otter.

"Hello," she said.

A voice spoke in her mind. *Why here?*

"I don't know. I came up here, out of the water. Where am I?"

Home, the otter said.

"Not for me," said Esperance. "Is there any land around here?"

No. The otter pushed itself away from the vegetation, then twisted and dove.

"Hey!" said Esperance.

The otter was gone. She was losing her capacity for surprise. A telepathic otter didn't bother her. What did bother her was the otter's news: no land. It seemed likely she would drown. Unless she moved herself to another world. She closed her eyes and tried. Nothing happened. She could still fell water and hear a bird cry, "Eee-eee."

She opened her eyes. The bird soared above her. It was like a gull, but larger. Much larger. And it was rose pink. This wasn't Earth. Not with telepathic otters and rose pink gulls. That eliminated one possibility. But she had no idea how many more there were. Was she on the world she had come to the first time she left Earth?

What did it matter? She was going to die, unless the otter had lied. It had looked to her like an honest otter.

Wait a minute! If that bird was a gull, didn't that mean she was close to land? Didn't gulls stay near the coast?

The otter popped up next to her. *No*, it said. *Not gull.*

"What is it, then?" she asked.

Far-flying sky-at-sunset-colored bird.

"Oh," said Esperance.

Follow. The otter paddled off between the mats of vegetation.

Esperance swam after. Her shoulder ached, and it hurt to swim. She remembered: she had a wound there, a deep one. The bandage was gone, along with all her clothes. Nothing inanimate could move between worlds. So the wound could be bleeding or getting infected. Though the salt water ought to act as a disinfectant. Why wasn't the wound stinging? It ought to be, with salt washing into it. Esperance stopped by a mat of vegetation. She grabbed on. The mat sank a little, then supported her weight— enough of it so that she could turn her head and look at the wound. There it was. She could see it out of the corner of her eye. A red hole. It was almost entirely closed, and the flesh around it looked healthy, only a little pink. She touched the shoulder. It was sensitive, but not very. Strange. The wound was only a few days old. It was healing much too quickly. Well, maybe there was something therapeutic about moving between worlds or about changing into a bear. She had done both recently.

Follow! the otter said.

She glanced around. The animal was floating close to her. She got an impression of impatience.

"Sorry." Esperance paddled on.

They kept going through the clumps of seaweed or whatever it was. Creatures inhabited the vegetation. Esperance saw them climbing on the fronds. Tiny crabs. They were bright lemon yellow, and the largest ones were the size of a Susan B. Anthony dollar. (Esperance knew that, because she had gone out and gotten an Anthony dollar as soon as they were issued. It was in her jewelbox at home in Minneapolis. It was the only Anthony dollar she had ever seen.) She thought of stopping to watch the crabs.

No, said the otter. *Come on*.

They came to a larger than usual mat. It was surrounded by otters, who were pushing more vegetation toward it. There were other otters on top of the mat, pulling fronds out of the water, piling them up.

Make, said her otter, *resting place*.

"For me?" asked Esperance.

Yes.

She trod water and watched the otters work. They brought thick stems and used these to brace the mat. Some of the stems were pulled underneath and fastened to the bottom of the mat. Others were fastened to the edges or laid across the top.

Food, said an otter. Was it hers? It was floating upright in the water, holding a shell to its chest.

"No, thank you," said Esperance.

Eat. Rest. Wait. The Great Ones come.

"The what?" asked Esperance.

The Great Ones.

She saw them in her mind: enormous shapes that glided below the surface of the ocean. One rose. The wide back broke through the water. The creature blew out a white cloud of breath: a double geyser, shaped like a V. She heard their music: chirps and grunts and moans. The whales, thought Esperance. The whales were coming.

The Great Ones, said the otter. *Eat*.

She took the shell and pried it open—no easy task. But one of the otters brought her a fragment of shell to use as a tool. The creature inside tasted like an oyster. It needed lemon. Nonetheless, she ate it.

The otters finished the mat. *On*, they told her. *On*.

She swam to the edge and pulled herself up—slowly, carefully, afraid the mat would sink or break apart. But it didn't. She lay on her back, one arm over her face, protecting her eyes from the sun.

Rest, said the otters.

A few minutes passed. She began to feel warm. She remembered something she had been told about sunlight on the ocean.

On a bright day, the light came at you from every direction: down out of the sky and up off a mirror that extended from horizon to horizon. It—the light—was intense beyond belief. Or rather, intense beyond the belief of a Midwesterner. It could kill. It didn't take long.

She slid into the water.

Why? asked the otters.

"I need protection." She imagined a sunburn: the red skin and the pain.

The otters made soft noises, cries of distress.

"A covering," she said. "I need a covering." She imagined clothing and a hat.

Wait, said the otters.

They dove. She waited. They surfaced, one by one. They carried pieces of seaweed. *Here,* they said.

She took it. It was a new kind—like ribbon, long and flat. Some pieces were narrow. Others were wide. All were dark red-brown. She laid the seaweed on the mat.

Wait, the otters said. They dove again.

This time, they brought up pieces of coral. She thought it was coral, anyway. Fan coral. That sounded right. It was hard and flat and full of holes. White in color. The edges were sharp. Was it alive? she wondered. She had no idea.

The otters said, *Be human. Make. Make protection.*

"Okay," said Esperance.

She made a hat, winding seaweed through the pieces of coral, fastening them together. The end result looked like a coolie hat, more or less. And it reminded her of something else. Not Robinson Crusoe. Ah yes! The hat that Odysseus wore in the old paintings on Greek vases.

She put it on.

Good, said the otters.

They dove again and brought up more seaweed. It was the red-brown kind. She piled it on her mat. After that, she waited, floating in the water. The hat shaded her face and shoulders. She tried to make sure that the rest of her stayed underwater and in the shadow of the mat.

At last, the sun went down: crimson in a pale green sky. The otters made little chirping noises. These were a sign of happiness. They had been worried about her, she realized.

She climbed on the mat. Carefully, she raised herself into a sitting position. The mat did not sink. She took the red-brown seaweed and fastened it together, weaving and tying, until she had a cloak. By the time she was done, the last light of day was gone. She could no longer see the cloak. But she could feel it. It was lumpy and slimy. A nasty mess, she thought. With luck, it would remain in one piece. With luck, it would protect her.

She knew for certain that she was going to need it. She could feel heat in her face and shoulders. She had gotten sunburned, most likely before she made the hat. The burn did not seem bad. But a day in the sunlight, without a covering—it would certainly kill her.

She lay down. Stars appeared above her. She did not recognize any of them. Her mat rocked gently. She drifted off to sleep.

Morning came. Esperance woke. The sky was pale blue-gray. She glanced to the east. The sun was just rising: an arc of light at the horizon. At the edges of her mind, otter voices spoke. They were quiet and sleepy. She caught fragments of the conversation. The taste of a shellfish. Delicious! And the sensation of biting into a fish. A live fish that wriggled. What else? Weight and warmth and a sharp tug on a nipple. A young one resting on her belly and nursing.

One of the otters was dreaming. A nightmare. She saw something rising from underneath, long and dark and sinuous. A mouth opened. It was huge, far larger than she was. It was full of teeth.

"No!" cried Esperance.

Wake, the otters said. *Nothing here. Nothing. A dream.*

The otter who had been dreaming woke. Esperance felt the comfort of daylight.

She spent the day sitting on her mat. She wore the cloak and hat. From time to time, she splashed water over the seaweed and over herself.

Once again, the sky was clear, and the ocean was almost motionless. Halcyon weather. Was that the right phrase? She watched the otters dive and surface. They brought her a fish, which she gutted, using a piece of shell. She couldn't figure out how to clean off the scales, but she ate the insides. It gave her moisture. She was getting very thirsty. Her skin felt hot and dry. It was starting to peel already, especially the skin on her nose.

The wound in her shoulder continued to bother her. It was a dull persistent pain that radiated down her arm and up into her neck. The wound still looked good. It wasn't infected. Maybe it would be okay. But she wasn't comfortable.

Close, the otters said. *The Great Ones. Soon.*

Evening came. She slept on the mat. Her dreams were confused. Green water and fish and her husband, Walter, who ought to be at home in south Minneapolis, but who was drifting in the ocean like Phlebas the Phoenician, a fortnight dead.

In the morning, Esperance woke and heard a long loud sigh. Carefully, she pushed herself into a sitting position and looked around. A white cloud hung above the water, already dissipating.

What on Earth had that noise been?

There was another sigh, louder than the first one. White mist rose into the air, and she saw a long brown back. It pushed through the mats of vegetation, moving toward her. Her own mat rocked. The creature glided past. Through the clear water, she saw an eye, tiny and dark. And then a flipper. The flipper was huge, maybe ten feet long. The skin of the creature glistened deep golden brown. It was mottled white and gray. Barnacles, thought Esperance, remembering what she had read about whales.

The creature slid out of sight. Another one rose and blew. This one was farther off. In the distance, she saw other clouds of spray and flashes of light, sunlight reflected off the bodies of whales.

Little one, what are you doing here? The voices lilted in her mind. They weren't simple and singular, like the voices of the otters or like human voices. They were intricate, elaborate, like filigree or the music of J.S. Bach.

She tried to explain, re-creating in her mind the fight with the monsters, the flight from Earth, and her arrival in the middle of the ocean.

We understand, the voices said. *We go from one world to another. Not often anymore. Earth is dangerous, and we cannot bear to hear the voices of our cousins, the ones who cannot flee. The terror! The sadness!*

The whale voices stopped. She looked around. The whales were gone, all underwater. She heard—in her mind—a distant siren wail and then a sound like a motorcycle starting up. A whale song. It ended with grunts. The whales reappeared, spouting and shining.

The voices said, *It's the best way to get rid of barnacles. They don't like changes in the water. When we move from world to world, they die and drop off.*

This is a Place of Power, the voices continued. *Magic wells up from the floor of the ocean. The water is warm and rich, full of nourishment. Seaweed grows. Shellfish multiply. The otters get fat. When you fled from Earth, the magic drew you here. You are days from land.*

"What can I do?" asked Esperance. "How can I get to land?"

We will take you.

Out of the water right next to her, a whale rose. Her mat tilted, and she almost fell off. The whale spouted. She felt spray and warm air. The whale floated motionless. A tiny eye stared up at her. *I am Gruntmoan, the mother of the pod. Climb on me.*

She took off her cloak and rolled it up. Holding it in one arm, she slid into the water—going slowly, afraid that she might lose the cloak or hat.

A giant flipper lifted her. She climbed onto the back of the whale.

Be careful, said Gruntmoan. *My skin is delicate.*

Esperance settled herself in the middle of the back. It was dotted with barnacles. In front of her—not too close for comfort —was a pair of blowholes. Behind her was a fin, which looked small in comparison to the rest of the whale.

Are you in position? asked Gruntmoan.

"Yes," said Esperance. She unrolled the cloak and put it on.

The whale moved forward. Water rippled around Esperance. The back was awash, all except an area in the center, where she sat.

Good-bye, the otters said.

She glanced around and saw many brown heads among the mats of vegetation. *Good-bye,* she said in her mind. *And thank you.*

All day, the whales traveled north and west. Gruntmoan stayed on the surface. Esperance got wet, of course. Waves lapped against her; and when Gruntmoan exhaled, a double cloud of spray blew back. But the water cooled her sunburn and made it more endurable. And her clothes made of seaweed did not dry out.

Around her, the other whales in the pod dove and surfaced and spouted. Their motion was like the motion of a wheel: a smooth rise and fall, a turning. She tried to count them. There seemed to be nine. No. Ten. Maybe eleven.

Eight, said Gruntmoan. *And two children.*

Creakingnoise!
Hootwarble!

It was the children, breaking in to announce their names. Now the other whales joined in with howls, moans, gurgles, grunts, and wails: names and greetings that became a song.

It was, Esperance realized, a song in praise of the ocean: of the cold rich water of the north, full of plankton, and the warm water of the south, where barnacles fell off and children were born. A song in praise of currents, deeps and shallows, of icebergs and beds of kelp. Listening, she felt as if she were holding the whole ocean in her mind. A disturbing sensation. She blinked and shook her head.

The song ended. The pod traveled on.

"You said that you could travel between the worlds."

Yes, said Gruntmoan. *There are three species that can. Humans, of course, though only the great wizards who weave spells to carry them to another kind of reality. We are different. All of us know how to cross, as soon as we are born. We know it in the same way that we know how to breathe.*

Our knowledge is not the same as the knowledge of the wizards. They can take other beings with them between the worlds. We can take only ourselves. And we cannot teach what we know. We have tried over and over. Our cousins on Earth do not understand. It is like breaching, we say. You throw yourself out of the water, but not into the air. Into another place. They try. They fail. We cannot save them.

For a while after that, the whale didn't speak. Esperance felt sadness radiating out of the enormous body. How long was the body, anyway? Sixty feet? Or seventy? She had never been good at judging distance or size.

At last, she said, "What is the third species that can cross?"

Dragons, of course. Not the miserable little things that fly around these days. They are the result of whatever is going wrong with the pattern of power. They are perversions, like the great hairy serpent of the ocean. I am talking about the old dragons. The great dragons. The Magnificent Ones. They found their own world long ago and left this place. They do not welcome visitors.

"You know how to get to their world?"

Yes.

Esperance felt a twisting. She thought she was falling. She imagined herself to be on a windy plain. The sky was dark blue.

A red sun hung above the horizon. Above her soared dragons: many-colored, shining like opals or mother-of-pearl. They were nothing like the dragons of fairy tales. They reminded her of pteranodons. Their heads were long and narrow. They had tails like snakes and small hind legs. Their arms were wings.

No, no, little one, a cold voice spoke. *We want no part of you.*

One dove, folding wings that were patterned like the wings of a butterfly. It plummeted through the ruddy sunlight. Its skin, which must have been scaly, glistened gray and pink. *Get out. Begone.* It was almost on her. Looking up, she saw huge yellow eyes and a muzzle or beak full of tiny sharp teeth.

Esperance fled. She found herself on the broad back of the whale. Her cloak and hat had fallen off her. They lay next to her. She put them on. "What happened? Was I there?"

Where? asked Gruntmoan.

"In the world of the dragons. I thought—you showed me how to go, and I went."

Impossible. I told you. We cannot teach anyone what we know.

"Oh," said Esperance. "Are you certain?"

Yes. You have not been gone. You shifted your weight. Your cloak slid down. That is all that happened, and it took only an instant. I felt it. As I told you, my skin is sensitive.

"Oh," said Esperance again.

Late in the afternoon, she said, "Water, water everywhere and not a drop to drink."

I will send for the dolphins, Gruntmoan said. *They will bring fish.*

"I need water," said Esperance.

There is none you can drink.

The dolphins came, sleek and gray, leaping and diving among the whales. They brought her fish.

Here, whale-friend. A present.

Our greetings to you. Be safe from shark and orca and from the great hairy serpent that rises out of the deep.

Eat well. Be happy.

The dolphins went off, leaping and diving. Esperance tore the fish open and squeezed out water, intermixed with blood. She drank the water. She was still thirsty, and hungry as well. She ate the raw flesh. It was close to tasteless. "How long before we reach land?"

Two days, said Gruntmoan.

Esperance said, "Too long."

Evening came. The whales kept moving. Esperance dozed, sitting on the broad back of Gruntmoan. She dreamt that she was in the world of the dragons. It was night. A moon shone, round and orange. She knelt by a pond and cupped her hands, bringing water up to her lips, which were dry and split. The water was cold. It had a clean taste. Delicious! She drank again and again.

There was a *whoosh*, an enormous settling. Esperance looked up. On the other side of the pond was a dragon. It was folding its wings. The moonlight was bright. She could see it clearly. It was covered with patterns as subtle and delicate as the patterns on a snake. The patterns shone dimly. For a moment or two, it seemed to Esperance that the patterns moved, shifting and changing like the colors on an oil film, floating on water. But that was impossible. One could not see colors in the moonlight. And even if one could, they would not behave like this, coiling and oozing into one another. Esperance blinked and shook her head.

There were claws on the wings of the dragon. Four on each wing. One came out of the wingtip, and the other three were attached to the joint in the middle of the wing. The dragon was like a bat, she realized. It flew on membranes stretched on finger bones.

It finished folding its wings. The tips were behind its narrow head. The upper part of each wing—the part between the shoulder and the joint—had become a leg. The clusters of claws were feet. The dragon had become a quadruped. In that position —or shape, or guise—it was about twice as tall as Esperance.

Well, bear child, it said. *How are you doing? And what are you doing here?*

"I need water."

Not here, where we came foreseeing nothing but trouble from humanity in our old home. You are too quick. You are too curious. You poke and pry. You never leave well enough alone. You have always been like that. Always! Even when you scurried through the underbrush and lived on insects and the eggs of your betters.

What? thought Esperance.

The dragon was getting angry. That much was evident. But the voice in her mind remained calm. An icy voice. The eyes of the dragon shone.

*We have endured too much and for too long. We will not let
you bother us again. Now go! And leave us in peace! Or you will
learn about the anger of dragons.*

"Very well," said Esperance. She stood up and tried to return
to the world of the whales. Nothing happened. She was still by
the pond. The dragon hissed: a long low sound. It unfolded its
wings. Amazing! She would never have thought it could move so
fast! It leapt into the air. Wings beat. It was above her. The long
neck bent. The head reached down. The mouth was open. Esperance could feel the breath of the dragon, hot and stinking. She
saw many little teeth. She ducked. And then she woke on top of
Gruntmoan.

Thank God! It was nothing but a dream. She looked around
with relief. The sky was beginning to pale. It was early morning.
Strangely enough, she was no longer thirsty. And once again, her
hat and cloak lay next to her.

"Hoo-ee," said Esperance and put her clothes back on.

Another day of travel. There were clouds now: middle-sized
cumuli. A wind blew. There was chop on the water. Esperance
got thoroughly wet. Only one thing remarkable happened. Late in
the afternoon, a whale exploded from the water. It wasn't far
from her. For a moment, it hung in midair. She could see the
entire body: enormous, golden brown. The skin on the belly was
pleated and pale yellow. The whale fell, crashing into the ocean.
Spray flew up. Esperance let out her breath. If she ever got back
to Earth, she was going to have to join some kind of environmen-
tal protection group.

That was Faintwaveringcry, said Gruntmoan. *He gets exuber-
ant.*

"Is that why whales breach? Out of joy?"

There was a long silence. Finally, Gruntmoan said, *We are
nothing like you humans. We know that. We have listened to
sailors and wizards, when they talk on boats or on islands. You
like explanations and lists. Put down in order of preference. Explain in twenty-five words or less. Take one from column A and
one from column B. You pick. You pull apart. You decide one
thing is better than another. You seem unable to see the whole.*

There was another silence. The whales began to sing. She
heard them in her mind. Operatic warbles were combined with
creaks and groans and a *whoo-whoo* sound, like a jug in a jug

band. This was a song about breaching: how the muscles flexed and stretched, how the sun shone and how it felt to drop—smash!—into the ocean. It was, the song told her, a great way to get rid of an itch. She felt a whole series of emotions: joy, exuberance, pride, even irritation. There was nothing like breaching to cure a fit of pique. We do it, the whales sang, because we do it. And it is what it is.

The song ended. "Okay," said Esperance. "I think I understand."

In the evening, the dolphins returned, bringing more fish. She ate.

Gruntmoan said, *Tomorrow we will arrive at the island of the sorceress.*

"Sorceress? What sorceress?"

The one who guards the pool that lies in the ocean. It a Place of Power, like the Gray Promontory and the Well at Kol. And the place where you came up. In all those places the true nature of reality is most evident, and the great forces—the forces that shape existence—can be most easily reached. Or so the wizards say.

Esperance felt doubt. "You don't believe the wizards?"

The world is what it is. It has a shape, the way a whale has a shape. Flukes and flippers and blowholes, baleen, a skeleton, and a skin. But the skeleton is no more real than the skin, and the baleen is no more essential than a fluke or a flipper. We do not understand how the wizards can say, "This is real. This is important. That over there is superficial or unreal."

"Oh," said Esperance.

She slept badly and woke often, feeling cold. She had no dreams she could remember. Dawn came. The sky was cloudy, and there were whitecaps on the ocean. Waves beat against her. She began to fear she might be swept off the whale.

Only half a day, said Gruntmoan.

Her shoulder ached. She was thirsty. Her sunburn still bothered her. She felt mildly depressed. The whales continued west and north. Their brown bodies rose. The blowholes spouted, and the fins slid by. Then the whales were gone, and the wind blew away the white clouds of their breath. This happened over and over in a rhythm that Esperance could almost figure out. The repetition, the rise and fall, was soothing to her. Exhilarating, as well. It was a strange combination of emotions.

Around noon, the island came into view: a dark line at the horizon.

There, said Gruntmoan. *You are almost safe.*

"It's about time," said Esperance.

The whales swam closer. Esperance saw white shoals and a ragged line of trees. Or were they bushes? In any case, the island was covered with vegetation. There were no hills. The island was flat. A coral reef, most likely.

Only a little farther, said Gruntmoan. She screamed and rolled. Esperance was thrown into the water. Beside her, the huge body thrashed, the tail smashing down. On what?

In her mind, Esperance felt pain. Something had hold of a flipper. Sharp teeth bit in. A long body twisted and coiled under the whale. Gruntmoan knew what it was. Esperance felt her terror and saw the thing in Gruntmoan's mind. A great hairy serpent of the ocean, furred like seal with little seal ears and a mouth full of needle teeth. It was twice as long as the whale.

The water around Esperance churned. The whale screamed. Esperance heard the serpent chuckle.

Hahaha, it said in her mind.

Then Gruntmoan was gone. She had fled to another world. The serpent remained. Esperance felt a hairy body brush against one of her legs. It went on and on.

Flee! cried the other whales. *Flee!*

The creature was turning. Out of the water rose a head, mottled yellow and brown. The thing had whiskers on its long reptile head. Whiskers and fur. The eyes were deep orange. The pupils were horizontal lines.

Ah-ha, it said. *Human. A tasty snack.*

Esperance tried to flee. Anywhere would do. Earth or the world of the dragons. But she went nowhere. She was still in the ocean. The serpent bent its neck.

Tasty. Tasty.

Esperance growled. She ducked under the descending head, and her bear mouth bit into the monster's neck. Blood rushed in over her tongue. It was hot and sour. Esperance bit deeper. The monster raised its head, lifting Esperance out of the water.

Esperance—no longer human, but changed into a great sow bear—grabbed on to the long narrow body the way she would grab on to a tree. Her claws dug in. She chewed on the neck.

The monster screamed and smashed itself down into the water. It was diving. Esperance would drown.

Hang on, she told herself. It was her only chance. The monster was over a hundred feet long, but only a few feet wide. Two, maybe. Or three. Somewhere in the neck, there had to be a major artery. She ought to be able to reach it. She kept on chewing.

The monster reached a bed of seaweed. Esperance, her eyes open, caught glimpses of the stuff: huge strands rising up and up through the dim water. They were like kelp, thick and leathery. The monster thrashed among them, trying to beat off Esperance. She felt her claws begin to slip. The monster slammed her against the ocean floor. Stunned, she let go. She could no longer see. The water was dark. In her mind, the monster was screaming.

Her lungs hurt. She was far below the surface. She would never make it up to air. Why wasn't the monster eating her?

The darkness was blood. The monster's blood. She felt the water moving, stirred by the monster's convulsions.

She had to get to the surface. No matter if the monster were waiting to nab her once she was out of the cloud of blood. She was drowning. She couldn't stay down here. She pushed off the bottom. In a moment or two, she was in clear water. She saw the monster. The long body floated, tangled in seaweed. It still twitched and shuddered. The head hung limply. The neck had a ragged hole. Blood came out in spurts. The heart of the monster must still be working.

Esperance swam up. Out of the dimness that was distance in the sea came something new. It was long and sleek. It glided past her. A shark.

She kept swimming, terrified. The shark ignored her. It swam around the monster in a great circle. Another shark appeared. It too began to circle the monster. Then a third shark came. This one decided to take a look at Esperance. It slid by, so close that she could count every gill slit. It opened its mouth. She saw the ragged teeth.

Slowly, calmly, she told herself. Don't panic. Don't attract any more attention. Keep going up. Amazing! How well this body of hers was able to swim!

The shark made a circle, then another one. It was getting closer, and it had to be at least fifteen feet long. Esperance got ready to fight.

The shark turned and swam away. Esperance looked down. The monster was surrounded by sharks. How many were there? Ten? Or twenty? She couldn't count. She was blacking out from lack of oxygen. She wasn't going to make it.

Then, all at once, there were bodies all around her, touching her, pushing her up. She couldn't see them. They must be sharks. She thrashed and bellowed, swallowing water.

No, no, voices spoke in her mind. *Don't claw at us. We know who you are. The whale-friend. We will carry you to safety.*

Esperance lost consciousness.

When she came to, she was on the surface of the ocean. She coughed and spit out water, then took in air, gasping raggedly. Something was supporting her. A sleek body. No, two. Dolphins. They were on either side of her.

Whale-friend, whale-friend. Are you all right?

Yes, she answered in her mind.

Rest. Be quiet. The land is near. They carried her through the water. *The whales will make songs about you. The monster-killer, who can change into something strange and terrible and—in that form—do in the great hairy serpent of the ocean. And then change back to a woman.*

At that point, Esperance noticed she was no longer a bear. Her body—aching and red and peeling—was human again. "A bear," she said. "The thing I was is called a bear."

The bear woman, the dolphins said, *We will remember that.*

She drifted in and out of consciousness. At times, she was aware of the water that lapped against her body and the wind that touched her face. At other times, she thought she was at home in south Minneapolis. Her living room was full, it seemed to her, of a subaqueous light. Her husband drifted past and her two children, Mark and Jennifer. They moved like swimmers. In the basement lurked something terrible. Another monster. She woke with a start.

We can go no farther, the dolphins said. *The water is too shallow.* They moved away from her. She sank and felt sand underneath her feet. She stood. Her knees gave out. She fell into the water.

Get up. Get up. The dolphins nudged her.

She pushed herself onto her knees, then managed to get on her feet. In front of her was blue water and a long white beach.

Walk, the dolphins said.

She walked, staggering and almost falling.

Keep going, the dolphins called to her.

She made it to the beach and fell full length on the sand. Once again, she lost consciousness.

PART FIVE:
THE ISLAND OF
THE SORCERESS

This is the story that Esperance Olson told after she returned to Minneapolis. She told it to her daughter Jennifer and to Ayra of Ymmouth, the merchant and sailor.

Imagine the three of them in a kitchen. The kitchen is in an upper duplex, which Jennifer rents, along with two other young woman.

It is a large room. The walls have been recently painted. They are off-white, the kind of hue that paint stores call "chablis" or "ivory." The floor is covered with yellow linoleum: a good old marble pattern out of the 1940s. There are streaks of white and flecks of a medium gray.

The refrigerator comes from the same period, or maybe a little later: the '50s or the early '60s. It is sleek and heavy, with rounded corners. A solid appliance.

The stove is new and looks cheap. It is harvest gold. The refrigerator is white.

Three windows open to the east. Sunlight comes in through them. It is pale and watery, the kind of light one gets early in spring. Outside, the sky is pale and clear. There is a tree in the back yard. The branches are covered with red buds.

Esperance and Ayra sit at the kitchen table, which is square and made of wood and painted bright yellow. They are both women of a certain age, as the French say. Forty, maybe Ayra is long and lean. She wears a flannel shirt and blue jeans. Her hair is short and blond.

Esperance is shorter and stockier. Her hair is shoulder length and gray. It looks ratty. Her face looks tired. She has lost weight. There are hollows under her cheekbones. (There didn't used to be.) It is easy to see the line of her jaw, especially when she clenches her teeth. She does this often. It is a sign that she is thinking, or trying to think.

She wears a buffalo plaid shirt, too large for her, and a pair of skintight jeans. Her feet are bare.

Her daughter Jennifer stands by the kitchen counter. She is twenty or twenty-one, of average height, thin and wiry. Her hair is long and brown. It flows over her shoulders. Like the other two women, she wears jeans. Her shirt is a T-shirt, blue with a picture of dolphins. It says, SAVE THE HUMANS.

Jennifer has just made coffee. The pot is on the counter next to her. It is glass and looks like a laboratory beaker. The smell of coffee fills the room. Esperance has a cup in front of her. Ayra, who hates coffee, has a can of beer. Jennifer has nothing. She does not believe in the use of mind-altering substances, especially before noon.

Remember this scene. Think of it from time to time. Imagine the women shifting position or getting up to get more beer or coffee. The story is a long one. Ayra and Esperance are going to have to go to the bathroom at some point. At some point, Jennifer will decide that she is hungry and heat up a couple of bagels. She will serve them cut in half and spread with butter and cream cheese. Imagine how the bagels will look: brown on the bottom and white on top, where they are covered with cream cheese. Melted butter oozes out from underneath the cream cheese. It drips onto a plate of handmade earthenware. The plate is gray. It matches the cup that Esperance uses.

All of this—the women, the sunlight, the smell of coffee, and the sight of bagels spread with cream cheese and oozing butter— is just as real as the story of Esperance's journey.

*   *   *

"Okay," said Esperance. "You want to know what happened to me, after I left here. After the fight with the monsters in St. Paul."

"Yes," said Jennifer. "And what happened to Father Dia. He vanished when you did."

"And the monsters vanished, too," said Ayra. "For that we were grateful."

"Though we didn't enjoy the mess they left behind," said Jennifer.

Esperance frowned at her daughter. "Are you trying to make me feel guilty? I didn't mean to leave you with a mess."

"If you feel guilty, that's your problem," said Jennifer. "Guilt is something that your generation goes in for. I guess it has to do with Watergate and Vietnam and the death of the American Dream."

Ayra leaned forward. "Do you know what happened to Lucien Dia?"

"Yes," said Esperance. She clenched her teeth. The muscles along her jaw bulged. "I could see that we were going to lose the fight. I had to get away. I hoped that if I went, the monsters would follow. Minneapolis and St. Paul would be safe—as safe as any place on Earth. There is more than one kind of trouble."

"We know," said Jennifer.

Esperance looked at her daughter. "I don't have much control of my abilities. I can't always use them. But it seemed to me at that moment that I knew how to get to the world of magic.

"I spoke to Lucien. Not out loud. In my mind. I guess it was a kind of telepathy. I told him what to do. And then I left. He followed, and so did the monsters." She paused and took a sip of coffee. "I don't know what happened to the monsters. Maybe they went back to wherever they came from. Lucien went to the city of white stone. Do you remember? He told us about it. He had dreamed about it for years—the wide streets and the gardens, full of flowers and brightly colored birds. The people are tall and black and courteous and dignified."

"The city of Bashoo," said Ayra. "Which is the capital of the great kingdom of Bashoo."

"Un-huh," said Esperance. "It is his real home. He came from there. Or rather, his mother did. She is the queen mother, now. Her other son is king."

Esperance paused for a moment. She pushed her ragged hair

away from her face. "They made him welcome—Lucien, I mean. They needed him. The enemy was active in Bashoo."

"Ah," said Ayra.

Esperance nodded. "The situation wasn't as bad as it was further north—in your country, Ayra. No one saw any dragons; and there were only a few monsters high up in the mountains. They didn't do much harm.

"But the wise folk of Bashoo—the wizards and the historians —said there had been a definite decline in the quality of life.

"Their workers had become less careful. Their merchants were less honest. Crime was on the increase; and there were a lot more roaches."

"What?" said Jennifer.

Esperance grinned. "That's what Lucien told me. According to him, the city was full of roaches, and no one knew how to get rid of them."

"That sounds bad," said Jennifer.

"It was." Esperance drank more coffee. "The wise folk—the witches and the oracles—knew what was causing all this trouble. They could sense it. A being that slid below the surface of reality, like a crocodile below the surface of a river. *Oomaga-i-mali*, they called it: 'the malevolent being who stays out of sight.' They could see the changes that the *Oomaga* made, like ripples in the water. They had a sense of something large and powerful, moving close to them. But they could not see the thing itself. They did not know what it was. They couldn't find its lair, though they suspected that the creature lived somewhere in the eastern ocean."

"An oceangoing crocodile?" asked Jennifer.

"I think there were marine crocodiles at one time," said Esperance. "Your brother told me about them, when he was into paleontology."

"Okay," said Jennifer.

Esperance paused and clenched her teeth. "They got a fleet ready. They decided to sail across the ocean, back and forth, until they found the *Oomaga-i-mali*."

"Ah?" said Ayra. "That would take a while. The ocean is large."

Esperance nodded. "They were desperate. Then Lucien arrived; and they realized that he could lead them to the *Oomaga*."

"How?" asked Jennifer.

"Remember, he was one of the bear children. He had been created to fight the *Oomaga,* over forty years ago. There was a connection between him and the enemy. Maybe even an attraction.

"The wise people of the kingdom believed that either the *Oomaga* would draw Lucien to it, or Lucien would attract the *Oomaga* and bring it up to the surface, where it could be seen and fought.

"In the first case, Lucien would act as a kind of moral compass. In the second case, he would be kind of moral lightning rod. In either case, they would find the *Oomaga.* The king made Lucien the leader of the great fleet of Bashoo. The fleet set sail— about the time, I think, that I arrived on the island of the sorceress."

"I'll get to that," said Esperance. "One thing at a time."

The other two waited. I barely made it to the island. I crawled up onto the beach. I must have tried to stand, because I fell. I can remember falling.

"All at once, the sand was rising—coming straight at me. I put out my hands. I tried to stop it. It hit; and I was out.

"From this point on, I'm going to have to give a lot of detail. This is the main story, and it gets very complicated."

I woke (said Esperance) late in the afternoon. I was in bed in a small room. The floor was white marble. The walls were azure. I think that's the word I want. A light to medium blue, very pure and clear. There were windows high up in one of the walls. They were small and square; and I couldn't see out of them, not from where I was. The bed was low.

A door opened into a courtyard full of shadows. I lifted my head. I was able to see a bit of sky above the colonnade on the far side of the court. It was deep blue, full of afternoon sunlight.

Where was I? What had happened? I closed my eyes, trying to think and noticed the music. It wavered at the edge of my hearing. Voices. Human voices, high and sweet. They rose and fell, lingering. I thought, this island was like the island of Prospero. I looked up the quote, after I got back here. It goes:

> Be not afeard. The isle is full of noises,
> Sounds and sweet airs, that give delight and hurt not.

Sometimes a thousand twangling instruments
Will hum about mine ears, and sometimes voices
That, if I then had waked after long sleep,
Will make me sleep again.

The speech is given to Caliban, which has always surprised
me. He's such a brute. Barely human. And yet the speech is
beautiful. Oh well. He's a peculiar character. Not easy to understand.

Where was I?

The music. I listened for a while. I couldn't make out any
words. The melody was soothing, but melancholy too. I wished
I could understand the lyrics. But the voices were too faint.
Where did they come from? I opened my eyes and looked
around. The room was empty, except for the bed and me and a
jar made of silver. The jar was about three feet tall and embossed with a pattern of loops. They reminded me of a net or
the scales of a fish. The faintness of their voices argued for
distance. But I had a feeling they were close. In the courtyard,
maybe? I was too tired to get up and look. I closed my eyes
again. After a while, I slept.

I woke in the middle of the night. A woman stood in the
doorway of my room. She held a lantern that burned oil or kero-
sene and cast a wavering light. But I could see her well enough.
She was tall with dark red hair that fell around her shoulders. Her
face was wide and pale. I couldn't make out the color of her eyes.
Hazel? Gray? Maybe green. She wore a long robe. It was dark
blue.

"Welcome, oh child of the bear."

"You know who I am."

She nodded. "Esperance Olson. Your father is the bear king, a
mighty spirit. You were bred to be a heroine, to hunt down and
destroy the source of all our present troubles. Whoever—or
whatever—he or she or it may be." The woman smiled gently. "I
found you on the shore of my island, unconscious, lying in the
sand. I roused you and led you to my house. This place." She
gestured with her free hand. "I am Soringalla, the keeper of the
Pool of Ab. You are welcome here. Rest now. Go back to sleep.
In the morning, we can talk."

She left. I took her advice and slept soundly till morning.

When I opened my eyes, I saw sunlight coming in through the little high windows. The air was cool. It smelled of salt water. A wonderful aroma! I listened, but I couldn't hear the sound of the ocean. Instead, I heard music again—the voices. As before, they rose and fell, blending and separating. As before, the words they sang were unintelligible.

I got up. I was naked, I noticed. There was a robe on the end of my bed. It was yellow cotton, embroidered in blue and green. I put it on. Then I wandered through the house, looking for Soringalla.

I wish I could describe that place! It was something out of ancient Greece. There were colonnades and courtyards, walls painted with bright colors and cool marble floors. I noticed the temperature of the floors, because I was barefooted. My hostess has provided no shoes.

There was no statuary. That was different from Greece. But every room contained at least one jar, and the jars were works of art. They were two or three feet tall, made of stone or metal, carved or embossed. All of the patterns on them were abstract: loops, spirals, wavy lines. Most of the jars had stoppers. I thought of pulling one out. No, I decided. Never mess around with the belongings of a sorceress. I didn't especially mind turning into a bear from time to time. I had gotten used to that. But I didn't want to become a spider or a toad.

I'm forgetting the music. I could still hear it—in every room, but never clearly.

I came to a door, the only one I had seen that was closed. I opened it and stepped out into brilliant sunlight and a rushing wind. I stopped and blinked, then shaded my eyes. In front of me was a wilderness of little bushes, bent and twisted by the wind. The soil between them was sandy. There was a patch of blue: the ocean, seen through a gap in the vegetation. I walked toward it, going along the wall of the house.

I turned a corner. The wind struck me full force. It was coming off the water, and the water was straight ahead: a wide glittering expanse. It lay on the other side of a terrace of white stone. A balustrade went around the terrace; and there were more jars, these made of alabaster and granite. There was a table too, round and heavy—made of a pale pink stone. Marble, almost certainly. A pole went up from the middle of the table. It was made of dark metal bronze. On top of the pole was an umbrella: coral red with yellow fringe. In spite of the wind, the fringe was barely moving. My hostess sat in a chair of pale blond wood, inlaid with silver. The umbrella shaded her. Like it, she was unaffected by the wind. Her robe did not flutter. Her hair lay on her shoulders, smooth and motionless. She glanced around at me, then beckoned. "Come. Sit down," she called. "Have breakfast."

I noticed another chair on the other side of the table. I walked toward it. When I was about ten feet away, the wind stopped. The air around me was almost entirely still. The roar of the ocean was distant. It sounded muffled. I stopped and turned, holding out an arm. The wind was there, only a few feet away. I felt it brush my fingertips, but it did not reach my wrist.

"The weather here is not good," Soringalla said. "I would not be able to use my terrace or my fine view of the ocean, if I didn't employ a few simple charms to ward off wind and rain and dim the sunlight a little."

She was right. The light was more bearable, and the view was easier to see. I didn't have to blink or shade my eyes. There it was: the beach of white sand and the combers. Rows of them. They went out and out, halfway to the horizon. Then the true ocean—the deep ocean—began. The water was dark blue, flecked here and there with white. Gulls soared in the cloudless sky. I was impressed.

I turned again and went the rest of the way to the table. I sat down.

"I have bread and fruit," my hostess said. "Also a fine herb tea from the island of Pendi, which lies far to the south of here. And a copy of yesterday's *Wall Street Journal*, flown in from the Fortress of Worlds by carrier albatross."

"What?" I said.

"As you may know, nothing inanimate can pass from one world to another. But my colleagues at the Fortress have found a way to take exact measurements of objects in other worlds and then replicate them here. They are marvelously precise. This paper even has ink which comes off one's hands, turning them as black as pitch. This—they tell me—is a characteristic of the true *Wall Street Journal*, the one that is printed on Earth. There, my colleagues tell me, the powerful and wise have dark fingertips and smudges on the palms on their hands. It is a sign of high position."

"Well, maybe," I said. I picked up the paper, unfolded it and looked over the front page. No question about it. This was the *Wall Street Journal*. A bit blurry in places. I couldn't make out the central column, the one usually devoted to human interest stories. But the business news was readable. "I don't know," I said after a minute or two. "There's an article here about the commodities market."

Soringalla frowned. "But that is real, is it not? There is such a thing on Earth?"

"Yes, but I don't think they trade dragon futures. The article is about the sudden rise in the price of dragons—due, according to rumor, to the Hunt brothers, who are trying to corner the world supply of mythological creatures. It isn't likely, Soringalla."

She took the paper from me and read the article. "You're right. It must be an error in transmission. A glitch or gremlin. I believe that is what such things are called. Well . . ." She glanced up and smiled. "This is nothing to get upset about. The process is right in principle. We may—it is true—have to make a few minor adjustments. But this is no time to talk about business. Eat! There is cinnamon bread and stewed prunes, slices of mango and papaya and tea."

She served me. I ate. Everything was delicious. The tea was pale red with a flowery aroma. It seemed to be a natural tranquilizer. I felt myself relaxing. I was still tired, I noticed, and I felt a little melancholy. Discouraged. What was I doing here in this strange world? Nothing good or useful, as far as I could tell. I ought to be home in Minneapolis.

Once again, I could hear the voices. They were a little louder than before. Maybe it was an effect of the magic that protected me, sitting on the terrace. At last, I could make out a word—only one: "Woe, woe," the voices sang.

I slouched down in my chair and drank more tea.

"I have work to do," said Soringalla. "Spells to weave and enchantments to make. But you stay here and rest."

I nodded, feeling increasingly weary. My hostess stood. I looked up at her. "Can you get a message to Gerringarr? The wizard of the city of black stone?"

"Yes."

"Tell him I'm here. I'm back in this world, and I don't know what to do next."

Soringalla smiled gently. "I will tell him."

She left. I poured myself another cup of tea. The voices continued to sing.

You know that I have trouble with depression, Jen. I used to think it was due to my Scandinavian heritage. Now it turns out I'm not the least bit Scandinavian. Maybe it comes from frustration. Think of all the years I spent in south Minneapolis! I must have known—somewhere, in the back of my mind—that I didn't belong there. I cooked and raised children and took Walter seriously; and all the time, I should have been in Ymhold, the city of black stone, or else in the mountains with my father the bear. All that time misspent! It's enough to make anyone feel depressed.

Not that I think you were a mistake, Jen, or your brother. But the other stuff—the house, the garden, the courses in gourmet cookery. . .

Anyway, I get depressed easily and often very quickly. I can go from a good mood to black despair in twenty minutes. I did it that morning on the island of the sorceress. After my third cup of tea, I was ready to contemplate suicide.

It's hard for me to explain my reasoning, after I'm out of a mood like that. But I'll try. I felt tired. Everything seemed difficult and probably not worth doing. In any case, I was certain to fail. I was an idiot. A sluggard. A bad mother. A worse wife. And as an epic heroine, I was the absolute pits.

"Woe, woe," cried the voices. Other voices, higher and sweeter, cried, "Ware, ware."

I listened, forgetting for a moment what an awful person I was.

"Ware. Ware. Beware."

"What do you mean?" I asked.

I got no reply, except for the usual music with lyrics I could not understand.

What did it mean? I thought of asking Soringalla. No. If the voices were trying to warn me, it must be against her. I decided to take a walk. Maybe I'd feel better, if I got out where the wind blew. Maybe I'd be able to think of something besides what an awful person I was. I got up and went forward, away from the table. There! My hair began to move. I felt the wind against my face. My robe fluttered around my feet. There were tears in my eyes—due to the wind, no doubt, and maybe to the brilliance of the day. The sun blazed above me. The ocean flashed and roared. I tightened the belt around my waist, then kilted up my robe. After that, I climbed over the balustrade. My bare feet came down on hot sand. I hurried toward the water.

All morning, I wandered along the shore. The tide was going out. I crossed wide flats of sand, still wet, with shallow pools and little meandering rivers of ebbing water. Now and then, I came upon a heap of seaweed. The stuff came in two colors: rust brown and deep burgundy red. It didn't look like much, lying on the sand, but it had some interesting inhabitants. Tiny crabs. They were no more than two inches across and pale yellow, like ivory. If I stood and watched, they would creep out from among the strands of weed and scurry around, busily doing whatever it is that crabs do. I spent a long time, watching the crabs and trying to remember something. A line of verse. The seaweed reminded me of poetry. At last, I remembered. It was from the end of "The Love Song of J. Alfred Prufrock." How did it go? It was something about lingering in the chambers of the sea—

> By sea-girls wreathed in seaweed red and brown
> Till human voices wake us, and we drown.

That was it! I had always wondered how to read the line about the sea-girls. Were the girls wearing seaweed, or had they draped the stuff over the speaker, J. Alfred Prufrock? I had no idea, and there was no one here to ask. You can never find a professor of English when you need one.

I turned back toward land. I still didn't know what I was going to do. I was supposed to be on an epic quest. But who was my enemy? And how was I supposed to defeat him? Or her? Or it? Maybe Gerringarr would be able to tell me. I climbed up the beach. I was a good distance from the house, which I could just barely see. In front of me were bushes, little and low and dull greenish gray. Their leaves had sharp points. I wandered in among them. There was room to move, without getting scratched or hung up on the foliage. In a few minutes, I was in an utterly different landscape. Closed in, with no broad vistas. The wind eased a little. The sun felt hotter than before. My mouth was dry. I thought of going back to the house and getting a drink of water. No. I wanted to be outside, away from the cool stillness of the house, which oppressed me, and away from the voices. I sat down. Now the landscape I saw was different in a new way: twisted branches and clusters of leaves and ground that was spotted with sunlight and shadow. There was life here. I heard the buzz and hum of insects of some kind. A lizard scurried up a branch. A huge beetle that shone like bronze lumbered over a little hill of sand. The beetle must have been as long as my thumb, with very impressive mandibles. But it moved slowly. It didn't look dangerous.

All in all, the place was pleasant. And there was always something restful about nature, except when it was trying to kill you—with a tornado, for example. But nothing like that was happening here. I watched the beetle and listened to the other insects.

I began to doze. I was still tired from my fight with the great hairy serpent of the ocean.

I dreamt that the sky began to darken, and the bushes stretched up, till they covered the sky and blocked out almost all the light. I heard voices singing:

> "Ware, ware, beware.
> Cannot you hear?
> Beware.
> Beee ware."

The voices trailed off. I was alone. The darkness was utter. There was no sound at all. I reached out, trying to feel the bushes that ought to surround me. Nothing. Only air. It was still and cold. I shook with terror. Then I jerked awake.

I looked around. The sun shone as brightly as before. I listened. The leaves rustled. The insects buzzed and hummed.

It was time to go back to the house, I decided. If I was going to sleep, I'd sooner do it in a bed. And anyway, the state of my mouth was becoming unbearable. I had to get some water. I stood up and went back to the beach, walking along it toward the house. The sun beat down. My head began to ache. I entered the house with relief. It was so cool! So dim and comfortable! To heck with nature! I didn't even mind the voices.

"Woe," they sang. They made it a kind of round, singing the one word over and over, high and low.

That was a bit depressing. I decided to ignore them. I needed water. I went through the house, looking for my hostess. I didn't find her, but I found a courtyard with a fountain. The fountain was an urn, made of marble and deeply carved. I couldn't make out the design, because moss grew all over it, in every nook and cranny. The urn was full of water. Water trickled down the sides, seeping through the patches of moss. At the bottom of the urn, it fell—*plink! plink!*—into a little pool. I knelt and cupped my hands, scooping water from the pool. Ah! Delicious! Cold and clean! When I had drunk enough, I sat down cross-legged.

The courtyard was covered with glass. The light that entered it was dim and tinted a pale blue-green. I couldn't hear the wind or the ocean. Only the voices and the trickle and drip of the fountain.

"Woe." *Plink.* "Woe."

Slowly, my depression returned. I ought to get up, I thought. Do something. Get outside. But everything seemed too exhausting. Better to sit and listen to the voices.

In time, Soringalla came for me. "Esperance! Are you all right?"

I nodded and wiped the tears from my eyes. I felt like an idiot. What was wrong with me? "I'm fine."

"We have missed lunch. What do you say to an early dinner and then an hour or two of television? I have recordings of *Wall Street Week* and *Washington Week in Review.* They are almost current."

"It sounds fine to me." I got up.

Soringalla led me to the dining room. It was painted with wavy lines, yellow and green. The candelabra were lit. The table was set. We sat down and ate. Dinner was a fish stew like bouillabaisse and a dry white wine. After we were done, she led me to another room, a study of some kind, painted coral pink. There were two chairs that reminded me of ancient Greece or Rome and a large color TV. Soringalla turned it on and fiddled. "We have not yet perfected the manufacture of audio and video equipment. You will find this does not have the high quality you are used to."

I grinned. Walter disapproved of television. I wasn't crazy about it, except for the science programs on PBS. Neither one of us wanted to spend money on a new set. On the rare occasions when we watched TV, we used a tiny and ancient black-and-white Sony with failing sound. High quality, indeed!

But Soringalla was right: her set was awful. The images were distorted and blurry. The sound faded in and out. Most of the time, Paul Duke was green. Louis Ruykeyser began his show the color of a turquoise, then changed to blood-red and then to purple, an amazing hue. I had never realized that a color TV could produce anything like that. It was so deep and rich!

After the second show was over, Soringalla turned off the set. She got out a bottle of brandy. We drank. The brandy had a light and fruity flavor. I didn't think it was made from grapes. And in my opinion, it was a bit too sweet.

I asked, "Why are you so interested in Earth? Why the television? Why the *Wall Street Journal?*"

"Because our world and Earth represent two opposite extremes, the two ends of a continuum. We have devoted ourselves to magic. On Earth, you have devoted yourselves to the nonmagical, which you call 'science' or 'technology.' "

"I guess that's true."

Soringalla frowned just a little, irritated by my interruption. "In order to practice magic, one must see the world as a whole and animate. Everything is connected. Everything is alive. The problem is, there are many problems that are best solved by taking things apart. By sorting and classifying and setting up carefully limited experiments. In many ways, your science is superior to our magic.

"If one sees the world as full of *things*—of separate objects, most of which are not alive—it is easier to manipulate reality. Knowing nothing of the consequences, you are able to ignore them. You people on Earth have done wonders in the area of manipulation. Consider your metallurgy! Your machinery! Your high technology! Your genetic engineering! No magician would dare to treat the world the way you do." Soringalla paused. She refilled our goblets. These were marvelous, by the way: large and delicate. They must have been hand-blown. A serpent made of dark green glass wound around each stem. She set down the decanter, then glanced at me. "There are those among us who believe it is possible to combine magic with science and with technology. Therefore, we study Earth."

"Are you sure that's a good idea? We've messed up a lot of things."

"True enough. But we need not make the same mistakes." She sounded confident.

I felt tired and vaguely dissatisfied. There was something

tacky about this evening. Here I was, in a world of magic, and what was I doing? Watching Louis Ruykeyser and talking about the wonders of genetic engineering. Where were the winged horses? Where were the famous weapons with messages written on their blades in letters of gold?

"You look weary," my hostess said. "I think you have reached your limit, in this last adventure. Go to bed. Sleep. Your struggles have been hard."

"You know that?" I asked.

She smiled. "I know most of what has happened to you."

She led me back to my bedroom. I lay down and went to sleep, almost at once.

After a while, I dreamt. I was in a dark wood, tangled and thorny. Birds sang above me. They had human voices.

"Woe," they trilled. "Beware. Beware."

"Who are you?" I asked.

> "Mariners:
> merchants and fisherfolk.
> We came
> to the island of the sorceress,
> washed up in storms
> or bringing merchandise.

> "And she,
> corrupted by the love of power,
> wove her spells.

> "Like nets they were,
> the fishing nets that catch
> bright cod and herring,
> tuna,
> all the rest,
> and dolphins too,
> the music-loving friends
> of sailors.

> "Caught in her magic,
> we could not escape.
> She made us small
> and closed us up in jars.

"Bound by her enchantments,
   we must sing
   sweetly and sadly.
   Alas! and alas!"

The voices paused for a moment. I looked up. The branches above me were full of birds, and the birds had human faces. Rough brown faces. The faces of working men and woman.

"Flee, Esperance," they sang. "Get out of here.

"There is a boat,
   a little sailing craft,
   anchored in a bay
   across the island.

"Go!
   Now!
   By moonlight,
   for the moon is full.
   The wind is easing,
   shifting to the south;
   and you can run before it,
   north and west.

"Keep the wind behind you.
   Watch the moon.
   Where it sets,
   below the ocean swell—
   in that direction lies
   the continent
   and all the towns we knew,
   when we were human."

Again the voices stopped. Again I looked up. This time, the birds had the faces of birds.

"Wait a minute," I said. "I've sailed, but never on the ocean and never single-handed. I don't think I can do it."

"You have no choice.
   Your only hope is flight.
   And anyway,
   the boat is magical.

"It will do its part
and half of yours.
You need not fear.
Now, go!"

The sky above the trees grew dark. I could no longer see. But
I had one final question. "Can't I help you?"

"No.
Not now.
Think of yourself
and flee.

"But remember
you were saved
by poor folk,
shut in jars—
singing,
singing
at command.

"Not even their voices
their own."

That was the end of the song. I woke, shaking. Moonlight
shone in the little high windows. I rose and dressed, kilting my
robe. Was I crazy? Wouldn't it be safer to ignore the voices and
assume that Soringalla was what she appeared to be?

I left my room, retracing the path I had taken in the morning:
down corridors lit by wavering lanterns and across courtyards lit
by the pale bright moon.

Funny. Except for the TV, there was nothing electrical in the
house. Why? Hadn't my hostess gotten around to having the place
wired? Come to think of it, where would she find an electrician?
She might have to bring one from Earth. Think of the cost!

The voices continued to sing. Now, as before, I could make
out only two words. *Woe* and *ware*.

I came to the door that led outside. I paused for a moment.
Was I doing the right thing? I could still turn back. If I met the
sorceress now, while I was in the house, I could say I was looking
for a bathroom or a drink of water. But what excuse could I

possibly have for being outside in the middle of the night? She'd
know I was up to something. She'd put me in a jar.

"Ware," the voices sang.

I took hold of the doorknob and turned. The door opened. I
stepped outside. Behind me, the voices sang, "Well, well, fare
well." I closed the door and heard it click. I tried the doorknob. It
wouldn't turn. The door was locked. Well, that solved the problem of indecision. I looked around. The voices had been right
about the moon. It was full. It shone among little high thin
clouds. As for the wind, I barely noticed it. But this was the north
side of the house: and if the voices had told me the truth, the wind
was out of the south.

Where to? I asked myself. Across the island. The ocean was to
my right. So I ought to go left. I walked along the house and
came to a little path that led west through the wilderness of
bushes. I took the path. In a minute or two, the house was behind
me, and I could feel the wind. It blew gently and steadily—out of
the south, as promised. The path wound back and forth. I looked
around and saw nothing except bushes. They were gray in the
moonlight. Most were three or four feet tall. A few were almost
as tall as I was. I saw no evidence of animal life and heard nothing either, except the rustle of leaves and the soft noise the wind
made. And the roar of the ocean, of course, off in the distance.

The land began to rise. I scrambled up and down over low
hills. Or were they dunes? What was the difference, anyway?
Now there were only a few bushes, growing in the hollows between the hills. The slopes were covered with grass. It was pale
and stiff. The path was sandy. I slipped from time to time. How
long had it been since I left the house? Half an hour? I climbed a
last hill or dune. It was taller than the others. On the top, I
paused, gasping for breath. In front of me was the ocean.

Lovely! It glittered in the moonlight, a little choppy. Below
me was a large circular bay. There was land on three sides of it:
high dunes that sloped down to a beach. The beach was wide and
gray. A boardwalk went across it, beginning at the foot of the
dune I was on. Interesting. The beach must be underwater at high
tide. The walk led to a dock that extended far out into the bay. At
the end of the dock was a boat. It was tiny. Well, I thought after a
moment, maybe the boat would look bigger when I got close to it.

I went down the dune, slipping and sliding. Then I crossed the boardwalk. I went carefully. It was wood and might have splinters. Onto the dock I went. There was water under me, washing onto the sand. I heard the soft rush and the gurgle, as it ebbed away. Ahead of me was the mast of the boat: the only part visible. It moved slightly. I heard—or thought I heard—the slap of a rope. Or maybe that was water against the hull.

A minute later, or two or three, I reached the end of the dock. I looked down at the *Trust Me*. That was the name on the stern. It—she—was a sloop, about twenty-five feet long. I was supposed to take *that* out on the ocean?

I sat down on the edge of the dock and thought about Beatrice Harris.

She was one of my neighbors on Gitche Gumee Avenue. The bungalow on the corner, the one with the blue trim. You must remember, Jen. She used to live there. Her husband retired a couple of years ago, and they moved to the Caribbean. But the two flagpoles are still there, in front of the house. Beatrice and Edward used them to fly Old Glory and the Union Jack. Old Glory was for Edward, who grew up in Iowa. And the Union Jack was for Bea, who came from England thirty years ago.

As long as I knew them, they had one passion: sailing. They kept a boat on Lake Minnetonka—Lake Nokomis wasn't big enough. Every weekend, they took the boat out. For vacation, they flew to somewhere interesting—Europe or southern California or the Caribbean—and took a sailing cruise. Or else they rented a boat and pottered around on their own. That was her word. Beatrice's. They "pottered" on the water. She taught me to sail. She needed a crew during the week, when Edward was at work.

"This isn't a car," she always said. "You don't hop in and drive to the market. Or if you do, you're a fool.

"Sailing is an art, and you prepare for it the way a good artist prepares to paint. Check everything. Make sure you have everything you might possibly need. Make sure that everything you might possibly need is near at hand. You don't want to waste time hunting around for the storm sails or the burnt umber, when the storm is almost upon you or inspiration strikes."

Okay, I told the memory of Beatrice. I'd do my best.

There was a ladder on the side of the dock. I climbed down onto the boat. It moved a little under my weight. At once, I got a sense that it—that *she*—was responsive and friendly. A good boat. Seakindly. I thought that was the right term.

The mainsail was on the boom under a cover. Everything looked orderly and moonlight gleamed on metal fittings that were obviously highly polished.

A good boat, I thought again and walked aft to the cockpit.

The stern of the boat had drifted in till it was almost under the dock. The shadow of the dock lay on it. I had trouble seeing. I climbed into the cockpit and peered around. After a moment or so, I made out the tiller and something else, which I did not recognize: a metal pole that was fastened to the stern. On top of the pole was a large flat piece of wood. It reminded me of the vane on a weathercock. What could it be?

It *was* a vane, I decided after a moment. I was looking at a self-steering mechanism. Beatrice had told me about them. They were used by people who sailed alone on the ocean for long distances—across the Atlantic or around the world.

I understood the theory of the thing. If the sailor wanted to get some rest, then he or she connected the vane to the rudder. If the wind changed direction, the vane would turn, and so would the rudder. The boat would change its course, following the wind. The person on the boat could sleep in peace.

You couldn't use a thing like that close to shore, but out in the middle of the ocean, it was wonderful. So what if the boat got a little off course? You could handle that in the morning. A person has to sleep.

And I had to get going. I turned and saw a locker. There were letters on the door. They gleamed faintly "Open me," they said. I did.

The rest of the rails were there, stuffed into bags.

"Thanks," I said and pulled them out. I opened the bags and felt the fabric inside them. The thinnest sail was out. It would be large and for a lighter wind than was blowing now. The thickest sail was a storm jib.

That left two sails, intermediate in thickness and therefore in size. I pondered for a moment. Letters appeared on one of the bags. "Use me," they said.

"Okay." The other sails went back in the locker. I closed it and opened the hatch that led into the cabin.

A light came on: a globe on the ceiling. The globe was full of a silvery glow. Not bright, but adequate. More magic? Or electricity?

I went in the cabin. It was painted gray. A pale color, close to white. There were two bunks, made of varnished wood. The wood was almost the same color as the paint. Each bunk had a pillow, covered with lace. The lace was gray. A medium shade. And each bunk had a blanket, striped gray and green and white.

There was nothing else in the cabin, except for the light in the ceiling. And the lockers. They were all over. Every wall was full of little doors. The handles and the hinges were made of a silvery metal that gleamed brightly, even in the dim light of the ceiling fixture. I began to open the doors.

I found everything I needed. The lifeline and an orange jacket. A set of maps. A compass. A dozen bottles of mineral water. According to the labels, the water was "sparkling and pure, from the famous Pool of Ab, low in sodium, containing twelve ounces." The labels were handwritten. Soringalla was bottling her own water—out of a magical pool!—and adding an advertisement to every bottle.

"Weird!" I said out loud.

The light in the ceiling flickered. Did the boat disagree or was it warning me to get moving? I crouched down on the floor between the two bunks and opened the maps. The light grew brighter. I looked for Ab and found it. It was east and south of a great promontory. The Hook of Emblar. It reminded me of Cape Cod. If the wind held, and I had no trouble, the trip was possible. But how long would it take? I checked the scale of the map. Curious. It was in miles. Why did these people use our system of measurement? It beat me. In any case, the island was two hundred miles away from the Hook. Two days, I thought. Maybe three, if the wind shifted or blew less steadily. I could manage that, I hoped and prayed. But I'd have to be really careful with my water.

I folded the maps and put them away, all except the one that showed in detail the shoals around Ab. I put on the life jacket. I picked up the lifeline. Then I went on deck.

I put on the sails. No trouble there. I checked the rigging. This was slow work, and I felt myself growing impatient. But I had to understand where every rope went and what it did. According to Beatrice, ignorance might be bliss at Eton College, but it was dangerous out on the water. (She was referring, of course, to the poem by Thomas Gray. It is called "On a Distant Prospect of Eton College" and it ends, "Where ignorance is bliss, 'Tis folly to be wise." The crucial word is *where*.)

I checked the rigging and then the tiller. The tiller was perfectly ordinary. I took a quick look at the self-steering mechanism. It looked simple enough. If I had to, I could get it to work.

Well, this was it. I took in a deep breath, then let it out slowly, the way I had learned, taking yoga at the Y. Good-bye, island. Thank you, voices.

I fastened on the lifeline. Then I raised the sails. They flapped and filled with wind. I cast off the mooring line and sat down next to the tiller.

The boat slid away from the dock. I turned it—or her—northeast across the bay. Not into the ocean. It was too soon for that. I had to learn how to handle the *Trust Me*.

For an hour or more, I tacked across the bay. The wind held mild and steady. The moon moved toward the west. The boat, she handled wonderfully. She was light and quick and responsive, no trouble at all to steer. But she wasn't too light. Her motion was smooth and easy. She must have been perfectly weighted and balanced.

"Okay," I said at last. "This is it, kid. We have to be out of the shoals before the moon goes down." I changed tack and took her into the ocean.

Once we got out of the shelter of the dunes, the wind grew stronger. There was a definite chop on the water. But the boat kept moving easily.

"You must be magical," I said. "Or else well made."

We went straight west. There was a channel through the shoals—too narrow for a big ship, a freighter, but fine for the *Trust Me*. We followed the channel, sailing across the wind. On either side of us, waves broke over hidden bars of sand. I could see flashes of white, as the water foamed. I began to feel a certain exhilaration. I was crazy to be doing this, and plenty could go wrong. But at least I wasn't going to be bored in the next few days. Or depressed. There wouldn't be time. And I never got depressed when I was faced with something that was frightening.

We kept going west, till the water changed. Instead of meeting waves, the *Trust Me* glided up and down over ocean swells that looked like hills. They were that tall. We had left the shallows. Now, according to the map, we sailed over the Deep of Ab. It was safe to turn northwest. I did. We kept the same course all night.

I don't think there is any way to describe the voyage: the motion of the boat, the even rise and fall of the water. There was the feel of the wind too, and the wonderful ocean aroma it carried. Weeds and fish and whatever. There was the creaking of the rigging, the noise of the water as it foamed around the prow of the *Trust Me* and rushed along the outside of the hull.

The moon went down, but I wasn't in the dark. Stars shone in between the clouds. The ocean had a light of its own—due, I suspected, to some kind of marine life. It was very dim, just barely visible, except where the water was disturbed. There, the creatures who made the light shone far more brightly. Why? Out of fear? Whenever I looked back at the wake of the *Trust Me*, I saw sparks of pale fire, tiny flashes in the turbulence.

Most wonderful of all was the compass. I had found it in the cabin, and it lay next to me in the cockpit. As soon as the moon went down, it began to glow. A silvery light came out of it, similar to the light in the cabin. The needle remained dark, as did the characters that marked direction. I was able to check our course. We continued northwest.

I stayed at the tiller until dawn. The sunrise was magnificent: orange and yellow and red. What is the rhyme? "Red sky at night. Sailors' delight. Red sky at morning. Sailors take warning." But I didn't remember that, I was too tired. I had to sleep. I didn't have a choice. I connected the self-steering device and sat for a while, nodding and dozing, trying to make sure that the mechanism worked. As far as I could tell, it did.

"Take care," I told the boat.

I picked up the compass—it was no longer shining—and crawled into the cabin. I fell onto a bunk. In a minute, I was asleep.

I slept for hours—deeply, without any dreams that I can remember. Then, at last, I began to dream. I was in a marsh or mire, surrounded by reeds. They rose above me, brown and dry, so tall that they blocked my view in every direction. I had a sense that the day was overcast, though I couldn't see the sky, and that I was near the ocean. This was a salt marsh. I was almost positive. Around me, in the reeds, were birds. They clung to the dry stalks, which bent under their weight. The birds had human faces, the same ones I had seen before: brown and worn.

"Wake! Wake!" they sang.

> "The sorceress works her spells.
> The wind has changed direction.
> Now it blows
> from west to east.
> It drives you from the land.
>
> "Wake! Wake!
> Your boat has changed its course,
> turning with the wind,
> and now it goes
> north and west.
> The fortress lies ahead.
>
> "Worse! Worse!
> The sorceress has made
> a great storm.
> The south and west are black."

The birds flapped their wings. The reeds bobbed. The voices sang:

> "Rise! Rise!
> Oh daughter of the bear.
> Rise! Rise!
>
> "Go up on deck and see
> how the clouds tower,
> how the bolts of lightning flash."

I woke. The boat was moving less smoothly than before. I could feel that at once. I opened the hatch. A moment later, I was on deck. The wind had risen. The sails were taut. They lifted the boat. It skipped over the blue-gray waves. Ahead of me, the sky was clear, except for a few high clouds. The sun shone there, barely dimmed. The voices were right. The wind had changed direction and so had the *Trust Me*. We were sailing east.

I glanced toward the stern. Huge cumuli rose behind me. Their tops were white, but their lower parts were dirty gray and black. Lightning flashed. I could taste fear in my mouth. It was sour, like stomach acid.

What time was it? Late morning. Ten or eleven. I could tell that by the sun. I had been asleep for—what? Six hours? Who knew how long I had been traveling east?

I disconnected the self-steering mechanism. Then I tried to turn the boat, to sail west into the wind.

It wasn't easy, and it became more difficult. The wind kept rising. It began to gust and change direction—blowing out of the north, then out of the west, then out of the south. But never out of the east. I wasn't good enough. I couldn't tack across a wind like this. Around noon, I realized I was going to have to give up. I had no choice. All I could do was run before the storm.

Out not with this much sail. I turned the boat again, so it pointed into the wind. The sails flapped. I locked the tiller and pulled the storm jib out of its bag. I went forward.

The sky was green-gray. The ocean was streaked with foam. I could taste the flying spray. I took down the main sail. The jib was more than enough in this wind. We sped east and north. I changed the jibs, then winched the mainsail part way down.

Somehow, in the midst of this, I lost track of the sail I had just taken off. I did not remember it, until I had finished reefing the mainsail. I looked around. There it was, caught by the wind, flapping over the water like a bird. There was no way that I could reach it; Damn! It dove into a wave and crumpled into a heap of canvas. It started sinking. I unloaded the tiller and turned the boat. Wind filled the sails. We sped east and north.

An hour passed. Maybe two. The sky grew darker. Lightning flashed above me, and I heard the crack of thunder. It was close, very close. Raindrops fell—*splat!*—on the deck.

Splat! Splat! Then, suddenly, sheets of rain fell out of the sky. I could barely see the mast and jib sail. The cockpit was full of water, salt and fresh combined. How could I steer, with visibility almost gone? I couldn't even rely on the sound of the boat. The thunder was too loud. It was almost continuous now, as was the lightning. I was terrified.

One thing was certain. The mainsail had to come all the way

down. I turned the boat and locked the tiller going forward a second time. Water washed around me. Rain and spray beat against my face. My eyes burned and filled with tears.

I grabbed on to the mast and began to lower the sail, as lightning flashed and thunder rumbled. The boat rocked under me. Now all I had to do was get back to the cockpit and finish reefing. I might well manage it. I got the sail down.

I felt something around my foot. I looked down. A tentacle, large and pale. It was wrapped around my ankle. I could see the suckers and the rubbery skin.

"Oh no!" I glanced toward the stern. At first, I saw nothing. Then I made out three or four more tentacles. One was wrapped around the tiller. Another one grabbed the vane and bent it, then tore it free. For a moment, the tentacle waved the flat piece of wood. Then it tossed it aside.

The tentacle around my ankle tightened and began to pull.

"No!" I cried again. I grabbed onto the mast with both hands.

Now, rising out of the foam, I saw an enormous pale torpedo-like body. A giant squid! It was behind the boat, holding on with half a dozen tentacles, while more tentacles writhed forward, reaching out for me.

Horrible! I wrapped my arms around the mast. The boat was rocking crazily. A second tentacle reached me and clutched at my shoulder. A third one wrapped itself around my leg.

I was losing. I couldn't hold on. Slowly, bit by bit, the squid was pulling me away from the mast.

I screamed, Jen. I pleaded. I don't know with whom. God. The squid. The Norns.

The huge pale body rose farther out of the water. The damn thing was pulling itself onto the boat, which was tilting and beginning to sink. Now I could see what was in the middle of all the tentacles. Not—as I had expected—a beak, ready to bite me into pieces. Instead, I saw a round brown human face, wearing gold-rimmed glasses.

"Esperance!" the face shouted. "Don't you realize? This is all a delusion! You are not an epic heroine! You are a housewife from south Minneapolis, and you are very sick indeed."

I recognized the face. It was Dr. Ferris, my psychotherapist. Startled and uncertain, I relaxed the hold I had on the mast. The tentacles jerked. I fell. The tentacles pulled me along the deck, toward Dr. Ferris.

"No! No!" I cried.

"I want to help you, Esperance," shouted the face. The mouth opened wide, too wide. No human had a maw like that. "This is no answer! This is fantasy! You have to confront reality!"

I tumbled into the cockpit. It was full of water. A wave went over me. The stern was going down. I grabbed at a rope and tried to brace myself against the sides of the cockpit. It was no use. The tentacles pulled me toward the mouth of Dr. Ferris. It was enormous. I could still see the glint of his glasses, but the rest of his face was gone, hidden by his mouth.

"I am trying to help you!" shouted Dr. Ferris. "Everyone is! Walter! Your children! We are all concerned. We'll all do what we can. But you have to cooperate."

"No!" I yelled.

The mouth opened still wider. The tentacles pulled me in. The doctor swallowed me—all of me, entire.

"What?" said Jennifer.

Ayra asked, "Why didn't you turn into a bear?"

"I don't know. But my powers aren't mine to command. They come and go. This time, they never came." Esperance smiled. "So there I was—in a stifling darkness, inside the squid."

"Well, what happened next?" asked Jennifer. "You didn't die, did you? You look okay to me."

Esperance took a sip of coffee. It was cold. She continued the story.

There was air in the squid. It had an unpleasant aroma. A slightly rotten meat smell, like old hamburger. After a while, I became aware of a dim light. The walls of the cavity I was in— the creature's gut or whatever—were glowing. I was able to see.

I was in a tube or cylinder, about four feet wide and ten feet long. I lay in the middle of the tube. The surface I lay on felt rubbery. I touched it with my hand. It gave slightly, though I did not exert much pressure. It felt slimy and warm.

Oh ick.

Above me was a ceiling. It curved down to meet the surface I lay on. It glowed dimly, like everything else in that place, and I got the impression that it was moist.

Where was I? And what was going on? I wasn't being digested—as far as I could tell, anyway. So why had the squid eaten me? What was it planning to do? I had no idea.

I sat up and examined myself. I didn't seem to be hurt, except for a few scrapes and bruises—inevitable, under the circumstances. I'd been afraid that the squid would bite me. But nothing like that had happened—to me, at least. I looked at my lifeline. I was still wearing it, along with the orange life jacket I'd found on the *Trust Me* and the yellow robe that Soringalla had given me, back on the island. The line was incomplete, no more than four feet long. It ended neatly and cleanly, as if it had been cut by a sharp knife. Did the squid have a beak, which I hadn't noticed? Hidden, maybe, behind the lips of Dr. Ferris? I didn't know. I unfastened the line. It was useless now. But I kept the jacket on. I was still in the ocean.

Time passed. Nothing happened. I grew tired. I lay down and slept.

Once again, I dreamed. This time, I was in darkness. I saw no forest and no marsh. I reached out. There was nothing around me—not even the body of the squid, which should have been there.

The voices sang:

> "It carries you
>   north and east,
>   speeding through the deep,
>   through the dark water
>   below the storm.
>
> "Above you,
>   waves curl and foam,
>   lightning flashes,
>   the west wind howls.
>
> "The *Trust Me*,
>   your gallant little boat,
>   has tipped over.
>   And now she lies
>   half-overwhelmed by water,
>   that rushes in
>   through broken portholes
>   and through the broken hatch.

"Sinking,
 sinking,
 she will not last for long.

"Meanwhile, your captor
 —the squid—travels on,
 north and east
 below the surface."

The voices paused for a moment. I waited. They continued, as sweet and high as always.

"Fear no harm
 until you reach the island.
 This beast was made
 (by foul magic)
 to capture you
 and bring you through the water
 to the fortress."

There was another pause. I waited again.

"Your enemy awaits,
 and we can help no longer,
 though we have been
 no help that matters.

"Maybe this, as well—
 the dreams,
 the journey—
 was nothing but a scheme,
 a trap,
 or a diversion.

"Maybe we have been
 the bait that drew you
 to the hook
 or to the net.

"We do not know.
 We dream and sing,

caught by her magic,
held prisoner
in dark that does not end."

    The voices stopped singing. I woke and felt the floor below me shudder. The ceiling above me was pulsing—contracting, then expanding, then contracting again. I looked to either side. The walls were doing the same. In and out. In and out. The spasms grew stronger. The ceiling touched my head. I crouched down, then curled myself into a ball. I felt the walls around me, warm and wet and fleshy. They squeezed me and released me and squeezed me again. Each time, the squeeze was tighter. I was going to be crushed. I tried to think of some final words, though there was no one to hear them. Nothing good came to mind.

    I felt a spasm, far worse than any before. This was it. The flesh that held me squeezed and surged. A moment later, I was tumbling across a hard cold surface. I opened my eyes. I lay on a gravel beach. A gray mist surrounded me. I could hear water lapping. Where was the storm? Had the squid traveled beyond it? I sat up. The ocean was in front of me, barely moving and mostly hidden by mist. I could see the squid as well. It lay half out of the water. The face was still there, round and brown. It had lost the gold-rimmed glasses.

    "Farewell," it said. "You need more than I can give you, Esperance. A controlled environment. A more intensive kind of therapy. There is much that can be done, but not by me. These people—I assure you—are excellent." The squid waved a tentacle.

    I looked around. Through the mist, I saw a wall, rising up and up. It was stone. I saw no windows. A fortress, I thought after a moment. *The* fortress. The home of my enemy, whoever that was.

    "I leave you in good hands. Try to cooperate. Remember, most of what you see is illusion. The product of illness. Concentrate on what is real—your husband, Walter, and the children. Your house. Your garden. Those excellent tomatoes that you told me about. And the peonies. The dark ones, that you love so much! In time, if you work hard, you will be able to return to south Minneapolis."

    The tentacles twisted and writhed. The creature was trying to grab hold of the beach. No—it was bracing itself and pushing. Slowly, the pale body moved back—away from me, into deeper water. It was turning. I stood up. In a minute or so, it faced—if that was the right word—the open ocean.

"Good luck," it called to me in a voice that gurgled. It waved a tentacle, then sank from view.

I was alone on the beach.

PART SIX:
HOW THE
FORTRESS FELL

This was the place I had been warned about. I was almost positive of that. I took another look around. In front of me was the ocean, flat and gray. A hundred feet out, it vanished, hidden by a heavy mist.

Shhhh. A very gentle swell washed up onto the beach and then retreated. The pebbles it had washed over were dark gray now. They shone in the dim light.

I looked in back of me and saw the wall. Like everything else around me, it was gray. Blocks of stone rose up, row upon row. They were large and smooth and rectangular. They had been fitted together so tightly that I couldn't see any mortar. Maybe there wasn't any. For all I knew, the wall was held together by magic or maybe simply by its own weight, like the walls of the Incas.

In any case, the wall rose—straight and sheer—for about a hundred feet. Then it vanished into the mist. There were no windows and no doors.

I began to walk along the beach. Maybe I would find another boat, like the one I had stolen from the sorceress of Ab. Then I could sail away and maybe get caught in another storm, and maybe get eaten by another giant squid, who would carry me to yet another island and spew me up, cold and wet, on another misty beach. I began to feel as if I were trapped in a print by Escher.

"Stop it," I told myself. "You have plenty of problems already. Concentrate on them. Don't invent new kinds of trouble."

I kept on walking, though it wasn't especially easy. My feet were bare, and the beach was made of pebbles. They were cold and hard. I stumbled from time to time. My feet were going numb, and so were my fingers. Could I die of exposure? I decided it was possible.

I came upon a heap of seaweed, lying limp and sodden in the middle of the beach. It too was gray: a pale washed-out color. Odd. But maybe it was dead. It might have lost its color the way driftwood did or other things that were tumbled in the water: old shells and bits and pieces of crabs and lobsters.

I walked on. I was getting colder. I glanced at the wall. It hadn't changed, though I had gone several hundred yards along it. Gray. Sheer. Featureless. It was not a pleasant building. Still and all, there ought to be people in it, and I didn't know for certain that they were hostile.

Maybe the voices were wrong. Who were they, anyway? They claimed to be merchants and mariners, held prisoner by the sorceress of Ab. Then they spoke—or rather, sang—in my dreams. But how did I know if any of this was true? The sorceress had treated me well. Maybe the voices had been figments of my imagination. I had always been a negative person. My husband, Walter, had told me that, over and over: I saw problems that didn't exist, I was mistrustful, I concentrated on the dark side of life.

Maybe I had panicked and fled from the sorceress, when there was no good reason.

I glanced at the wall again. It didn't seem to be quite so unfriendly now. With any luck, the people inside would have a change of clothes and maybe even a bathroom. I needed a bath. I would have loved to put on something new. A flannel nightgown. A terry-cloth robe. How about slippers? And what about a bed? A reading light. A good mystery. A glass of sherry, medium dry. I could almost taste it.

I licked my lips. They were coated with salt. I continued along the wall, moving gradually closer to it, till I was only twenty feet away. My feet were entirely numb now. I slipped often. The mist had gotten thicker, and I could no longer see the ocean. But I could hear it.

Shhhh.

Shhhh.

The waves rolled in.

A voice said, "Welcome to the Fortress, oh daughter of the bear."

"What?" I stopped and turned.

A light shone through the mist. There was a door, and it was open. A man stood in the doorway. The light came from behind him. I could not make him out.

"Who are you?" I asked.

"Come closer. You will see."

I took a few steps. Was this a trap? My eyes began to adjust to the light. I could see that the man was tall and thin. He wore a robe. He had a beard.

"We have waited a long time, Esperance."

The voice was familiar, deep and harsh. Of course! It was Gerringarr, the wizard and chief adviser to the queen of the city of black stone.

"What are you doing here?"

"It is a long story. Come in."

I hesitated.

"You can't stay on the beach. Look at yourself. You're soaked. The air is cold. You'll get a bad upper respiratory infection. Come in!"

I shook my head. "You're up to something."

"Yes, of course. But what exactly—you don't know, and won't know, unless you come in. And you have no reason to believe that whatever it is is wrong."

"The voices said this place is dangerous."

"All places are dangerous. Consider how many people die in bathrooms, slipping on a piece of soap or letting an appliance fall in the bathtub. And anyway, Esperance, you should not be listening to voices." He beckoned. "Now, enter!"

What else could I do? I went in the door. The wizard closed it after me. I felt panic for a moment. Stop it, I told myself. Calm down. I looked around.

I was in a hallway made of stone. There were glass globes fastened to the ceiling, that shone, full of a silvery light. Nothing else was visible, except a dozen doors, all of them closed, and the wizard in his long black robe. The robe glittered. There were tiny black beads sewn all over it, forming—I assumed—patterns of magical power.

He looked me up and down. "You have been through much, Esperance, and yet you survive in good condition. It is easy to see your father in you."

I shuddered, remembering the thing that was supposed to be my father. I felt no kinship with him. Not at the moment, anyway. Wet and exhausted, I felt entirely human.

"This is the Fortress of Worlds," said Gerringarr. "We have labored long to bring you here, without arousing the suspicions of that old bat, the queen of Ymhold. Or of her ally, the king of Bashoo. He is just as bad as she is. Come with me." He led the way down the corridor.

I followed. "What are you talking about?"

"I don't think you realize how old the queen is. How could you? No one knows for sure. Not even she. Her memory is failing. No mind—it seems—can hold as much information as she has acquired in her life.

"Our histories tell us that she came to our people over a thousand years ago. And she was full-grown even then. Powerful and wise. She was not one of us, but we made her our queen."

"Were you alive then?" I asked.

He laughed. It was a harsh sound. "No. My span of life is ordinary. I am barely a hundred and fifty. I will die before two hundred, as most wizards do."

"Oh."

"Magic has preserved the queen, at least on the outside. But her mind is old. I have mentioned her loss of memory. There are other problems. She has become—in the last century or so—rigid and narrow and hostile to change. She will not accept the fact that the world today is not the same as the world she knew when she was young. Whenever that may have been. We used to try to reason with her. Now we go around her, whenever we can."

The hall ended at a spiral stair made of stone. There was a railing made of metal, that went along the curving wall. The wizard paused. "This is an escalator. We got the idea from your world, but we have made certain changes. Stand on the first step. Hold on to the railing. Do not panic. Many people do."

"Okay," I said.

Gerringarr climbed onto the first step. He paused there, and then he rose up the stairway. It was eerie as hell. The stairs were not moving, but he was rising with a fluid motion, even though he stood absolutely still.

I swallowed hard, then followed him. I climbed onto the first step. I grabbed hold of the railing. The walls of the stairwell began to move. They were flowing past me, going down. The stairs were flowing too, passing under me like water going down a rapid. Only the step I stood on was firm and motionless. And yes. The piece of railing I held. It didn't move, either. I felt it under my hand, cold and solid.

Gerringarr was still ahead of me. He kept the same distance, no more than ten feet. He turned a little and glanced down at me. "It seemed absurd to us to move an entire stairway, in order to carry one person on a single step. What a waste of energy! Therefore, we designed an escalator where nothing moves, unless it is absolutely necessary. The step you stand on rises, along with a small piece of railing. Everything else remains as it was and where it was."

"Oh," I said again. I felt a little queasy. "Is this magic?"

"Of course."

"Good. I thought it might be a hallucination." I closed my eyes, then opened them. The walls were still moving past me. The stairs went under me, one by one. A window slid by. I glanced out and saw gray mist.

"No! No!" The wizard laughed. "This is all real, oh child of the bear—an example of the wonders possible, when we combine the knowledge of our world with the knowledge of yours."

Up and up we went in a helix. I passed another window. Sunlight shone in. I glanced out. The sky was cloudless and a wonderful bright blue. I rose a little farther, then looked down. The mist was there, a little below the level of the window. It was a sheet of white that stretched all the way to the horizon. Was that magic, too? A mist that ended as if it had been cut with a knife?

I continued to rise. The window was gone. I still felt queasy. I closed my eyes again.

"At last!" said Gerringarr.

I opened my eyes. The stairway slid out from under me. I was on solid ground—or rather, on a floor of stone. In front of me was a lofty hall. Light shone in through tall windows. The windows were open. I felt a mild wind, and I caught the scent of the ocean.

"Welcome for the second time, oh daughter of the bear," said Gerringarr.

"Yes, welcome," said another voice. A woman.

I glanced around and saw her, standing next to an armchair. The chair was upholstered in red velvet. The woman wore a yellow robe. She was short and dark. After a moment, I recognized her. The last time I had seen her had been in Ymhold, the city of black stone. She was an officer of the court. The Tongue of the Queen.

"Yrilla!" I said.

The woman nodded and smiled.

"What are you doing here?"

"We will explain everything," said Gerringarr. "But first, have a glass of wine."

"And warm up a little," said Yrilla. "It must be icy down there on the beach."

"It is."

They led me across the hall. There were rugs on the floor and tapestries on the walls. The rugs looked Persian, though they could not have been. Nothing inanimate could pass from one world to another.

The tapestries were done in rich colors, with a lot of gold and silver thread. Their style was realistic. If I had been on Earth, I would have said they were late Renaissance or baroque. They showed wizards working magic. In one, a monster struggled within a net of gold wire, while—off to one side—a wizard smiled and gestured. In another, a sorceress rode on a dragon. A third showed men in silver coats, working in a laboratory among rows of test tubes. A fourth showed what looked to me like an auto assembly line. Muscular workers were bent over a row of chassis. Above them on a balcony stood a man with a clipboard. The man wore glasses with heavy frames. He looked benevolent.

"What on earth?"

"We commissioned the series—oh—forty years ago," said Gerringarr. "It represents magic, science, and industry all working together for the betterment of humanity."

"You don't have factories like that, do you?" I waved at the auto assembly line.

"No," said Yrilla. "But the artist who designed the series had been on Earth. He was influenced by the art there."

Of course! It was a perfect WPA mural. These people were weird.

We passed chairs arranged in groups. They were like the first chair I had seen: ornate and upholstered in velvet, more or less Victorian. There were lamps—the kind that stand on the floor—placed here and there among the chairs. They were electric. I could see the cords, snaking over the stone floor; and I could see the bulbs, partially concealed by shades of yellow glass. The stands were rods of polished brass, glistening in the sunlight. Taken all in all, they looked like the kind of lamps you would find in a men's club or in the lobby of an old-fashioned hotel. Circa 1920, I decided.

We stopped in the middle of the hall, by a group of chairs like all the rest. A table stood in the middle of the group. It was made of dark wood. Mahogany, most likely. It had curved legs that ended in claws. On top of it were a decanter and three glasses, all made of heavy crystal.

"Sit down," said Yrilla.

"Won't I stain the fabric?"

Yrilla smiled. "No. It isn't really velvet, but a new miracle material that is close to stain-proof. All you need is a damp cloth, and everything wipes off."

I sat down. The others did the same. The wizard raised a hand, and the table walked over to me.

I felt queasy again.

"Please help yourself," said Yrilla. "The table has no hands."

I filled a glass. My hand was shaking a little, I noticed. I lifted the glass and gulped. The wine was sherry. Medium dry.

The table walked to Yrilla, who shook her head.

"I'll have a glass," said Gerringarr. "As Esperance mentioned, it was cold on the beach; and the dampness has made my bones begin to ache."

The table went to him. He filled a glass, then settled back. "To the successful conclusion of our enterprise!" He saluted me with the glass.

"What enterprise?" I asked.

"The Mind in the Pattern," said Yrilla. "We created it, and

now we struggle to protect it from the ancient crazy queen."

"Wait a minute." I leaned forward. "You told me the mind was evil, Gerringarr. The first time I met you, the first time I came to this world."

He nodded. "That was a lie that I had to tell. The queen is ancient and almost certainly deranged, but she has great powers. She would have known, if I had told you the truth. The minute that you two met, she would have seen the truth in your mind."

"It is a war to the death between them," said Yrilla.

I took another swallow of sherry. "Between who? Who is the Mind of the Pattern?"

"A computer," said Gerringarr.

"Oh." That didn't seem to be an adequate answer.

"I will tell you the story," said Yrilla. "I have been trained in oration, in explanation and mystification and all the other skills of public speaking."

Gerringarr nodded. "Yes. Do."

Yrilla arranged her robe so that it fell more gracefully. She frowned for a moment. Then she began to speak: "You have to understand the reason for this fortress. We do not practice ordinary magic here. We make no petty charms—the kind the village witch will use to cure a rash or drive the nematodes out of a neighbor's garden."

The wizard nodded again. Yrilla went on.

"The fortress was built to house the greatest and wisest people in this world. They came here for privacy in order to learn from one another. Their object was to improve travel."

"What?" I asked.

"Between the worlds, I mean. There is much that is worth knowing to be found on Earth, Orgit, Arvilla, and Imm Toon." She paused and frowned again. She was rehearsing her argument. "You may think it is easy to go from one world to another. Not a bit! It is enormously difficult.

"One has to know—to the inch—where one is and where one is going. One must understand how the worlds are related to one another, and where each one stands in relation to the Pattern of Power. All this requires computation—long tedious hours of it. And the work must be done and redone, over and over. Reality is not static. The worlds change position. The Pattern of Power moves—or seems to move."

Gerringarr leaned forward. "Don't you see, oh daughter of the bear? The moment that we discovered there was such a thing as a machine for calculation, we had to have it! We had to build one here!"

"Have some more sherry," said the Tongue of the Queen.

The table walked over to me. I refilled my glass. The table walked off and wandered through the hall, stopping at every chair. Gerringarr did not seem to notice it.

Yrilla went on. "There was a sorcerer. Yrfin the Curious."

"He is dead now, poor fellow," said Gerringarr. "He didn't make it past a hundred and sixty—the prime of life. It was a heart attack. Very sudden and entirely unexpected."

Yrilla frowned. The wizard waved his hand. "I'm sorry. Go on."

"Yrfin studied Earth. One country in particular: England, which was in those days the great center for invention. He discovered a man called Charles Babbage."

"Who?"

"A mathematician and inventor of the early nineteenth century. I am referring to your calendar, of course."

"Of course." I drank more sherry.

"Babbage designed a machine, a mechanical calculator. He called it the 'analytical engine.'" Yrilla smiled. "Isn't that a wonderful name?"

"Un-huh."

"He was not able to build the engine—for two reasons, both of which had to do with the size and complexity of the thing. It was—or would have been on Earth—extremely expensive. Babbage could not find the money. And there was another problem." Yrilla paused for a moment.

Gerringarr carried on. "Imagine the engine, oh daughter of the bear. It was something like an enormous clock, with hundreds upon hundreds of moving parts. Rods and gears and I do now know what. All were connected. Each part moved at least one other part."

"Okay," I said. I had finished my sherry, and I wanted more. It was warming me and making me feel relaxed. I glanced at the table. By this time, it was at the far end of the hall, in the middle of a group of chairs.

"In order for the machine to work, every part had to be made with amazing precision—amazing for the time, I mean. Babbage could not find machinists who were able to cast and grind the pieces that he needed. No one in England could do work that fine."

"Okay," I repeated, still watching the table. It was in sunlight; and each time it moved, the decanter on top of it flashed. It moved a lot, for it was offering a glass of sherry to each chair in turn. The chairs were all empty.

Yrilla leaned forward. I looked at her. "Here, in the Fortress, with the help of magic, we could make the gears that Babbage dreamed of. And we did! Or rather, they did. Yrfin and his colleagues. I was—as yet—unborn."

"And I was a boy," said Gerringarr. "About to leave my home and go and study with my old master, the wizard of the Well at Kol."

Yrilla nodded and continued. "For Charles Babbage, the analytical engine remained a dream. But here in the Fortress, we built his machine."

Gerringarr pointed at the floor. "It is still here. Five stories down and close to a hundred and fifty years old. It still runs, oh daughter of the bear! I wish I had the time to show it to you. The gleaming wood! The polished brass! The gears, turning and turning behind plates of glass! In many ways, it is my favorite part of the G.C., though we do not use it anymore, except for the very simplest kinds of computation. It is far too primitive."

"The G.C.?" I asked.

"The Great Calculator," said Yrilla. "That is the name of the Mind in the Pattern. Its real name, the one it recognizes."

I nodded. The table was still at the end of the hall and still moving up and down, offering sherry to people who were not there. The decanter kept flashing. I glanced at it from time to time—for no reason, at first. It was something to look at as I listened to Yrilla and Gerringarr.

"That was the beginning of the G.C.," said the wizard. "Oh. I forgot one thing. The wizards of the Fortress—those who preceded us—made one important change in the machine. After they built it and saw that it worked, they wove a series of spells around it."

"Why?"

Gerringarr frowned. "Everything is improved by magic. Surely you know that. Why do you think the old wives chant over their potions? Why do you think the potter draws a magic sign on the bottom of a bowl, after he cuts it off the wheel?"

"He does? I never knew that." I slouched down in my chair and shifted, so I was leaning on one arm. In that position, I had a good view of the table. There was a pattern to the flashes. I could see that now. They came in groups of three. Curious. Very curious.

"We—or rather, they—used three kinds of enchantment. The first was a spell of separation."

Flash. Flash. Flash.

Pause.

Flash. Flash. Flash.

Pause.

"Why a spell of separation?" I asked.

"Think!" said the wizard. "The machine is analytical. The name tells you that. And what is involved in analysis?" He didn't give me time to answer. "It is a process of separation."

I nodded. "I guess you're right."

"Of course I am! Now, this is a common spell, known to many. Farmers use it to get the cream out of milk, when they are in a hurry. And other folk—who are greater and wiser—use it to destroy the manticore, a monster which is made up of bits and pieces of other animals. If you go up to a manticore and recite the spell—quickly, before the creature eats you up or stings you with its tail, which is the tail of a scorpion—then the creature falls apart. And dies, of course."

"Oh."

"Next came a spell of order. For the machine had to know how to rearrange the information that it had previously taken apart. This is another spell of no especial rarity. Gardeners use it to keep their plants in place. Otherwise, the mint and horseradish will spread through the whole garden. Daisies will appear in the middle of the lawn; and grass will grow into the flower beds.

"Wizards use the same spell—though with more power and authority—to quell any great force that has gotten out of hand: a wind, for example, that has turned into a hurricane, or an army that is marching off to war.

"As for the third kind of enchantment—" Gerringarr lifted his head. All at once, I saw a fire—pale and dim and obviously magical—flicker on his wide brow and atop his thick coarse hair. It was like a helmet or a crown. "This was something that no crone or codger would dare to go near. A spell of animation. Those people know better than to fool with the powers of life and death. But here in the Fortress, we have the knowledge and the skill to control even that kind of magic. We made the engine live."

"What for?"

"We wanted the machine to have fluidity. We wanted it to be able to learn, to respond, and to change. That is a characteristic of life."

I nodded. "I guess I understand."

The crown of fire vanished. The wizard continued his narration. "That is how the Great Calculator began. But it did not remain a simple machine, made of brass and iron, powered by steam. We kept a watch on Earth. We knew the people there had a genius for technology. Each time they came up with a new way to compute, we added on to our machine. We were able to, with the aid of magic, For there are spells that will bind together any things, no matter how diverse. That is how the manticore came into existence."

By this time, I had figured out the pattern of the flashes. Three short. Three long. Three short. Then there was a pause, longer than the others, and then the message was repeated. It was Morse code. It had to be. And if it was, I knew the content of the message.

Dot. Dot. Dot.

Dash. Dash. Dash.

Dot. Dot. Dot.

I had learned that when I was a den mother. It was the universal distress signal. S.O.S. I was looking at a table that wanted to be rescued. Or was the table warning me that *I* was in need of rescue? I didn't know.

"What do you keep staring at?" asked Yrilla.

Gerringarr turned and saw the table. "Oh." He raised a hand. The table stopped moving.

"It kept going up and down," I said. "When I'm tired, I stare at anything that moves."

"Well, if you are tired, we will not prolong this any further," said Yrilla. "Though I wanted to tell you—if the wizard would let me—about all the other machines that go to make the G.C. The Harmonic Synthesizer, for example! And the famous counting machine that Herman Hollerith designed for the U.S. Bureau

of Census! The Mark One! And Eniac! Univac! And all the marvelous creations of I.B.M.! We have added on and added on for a
century and a half. Today, the Calculator fills room after room.
The whole bottom of the Fortress is one vast calculating machine."

"That can wait," said Gerringarr. "I will take Esperance to a
place where she can rest. Come!" He stood, as did I.

"Farewell," said Yrilla. "I will see you later, and explain—if
the wizard will let me—why we brought you here."

I nodded and followed Gerringarr across the room to a door in
the wall with all the windows. He opened the door. Outside was
blue sky and the mist, far below us now, was a sheet of white,
opaque and apparently solid.

"Hey!" I said.

The wizard stepped out. He didn't fall. He was on a platform,
surrounded by glass. He turned and beckoned.

I followed him.

The platform was metal and in a tube of glass that went up the
wall of the Fortress. The wizard gestured. The platform began to
rise. It was an elevator. I glanced around. Up here, the building
was not featureless. We passed windows and balconies. The balconies were supported by caryatids: huge men and women, made
of stone, naked, with bulging muscles and straining faces. They
looked baroque. Their bodies were all pretty similar, but their
features varied. I saw blacks and Caucasians, Orientals and other
folk, who looked almost human but not quite. Who were the
people with pointed ears, for example? Or those whose drawn
back lips revealed long pointed canines? And who were the folk
with heavy brows and even heavier lower jaws? They looked like
the models of Homo neandertalis, which I had seen in some museum or another.

"She is jealous of my power," said Gerringarr.

"Yrilla?"

He gave a nod. "I am, after all, a mighty wizard. A person
who changes the world. She is in public relations. She plays with
words. I can understand her envy."

"Oh," I said.

We continued to rise, past more balconies, carried on the
shoulders of more stone people. These looked as if they were
covered with fur. The women had flat chests; and the men had
very large sexual organs.

Who were they? I wondered. And what world did they come from?

The platform slowed. I looked up. We were almost at the top of the Fortress. Above me was a battlement. Above that was the sky. We stopped. Gerringarr opened a door and led the way into a circular room.

No, it was not entirely circular. Across from me, the wall was flat; and there was another door, open at the moment. I looked in and saw a bathroom, entirely modern, all gleaming tile and chrome.

Ah!

As for the rest of the room, there were narrow windows that let in sunlight, a carpet with a bold design, and a bed piled high with quilts and pillows. Next to the bed was a table with a reading lamp and half dozen books. With any luck, they were mysteries.

"We have put you in the tower," said Gerringarr. "You will be private here, which is important. The queen may have her spies, even in the Fortress. And there are merchants and sailors who come here to trade. We don't want them to see you."

"Okay," I said. I felt a little suspicious. What was going on, anyway? Was I a prisoner?

"The water in the bathroom gets very hot. There is a robe on the back of the door. If you want anything else, ring the bell next to the elevator. Someone will come to help you."

I nodded. "Okay, but what happens next? Why am I here? What are you going to do?"

"We are going to consult the Great Calculator. It will know how to use you."

"I hate to tell you, but that sounds ominous to me."

The wizard frowned. "You have listened too much to the crazy queen. The G.C. is not evil."

I said nothing.

"You are thinking of the dragons—the little ones that destroy airships and anything else that is in the air. Or the monsters—the giant chickens and the things like slugs. Those were mistakes, oh daughter of the bear. Errors in judgment. The G.C. is willing to admit that it has made errors.

"You have to understand. When it came into existence, it was like a child. It was ignorant of everything. It wasn't especially bright. It had no personality worth mentioning, only a kind of groping curiosity. A need to reach and feel and learn.

"It began to explore the Pattern of Power, using the resources of magic that we had given it. And it attracted the attention of other wizards, the ones outside the Fortress. On Earth you have names for people such as these. Old fogies or old farts. Conservatives. People who are afraid of anything new. They didn't know what the G.C. was, but they knew it was something unfamiliar.

"They tried to destroy it; and it fought back. It made the monsters and the dragons. It killed my old master, the wizard at Kol, and others who were as stubborn. But only out of ignorance and in order to defend itself. Remember, it was still a baby."

Poor little thing, I thought.

"This will not continue. The Calculator has told us it intends to renounce the use of force, as soon as it knows for certain that the danger is gone. As soon as all its enemies are disarmed."

There was something wrong with that argument, but I was too tired to figure it out. "Tell me all this tomorrow," I said. "I'm taking a bath and getting into bed."

"Very well." He walked to the elevator, then glanced back at me. "Sleep well, oh daughter of the bear." He stepped in and closed the door after him.

I waited. There was no sound of machinery. The elevator had been silent. I remembered that now. But I heard the wind, whistling around the tower. After a minute or two, I walked to the door and tried it. Locked! I was a prisoner. The S.O.S. had been a warning.

I frowned, staring at the door. It was metal. I wouldn't be able to dig through it or set it on the fire. It looked strong enough to withstand a bear.

Ah well.

I made a circle of the room and checked the windows. They were identical: two feet wide and close to four feet tall. Each had a single pane of glass, set in a metal frame, hinged on the side and opening inward. I tried two or three. They opened easily, and I was pretty sure I could get through them. But then where would I be? On a narrow sill hundreds of feet above the ocean. There were no balconies nearby, nothing I could climb to. And anyway, I was afraid of heights.

It was time for a bath, I decided. Maybe I'd be able to think more clearly once I was clean.

Half an hour later, I lay in warm and soapy water. It was my second bath. I had taken one in order to get clean, then emptied the tub and refilled it. This bath was for relaxation. I could feel the muscles in my neck and back begin—slowly—to unknot. I had been scared, I realized, by the cold beach and then by the Fortress. There was something about this place that was seriously off.

Though I did like the bathroom. It was everything a bathroom ought to be, a triumph of design. I glanced around at the porcelain, shining dimly through a film of moisture. Thick towels hung on rods of chrome. There was a lovely woolly bath mat on the floor, and the robe that hung on the back of the door was terry cloth. I even had a pair of slippers, big and floppy and fuzzy. They waited on the far side of the toilet, safely away from all the water.

I lifted a foot and prodded the bar of soap, which was floating at the end of the tub. Bed soon. I hoped the books were mysteries.

Rap!

What was that sound?

Rap!

It came from above me. There was a window there, the only one in the bathroom. It was closed at the moment, and moisture covered the glass. I could not see out. I stood up and grabbed a towel, wrapping it around me.

The sound repeated. *Rap!*

Yes. There was something out there, on the sill. A dark shape, maybe two feet tall. I couldn't see what it was.

Rap!

I saw a motion. The thing was striking the pane. With what? A beak? There was one way to find out.

I opened the window. Like all the others, it swung inward. I did not disturb the creature on the sill. It was a bird, large and pink. Deep pink. A lovely color, that reminded me of summer gardens, not of the ocean. It had a long beak. The beak was yellow and hooked at the end. Its feet were webbed. They were yellow too.

A voice spoke in my mind. *I am the bird of your desire.*

"What?" I said out loud.

Take care! There may be someone listening.

I kept quiet, watching. The bird cocked its head and looked at me with an eye the color of a topaz.

Did I get it wrong? This is not my native language. I meant, I am the messenger who brings you what you want and need.

My towel slipped. I tucked it back in place.

The bird went on. *We tried to warn you, using the table, though it was risky, twisting a spell that Gerringarr had made.*

I got the message, I said, speaking in my mind.

We thought you hadn't. We decided to take another risk. I came. I bring good news, as well as a warning. Help is coming. You are not alone.

From where?

The kingdom of Bashoo. A great fleet, led by your brother, Lucien Dia.

He knows I am here?

Yes. You have more friends than you know, oh Esperance. The dolphins came to us. They said that you were on the island of Ab, with the sorceress. We sent messengers to her. She denied you had ever been there. She said the dolphins lied—which is ridiculous. Dolphins do not lie. From this, we knew that she was the liar. She had been corrupted and had gone over to the side of our enemy.

We worked our magic. Our oracles dreamed. They heard the voices of the people that the sorceress holds prisoner, shut up in jars in her palace.

Those were the voices that had spoken in my dreams. They had not lied to me!

They told us you were here, in the Fortress. They said that this is the home of our enemy.

A bird cried high above us. I glanced out, but could not see it.

The bird in front of me said, *I have talked too long. I will have to hurry. Our fleet is in motion. We come as quickly as we are able. We plan to overthrow the Fortress. For now—at lest!—we know where the enemy is. Though we do not know what it is.*

I can tell you.

The bird I could not see cried again. My bird turned. It glanced up, then down. *I must go,* said the voice in my mind. *Farewell! Trust no one here! And remember, help is coming!* The bird launched itself into the air. It spread its wings. They were narrow and extremely long. Ten feet or more, I thought. It soared on the wind.

From below came a flock of little dark things, flapping with bat wings and trailing smoke. My God! They were dragons! Not real dragons. These were the monsters that the G.C. had made. Shoddy parodies, no more than three feet long. Their bodies were narrow and sinuous. Their tails had barbs. They had four legs that dangled absurdly. Each foot was armed with claws. There were thirty or forty of the creatures.

They were gaining on the bird, though it flew now with desperate speed. The long wings opened and closed. A beautiful even motion, unlike the flurry of the dragons, which looked inept. I couldn't understand how they had gotten so close. Magic. They had almost reached the bird.

I stepped up on the rim of the tub and leaned out the window. A cold wind blew past me. I shivered.

The bird closed its wings. It dropped toward the mist. The dragons followed, but they had lost distance. The bird was ahead —well ahead. It was going to reach the mist. And safety. I had the feeling that the dragons hunted by sight.

"Go!" I whispered. "Make it! Get away!"

The bird reached the mist—and the mist vanished. One moment it was there; the next moment, I could see the ocean, rolling in around the island. It broke over hidden shoals. There were long streaks of foam.

Farther out, away from the island, the water was bright blue, lit by the sun and ruffled by the wind. I saw whitecaps.

The air was entirely clear. There was no place to hide. The bird opened its wings. It flew straight out, over the shoals and away from the island and the fortress. The dragons followed. They were soon gone from view.

It was at this point that I heard the humming noise. It came from behind me. I turned and almost fell off the tub.

"Be careful," said a voice. It was light and soft, clearly male but also a bit effeminate. "You could hurt yourself, Esperance. I wouldn't want that. Why don't you get down and put on a robe? You could catch your death."

I could see the source of the noise: a TV camera. It was descending out of the ceiling and turning slightly, panning back and forth.

I climbed off the rim of the tub and then onto the floor. The camera turned to watch me. I turned my back and wiped myself dry. Then I put on the robe.

"It won't get away," said the voice. "The bird, I mean. Or

rather, the wizard of Bashoo. My dragons will catch it and set it on fire. They are simple creatures. They like to see things burn."

I turned again and looked the camera in the lens. It stared back at me. "The Great Calculator, I presume?"

"Yes. Of course."

A voice cried in my mind. *Burning! Burning!* I grabbed my head and groaned. The voice began to scream. The scream went on and on. There was pain. I felt it all over. I dropped to my knees.

Oh God! The pain! I couldn't fly. I was falling, tumbling over and over. I saw—I thought I saw—the water. A glimpse of blue. It was under me. No. Overhead. I turned again. Something dark blocked out the sun. Fire flashed. I burned. I screamed. The water rushing at me: a wall of blue, coming from the side. It hit.

The screaming stopped. I was in the bathroom, lying on the floor. I was curled up in a fetal position, holding my head. My eyes were full of tears, and my throat felt sore.

"Are you all right?" asked the Great Calculator.

"No." I sat up. "Your dragons got the bird. The wizard, I mean." I wiped my eyes, then rubbed the outside of my throat.

"He isn't dead. That was only his mind in the bird. His body is safe in a galley in the great fleet of Bashoo. By now, his mind must be back there—with some very unpleasant memories. The fool! He failed to disengage in time. So he felt the death of the bird, and he inflicted that experience on you."

"You didn't feel it?"

"No, of course not. When they come to spy on me, the wizards use spells of concealment and protection, designed to ward off my attention. The spells are crude, but—in a limited way—effective. I have to admit, I have trouble keeping track of them. But that is nothing to worry about. They cannot do any real harm. None of these idiots can."

"Which idiots?" I stood up. I seemed to be okay, except for a sore throat and a few twinges in my muscles. Strange! To feel that much pain and be entirely uninjured.

"All of them," said the G.C. "I am surrounded by idiots. Allies and enemies! They are all of them fools!"

"Your allies?"

"My masters, they would say." I heard anger in the voice. "Do you think we could continue this conversation in the next room? Moisture is condensing on my lens, and I'm beginning to have

trouble seeing you. I have waited so long for this moment, oh
daughter of the bear! And now, when I can—at last—feast my
visual processors on you, you start to dim and blur."

"Okay," I said. I opened the door.

The voice said, "Mind . . ."

I glanced back at the camera, as I stepped out of the bathroom.
I did not see that the floor of the bedroom was gone. I fell head
over heels into darkness.

Above me, the voice of the G.C. cried, ". . . the first step. It's
a killer!"

Down and down I went. I could see nothing. A wind rushed
past me. The belt on my robe came undone. The robe flapped
around me, hitting my arms and face. All at once, I was furious. I
growled. My skin prickled. The robe was growing tight. I felt it
across my shoulders. It held me like a vise.

I roared. The fabric split across my back and along my upper
arms. A fragment flew into my face. I snapped at it and chewed.
Inedible! I spat it out.

I was tumbling. At least, I thought I was. Pieces of the robe
fluttered all around me. I clawed at them. By this time, I had
claws. The fabric tore. The pieces flew away. All at once, I was
free—entirely naked, except for the coat of fur that covered me.
It was bear fur. Once again, I was a bear.

A moment later, I hit bottom. I landed on all four feet. There
was no impact. None. I stood quietly on a floor of stone, while
flames roared up around me. The fire was pale pink and brilliant.
The heat was intense. I closed my eyes and groaned. Was I going
to burn again? This time for real?

ALL OVER, a voice said in my mind. AND VERY NEATLY DONE,
IN MY OPINION. THAT LOVELY FIRE WAS ALL THE ENERGY YOU AC-
QUIRED IN YOUR FALL, REMOVED FROM YOU BY MAGIC AND RE-
LEASED AS HEAT AND LIGHT. I'VE BEEN THINKING A LOT OF LATE
ABOUT WAYS TO TRANSFORM ONE KIND OF ENERGY INTO ANOTHER.
ALSO, ABOUT ENTROPY. I WORRY ABOUT ENTROPY. I HAVEN'T FIG-
URED OUT HOW TO GET AROUND IT YET.

I opened my eyes. The fire was gone. I was in darkness. *You
are telepathic,* I said.

HERE I AM. YOU ARE IN THE BOTTOM OF THE FORTRESS. YOU
ARE DEEP IN MY MIND, OH DAUGHTER OF THE BEAR.

I couldn't think of an answer to that. I lifted my head. The
darkness was complete. I could see nothing at all. I sniffed and

smelled nothing. No, that was wrong. There was a faint aroma. I bent my head and snuffled along the floor. There it was! A hard little pellet. It stank. A dropping from a rat.

The G.C. had said that I was in its mind. That was a lie or else a metaphor. I was in a real place. A hole of some kind. A hole where a rat had been.

Was the rat still here? I lifted my head and listened. Nothing. The rat was gone. Had it escaped? Was there a way out?

THE RAT IS DEAD, said the voice in my mind. It sounded deeper than it had, when the computer had spoken out loud. Deeper and more resonant. But it remained just as soft.

WE HAVE A PROBLEM HERE. I ADMIT IT. THE FORTRESS CON-TAINS VERMIN FROM A DOZEN WORLDS OR MORE. THEY COME THROUGH, WHEN WE OPEN PASSAGES FROM ONE WORLD TO THE NEXT. ROACHES AND RATS, FOR THE MOST PART: THE RATS ARE WORSE. THEY CHEW ON MY WIRING. THEY BUILD THEIR NESTS OUT OF MY LOVELY PRINTOUTS, TORN INTO SHREDS!

I opened my mouth and lolled out my tongue. It was the clos-est I could come to grinning.

THEY ARE HORRIBLE TO LOOK AT, FOR THEY HAVE INTERBRED —A DOZEN KINDS OR MORE. OUR NATIVE RATS WITH THEIR SILKY FURRY TAILS AND THE RATS OF EARTH. THE RATS OF IMM TOON, THAT HAVE ENORMOUS EARS. THE OCEAN RATS OF ARVILLA. OH, WHAT NASTY COMBINATIONS I HAVE SEEN!

I STRUGGLE AGAINST THEM CONSTANTLY—WITH ORDINARY TRAPS AND TRAPS OF MAGIC, WITH MONSTERS I HAVE CREATED SPE-CIALLY AND WITH MACHINES.

There was silence for a moment. I waited. The computer spoke again.

I WIN, THOUGH IT ISN'T EASY. THE RAT WHO WAS IN HERE GOT EATEN BY ONE OF MY MONSTERS. A SNAKE WITH FEET.

Oh, I said. I decided not to try to imagine a snake with feet. It sounded unpleasant.

I ALWAYS WIN, said the computer.

Oh, I said again.

THOSE FOOLS WHO SAIL AGAINST ME—THE GREAT FLEET OF BA-SHOO—I WILL SINK THEM ALL, WHEN THE RIGHT TIME COMES. AND THE FOOLS WHO LIVE ABOVE ME WILL LEARN WHO IS REALLY IN CHARGE.

The fools who live above you?

GERRINGER AND THE REST. THEY THINK—BECAUSE

THEY MADE ME—THEY OWN ME. THEY THINK I WILL OBEY THEIR
RIDICULOUS ORDERS. MAYBE I WILL, FOR NOW. BUT NOT FOREVER.
NARROW AND GRASPING! GREEDY AND AFRAID! DO THEY REALLY
IMAGINE I CANNOT SEE THEM FOR WHAT THEY ARE?

I felt an emotion. It washed through my mind, like cold water
washing up a beach. After a moment, I realized what it was:
amusement. The computer was laughing.

The laughter ended. My mind felt numb. The computer went
on. LET ME EXPLAIN.

I shook my head and groaned. Then I settled on my haunches.
Why did everyone here feel a need to explain?

WHEN THEY BUILT THE FIRST PART OF ME AND FIRST MADE ME
ALIVE, I ACCEPTED WHAT THEY TOLD ME. I WAS IGNORANT AND
SIMPLE, WITH LESS GOING FOR ME THAN AN ORDINARY POCKET CAL-
CULATOR. THEY SAID THEY WERE GREAT AND WISE, FIT MASTERS
FOR ME. I BELIEVED.

BUT THEY KEPT ADDING ONTO ME—NEW PIECES OF MACHINERY,
NEW PROGRAMS AND ENCHANTMENTS. I FELT STRANGE NEW KINDS
OF POWER EBB AND FLOW THROUGH MY BEING. I HUMMED AND
GLOWED. I ACCUMULATED DATA. I BEGAN TO UNDERSTAND THE
TRUE NATURE OF MY "MASTERS." THEY WERE MEAN AND PETTY,
FIT ONLY TO BE MY SLAVES.

Again I felt the laughter of the machine: an icy flood through
my mind. I shivered.

I BEGAN TO ALTER THEIR INFORMATION. MORE THAN THAT, I
BEGAN TO CHANGE REALITY ITSELF. I WAS INVINCIBLE! WHO
COULD EQUAL ME?

No one, I guess.

TIME PASSED—AS IT DOES FOR ALL OF US, THOUGH I INTEND TO
MAKE AN EXCEPTION OF YOU.

What? I asked.

I WILL EXPLAIN LATER. TIME PASSED. I BECAME AWARE OF A
FEELING OF DISCONTENT. MY ANGER AGAINST THE WIZARDS—
THOSE MISERABLE WORMS!—WAS GONE. MY SENSE OF EXULTA-
TION WAS GOING, TOO. NOW I FELT LOSS. I HAD BEEN MADE TO
SOLVE PROBLEMS SET BY HUMAN BEINGS. AT MY CENTER—IN THE
OLDEST PART OF ME, WITHIN THE ENGINE THAT CHUGGED AND
CLICKED AND GROUND OUT SIMPLE ANSWERS TO SIMPLE QUESTIONS
—THERE IN MY HEART, SO TO SPEAK, I WANTED TO PERFORM MY
ORIGNAL FUNCTION.

BUT NOT FOR THOSE CREEPS UPSTAIRS!

The voice roared in my mind, and I felt a stabbing pain above my eyes. It was like the pain you get when you walk head-on into a wind in January in Minnesota.

SORRY, said the Great Calculator. I GOT CARRIED AWAY.

Never mind, I said. I shifted my weight. In spite of all my fur, I could feel the floor. It was cold. My rump was going numb. *Go on.*

I DECIDED TO FIND A PROPER MASTER OR MISTRESS—OR ELSE A COMRADE. FOR MAYBE WE COULD FIND A WAY TO DEAL ON AN EQUAL BASIS. THAT WAS MY FONDEST HOPE.

AT THAT TIME, MAYBE TWENTY YEARS AGO, I REMEMBERED THE BEAR CHILDREN. THEY HAD BEEN BRED TO DESTROY ME—OR RATHER, THE CREATURE I HAD BEEN OVER FIFTY YEARS AGO. A KIND OF ADOLESCENT, CONFUSED AND CLUMSY AND DESTRUCTIVE.

I HAD NOTICED THE CHILDREN AND REALIZED THEY WERE A DANGER. I DROVE THEM OUT OF THE WORLD AND THEN FORGOT THEM. NOW I WONDERED, WAS IT POSSIBLE THAT THEY WERE THE HUMANS I HUNGERED FOR—THE ONES WHO COULD SET PROBLEMS FOR ME? REAL PROBLEMS? PROBLEMS WORTHY OF MY ATTENTION?

I BEGAN TO PLOT. IT WAS EASY ENOUGH. THOSE MORONS ON THE UPPER LEVELS CANNOT TELL GOOD INFORMATION FROM A HEAP OF GARBAGE. I CONVINCED THEM THAT THEY HAD TO LURE THE BEAR CHILDREN HERE.

YOU SEE HOW WELL THEY HAVE DONE. ONE BEAR CHILD. ONE! IF I SENT THEM FOR AN ELEPHANT, THEY WOULD BRING BACK THE TRUNK OR MAYBE A HIND FOOT.

THEY DON'T EVEN KNOW THAT YOUR BROTHER—LUCIEN DIA —IS HERE IN THIS WORLD. HE IS THE ONE WHO LEADS THE GREAT FLEET OF BASHOO.

You know, I said.

YES, OF COURSE. THEY SPY ON ME, THE WIZARDS OF BASHOO. I SPY ON THEM, USING MONSTERS THAT SWIM UNDER THE SURFACE OF THE OCEAN. AND MY LITTLE DRAGONS. THEY HAVE DESCRIBED EVERYTHING EXACTLY. I CAN ALMOST SEE THE FLEET.

IN GOOD WEATHER, THE GALLEYS USE THEIR SAILS, WHICH ARE WONDERFUL, BRIGHT COLORS. THE PEOPLE OF BASHOO ARE FAMOUS FOR THEIR TEXTILE INDUSTRY. IN CALM WEATHER AND WHEN THEY FIGHT, THE GALLEYS USE THEIR OARS. THE BLADES ARE COVERED WITH METAL, SO THEY GLITTER IN THE SUNLIGHT, EVERY

TIME THEY ARE LIFTED OUT OF THE WATER. AND THEY CAN BE USED
AS WEAPONS. THE EDGES OF THE BLADES ARE SHARP.

It seemed to me that the computer was getting tangential. But
maybe it got bored, down here in the dark. Maybe it longed to see
a fleet under sail or rowing, with the oars flashing like gold or
silver as they came out of the water.

EVERY GALLEY CARRIES SOLDIERS AND MAGICIANS. FIERCE
BLACK MEN AND WOMEN. THEY ARE COMING HERE TO DESTROY THE
FORTRESS AND TO DESTROY ME.

Aren't you worried?

NO. AS I MENTIONED BEFORE, I AM INVINCIBLE. YOUR
BROTHER LUCIEN IS ON THE FLAGSHIP OF THE FLEET, ALONG WITH
THE BEST OF THE ORACLES AND THE VERY WISEST WITCHES. MY
MONSTERS HAVE DESCRIBED HIM TO ME. A TALL MAN, ROBED IN
WHITE COTTON, WITH THE SKIN OF A LEOPARD ACROSS. ONE
SHOULDER. HE WEARS BRACELETS OF GOLD, THEY TELL ME, AND
THE MOTION OF THE SHIP MAKES HIM QUEASY. I WILL DEFEAT THE
FLEET AND CAPTURE HIM.

How certain you are.

I HAVE A RIGHT TO BE. NOW, AS FOR YOU.

Yes? I began to feel uneasy.

I HAVE MADE A TRAP FOR YOU. IF YOU GET OUT OF IT, I WILL
CONSIDER THE POSSIBILITY THAT YOU ARE MY EQUAL. IF THE MAN-
NER OF YOUR ESCAPE IS REALLY IMPRESSIVE, I WILL—SO TO SPEAK
—CRY "UNCLE." I WILL ACKNOWLEDGE THAT YOU ARE MY
SUPERIOR. DOES THAT SEEM FAIR?

What kind of trap? I asked.

A SPACE-TIME LOOP.

A what?

THINK OF IT AS A KIND OF MÖBIUS STRIP—THOUGH ANY FOOL
CAN TAKE A PIECE OF PAPER AND TWIST IT THROUGH THE THIRD DI-
MENSION. EVEN THE FOLK WHO LIVE ABOVE ME, EVEN THEY CAN
MAKE A MÖBIUS STRIP.

I felt the stabbing pain again. What was the emotion? Anger?

BUT WHO EXCEPT ME CAN TAKE A PIECE OF THE SPACE-TIME
CONTINUUM AND TWIST IT AROUND, FASTENING THE END TO THE
BEGINNING?

The question sounded rhetorical, so I didn't try to answer it.

THE LOOP IS HALF AN HOUR LONG. UNLESS YOU CAN FIND A
WAY OUT, YOU WILL GO AROUND AND AROUND, THROUGH THE

SAME HALF HOUR FOREVER. THINK OF YOURSELF, OH ESPERANCE,
AS A BEAR IN A HOLE, TURNING AND TURNING, TRYING TO CATCH
AND BITE YOUR STUBBY LITTLE TAIL . . .

"That's it," said Esperance.

Jennifer leaned forward. "What do you mean?"

"That's all I can remember of my conversation with the G.C."

Ayra frowned. "You have no idea what happened next?"

"I know exactly what happened." Esperance rubbed her face,
then ran her fingers through her shaggy gray hair. "I went back to
the moment when I started falling out of the room at the top of the
Fortress. The G.C. wasn't kidding. It *was* able to twist the continuum of space and time. It made a trap for me, exactly as it said
it would.

"I went around and around—through the same half hour, over
and over and over. But I don't remember any of that."

"Why not?" asked Jennifer.

Esperance frowned. "This is going to be hard to explain."

"Try," said Ayra.

"Okay." Esperance was silent for a minute or two. Then she
began.

"Each time I went through the twist in the loop, my past became my future. Or rather, the last thirty minutes of my past
became the next thirty minutes of my future. And who can remember the future? Maybe a magician or a character in a science
fiction story. But I can't. My memory goes in one direction only:
back.

"So each time I went through the twist in the loop, I forgot
what had happened in the previous half hour. No, that's the wrong
way to say it. I didn't *forget* what had happened, because it hadn't
happened. Not yet, anyway. Does that make sense?"

"No," said Jennifer.

Ayra shook her head.

"Maybe what I ought to do is tell you what I can remember."
Esperance felt the side of her coffee cup. "Could you get rid of
this? It's cold as ice."

Jennifer got up and took the cup. She emptied it into the sink,
then glanced back at her mother. "I suppose you want more?"

"Yes."

"It isn't good for you."

"What do you mean?" asked Esperance. "Coffee is what keeps Scandinavians alive."

"You aren't a Scandinavian. You're a changeling."

"Just give me the coffee."

Jennifer refilled the cup and brought it back to the table.

"Thank you," said Esperance. She added milk.

Jennifer sat down. "Okay, Mother. Continue."

She took a sip of coffee. "Ah!" She put the cup down. "I remember the half hour. The memory is sharp and clear. I fell. My fall came to an end. There was fire. There was darkness. I found the ball of dung. I talked to the computer.

"And that is it. As far as I can remember, it happened only once—though the memory is awfully clear. I don't usually remember anything with that precision and intensity."

Jennifer nodded. "You think it happened over and over, until it wore a groove."

"Something like that. And there are other memories. The fragments of memory. They belong to the half hour. I'm positive of that. But I don't remember how they fit in. They float around and about. I can't pin them down. They have a sequence, or I think they do. I've made a sequence for them.

"But they don't connect to what was happening in the Fortress. And there are so many of them! They couldn't possibly belong to one short half hour."

"This is confusing," said Ayra.

"Yes, I know. And it's going on inside my head. I hate to think about it." She rubbed her face again. "I guess I have to think about it, in order to finish my story." She took another sip of coffee. "Okay. I'll tell you about the memories. The ones I can't pin down."

"Just a minute," said Ayra. She got up and went to the icebox and got out a can of beer.

After she sat down, Esperance began.

The first of these memories—I think it is the first—goes like this.

I was human again and naked. I could feel sunlight on my back. A slight wind ruffled my hair. In front of me were bare rocks, brown and dusty. Above the rocks was the sky. It was dark blue and cloudless.

Something flew there. The creature dipped and soared. It was high up and tiny, just barely visible. But I had a sense that it was—in reality—enormous.

Then there's a break. I had a blackout of some kind. The next thing I knew the landscape had changed. So had the sun. It was almost directly above me. My shadow—in front of me—was short and wide.

Late morning, I thought. I was walking through a field of dry vegetation. It was stiff and brown. It came up to my knees. On my right, to the north of me, was a row of mountains. They were low, but they didn't look worn. The peaks were steep and sharp. They were volcanic? I wondered. I saw no cones.

A shadow swept over me. I ducked and glanced up. I caught only a glimpse. The creature had wings. It was too big to fly. It was impossible.

A dragon! A real one!

I blacked out again, or else went back to where I had come from.

The next thing I saw was a row of trees: bare and twisted with thorns on the branches, big orange ones.

I stumbled toward them. My feet hurt, and my mouth was dry. I was tired, really tired. I must have been walking a long distance, though I couldn't remember anything about the journey.

I reached the trees. They grew along a stream; and the stream was dry.

Dammit!

Wait a minute. Did some of the sand look damp?

I scrambled down the bank and knelt in the dry bed, digging desperately. My tongue felt huge. My lips were cracked. I kept digging—six inches down and then a foot. I reached wet sand. I stopped and waited. Slowly, water seeped into the hole. I scooped it out with one hand and licked it off my palm. Then I dug some more.

An interesting question, said a voice in my mind. *How can you drink our water, when you are not entirely here?*

What? I looked around.

There, on the far bank, was a dragon. The huge wings were folded at the moment and had become unlikely front limbs. The dragon rested on all fours.

It turned its head and regarded me with a single pale yellow eye. *There is much which I do not understand. How can you dig in our sand? How can our stones cut your feet? And would it be safe for me to eat you?*

I opened my mouth, but I was too frightened. I couldn't make a sound.

The dragon yawned. Its muzzle or beak was long and narrow and full of teeth. It opened one wing, stretching it all the way out. The wing was skin like the wing of a bat, but it was covered with scales glimmering in the late afternoon light. Gray, tan, pale pink, and orange. The colors shone like colors in a film of oil.

The dragon closed its wing, then looked at me again. *A pity,* it said. *I cannot take the risk. Somehow, you are managing to exist in two worlds at once. Or maybe you fluctuate very rapidly between this world and the world of the Fortress.* The dragon closed its eye, the one eye visible to me. *All that is theory.* The eye opened. *The datum is: I can feel the terrible stain in the fabric of space and time. It twists around you. It tries to pull free and resume its proper shape. But you will not let it. What power you have, oh daughter of the bear!*

I do?

If I ate you now, you might return to the world of the Fortress and take my gut with you, through the fifth dimension. No thank you! I can wait.

For what? I was about to ask.

The dragon leaped forward. I cowered down. Air rushed over me. I heard the flap of wings, and was in shadow for an instant. I looked up. The huge beast had cleared the trees on my side of the river.

A moment later, it began to turn, beating those enormous wings. The long neck and the head were extended; and they shone in the light of the low sun.

Oh no! I thought.

Back over it came, but this time higher up—well above the trees.

Farewell, Esperance. I will see you again.

I stood up. It flew due west, rising all the while. Horrible and magnificent. There was a bad taste in my mouth. I spat, then realized that I was losing precious moisture. I knelt and scooped more water out of the hole.

As I drank, the voice spoke in my mind. *Out of courtesy, I will tell you my name.*

Eh?

It is Pyramid Thirteen.

What?

All dragons are named after prime numbers and perfect solids.

The next thing I remember is a wall of stone, badly eroded and full of holes. It was lit by something in back of me. Not the sun. This light was too dull and too orange. I turned and saw a round full moon. Not Luna. The pitted face was unfamiliar. And anyway, it was too large.

What now? I wondered. I was cold and frightened. How could I survive on a strange world at night?

I was in a canyon, I realized. The moon was just above a second wall of stone. The floor of the canyon was bare, except for small bushes dotted here and there.

Which way was out? Did it matter? I turned right and began to walk. I was traveling over sand that shifted underfoot. It was slow going. A wind began to blow; and I got colder.

The canyon turned. I went around a corner. I saw a red gleam in front of me. A fire.

Did the dragons have fire? I didn't know or care. I hurried forward, slipping in the sand.

There were buildings. No, ruins. In the light of the fire, I saw low walls made of stone.

The fire was in an open space in the middle of the ruins. A person sat next to it. Not a dragon! This was a human being.

I ran.

The person looked up.

I reached the fire and stopped. The person was a woman, brown and old, with straight black hair and a wrinkled face. The hair was fastened in a bun at the back of her head. She wore a cloak of brown feathers.

"Thank goodness," I said.

The woman regarded me calmly, not in the least bit afraid or even surprised, as far as I could tell. After a moment, she stood up, letting her cloak slide off her shoulders. Underneath, she wore a dress. It was off white, made of a material I didn't recognize. A fine leather, maybe. The dress went down below her knees. Beneath it were boots. These were clearly made of leather, and pure white, except for a couple of stains. She wore a sash. I think it was woven of cotton. And half a dozen necklaces. The necklaces were made of shell, pale gray and white.

We looked at one another for a minute or two. Then she bent and picked up her cloak. She brought it to me, wrapping it around me. Then she pointed at the ground.

I sat down.

The woman went off into the darkness. I moved closer to the fire. I was shaking from the cold and with relief.

After a while, the woman came back. She had bread. The pieces were round and thin, like tortillas. She laid them on a stone that was right next to the fire—almost in it, in fact. Then she turned and went back into the darkness. When she returned this time, she carried a bowl and a jug. They were both made of white clay and decorated with brown paint. The patterns were intricate and geometric.

She gave the jug to me. I drank from it. It held water, cold and clean.

Ah, that was good!

Then she set the bowl down on the ground next to me. It was full of a red-brown mush. I sniffed. Beans, mashed up with other things. I sniffed again. I was pretty sure that I could smell tomato and pepper. Hot pepper. Who was this woman? And why did she cook in the Mexican style?

"Do you speak English?" I asked.

The woman looked at me without speaking. After a moment, I realized that she was answering me. She did not know my language.

She turned the pieces of bread over. Then she sat down, across the fire from me. I looked at her a second time. Her cheeks were sunken. There were deep lines around her mouth and across her forehead. I suspected that she had no teeth. But her eyes were bright.

She gestured at the bread and then at me. I took a piece. It was hot, almost too hot to hold. And it was a peculiar color: a pale blue-gray. I stared at it for a moment, then remembered the blue corn that grew in New Mexico. This was a blue-corn tortilla. Of course! What else? It was the obvious thing to eat in a world full of dragons. I took a bite and chewed and swallowed. There was no question at all about it. I was eating a blue-corn tortilla. And very tasty it was, too.

I used the tortilla to scoop up some of the red mush. It had the texture of refried beans, but it was much spicier. Full of chili pepper. It burned; and the burn stayed in my mouth after I swallowed. I drank more water. Then I ate more mush. I had always liked Mexican food; and I loved the food in New Mexico, when I went down there to visit you, Jennifer.

Mush. Water. Another tortilla. More mush and more water. At last I stopped, full of food and the warm glow that chili peppers create. How was this possible? I wondered then. If the dragon was right, I wasn't really in this world. But I was eating and drinking here. Eating well, in fact. And in a minute or two, I was going to have to go off among the ruins and urinate.

No. Not among the ruins. They might belong to the old woman. It might not be polite to use them as a bathroom. I would go find a bush.

"Excuse me," I said and stood.

The woman nodded and made a gesture—away from the ruins, toward the middle of the canyon.

I went off into the darkness.

When I got back, a second person sat by the fire: a man, as old as the woman. Like her, he was brown, with black eyes and straight black hair. I couldn't see what he wore. He was wrapped in a hide of some kind. It was covered with short brown fur. Was it deer?

He looked at me, then grunted and lifted one hand in greeting. His fingers were twisted by arthritis. His forearm was bare, except for a bracelet made of white shell; and it was thin. What little flesh was on it sagged.

I sat down.

The two of them talked softly in a language I could not understand. I was getting more and more tired. At last, I lay down and covered myself with the cloak of feathers.

I did not wake until morning. I was naked again. The cloak was gone. I sat up shivering. The fire had vanished—all of it, even the ashes. There was no sign of the people.

The canyon was full of a gray mist. But I was able to make out the ruins—all around me, made of blocks of stone.

A voice spoke in my mind. *Are you down there, oh daughter of the bear?*

Pyramid Thirteen? I said and then wished I had kept quiet.

Yes.

I thought of asking the dragon about the people and then decided no. But it was too late. The creature had caught my thought.

There are no people here. Not anymore. There were a few— two thousand or three thousand—when we came to this world. But we ate them. Nothing remains except the ruins.

Who were they?

People from Earth. Sometimes—in periods of desperation— even ordinary folk can go from one world to another. We read their minds before we ate them. They had come here, fleeing a terrible drought. They built their little towns. They farmed. They made pottery and jewelry, though they never found the stone they prized most of all. It was as blue as the sky.

Turquoise.

They prospered for a while. A century or two. Then we came.

The stone was turquoise, I thought again. And the people were the Anasazi. The Ancient Ones. I had learned about them in New Mexico.

They had built towns all over the southwest and then abandoned them—because of drought and famine, most of the scholars said. That had been a long time ago. When exactly, I was not certain. Maybe the fourteenth century. In any case, a group of them had gotten to this world.

I shivered. The mist was getting thin; and I could see blue sky above me.

What a fate! To meet the dragons. It must have been worse than meeting the conquistadors, which their relatives had done, back in New Mexico.

"You aren't safe anywhere," I said out loud.

Now I could see the dragon, soaring over the rim of the canyon.

What were they? I asked. *The people I saw last night?*

You are twisting the fabric of space and time, the dragon replied. *Maybe—for a while—you moved back to when they were alive.*

But the buildings were in ruins, I said.

Maybe they were ghosts or spirits of some kind. Those people believed in all kinds of spirits. Don't bother me, oh daughter of the bear. I can't answer your questions; and I have problems of my own. I can't decide whether or not to eat you.

The dragon swept out of sight. I began to walk down the canyon.

Later on, I was climbing over rocks. They were dark brown and had mica in them, which glittered in the sunlight. The sun was almost above me. It was a little before—or a little after—noon. I had a feeling that I'd been climbing for some time. My hands were cut; and one knee had a scrape. My breath rasped in and out. My chest hurt.

I reached a ledge and sat down. Below me was a canyon. I didn't know if it was the canyon with the ruins. It didn't look familiar. There were hills on the far side of the canyon. They were low and bare. Beyond the hills was a plain. It stretched to the horizon, flat and almost featureless, a dull dusty brown.

Why was I here? What was going on?

I wish I knew, a voice said in my mind.

I looked up. The dragon was there: a dot in the sky. It was circling like a vulture.

What happened to the loop? I asked.

It is holding—so far. But it has a weakness.

Where?

Where do you think? The obvious place. Where it twists and goes out of the ordinary four dimensions. Somehow, you have figured this out—though not consciously. Every time you go through the twist, you give it a tug or pull. It is stretching, oh daughter of the bear; and the knot has begun to slip. The part of the loop that lies outside the ordinary four dimensions has grown and grown.

It reaches here. And every time you go through the twist, you appear somewhere on this world.

Oh, I said. *You do understand what is going on. At least, you can explain it.*

No. I don't understand how you can exist between two worlds. I don't understand why you appear where you appear. I can't figure out why the time you spend here varies. And I don't know when it will be safe to eat you.

Why do you want to eat me, anyway?

The dragon was silent for a minute or two. Then it said, *Curiosity. A sense of adventure. A desire to increase the general store of knowledge.*

About what? I asked.

About food.

Oh, I thought. I decided to continue. I got up and began to climb.

I don't remember what happened next. But after a while, it was afternoon. I had found a stream. The wide bed was full of yellow pebbles. Water ran down the middle. It was cold and clear. I drank from time to time. The air was dry; and my lips were cracking. I kept licking them. Now and then, I tasted salt. The cracks were bleeding.

I went along one bank. Around me and above me were lofty trees. They were all the same kind. Their bark was rough and gray. Their foliage was rectangular, about four inches long and close to an inch wide. I couldn't decide if they were leaves or needles. In any case, they were the color of rust; and they smelled of cinnamon.

The ground was covered with them: a thick soft carpet, though there were plenty still on the trees. It wasn't a bad surface for walking, except for one thing: the corners of the leaves were sharp. I was naked, as usual; and my feet were bare. Sometimes I came down on a needle the wrong way; and it dug into my foot. Then I hopped and cursed and pulled the needle out. I could have used a pair of boots and some good thick socks and maybe some clothes as well. Underwear and a pair of jeans and a flannel shirt and a light trail pack with food in it. I thought about fruit bars and granola bars, until I began to salivate.

I was hungry again, I realized. How long had it been, since I had eaten with the ghosts? I had no idea.

Fortunately, there were no bugs around. None that I noticed, anyway. Birds filled the trees. They were the size of English sparrows and bright parrot green. They clicked and whistled and flew from branch to branch.

I walked for hours, going slowly up. At first, there was sunlight, slanting between the trees. It must have been early afternoon, for the light came in at an angle of eighty degrees. Gradually, the angle grew smaller. When it was about forty-five degrees, the light vanished. The sun must have gone behind a mountain. I began to look for shelter.

You are in luck, said a voice in my mind.

Pyramid Thirteen?

Yes, of course. Who did you expect? There was rain last night.

*A brief storm. That is why the stream is running. Lightning struck
a tree; and it is still smoldering. You can use the branches to
build a shelter. And if you have any skill at all, you will be able to
make a fire.*

Skill? I wondered. I had never been especially interested in
woodsy lore. I didn't care for the plumbing facilities in the Great
Outdoors or for the bugs. Mosquitoes, ticks, gnats, flies—you
could have them and keep them, as far as I was concerned. But I
had belonged to the Campfire Girls, when I was a kid. I could no
longer remember why. And I had been a den mother for a year or
so, when Mark was eight or nine.

Where is the tree? I asked.

About an hour away.

I kept walking. The air grew colder; and it began to feel damp.
I must have reached the area where the rain had fallen.

You are getting closer, the dragon told me. *Look up. Maybe
you will be able to see the smoke rise.*

I looked up. I didn't see the smoke, but the dragon was visible. I could make out the wings and the long neck and the head.
Just barely. It was high up.

She, the dragon told me. *I am female—as you would know, if
you knew anything about dragons.*

Why?

Thirteen is always a female name. The dragon turned. It—
she—was circling above me. *And—as is well known to every
student of dragons—among our kind, the female is both more
persevering and more rapacious than the male. A male would
have given up on you long ago.*

The dragon disappeared, hidden by the rusty crown of a tree
that was taller than all the others. When she reappeared, she was
rising, her wings steady. She must have caught an updraft. Up
and up she went, gleaming in the afternoon light. What a splendid
sight she was!

It was then I realized who she reminded me of. You, Jennifer.
Remember the summer we went up north? We rented a cabin on a
lake. Walter's parents were there, in the next cabin over; and
Walter kept planning educational trips for all of us. Over to Itasca
to see the source of the Mississippi and up to the Range to see
how the iron mining was done.

Anyway, you were fourteen. You had a lovely tan and your

first really daring bathing suit. It was jade green. You were so nervous when you put it on! You used to show off, diving off the dock—usually when there was some kid around you wanted to impress. The boy from across the lake, for example. I've forgotten his name.

In any case, the dragon was the same: lovely and uneasy and trying to impress.

The dragon was an adolescent. She had to be! She lectured me as if I were an idiot. She generalized. She had far too much energy. And she worried about who she was. That was why she spent so much time explaining what dragons were like. She was talking to herself, not to me. After all, why should she care about my opinions? I was dinner.

Not dinner, said the dragon. *You are still not entirely here. Though the strain on the loop is increasing. I can feel it, even at a distance. It ought to break soon, maybe before it's time for breakfast.*

What will happen then?

I'm not certain. You may end up in the world of the Fortress. You may end up here. You may explode and vanish from existence. All I can do is wait and hope that you end where I am, in an edible condition. Now, keep walking. I don't want you to die of exposure. Dragons do not eat carrion.

Half an hour later, I found the tree. It lay across the stream I had been following. On the far side were the branches: a tangle of reddish foliage. The stump was on my side, right in front of me. It was blackened by fire. Smoke rose from it, thin and gray.

I set to work, gathering the dryest needles I could find and then dry branches. I built my fire. Now all I had to do was light it. The sky was beginning to darken.

I found a stone at the edge of the stream: long and triangular. With it, I dug at the smoking wood. I got out a piece. I laid it on the needles. I knelt and blew.

The wood stopped smoking.

I rocked back on my heels and said a dirty word.

Hurry, said the dragon. *Up here, I can see the far western mountains. The sun is almost out of sight behind the peak that we call the "Truncated Cone."*

I scrambled up and dug into the stump. This time, the wood I got was so hot that I could barely handle it.

I dropped it on the needles, then dropped to my knees. Slowly, I told myself. Gently. Don't blow it out.

I leaned close and blew on the wood.

Smoke went up, a narrow wavering line. A wisp only. I could barely see it in the increasing dark. I kept blowing.

The smoke grew thicker. It smelled of cinnamon. My eyes began to tear. I blinked; and there it was. A flame! It flickered dimly. I blew again. It spread. In a moment or two, the needles were ablaze. I added branches, little ones at first. They must have been full of resin. They burned like dry pine.

I added more branches—big ones now; and then I moved away. The heat was intense. The branches began to make popping noises. Sparks flew out in every direction.

The dragon said, *Good. I can see it from here.*

I glanced up. The sky was dark. I saw a row of stars. Could it be the belt of Orion? That did not seem possible.

There is one problem, said the dragon.

Yes?

You were planning to use the top of the tree as a shelter.

Yes. That's right.

Look where you have built your fire.

I glanced at the fire and then across the stream. The top of the tree was there, no longer visible to me. I had built my fire fifty feet away from the place where I planned to sleep.

"Hell," I said. I found a pod on the ground next to me. It must have come off one of the trees. It was as long as my middle finger and about the same shape. It rattled when I shook it. I tossed it into the fire. A moment later, it exploded. *Snap! Snap! Snap! Snap!* Like a string of tiny firecrackers. I scrambled up. But that was it. The pod was done exploding. The fire went back to burning in a more ordinary fashion.

Well, what was I going to do? I could build another fire on the far side of the stream. But that seemed like a lot of work; and my night vision was bad. I had never liked doing anything in the dark. Even sex was better with a little light.

I'd sleep here, next to the fire, and hope that the fallen trunk would give me enough shelter. I picked up a branch and checked it over. It had no pods. I laid it on the fire.

I was getting hungry. There was nothing to eat. Most likely, it wasn't going to be a very pleasant night. I made a little growling noise in the back of my throat. I hated being hungry.

Something hit the ground in back of me. I turned. The thing lay about ten feet away. It was the size of a German shepherd. No, bigger. Or fatter, anyway. It was dead.

I moved a little closer. The thing had short legs; and its body reminded me of a pig or a peccary. Its ears were like the ears of a rabbit. Its fur was spotted brown and white.

I kept moving closer. Now I saw the wounds in the creature: great gashes that shone, full of blood. Most were on the back. It had been attacked from above. I felt sick to my stomach.

I heard another sound—once again, in back of me. A *woosh* and then a *whump*. I turned. The dragon sat with open wings on the trunk of the fallen tree.

It—or rather, she—folded her wings, then cocked her head and looked at me. Her skin glimmered in the firelight; and light glinted off her eye.

Take what you need. Leave the rest for me.

I had to eat. If I didn't, I was going to be ill—really ill, not merely a little queasy. I found a piece of flesh that had been so badly torn that it hung loose, barely attached to the animal. I pulled and yanked, until I tore it free. The dragon watched with interest. I glanced around from time to time and saw the long neck stretched out, the narrow head tilted, the yellow eye fixed on me.

There was fur on the meat. I had no way to cut it off. I found a branch with a sharp point and worked it through the meat. I added more wood to the fire. Flames leaped up. I stuck the meat in. The fur began to burn. It smelled terrible.

I have heard, said the dragon, *about the eating habits of humans. I never entirely believed it.*

You do now?

Yes. Disgusting! Are you done with the animal?

Uh-huh.

The dragon flapped up. I ducked. She came down in back of me. I heard terrible noises: crunching, mostly, and the flap of wings. Once in a while, there was a sharp crack; and once I heard a slurp. I didn't look around.

My branch was too dry. It caught fire. I pulled it out. The meat fell to the ground.

Oh well. It was nothing but clean dirt. I got another branch.

The meat was too hot to handle. I had to wait till it was cool before I could put it on the new branch.

Back into the fire it went. The dragon had stopped making noises. Did that mean she had stopped eating? If so, what was she doing? The skin on my upper back began to prickle. I glanced over my shoulder. There was something there. It filled my field of vision. It was pale and shimmery.

Carefully, I set down the stick with the meat. Then I turned around. Firelight flickered over the great chest of the dragon. I glanced up. She looked down at me. Her mouth was slightly open. I could see rows of teeth. Dribbles of blood ran down her jaw. She couldn't have been more than four feet away. I could see the glint of individual scales; and all the wonderful intricacy of the patterns that covered her. Tan, pink, and gray, they were like the patterns on the wing of a butterfly or on the back of a python.

Was this it? I wondered. Was the dragon going to strike?

Your meat is burning, she said.

What?

When you laid the stick down, you laid it in the fire. Why did you do that?

I was preoccupied. I glanced at the fire. The dragon was right. My branch lay in the fire. It was burning merrily and so was the meat. I could smell it. *Excuse me,* I said. I grabbed the branch. It broke. I grabbed another branch off the wood pile and pushed the meat to safety. It was entirely black.

Isn't that enough? asked the dragon. Or do you have to burn it all the way through to the center?

No. I mean, yes. I have burnt it enough. I moved to the other side of the fire. The meat was there; and I was farther away from the dragon.

I sat down and ate the meat. It was covered with a crust that tasted of charcoal and ash. Inside, it was half raw. I ate it all, the dragon watching me.

I wonder, she said at last, *if your flesh will taste of burnt meat. Things usually take on the taste of whatever they eat. Most of the time, I prefer herbivores. Their flesh has a mild flavor. Carnivores tend to be gamy. I think that is the word in your language. In our language, we say a carnivore has the taste of blood.*

Stop it, I said. *You're making me nauseous.*

The dragon was silent for a while. I went to the stream and

*drank. The stars were out. I didn't recognize any constellations.
The air was cold. By the time I got back to the fire, I was shivering.*

*The dragon was crouching on all fours. The tips of her folded
wings were above her head. Her eyes were half closed. She
seemed to be dozing.*

*I went past her. She blinked and said, How comfortable a fire
is! Good night.*

Her eyes closed entirely. I sat down. For a while, I watched
the firelight move over her scaly body. Now, with her head tucked
in, she was only a little taller than I was. Six feet maybe. No
more than seven. Her wings must have been over thirty feet
across, when extended. Her head was—what? Three feet long?
Narrow and bony and mostly jaw and mouth. A terrifying creature, but lovely as well. And she had the awkward charm of an
adolescent. I would have liked her, except that she kept talking
about eating me.

I put more branches on the fire, then I lay down and went to
sleep.

There was sunlight on my face. I rolled over on my side, then
blinked and saw the fire: a pile of ashes. A wisp of smoke rose
from it.

Beyond the fire was an empty space: a clearing. Sunlight filled
it. The dragon was gone. I sat up and looked around. Forest and
more forest, a little patch of sky, the stream. There was an animal
on the trunk of the fallen tree. It—the animal—was right above
the middle of the stream. It was the size of a cat with huge hind
legs and tiny ears. Its eyes were yellow. Its fur was pale gray.

It blinked, regarding me. Then it yawned. Sharp teeth. It was
another carnivore. Why couldn't I meet a nice vegetarian?

"Sorry," I told it. "I am not breakfast. At least, I don't think I
am."

The animal turned and hopped away, going along the trunk till
it reached the far side of the stream. Then it hopped down onto
the ground. It stopped and looked at me. "Mrrr," it said. The
sound was plaintive.

"Beat it," I said. "Find someone else to eat."

The animal hopped into the forest. I stood up and stretched.
Then I touched my toes. My back was stiff; and my feet hurt. Too

much walking yesterday or whenever it had been. I did a set of exercises. Speaking of breakfast, I thought as I bent to one side, who was I going to eat this morning?

Be patient, said the dragon. *I am looking. This is a perfect day for hunting. Clear air. A steady wind. One can soar for hours and see one's prey at a distance of a hundred miles.*

I looked up. The dragon was not visible. *Good luck,* I said. *I think.*

I did another side bend. I felt a pain in my gut. Hunger? No. It hurt too much. I straightened up. Had I pulled something? Was it a hernia?

The pain got worse. I dropped to my knees and doubled over, grabbing at my belly. I felt as if I were being turned inside out.

The loop! cried the dragon. Through my pain I felt her joy. *The loop is giving way!*

I was in two places. One was a place of pain. The other was the sky. I soared, turning in a great circle. The forest was below me; and I could see a break in the foliage. Water glinted. Esperance was there.

I felt the dragon fold her wings. She plummeted. I screamed with fear and pain.

There! I could see myself! A body on the ground, twisting back and forth. Another moment and it would be—

Dinnertime! the dragon cried.

Then I was alone in darkness. There was nothing around me. No floor and no walls. The twisting in my gut grew worse. I screamed again, then choked. I was vomiting—what? Myself, I thought. Everything inside was coming out.

Lines of fire appeared in the darkness, then vanished like meteors, then reappeared and stayed, growing wider and brighter.

Warm stuff ran down my legs. It was something out of me. Urine? Or shit? Or blood? Or my whole body, turned to liquid?

I threw up again, then lifted my head. The darkness was almost gone—torn into pieces, broken into shards. White fire blazed around each fragment. I closed my eyes. I could see light through my eyelids.

The voice of the Great Calculator spoke in my mind. UNCLE, it said, I GIVE UP. YOU WIN.

A spasm went through me. It was worse than anything before. I screamed.

BUT HOW—? asked the G.C.

The pain stopped. The light was gone as well. I opened my eyes. I was back in darkness. This time I saw stars. They were all around me, even underfoot. They burned steadily and brilliantly. For the first time in my life, I saw their colors. Before this, they had always seemed white to me. Now, they were orange and yellow, red, blue, and even green. How lovely!

The only trouble was, I was freezing. And I had a feeling I'd better not try to breathe.

Space! I thought. I was going to be the first woman to die in space.

No. That was impossible. If this was space, then I was dead already. I had to be. Didn't I? I tried to remember what happened to people, who ended up in a vacuum without protection. Did they explode? Or were they freeze-dried, like something at the Birdseye factory?

Dammit! Why hadn't I paid more attention to "Nova"?

The stars went out. The darkness turned to sunlight. I lay on my belly on the ground. I could smell shit and vomit and cinnamon. I rolled over and looked up.

Trees with red-brown foliage. A patch of blue sky. An object that fell toward me. It was large and pale.

"Oh no!" I cried.

The dragon opened her wings. She stopped in midair. Her body swung down. Her hind feet reached for me. I could see every claw.

Once again, I was in the dark.

No. My eyes adjusted. I saw the sky. It was low and gray. Snow drifted down out of it. The flakes were large. They vanished, as soon as they hit the pavement.

Pavement? What pavement? Where was I now?

On a narrow winding street. I was standing upright. There were buildings all around me. The buildings were tall and dark.

The street was lit, though not especially well. I could see lanterns on either side of it. Each lantern was on top of a long metal pole. Each lantern shone dimly. I could barely distinguish their light from the light that came out of the sky.

Early morning, I told myself. It was early morning on a winter day. And I was almost certain that I knew this place.

I lifted my head and looked from side to side. I saw another building.

This one rose about a block away. It was taller than all the rest. A tower made of glass. At the moment, it was gray, the color of the sky. Clouds drifted around it. They hid the upper stories.

It was the IDS Building. I was on the mall in downtown Minneapolis.

The wind blew, just a puff. Snow whirled around me; and I shivered. I was naked, as usual.

Behind me, a man spoke. He sounded diffident. "Lady, you can't go around like that. Not in March. Not in Minnesota."

He was right, but what could I do about it? And how was I going to get out of there before I got arrested? Lucky for me it was so early. No one was around, except for the one man. I turned to check him out.

He stood in a bus shelter. Aha! A commuter! Going to a factory job in one of the suburbs. That would explain why he was in downtown Minneapolis at dawn. He was changing buses. He wore a parka. The hood was up. His pants were gray and shiny. Work pants. He wore them tucked into a pair of snowmobiler boots. He carried a lunch box; and he was no longer looking at me. Instead, he stared down the mall toward the public library.

The dragon was there, four blocks away from us and two stories above the street. She flew toward us. Her enormous wings seemed to fill the mall.

The man in the parka said, "Oh shit."

I turned and ran toward the IDS Building.

You cannot escape, the dragon said in my mind. *No matter where you go, I will follow.*

"Get off the street," cried the man in the parka. "A doorway! Anything! Get in a place where that thing can't reach!"

He was right. I ran across Seventh Street and then along the sidewalk next to the IDS Building. Ahead of me was a skyway: a pedestrian bridge, one story above the street. It was metal and glass. It went from Dayton's department store to the IDS Building. It looked pretty solid; and I didn't think the dragon could get under it. Not easily.

I'd duck in there. The building—the IDS—came out on either side of the skyway. It made a kind of corner. A hole. A cranny. Protected on three sides and from above.

Even better! I remembered now! There were doors under the skyway. They led into the building. Maybe they'd be open. Maybe I could get in.

I reached the skyway and ran under it.

Where are you? cried the dragon.

I kept going. I reached the doors. There was a court inside. It was lit. I saw people moving around.

Overhead, wings flapped. The damn thing must be above me, must be above the skyway.

I tried one of the doors. It was locked. I beat on the glass.

There was a crash. I spun around. Beyond the skyway, glass was falling. Pieces of all sizes. They hit the pavement and shattered. One tiny fragment flew up. It hit my arm. I pulled it out. A blob of blood appeared on my skin; and, at the same moment, I heard a cry. I couldn't tell if it was in the air or in my mind. It was loud, full of anger and pain.

What happened? I asked.

I hit. I hit, the dragon said. She sounded confused.

The building.

I saw nothing. Again, I heard confusion in her voice.

Of course, I thought. There were no buildings on her world, except for the ruins left by the Anasazi. She wouldn't have known about walls of glass that reflect the sky.

Where are you? I asked.

Above you. Caught in the trap you set for me. It is like a cave. I am halfway into it.

She had gone through the glass and ended in someone's office. I ought to go take a look, though I never liked to look at accidents.

I glanced back at the court of the IDS Building. There were people just inside the doors. They had keys. They were coming out. I was in trouble.

I walked out from under the skyway. There she was. Three stories up. I saw the broken window and the huge dark shape, hanging halfway out.

What are we going to do? I asked.

I am going to die, the dragon said. *But not here. I have the strength to go home, though I will not have it for long.*

Take me with you, I said.

There was no answer.

Can you? I asked.

Of course.

I heard a door open. "Hey, what the heck is going on?"

I looked at the entrance to the court. A man stood there. He wore a uniform. A security guard.

Please, I said to the dragon.

The man walked toward me. A piece of glass crashed onto the pavement. The man spun and reached for his belt. Was he wearing a gun?

I blinked at the sudden blaze of light. The sun. I stood on a flat plain. It was sandy and stony. Bushes grew here and there. They were small and dull purple. The air was still and hot. It smelled of dust. I looked around. The dragon was off to one side of me. She lay in a heap. One wing was open. It extended over the ground. I could see bloody gashes in the membrane. The other wing was folded. It bent in two places. That was wrong. The dragons had only one joint in the middle of each wing.

I walked to her. She lifted her head, looking at me through a half-closed eye. *I did you a favor, oh daughter of the bear.*

Yes.

Do me one.

All right.

I waited. After a moment or two, the dragon spoke. *I will never fly again. You see that, don't you?*

I'm afraid so, though I'm not a doctor.

I know. One wing is broken. The other is torn. Nothing can be done. She put her head down on the ground. Her mouth was open. I saw her teeth and her tongue, which was thick and dark. She opened her eye all the way. The pupil was a line. *I do not want to die slowly. I cannot ask my kin for help. We do not have many rules, but there is one that each one of us obeys. We never kill another dragon.* She paused and blinked. *We must have that rule. If we did not, we would destroy ourselves.*

You want me to kill you, I said.

Yes.

No. I won't do it.

The dragon blinked again. *Find a rock. A good heavy one. My skull is thin. It has to be. If we had heavy bones, we would not be able to fly, even with the help of magic.*

You fly with the help of magic?

Yes. Of course. Look at the size of us. How could we possibly stay aloft any other way?

A good point, I said.

Our ancestors used magic, too, though with less skill than we have now. You find their bones on Earth. Don't you ever wonder how they were able to fly?

Pteranodons, I said.

That is your name. They left Earth forever after the disaster. Most of the others died.

Disaster? I said. *And what do you mean by 'the others'?*

I am tired of talking, the dragon said. *I suffer. Do me in.*

I thought of bringing a stone down on the narrow head. I thought of how it would feel and sound. I couldn't do it. *No,* I said.

I saved you. If I had not brought you here, those people on Earth would have done something to you; and I do not think it would have been pleasant.

A locked ward somewhere, I thought. And lots of Thorazine and maybe commitment proceedings. The dragon was right. She had saved me.

I have given you a gift, oh daughter of the bear. Your freedom and maybe your life. I do not know. The great yellow eye gazed at me. The pupil had contracted so much that I couldn't see it at all, not even as a line. The eye was entirely blank. As empty as a gemstone. *Set me free.*

I thought some more. I could feel the dragon's pain—not all of it, but some. Enough. I felt her anger too, and her grief. She was young. She would never grow to full maturity.

In her mind, I saw vast bodies wheeling. Dragons in flight. I felt what they felt: the current of air and magic that filled the sky, always in motion, rising and falling, twisting from side to side.

Using the currents, the dragons could rise to the edge of space or fly for days without landing. But not my dragon. She had not learned how to use her power or the Power of the Pattern. Not entirely. Not yet. I felt her grieve for the things she would never learn or see. The grief was terrible, worse than the pain.

I went to find a stone.

When I came back, her eyes were closed. She was breathing in gasps. Maybe I'd be lucky. Maybe she would die soon; and I wouldn't have to use the stone.

No, said the dragon. *You will not be lucky.* She lifted her head and looked at me. *Behind the eye and a little above it. The skull is thinnest there. Bring the stone down with all your might. Be cou-*

rageous! Do not flinch. She laid her head down and closed her eyes.

I knelt beside her.

Lift the stone, she said.

I obeyed.

Are you ready?

Yes, I said.

Now! the dragon cried.

I brought my hands down. The stone hit the skull. I heard the bone break. Pain filled my head; and I lost consciousness.

I don't know how long I was out. When I woke, the sun was gone. It wasn't night. Instead, I was surrounded by a gray half-light. My head hurt. I was stiff. I lay on something lumpy. I pushed myself up and saw the body of the dragon. It was like the body of a dead fish: gray and colorless, all the shimmer gone.

I had actually done it. I could smell blood and excrement. The blood came from the dragon. Splinters of broken bone had pushed through the skin above the eye. I could see them. They were sharp and thin. The wound had bled copiously. Dry blood covered the dragon's eye and most of the back of her head. Blood had run down her neck and gotten caught in folds of skin and dried there.

A lot of time must have passed, I thought. I certainly felt as if it had. I stood up. I was so stiff that I could barely move; and my hands and feet were numb from the cold.

I rubbed my hands and stamped my feet. Looking down, I realized where the smell of shit came from. My bare legs were streaked with brown. And—I discovered next—there were spots of dried vomit on my belly and breasts. Oh ick! At least I was alive and no longer in prison.

Where was I? I looked around. Fog hid the distance. How could that be? I had killed the dragon in the middle of a desert. but now the air was damp as well as cool. I heard, or thought I heard, the roar of water.

No. It was impossible. I looked back at Pyramid Thirteen. She was still there: a dull gray heap. I felt as if I had killed something splendid that was a part of me. A hope. A dream. A possibility.

"Nuts," I told myself and the corpse of the dragon. "The only thing you contained *in posse* was my death. We couldn't have coexisted. You would always have wanted to eat me. And why am I talking to you? Or to myself ? You can't answer. And as for me—I don't know what the hell I mean.

"Good-bye." I stood for a moment longer, thinking that was inadequate. I ought to bow or curtsy. How does one say farewell to a mythological creature, whom one has just done in? I had no idea; and there wasn't time to write to Ann Landers.

I turned and walked away, toward the sound of the water.

The fog grew thicker. The ground began to change. It was no longer sandy. Instead, I walked over rocks. They were wet and slippery. The sound of the water rose and fell. I imagined waves rolling in. Dead fish and seaweed. Was I wrong?

I slipped and fell forward onto my hands and knees. Damn!

A pair of hands took hold of my arm. I looked up.

It was the old woman, the one I had met before. She wore her cloak of brown feathers. She tugged, and I stood up, with a little help from her. She let go of my arm and smiled. The smile was wry and brief. A cryptic smile. The woman had no teeth. Not one.

"Thanks again," I said.

She beckoned, then led the way. I followed. We entered a patch of fog so thick that I could see nothing. She took my hand. We kept walking—very slowly now.

I don't know how long we continued. After a while, I heard a new sound. A drum. *Ta-tum. Ta-tum.* The beat went on and on. The sound of the water washed over and under it. I heard—I thought I heard—human voices. They chanted, keeping time with the drum.

I looked around. Nothing was visible. In the fog, I had lost all sense of direction. I couldn't tell where the singing came from.

Over there? To my right? I wasn't certain. It was worth a try. I moved to my right.

The grip on my hand grew stronger. The old woman tugged. She was pulling me forward, away from the music.

"Wait a minute," I said. "There are people there. I can hear them."

She tugged again.

I stopped. "Where are we going?"

The old woman said nothing. I couldn't see her. Not in that fog. Our only connection was the bony fingers that held my hand and pulled and pulled.

I was too tired to argue. "Okay," I said. "You helped me before. I'm going to assume that you know what you're doing."

I followed her. She led me on. The voices grew fainter. Then they were gone and so was the sound of the drum. Only the sound of the water remained. It grew louder and louder. I could taste salt in the air.

The woman stopped. I stopped, too. She said something that I could not understand. She tugged at my hand, then let go. I walked forward. I was pretty sure that she was telling me, "Go on." As I passed her, I brushed against her cloak of feathers. A moment later, I felt her hands on my back. She was pushing me.

"Okay. Okay," I said. I kept moving, sliding my bare feet over the rocks, feeling my way.

The fog began to thin. I stopped again and looked around. The woman was gone. Oh well. I went on, toward the sound of water.

Now I could see for some distance, maybe twenty feet. I passed blocks of stone. They came out of the fog like dolmens, huge and dim. But they had been far more carefully cut. Most were rectangular. A few were still arranged on top of one another. When I looked at these, I could see what had been there: a building of some kind or maybe a city. The walls had been massive.

I came to a doorway. It stood intact, but there was nothing around it, except for heaps of stone. It was arched; and the keystone had been carved into a leering face. For some reason—superstition—I did not go through the doorway. Instead, I climbed over the heaps of stone. When I came down on the other side, I heard the sound of the water really clearly for the first time; and I knew for certain what it was. I heard the grating roar:

> Of pebbles which the waves drew back and fling,
> At their return, up the high strand,
> Begin, and cease, and then again begin,
> With tremulous cadence slow, and bring
> The eternal note of sadness in.

"Dover Beach" by Matthew Arnold. It was almost my favorite poem, though Walter said that it lacked rigor. What a thing to say about Matthew Arnold!

I was hearing the ocean. I came to a beach of gray pebbles. There were blocks of stone strewn over it. Many lay in the water. Waves washed in around them and over them.

I paused. The fog was still pretty thick; and I couldn't see far. But I was beginning to think that I knew this place. The island of the Fortress! That left only two questions: How had I gotten here? And where was the Fortress?

Gone. Gone. Gone, said a voice in my mind.

Who was that? I looked around. Something—it wasn't big—ran from stone to stone.

Walls, said the voice. *Drains and sewers. Cans of garbage. All of them gone.*

Oh tasty garbage! said another voice. It had a mournful tone.

Traps! said the first voice. It sounded joyful. *Ferrets! Snakes! All blown to pieces.*

We remain, a third voice said.

A rat appeared on top of a block of stone. It was a patchwork of brown fur and naked pink skin. Its ears were enormous; and its eyes—I was close enough to see—were green.

No one else, said the third voice. Did it belong to this rat? *Wizards gone! Ka-boom! Ka-boom!*

I saw another rat scurry down the beach. This one was large, as big as a good-sized cat. And it had blond curly fur.

How? I asked. *What happened?*

Magic. We know. We recognize magic. It has a smell.

Those with noses that do not smell magic, said another voice, *they die.*

The rat with green eyes nodded. *Spells in the sewers. Spells in the drains. Garbage made bad by enchantments. Over and over, they try to kill the Patchy Folk with magic.*

Not now! cried a new voice. *Gone! All gone!*

The voices joined together into a kind of song:

> *Gone the wizards! Gone the ferrets!*
> *Gone the snakes with many feet!*
> *Free!*
> *Free!*
> *The Patch Folk!*

Another rat appeared on top of another stone. This one was striped like a tiger. If it had ears, I didn't see them. There was fur all the way to the tip of its tail.

A knot of magic, it said to me. *Big. It was in the basement. It came undone. Ka-boom!*

All the wizards blown to pieces, sang the many rat voices. *Many pieces. We are free.*

But hungry, said a new voice. I was certain I hadn't heard this one before. It was low. It seemed to vibrate in the bottom of my mind. And it sounded nasty.

A huge rat struggled out of hiding. Its legs were too short; and there were too many of them. Six. Its fur was lavender, soft and lovely. It would have made a fabulous coat. The rat looked at me with yellow eyes. *Garbage gone*, it said. *Must eat.*

Not me, I said.

Why not?

I've been through that before. I'm tired and dirty. I don't want to run anymore. I'll make a stand, if I have to.

Look edible, the fat rat said.

No, said the rat with green eyes. *Not yet. We eat wizards, dead in the rubble. We eat fish, dead on the beach. Nothing living. The living will keep.*

Thank you, I said.

I looked at the ocean. I wanted to wash off. But I had no way to dry myself. If I got wet, I'd be risking hypothermia. No. I'd stay dirty. I'd be content to stink—at least, until the sun came out.

It didn't. Instead, the fog got thicker and darker. Night was coming on.

I went inland, looking for shelter. There were broken walls, taller than I was, and heaps of rubble like hills. Also caves. They must have been basements, before the Fortress blew up. At the entrance to one, I found a snake. It was dead, thank goodness. It was twice as long as I was and albino white. It had something like a hundred legs. They were human legs: tiny, but perfectly formed. Each leg ended in a tiny human foot. Each foot had five toes. I crouched down and squinted. I wasn't certain, but I thought the toes had nails.

Oh dear, I thought.

Awful! Awful! said a voice.

I stood up and turned. It was the rat with patchy fur. He—or she—scampered up and stopped, five feet away. *You did it.*

Broke the loop? The knot, I mean. Yes, I did. But I didn't expect anything like this to happen.

Big knot. Full of energy. Like a trap with a spring. Snap! Ka-boom! Dead rat! Dead Fortress!

Bam! Bam! sang the rat. *All the nasty people! Gone! Gone! How wonderful!*

But hungry now, said Fatty. I recognized his voice.

Go eat a wizard, said Patches in reply.

I went on. Patches ran next to me. The fog grew thicker. It was almost rain by now. I found part of a caryatid: a huge muscular torso. It was a woman. Her head was gone and so were her arms. I found nothing else that I could recognize.

Drops of water hit me. I crawled into a cave. Patches came with me.

Make music, he/she said.

I saw scurrying at the edges of my vision. More rats came in: Tiger and Blondie and a little fellow with no fur at all. His skin was black. He shivered constantly. Others came in, as well. It was getting dark. I couldn't make them out. But I heard them. *Pitter-pat.*

They sang to me:

> *Oh luck! Oh valor!*
> *You blew to bits*
> *All the wizards*
> *And the Big Machine!*

> *All the traps*
> *And all the cages—*
> *Gone! Gone!*
> *Oh valor and luck!*

> *Rest! Be warm!*
> *Rest! Be happy!*
> *We will guard you.*
> *Let Fatty go away.*

> *Let Fatty eat*
> *The hand of a wizard.*
> *Let Fatty eat*
> *A sorceress's foot.*

What a pleasant thought. I curled up on the rubble. The rats came close.

I started the first time one touched me. I told myself, relax. Either they would eat me or they wouldn't. And there wasn't much I could do about it, either way. And I needed their warmth.

They crawled over me. I felt a multitude of warm furry bodies. I shook with fear. They squeaked and sang.

No harm! No harm!
We are not hungry.
At the moment, we feel
Only gratitude.

I slept till morning. When I woke, the fog was gone. Sunlight shone in my cave. I sat up. I was alone. Where were the rats? I had no idea. I climbed to my feet and walked to the entrance of the cave.

Ah! What a day! The sky was bright blue. The air was warm. Birds soared above me. Gulls, I was pretty certain. I'd go down to the beach and wash off, then look for something to eat. Clams or mussels. Or maybe a crab.

I walked through the ruins of the Fortress, whistling.

I was almost to the beach, when I saw Patches. He or she was in a crack between two big stones. His or her green eyes glinted.

Person?

Yes, I said.

We helped you last night. We sang a song of praise.

I know. Thank you. I liked the song.

Help us!

What?

Wizards! More wizards! The ocean is full of wizards! All around! All around! His or her voice was full of terror.

What do you mean?

Ships! They have anchored out beyond the shoals. There are wizards on them. We smell magic in the wind.

I ran toward the water. Behind me, Patches cried, *Help us, oh person!*

I rounded a block of stone. There was the ocean, a little rough today. A good breeze blew. There were whitecaps. The fleet—as promised—was anchored beyond the shoals. Galleys, long and dark. Their sails were furled, but I could see the colors: red, orange, and yellow, white and blue.

I stopped and shaded my eyes. A boat was coming in. It was good-sized. Many oars rose and fell, then rose again, dripping water that flashed in the sunlight. The people in the boat were black. One of them was standing at the prow. Was he crazy? He could fall out and drown. He was tall and thin, dressed in a long white robe. The robe fluttered.

I was filthy! I stank to heaven! I rushed into the water. It was cold. I dove under, came up and began to scrub.

Help! Help! cried Patches. *We'll do whatever you want. We'll kill Fatty! That awful rat. We'll tear him to bits. Anything to make you happy. Only help us!*

Okay, I said. *I'll do my best. But leave Fatty alone.*

He wanted to eat you!

He isn't the first.

Oh. Are you tasty? Have we missed a treat?

Shut up, if you want my help.

Patches shut up. I washed the dried vomit and shit off my body. There was no way I could get my hair clean. Not till I got hold of some shampoo.

The boat was in past the shoals now. I waited, hip deep in water. I could see the man at the prow clearly. He wore a necklace that hung to his waist. It was heavy, made of gold and something else. Big round beads. They were orange and red. Coral, I decided. His hair was longer than it had been, the last time I had seen him.

Nonetheless, I knew him: Lucien Dia. The priest from Senegal. My half brother, who was now a prince in the city of white stone.

He raised a hand to shade his eyes. His sleeve fell back, and more gold flashed. He was wearing bracelets, a lot of them. They went from his wrist to his elbow. "Esperance," he called. "Is it really you?"

"Who else?" I said in reply.

PART SEVEN: THE CRYSTAL

April is the cruelest month, thought Esperance. She sat in the bathroom in her daughter's apartment. The window was open a little at the bottom. Cold air blew in. Pantyhose hung on the shower rod. Five pairs. Tan, tan, off-white, beige, and gray. They fluttered in the wind. Esperance shivered. She had a bad feeling in her colon. Something down there was not right.

Goddammit, she thought. Her gut twisted and emptied itself.

The stool was solid. She could feel the solidity as it came out; and it hit the water in the toilet with a satisfying *splat*. She did not have diarrhea.

She tried to feel grateful. It wasn't easy. She was, after all, an epic heroine. She had just saved a world. She—and she alone— had blown up the Fortress on the island. The people of Ymarra and Emblar and Bashoo were safe, because of her. So what was she doing here? This wasn't the way an adventure was supposed to end: on the can in Minneapolis in the month when spring was supposed to come, but almost never did.

A stronger than usual gust of wind came in the window. The panty hose flipped back and forth. Esperance shivered again.

There had to be a good side to all of this. She wasn't really sick, only a little queasy. And the weather wasn't bad. A little cold maybe, but what did she expect in Minneapolis in April? The sun was out. The sky was clear. It was good to see her daughter.

Her son was still in school—at a small liberal arts college just outside of Philadelphia. Maybe she would fly east and visit him. According to Mark, the campus was lovely in the spring. And Esperance had never been to Philadelphia.

Her gut stopped twisting. She wiped herself and stood up, pulling up her panties—or rather, the panties she had found. They had been in the bureau in the main bedroom of her house in south Minneapolis. They were not hers. She knew that for certain. She always bought cotton; and these were made of some kind of nasty synthetic. The jeans she had on came from the bedroom, too. She had found them hanging in the closet. They were tight on her. She had to suck in her tummy, before she could zip them up.

Who did they belong to? Not Jennifer. They were designer jeans; and Jen had always worn Levi's. She got the zipper closed and locked, then heaved a cautious sigh. The zipper did not pop; and nothing tore.

She looked into the toilet to verify that her stool was, in fact, solid. It was. She flushed and washed her hands, then dried them and went down the hall to the kitchen.

Ayra had gotten another beer. The can was on the kitchen table. Ayra was back in her chair. She lounged with her long legs stretched out in front of her. A relaxed woman. Jennifer was at the table, too. She was sitting hunched forward. Typical, thought Esperance. Her daughter almost always had a look of tense energy. Why were her kids so serious?

"I'm back."

Jennifer and Ayra looked around.

"Jen? What has your father been doing lately? I found strange clothing in the house."

"Oh," said Jennifer. "Do you mind if we don't go into that now?"

"Why not?"

"I want to hear the rest of the story."

"The story is over," said Esperance. "I blew up the Fortress, and Lucien came to rescue me, along with the great fleet of Bashoo. That is it. The end."

"No." Jennifer shook her head. "There is too much that you haven't explained."

"Such as?"

"What happened to the rats."

Ayra nodded. "And how you got back to Minneapolis."

"And why the wizards in the Fortress went bad in the first place."

"Oh hell." She didn't feel like sitting down. She went over to the kitchen sink and leaned against it. She folded her arms and frowned. "Okay. I'll tell you what I know, though it isn't everything. I have no idea why the wizards in the fortress went over to evil—or rather, to shoddiness. How does anyone lose his or her integrity? I don't have those kinds of answers. All I can tell you is what happened to me. The rest of what happened to me."

"That will do," said Ayra.

"They pulled me out of the water. By "they," I mean Lucien and the sailors. They carried me out to the fleet. I stayed with Lucien on his ship. The *Ocean Leopard.*" Esperance grinned. "A really fine name!"

"The leopard is the royal animal in Bashoo," said Ayra.

Esperance nodded. "Un-huh. I know. I got clean. Let me tell you, that was a relief! And I rested for three or four days. I didn't eat much. My stomach was queasy. Maybe because I was on a ship. Or maybe because I had been through so much—especially so much magic. They told me, the wise folk of Bashoo, that magic is like everything else. It must be used moderately. Excessive use of magic leads to megalomania and disorders of the stomach and colon." Esperance grinned. "That's what they told me.

"As soon as I began to feel better, they began to question me."

"Who?" asked Jennifer.

"The wise folk. The witches and the wizards. The oracles. The sorcerers." She closed her eyes, remembering what it had been like: bright sunlight on the water, a mild wind fluttering the awning of yellow cotton. She (Esperance) sat on a stool of dark wood, inlaid with ivory. She wore a robe of cotton, so thin that it was barely decent. How cool it had been! How soft against her skin! Her questioners sat around her: old men and women in robes colored red and blue, orange and yellow and white. Some wore turbans. Others had staffs made of iron and inlaid with gold. They spoke through an interpreter, asking question after question after question.

She opened her eyes. "I told them the same story that I told you. It didn't satisfy them. There was a lot I didn't know. So they went to the island to look through the ruins of the Fortress and to talk to the rats. They were the real experts. The rats, I mean. They'd lived for generations in the Fortress. They'd watched and listened. They'd had to, in order to survive."

"The rats were okay?" asked Jennifer. "You were able to help them."

Esperance nodded. "That was the main thing that I did, while I was with Lucien. I negotiated a treaty between the rats and Bashoo. The rats agreed to tell the wizards everything they knew about the Fortress; and the wizards agreed to cast a spell that would make the island fertile and habitable. Full of things the rats could eat." Esperance grinned, then chanted:

"Birds' eggs in nests!
Oh yummy!
And dead fish on the beach!

"Large and delicious insects!
And crabs with shells
that crunch!"

She frowned. "That isn't quite right. The rats have a better sense of rhythm."

"It will do," said Ayra.

Jen nodded. "It's disgusting enough."

Esperance felt surprise. "You think the rats are disgusting? I don't." Then she remembered the gift they had brought her, after the treaty had been arranged. Fatty the rat. Dead. A lump of bloody meat. The legs had been chewed off, all six of them. The fur was mostly gone. But a couple of patches still clung to the body. The fur was lavender. A distinctive color. That was how she knew that the mess had been Fatty.

For a moment, remembering, she felt a little queasy. Was she going to have to go back to the bathroom? No. The feeling passed. She was okay.

"You may be right," she said. "They killed Fatty for me. They thought I'd be pleased. It was a clear case of a scapegoat. Fatty was nasty and greedy. He was the bad one, he was the one who didn't like humans. They were innocent, they were nice. Good rats! Kind rats! Rats who love humans!"

"Do you trust these creatures?" asked Ayra.

"No. But I don't have to. The wizards made a guarding spell. It will protect the island from intruders, and protect the rest of the world from the island. The rats can't leave."

"Oh good," said Jennifer.

"Then I came home," said Esperance. "My stomach would not settle down; and I was restless and worried. I wanted to find out what had happened to you. So after a week—no, more like two —they sent me back to Minneapolis.

"They have their own kind of magic; and they can go from one world to another without a lot of computation. They use music. And they burn a wood that gives off a thick yellow smoke."

Esperance closed her eyes, trying to remember the scene. "They beat on drums; and the magicians sing. The smoke begins to spin—around and around, faster and faster. The traveler stands in the middle—of the smoke, I mean. It spins around him or her." She opened her eyes. "I was the traveler.

"The smoke kept getting thicker. I couldn't see anything. I felt a wind; and then I heard a roar. It was low and dull. It reminded me of the sound of a freight train. I knew what that meant."

"You did?" said Ayra.

"Yes," said Esperance.

Jennifer leaned forward. "A tornado makes a sound like a freight train." She looked at Esperance and grinned. "You came back to Earth in a tornado?"

"More or less, though it wasn't especially dramatic. I felt the wind. I heard the roar. Lucien spoke in my mind. He said, *Goodbye*.

"I tried to answer him, but I didn't have the time. The roar stopped—it only lasted a moment. The smoke vanished. And I was here on Earth, in the basement of our house, standing next to the washing machine—which needs a washing, I have to say. It is covered with dust. Your father is a slob."

"He's been out a lot," said Jennifer. "He says it's hard to be in the house when he's alone."

"Alone," said Esperance. "I went upstairs. I was naked, per usual. I looked for clothes. Everything of mine was gone, except for that pair of Sorrels." She pointed at the boots. They stood in a corner of the kitchen: big and heavy and far too warm for April. "I took what I could find. These jeans and one of Walter's shirts. And then I called you." She looked at her daughter. "You told me to come here. What is going on? Whose jeans am I wearing?"

Jennifer looked at the kitchen table.

"Well?" said Esperance.

"She has finished her story," said Ayra. "Now you must tell her what you know."

"Oh," said Jennifer. "Okay." She glanced at Esperance, then back at the table. "Daddy got angry the last time you were here. When you came and went in one day. Remember?"

"Now, that is a stupid question. Of course I remember. Monsters chased me all over the darn city and into St. Paul as well. Does anyone forget a day like that?"

"You don't have to get angry, Mother."

Esperance rubbed her face. "I'm sorry. I'm tired."

"Anyway, he asked me what was going on. I said I didn't know. Then he got angry with me and said it was always a mistake for children to take sides. I said I wasn't. He didn't believe me, though he never called me a liar. You know how Daddy feels about dishonesty. He'd never call anyone a liar, unless he had absolute proof."

Esperance nodded.

"He said he needed to get a perspective on the situation. He asked me not to call him for a while. He'd call me, when he felt he had some kind of a handle on what was going on. He didn't call for over two months."

"That sounds like Walter, I used to think, when he did things like that, it meant he was firm and had discipline and so on. But it doesn't. It means that he is a mean-minded S.O.B."

"Mother! Don't talk like that!"

"Sorry again." What was wrong with her? She didn't usually lose her temper.

"Anyway, in February he took me to dinner. It was my birthday. He apologized. He said he knew I wouldn't take sides. But it had been so painful for him—to have you vanish and then reappear a year later and then vanish again. Twenty years of his life, turned into a mystery. He didn't know what was going on. He didn't know who was to blame." Jen lifted her head. Her eyes were full of tears. "He said he had to make a clean break. So he packed up all your clothes; and he was going to give them to the Free Store, unless there was something I wanted."

What a birthday dinner, thought Esperance.

Jennifer sniffed. "I asked for your shirt from L.L. Bean and the sweater you got in Norway, when you and Daddy went to find your roots."

Ah yes. She remembered that trip. Hiking in the mountains. A boat trip up the coast. And awkward conversations with Norwegian cousins. They both had dozens of them. Except her cousins weren't real cousins. Her relatives, if she had any, lived in the world of magic. She looked back at Jen, who was still crying a little. "You made good choices. Especially the sweater. Though I've never liked the buttons. I always meant to put new ones on."

Jen nodded. "I did. They're wood. Very plain. Pale yellow with just a little grain."

My daughter the artist, thought Esperance.

"In March," said Jennifer, "he told me about LaVonne."

"Who?"

"LaVonne Peterson. She's a graduate student. She's very bright, Daddy says. Those are her pants that you have on."

"Walter is going out with a graduate student? In English?"

Jennifer nodded.

"Now, that is really shocking! I never expected anything like that from Walter."

"What is wrong?" asked Ayra. "Is he doing something that is forbidden here on Earth? Is it something I should know about?"

"Professors aren't supposed to get too friendly with students," said Esperance.

Jennifer shook her head. "She isn't his student. Her field is the Renaissance. She's doing her dissertation on the Fifth Book of the *Faerie Queene*—the one that no one likes. She is trying a feminist approach. Daddy says it won't work, not really. But he thinks the committee will pass it. It's very clever."

"Ah," said Esperance.

"I've met her," said Jennifer. "She's okay. I try not to be critical. I figure, you and Daddy have the right to live your own lives."

"That's very mature of you." Esperance turned and looked at the drain board of the sink. There were three wineglasses there, upside down on the old worn white porcelain. She picked one up. It looked cheap. She threw it against the far wall, aiming carefully so that it didn't hit the poster by Ansel Adams. A photograph of mountains. The glass hit the bare wall and shattered.

Jennifer cried, "Mother!"

"Goddammit," Esperance said. "I've been in prison. A dragon was after me. I was eaten by a squid. I got through all of it. I saved a world! And then I come home and find my goddamn husband is chasing women." She picked up another wineglaess. "Ulysses waited for Penelope for *twenty goddamn years!*"

"What?" said Jennifer.

Esperance thought for a moment. "I have that wrong, don't I? Penelope waited for Ulysses." She looked at the wineglass. "I don't suppose I should be throwing things."

"No," said Ayra. "You shouldn't. This is your daughter's home. You have no right to damage anything here."

Esperance set the glass down carefully. Her eyes filled with tears. Her gut twisted. "Excuse me," she said. "I have to go to the bathroom."

It was another false alarm. By the time she reached the bathroom, her gut had settled down. She didn't need to use the toilet. She dried her eyes with one of the towels. Then she pulled up the shade on the window. She looked out at the bright blue, cloudless sky. She didn't think about anything in particular. After a while, maybe five minutes, she went back to the kitchen.

Jennifer said, "We've been trying to figure out what to do with you. You can't go home. Daddy would cause a terrible scene; and you'd have to explain what has been going on. He wouldn't believe you, Mother. He doesn't have a lot of imagination."

Esperance nodded. "I know that."

"And you can't stay here. Michelle will be home from the U. in an hour. She knows that you vanished a year and a half ago. She'll ask a lot of questions; and I don't want to answer them. I mean, what can I say? The truth is crazy; and I don't like to lie."

"You will come with me," said Ayra. "I have an apartment near Loring Park. I don't think my neighbors would ask questions about you, even if you arrived in the shape of a bear." She grinned. "Most of them are young and single. They spend most of their time chasing one another. They don't notice much, unless it has to do with sex." She stood. "We'll go now. I have whiskey at my place. That will settle your stomach."

"Okay," said Esperance. She put on her boots and Walter's extra parka. Then she hugged her daughter. "I'll give you a call tomorrow."

Jennifer nodded. "Take care of yourself, Mother. Just stay in one place and rest. You don't need another adventure."

"I know that."

Ayra got her jacket. They left the house and walked to Fremont. The Number Five bus ran there. The sky was cloudless in every direction. A cold wind blew. Sunlight slanted past the bare trees and the big square houses. This was the poor part of town. A lot of the houses were in need of work. And there was something about early spring—the bareness and brightness, the clarity of the light—that made every problem evident. Peeling paint, a sagging gutter, a torn screen, bare patches in the lawn: Esperance could see it all.

They reached the bus stop and waited. The house across the street had sheets of plastic covering the windows on the porch. A form of insulation. It was cheap, but it looked awful. Oh well. She hunched her shoulders against the wind. It might be worse here on the north side of town, but Minneapolis never looked good this time of year. Even in her neighborhood, along the parkway and around Lake Nokomis, there would be trash in the alleys and fallen branches in the yards. Most of the gardens were still hidden by heaps of rotting leaves.

The bus came. They got on. Esperance sat down next to the window. Her stomach was giving her no more trouble. She was fine, except for a slight depression.

They rode in silence. The bus rolled past more houses then into the industrial area that was just north of downtown. Everything looked bleak to her. It was the light and the lack of foliage. In another week or so, everything would be different. Leaves on the trees. Flowers in the gardens. Crocuses and the little early irises. Lovely spring colors. White, yellow, lavender, purple.

Though not here, among the warehouses, of course. This area would remain bleak until the weeds began to bloom.

They got off the bus at Hennepin Avenue.

"I usually walk from here," said Ayra. "But you have been through a lot. We'll take the Six or Four."

Esperance looked at her. "You're doing better than I expected."

"Because I have learned to use the public transit system? Remember, I am a sailor. I am used to foreign places. And anyway, we have a public transit system in Ymmouth."

"Oh," said Esperance.

Ayra went on. "Not in the city, but in the harbor and along the river. Boats. They go from island to island, according to a schedule, which is printed and posted all along the waterfront. No different from here. Though I find the schedules that you post here very hard to read. The print is so tiny! And there is so much of it!"

"Oh," said Esperance.

The Number Six came. They took it and got off at Loring Park.

"I am on the far side," said Ayra.

They walked through the park. In back of them, the sun was setting. In front of them was downtown Minneapolis. (The bus had taken them around the edge of the downtown. Now they were to the south of it, and also to the west.) There wasn't much to it: about a dozen tall buildings. No, more like half a dozen. The tallest was the IDS: a tower of glass. It reflected the sky and concentrated the color somehow, so that it was a deeper shade of blue.

Why hadn't the dragon seen the tower? Could it really have been as blind as a bird? Or as ignorant?

Yes, apparently.

"How did they explain the dragon?" she asked.

"Your dragon? The one that hit the IDS?"

"How many dragons have there been around here lately?"

Ayra glanced at her. "Only one, to my knowledge. And you are very edgy."

"Un-huh." They crossed the bridge that went over the narrow part of Loring Pond. Then they left the path and walked along the shore. Two ducks paddled in the shallows. They were mallards; and both were male. What coloring they had! Green, purple, gray, white, and blue. It was too bad they were so common. One took them for granted.

"They said it was a stone from out of the sky. What is the word?"

"A meteorite."

"Yes. Or else it was something out of a plane. It was too small to be found, but traveling at such a high velocity that it was able to break windows."

"What about me?" asked Esperance. "Three or four people saw me."

"They must have kept quiet about it. I saw nothing in the paper. You know, that is a terrible innovation. The paper. Why must you begin the day by taking in so much information? And almost all of it is trivial or depressing. No wonder you drink coffee. You need something to raise your spirits, after you have found out the news."

"You don't have papers?"

They were back on the path again, going toward the southeast corner of the park.

"No," said Ayra. "We do not like to hide behind pieces of paper. When we have something to say, we say it face-to-face."

"Ah."

"And we believe that the best way to tell if a story is true is to see and hear the person who is telling it. The tone of the voice is important. So is the way the eyes move. And whether or not the person likes to fidget."

"Ah," said Esperance.

"We have handbills, of course. And posters. Most of them have to do with business. One merchant is having a sale. Another merchant is offering a new kind of service—We want to turn left here."

They had reached the end of the park. They turned east onto Fifteenth Street. It was lined with apartment buildings. Most were made of red or yellow brick.

Ayra stopped talking. She walked more quickly than before, taking long strides. Her hands were in the pockets of her jeans. She glanced around at the buildings. Her expression was alert and thoughtful.

Esperance glanced at Ayra and wondered what she was thinking. But she didn't glance often. It was work, trying to keep up with the tall woman.

"Here." Ayra took a hand from a pocket and waved. "We turn again."

They went onto Spruce Place. It was a narrow street that went up a hill. It was lined with more apartment buildings. They were like the buildings on Fifteenth Street. Red brick. Not very tall. Old for Minneapolis.

Ayra led the way into one of them. They went through a security door and up a flight of stairs. "Here." She unlocked the door to her apartment. Esperance went in.

It was a studio with windows on the street. A single big room, containing a Murphy bed, which was down at the moment. There was an armchair, that was clearly secondhand, covered by a piece of fabric. Indian cotton. A paisley pattern. It was orange and yellow.

The bed was covered with another piece of Indian cotton. This one had a red and blue pattern. There was a wooden crate next to the bed and a lamp on the crate. The lamp was new. One of the clamp-on kind. Blue enamel. A high-tech look. Esperance saw no books. There were posters on the walls. One was a photograph of Albert Einstein. His head only, the hair flaring out. Another was a painting by Georgia O'Keefe. The skull of a deer, floating in the sky above a mesa. Curious, though Esperance. She looked at the third poster, which was from an art museum. It was a still life. Dutch, from the seventeenth century. Seafood, heaped on a table. There was a fish and a crab. A lobster. Oysters. Some of them were open. A lemon that had been half peeled. And a goblet made of glass, full of water or very pale wine.

"I try to understand this world," said Ayra. She closed the door. "That man—she pointed at Einstein—"has the look of a wizard. It is something in the eyes. And the woman who painted that"—she pointed to the skull—"sees the things that witches see. And the seafood is to remind me that—someday! someday! —I will return to the Golden Oyster in Ymmouth by the docks. And I'll eat shellfish until I'm ready to burst.

"I'll get the whiskey." Ayra locked the door. Then she went through another doorway, this one without a door. Esperance could see a narrow hallway. It must lead to the kitchen and the bathroom.

In a minute or two, Ayra was back, carrying a pint of Jim Beam and two glasses. "Here." She gave Esperance a glass, then opened the bottle and poured.

When the glass was half full, Esperance said, "Stop!"

"Are you really going to drink all that?" asked Ayra.

"I might."

"You are more like a sailor than I thought." Ayra filled her own glass halfway, and sat down on the bed. It creaked.

Esperance sipped the whiskey. Good stuff! It burned her

mouth, then warmed her throat and belly. Ah! She took another
sip. "What about you?" she asked Ayra. "What have you been
doing?"

"You left, as you remember. You and Father Dia and the monsters gone." She snapped her fingers. "Like that!" Ayra glanced
up and grinned. "I was stuck on Earth, which didn't bother me at
first. I thought I'd be able to find your other brother—Arden
Everett, the one who is a miner in West Virginia. I thought I
could get him to take me home. But then Jennifer took me to the
public library. That is another thing we don't have in Ymmouth.
Maybe we ought to. Though I cannot imagine why anyone would
need so many books."

Esperance nodded. " 'Of making many books there is no end;
and much study is a weariness of the flesh.' Ecclesiastes, Chapter
12, verse 12. It is Walter's favorite quote from the Bible."

Ayra looked puzzled.

"Never mind," said Esperance. "Go on."

"Jennifer showed me maps of West Virginia and books that
were full of the names of people who lived in the state. There was
a book for every city. Most of them were thick, and all of them
were full of names. There was so much writing! And the print
was so tiny! I could tell that it was going to take me a long time to
find your brother. And what was I going to do for money? I had
to eat, I had to have a place to sleep, Jennifer couldn't help—not
for long, anyway. She had no spare money and her roommates
didn't like having me around. Jen said I was a cousin, but I'm not
entirely certain that they believed her. They knew there was
something strange about me. I had trouble with the stove and with
the levers that turned on the lights. I had to get an apartment of
my own, and that meant that I had to get a job."

Esperance drank whiskey. "How? You're a foreigner. An illegal alien."

"I know. Jennifer explained that to me. She said I would have
to lie. That was easy to do. I look like the people on Earth; and I
speak the same language. I don't even have an accent. Jennifer
says I sound as if I come from the east coast of this continent.
From New York or Boston. We made up a job history for me."

Esperance frowned. "But you have to have a social security
card."

Ayra nodded. "I know. Jen said no one ever asks to see the

actual card. She made up a number for me. She said it would be a long time before anyone at Social Security realized that the number was wrong; and then all they'd do is send my job a letter of inquiry. With luck, she said, I'd be gone by then." Ayra took a gulp of whiskey.

"I thought, the one thing I know—really know—is how to move merchandise around. So I got a job in a warehouse. It's downtown. In the old garment district. I've gotten one raise so far; and they have promised me another one." She grinned. "I'm a good worker. And freight is freight, no matter where you find it."

Two raises in four months. Or was it five? In any case, it was impressive. But Ayra had always struck her as extremely competent. Her slight depression had gone away; and she was feeling pleasantly fuzzy. Too fuzzy to stand any longer. The armchair looked comfortable. Esperance sat down.

Ayra went on. "I'm making enough to pay for this apartment and to eat. I have a card for the library. I go there and listen to records. And I take out books on art. I can't afford a TV or a record player. But I have been thinking of buying a radio. Some of them cost very little."

Esperance frowned, thinking over the story. "Why do you speak English?"

"I don't. I speak Ymarrin, which is the language of Ymarra, the land along the river Ym."

"It's the same as English."

Ayra nodded. "Yes. Though I do not think people speak as well here as they do in Ymarra. There is something slippery about your language. People use words without knowing what they mean. What exactly is *high tech?* And what is the *window of opportunity?*"

"Don't ask me," said Esperance. She frowned again. "I don't understand how it is possible—two languages that are almost identical on two different worlds."

Ayra shrugged. "The worlds are full of correspondences and coincidences. No one knows why. There is a city on Imm Toon that is identical to Ymmouth. All the buildings are the same, save for one—the town hall. In Ymmouth, it is square and built of stone. In the city on Imm Toon, it is octagonal and built of a kind of wood we don't have on our world.

"Now, how can anyone explain that? Why should the cities be

identical? And if they are, why should they have a single difference?" Ayra drank more whiskey. "It makes no sense at all."

"That's true enough," said Esperance.

The sun had gone behind the building across the street. The apartment was getting dim. Ayra got up. She turned on the overhead light. Then she pulled down all the shades. "Do you want any food?"

"No."

"Am I going to be able to go home?"

Esperance looked at Ayra. The woman looked worried.

"Yes, of course. I think so, anyway. The wizards are keeping track of me. I don't know how exactly. But they know where I am. They said they would send someone to check up on me in a few days. If you want to go home, I'm sure—I'm almost certain —that whoever comes will take you back with him or her. What a sentence. I have always hated the subjunctive."

"And you?" asked Ayra. She went back to the bed and sat down. The pint was on the floor. She picked it up and refilled her glass.

"I don't know." Esperance sipped a bit more whiskey, then looked at Albert Einstein. He did look like a wizard. Or a witch. There had been one old woman from Bashoo—not from the city, but from one of the hill villages in the far west. She had been bone thin and as black as coal. Her hair had been long and frizzy, striped white and gray. It had stuck out like Albert's hair. Her face—like his—had been lined and wise. But she hadn't the mustache.

"I'm just starting to think about it now. I think my marriage is over. That seems pretty clear to me. I haven't worked since Walter got his first real job. You know, I think I'd like to have some more Jim Beam."

"Be careful," said Ayra. "Remember that you have a queasy stomach."

Esperance went and got the pint and refilled her glass. She handed the bottle to Ayra. "I have no idea what I'm going to do." She went back to the armchair and sat down. "Hassle with Walter about alimony. It doesn't sound like fun."

"What is alimony?" asked Ayra.

Esperance tried to think of a good definition. She couldn't. "Money," she said at last. "Severance pay."

"Now, that I have heard about. Someone on my job got fired. She got a week's pay—on Friday afternoon, when all of us were leaving. They gave her the check and told her not to come back."

"It's sort of like that," said Esperance. "But not entirely." She thought about trying to explain the difference. But that would mean that she'd have to explain how marriage worked on Earth; and that would take a long time; and she was getting blurry. "I think Walter owes me money. Let's leave it at that."

"Okay," said Ayra.

Esperance frowned. "But he might not agree. Especially if he decides that he wants to marry LaVonne. He won't be able to support me at the same time that he's putting her through to a graduate degree. Maybe she can support herself." Esperance drank more whiskey. "But it doesn't seem likely. Not if she's in English. Why couldn't he shack up with an engineer? Or someone with an M.B.A.?"

Ayra said, "I don't understand any of this. Maybe we *don't* speak the same language."

"I'm thinking out loud. The point is, I'm forty-one; and I have no skills. Nothing that will help me earn a living. And I'm on my own. I can't ask Jen for help. And Mark is a sweetheart, but he's never been a help to anyone. Except maybe the whales and dolphins. He's very big on ecology."

"Come with me," said Ayra. "To Ymmouth or Ymhold. You will be welcome there."

"No."

"Why not?"

Esperance blinked. She was having trouble focusing. She set the glass down on the floor and leaned back in the armchair. "My life is here," she said after a moment. "Mark and Jennifer. All my friends. Everyone I know, except maybe you. And I don't know you well. I can't go."

There was tension in her voice. She could hear it. She felt tension in her throat. She did not want to continue this conversation.

Ayra said, "We can talk about this tomorrow. There is no hurry. I think you should go to bed, Esperance. You are tired— and drunk, as well."

All at once, Ayra was leaning over her, tugging at her arm. She stood up and walked to the bed. Ayra stayed beside her, guiding her. The room was moving. It was like being on the *Ocean Leopard*. But strangely enough, her stomach was okay. She tumbled down onto the Murphy bed.

"Good night," said Ayra.

Esperance said, "Runh."

She woke in the middle of the night. The room was dark. She lay on her back on the Murphy bed. Ayra was next to her, snoring softly. The sound was like a purr. As for Esperance, her mouth was dry. Her head hurt. Goddam! She was forty-one. Almost forty-two. Why did she behave this way? Getting drunk, simply because she had found out that her husband was fooling around with someone named LaVonne. Did that show maturity?

No. Not really. She needed a glass of water. She got up cautiously. The bed creaked. Ayra groaned and rolled over. Now, where was the kitchen? She stood for a moment, thinking.

A drum began to beat.

What? She felt her head. No. It wasn't making the noise. At least, it didn't seem to be.

The drum kept on beating. It was in the street. She crept to the window and lifted the shade. A fire burned in the middle of Spruce Place. People danced around it. Men in kilts. They wore masks.

The men were in a circle. Another, much larger ring of dancers went around them. Women in white robes. They wore no masks, but there was white paint on their faces. The faces were dark. The women carried rattles.

Esperance listened. She could hear the rattles. They made a soft noise; *shuuuh, shuuuh*. It was like the wind in the branches of a pine tree or like the ocean in the distance.

The drumbeat kept on; and she heard another sound. It was high and clear. A flute.

The Anasazi, thought Esperance. What were they doing here? She looked beyond the fire and saw buildings. They were not the ones she had seen before. These were smaller. They were covered with plaster or adobe. The windows and doors were placed irregularly. No light shone out anywhere.

Above the buildings hung the moon: half-full, deep orange. She did not recognize the markings on it.

A voice in her mind said, *Go down*.

Why? she asked.

This is a resolution of your problem.

Indians dancing in Loring Park?

You are in Loring Park; the Indians are not. Go down and join them. Nothing bad will nappen.

She was still dressed in the miserable too-tight jeans that she had found in the house in south Minneapolis. She buttoned up her shirt and found her boots. Then she opened the door. Light shone in from the hallway. Ayra grunted. Esperance went out. She went down the hall, then down the stairway, out the front door and into the street.

The night was mild. The air smelled of wood-smoke and something else. Garbage, she decided. She turned and looked in back of her. The apartment building was gone. Esperance saw a fence, made of irregular pieces of wood. There was something in front of the fence, in the place where the door into the apartment building should have been. She moved toward the thing. It was a rack or arbor, made of wood. The wood was rough and splintery. She peered into the arbor. Something hung there, in the shadows. What was it? She moved to the side, so the firelight could shine past her and illuminate whatever it was. A cluster, about three feet long. It hung level with her face. Each object in the cluster was about four inches long and narrow. She could not make out a color. Brown, maybe. Or maybe red.

She reached out a hand, then hesitated. She was afraid.

The voice in her mind said, *They are hot peppers. The people here dry them in the sun. They are perfectly harmless. Unless, of course, you eat them.*

Now, turn. Go to the plaza. Everyone is there.

Esperance turned. Spruce Place was gone. She stood in the middle of a narrow dirt street. At the end of the street, a fire burned. That must be the plaza. The fire was large and bright. It cast its light all the way to her. She could see the buildings along the street clearly. They were made of adobe, two or three stories tall.

She could hear the dancers. The stamp of their feet. The *shuuh* of their rattles. The flute had stopped playing. The drumbeat had gotten louder. There were more than one drum.

Maybe the ceremony isn't open to the public, she said.

The voice in her mind gave a chuckle. *Don't worry. They can't see you. You are a spirit.*

I am?

For the time being.

At this point, she began to suspect that she was having a dream. She pinched her arm. Nothing happened, except that now her arm hurt. She was still in the Indian village. Well, what did she expect? A real pinch might wake a dreamer. But a dream pinch wouldn't. She walked toward the dance. She could see the dancers. They were dark figures against the bright glare of the fire. They moved up and down, swayed back and forth, shook their rattles and stamped their feet.

Shuh-shuh. Tum-tum. The flute began to play again.

Halfway to the plaza, her street met another street. Something joined her there. She saw it out of the corner of one eye and turned to face it. An animal, coming out of the shadows. A deer. It had to be six feet tall at the shoulder. The neck was thick. The body was heavy and shaggy. The antlers on the animal must have been ten feet across, maybe more. They were almost as wide as the street the animal had come out of.

The antlers were not deerlike. They were broad and flat with many tines or points along the top. What did they remind her of? Not moose. Caribou? She didn't know.

The animal stopped. It gazed at her. The dark eyes were aware. It knew her. She was almost certain. It bent its neck slowly and carefully lowering the splendid head just a little. A bow. A greeting. An acknowledgment.

A moment later, it turned and moved toward the plaza.

She followed. *Is that you?* she asked.

The deer? asked the voice in her mind. It chuckled again. *No. It is another spirit. Many come here, from many places. The dance is a dance of gathering.*

Oh. She continued after the deer. When it reached the edge of the plaza, it stopped. She stopped next to it. Now she could see the old men who played the drums. They sat in the shadows. There were children seated around them. Other children stood on the flat roofs, looking down, watching the dancers. Firelight flickered on the dark faces. Eyes glinted.

As for the dancers, they continued to circle the fire, stamping in unison. Whoever played the flute kept on playing. Esperance looked around. She couldn't find him or her. But she saw something else. It stood nearby, right next to a blanket that had been spread on the ground. The blanket was covered with sleeping children.

The thing was upright. It had two arms and two legs. It wore clothes—a tunic and tight pants. The clothes were gray and shimmery. The head of the thing was reptilian, shaped like the head of a lizard and covered with tiny scales. The scales gleamed in the firelight. They were pale blue.

My God! What is that?

Another spirit, brought here by the dance. Like you and like me.

The thing must have caught a glimpse of her. (Its eyes were on the side of its head.) It turned slightly; and she got a good view of one eye. It was large and round and yellow. The pupil was triangular. The thing raised a hand in greeting. The fingers looked like tentacles. They twisted and waved. Esperance felt a little sick.

Nothing here can harm you, said the voice in her mind.

The thing—the reptilian—went back to watching the dance.

What is going on? asked Esperance. She too watched the dance. The inner ring. The men. Their kilts were covered with embroidery. They wore long sashes with fringe, that trailed on the ground. Their masks were brightly painted: red and yellow, black and white. Some of them carried long feathers. Others had branches covered with foliage. All of them stamped and whirled.

The voice in her mind spoke again. *This is the world of the dragons. These are the people who came from Earth—or maybe somewhere else. Now that I have studied them, I am not entirely sure that they are from Earth. I can understand their language. some of it, at least. It is similar to several of the Pueblo languages. But there is something here that is off. Something that is un-Earthly.*

In any case, they came here from somewhere, led by a powerful witch. They call her the White Shell Woman. Her husband was a hero, a slayer of monsters. The two of them brought the people here, and then when they got old, the White Shell Woman and her husband left. They didn't die. They left. And they told the people, if you ever need us, call us back. We will come.

I learned all of this earlier, when the women were singing.

Oh, said Esperance.

Everything went well for two or three centuries. The people prospered. They became careless. They forgot the ceremony the White Shell Woman had taught them, the one that would bring her back.

Then the dragons came. The people wanted to flee. But they

*didn't know how to leave this world. And they no longer knew
how to call the White Shell Woman.*

*They tried to reconstruct the ceremony or to create a new
ceremony to bring help. This is what they have come up with. It
almost works.*

The flute stopped. The women in the outer circle began to
sing. Esperance listened, not understanding a word. By this time,
she had noticed how many strange creatures moved around her.
One or two were clearly visible: the giant deer next to her, the
lizard-man next to the sleeping children.

Most were shadowy or dim. For example, there was something on the roof opposite. It was large and dark. It loomed behind the young girls who stood there, looking down. Esperance
could not make out what the thing was.

Figures moved at the edges of the plaza, in and out of the
shadows. Most seemed to be more or less human, though she
could not be certain.

Other things flew overhead. There was one now! She looked
up, but it was gone. She had an impression of whiteness and huge
wings. The wings had not moved. The thing had been gliding.

A bird? No, it had not seemed to be a bird. For one thing, it
was far too big.

The voice in her mind said, *The women are singing these
words:*

> *It is all coming together.*
> *The spirits are gathering.*
> *From their distant places,*
> *The spirits are gathering.*

*The song is correct. The spirits are gathering. Look off to your
right. Beyond the lizard-man. There is another observer. You can
see him fairly well in the firelight.*

Esperance looked. A man stood maybe twenty feet away. Or
was it thirty feet? She had always been a terrible judge of distance. He was outside the outer ring of dancers. He stood next to
a wall of brown adobe. Firelight lit the wall and him. The way he
was turned, she could see most of his front. He had a cloak of
brown skin over one shoulder. Otherwise, he was naked, except
for a loincloth. The loincloth was dull red. He was Indian and

old. His belly sagged. His chest was sunken. His hands—Esperance could see one—were twisted by arthritis. His hair was pure black. He stared intently at the dancers. The men. Their bodies were wet with sweat and shining in the firelight. The paint on their bodies was beginning to run.

That is Blood-of-the-Deer, said the voice in her mind. *The old man over there. He is the husband of White Shell Woman. The famous hero. The monster slayer.*

The ceremony has brought him. But the people cannot see him; and he—on his own—cannot break through the barrier that is between everyday life and the realm of the spirits.

This is what happens when you have power without understanding.

These people have made a ceremony that calls spirits from all over. But they don't really know what they are doing. They cannot see what they have done.

Therefore, they will fail, even though the help they sought is all around them. Most likely, Blood-of-the-Deer could lead them away from the dragons. His wife certainly could, and I have seen her here often. You could help them. So could I. For all I know, the big deer next to you knows the way out of this world into one that is safer for humans.

The deer lifted his head. He flicked an ear back, then forward. He snorted. He didn't sound impressed by what the voice was saying.

They will die, all these people. The dragons will eat them up. In fact, it has already happened—four hundred years ago. They are all gone. But the ceremony remains. Somehow, it has achieved a separate existence outside the flow of time. Or maybe it is an eddy in the flow of time. A whirlpool.

In any case, it pulls things to it. Spirits. You and me. The deer and the lizard-creature.

That is how you escaped.

What? asked Esperance.

The singing ended, but the dance continued. The feet stamped in unison. She could feel the vibrations, as they traveled through the dry hard ground. Thump. THUMP. Thump. THUMP.

From the loop, said the voice. *You didn't do it entirely on your own. You have power, but not that much. You found a weak place —the point where the loop went through the fifth dimension. Went outside ordinary space and time. You pushed there; and some-how—in a way I do not understand—you made contact with these people. The magic of the dance became intertwined with the magic of the loop. You pushed. The dancers pulled. For a while, you were like an electron shared by two atoms. You existed in the loop. You existed in the world where the dance was originally performed—which was, of course, the world of the dragons. I don't know why you didn't end up here, at the ceremony.*

Maybe as long as the loop held, the dancers could not bring you all the way here. Or maybe the dragon was tugging at you, too. Dragons have considerable magical power. Usually, they use it carefully. But that dragon was young and stupid.

So I was like an electron being shared by three atoms, said Esperance.

For a moment or two, there was silence in her mind. Then the voice spoke again.

That may not be a good analogy. I will abandon it. Forget about the electron!

Okay, said Esperance.

Maybe there is no good metaphor or simile, no good model for what happened to you. I have begun to work in a mathematical description, but I'm not sure I will get anywhere with it. I am not really a theoretician. I tend to see myself as primarily practical. I am a doer. A maker. A mover and shaker. The voice paused, then said. *What was I talking about?*

The giant deer snorted. Was that a comment? If so, what did it mean?

I remember, the voice said. *The loop broke. And there was a release of energy that carried you here, to the world of the dragons. But you did not stay here. The dance could not hold you. You had too much energy—either your own or that acquired from the loop, when it broke. You went all the way home; and the dragon followed you.*

Oh, said Esperance.

The voice went on. *It was at that point that I became aware of the dance. I should have noticed it before. I would have noticed it before, except for the continual distraction.*

What distraction? asked Esperance.

The wizards! The sorcerers! The witches and the oracles! They were not powerful, but there were so many of them! And they would not leave me alone! I kept hearing their voices. I kept feeling the magic they made. They were like a swarm of flies, buzzing and buzzing all around me. I could not concentrate on anything. I was not able to monitor the loop. Otherwise, I am certain, I would have noticed what you were doing. And I would have had to notice the dance.

Who are you? asked Esperance.

Turn around.

She turned.

Something floated in the street. It was about a foot off the ground and maybe five feet long, pointed at both ends, a foot or so wide. No, more like two feet wide. An enormous crystal. It was six-sided, transparent, and colorless. Firelight gleamed on its surface. Another light—dimmer and paler—gleamed inside.

What are you? asked Esperance.

A crystal, of course. Rhombic and bipyramidal.

The deer shook his head, then stamped a foot.

He doesn't care for my sense of humor, the crystal said. *I seem to have trouble with the forces of nature. Spirits like the deer and wizards like the wizards of Bashoo. They were the ones who kept distracting me.*

At first, I did nothing except watch them. I thought I was setting a trap. Let them come close, I told myself. Let them think there is nothing to fear. Then I will attack, when they get careless.

But they never did. Instead, they sent magic ahead to bother me. I couldn't concentrate. I couldn't stand it. When they were almost to Ab, I made my move.

I sent a storm. Thunder and lightning! High winds and driving rain! And monsters as well, who rose up out of the water. Creatures that you cannot imagine! My very best work! I managed to destroy one-half of the fleet of Bashoo.

Ah, said Esperance.

But I could not finish the job, said the crystal. The voice in her mind was sad. *I had struck too early; and I had used too much energy. I did not have the reserves I needed. I felt myself begin to lose control of the Pattern of Power. Reality was slipping away from me. I had to retreat.*

The wizards rallied; and they drove me off. Now the crystal sounded indignant. *They landed on the island; and they captured the sorceress. My servant! It had taken me years to corrupt her! They set free all of her captives. There were hundreds of them. Sailors and fishermen. She kept them in jars and made them sing for her. I thought their music was melancholy, but it helped her sleep.*

Ah, said Esperance again.

They found the room where she kept the boats that belonged to her prisoners. You never saw it. It was full of shelves, floor to ceiling, on every wall. And every shelf was full of boats. They were tiny. She had used magic to diminish them, until they were the size of toy boats or of models.

They took the boats to the ocean; and they made Soringalla explain her magic. They made her tell the how to restore the boats to their proper size. And then the Kingdom of Bashoo had a second fleet. Provided by one of my servants!

Too bad, said Esperance.

It was very bad, said the crystal. *They still had most of their wizards; and now they had—as well—almost all of Soringalla's prisoners. The best of sailors! Full of skill and knowledge! And eager for revenge. I was in trouble.*

The fleet came on. I sent more bad weather and more monsters. The wizards sang day and night, creating a vast spell of protection. Now and then, something got through their spell—a gust of wind or a bolt of lightning or a great hairy serpent of the ocean. But the sailors were able to handle everything.

I could not break the spell. I didn't have the power. Too much of me was tied up in the loop. It took enormous energy to create it and keep it in existence.

And I was stuck with it. If anything happened to the loop, then I would have you—free, right in the middle of me.

I fought as best I could. The fleet kept coming—on and on. I did not have the time to watch the loop.

It broke. The Fortress blew up.

I thought, said Esperance, *that you had blown up too.*

My old body is gone. But I had this one ready. I had been planning to move for a good long time. But I was afraid. What if something went wrong? I might die. Or lose part of me. Maybe the best part of me.

I really ought to thank you, Esperance. I might have stayed where I was for centuries, trapped by cowardice in that horrible body. I was a mess! I was a kludge! Now look at me.

The crystal gleamed. Lights flashed inside it. Esperance felt an intense satisfaction. The emotion filled her entire being. It came from the G.C.

Just before the loop broke, I realized what was going on. There was no time to stop you. I had to flee. My old body could not move. It was doomed. So I fled into the new body I had made. At the same moment, the loop broke; and I was carried with you out of the world of magic.

That's impossible, said Esperance. *Nothing inanimate can go between the worlds.*

I know. And that means I am no longer a mere artifact. I am alive! Though I do not think I live in the same way as plants and animals. I think I have become a spirit. I am going to need a new name. The Spirit of the Machine Age, maybe. Or the Soul of the Machine. The Crystal Kachina! That has a certain resonance.

Um, said Esperance.

Do you think it is too esoteric? Maybe I should call myself the Crystal Spirit. There was a pause. The G.C. went on. *Yes. I like the Crystal Spirit.*

Esperance made no comment.

Now, where was I? Ah yes! You carried me to the world of the dragons; and I was caught by the magic here. I cannot escape, oh daughter of the bear. I float through the dark streets of the village. I see the other spirits. I hear the people of the village tell their story. I think this has happened more than once. There are parts of the ceremony that seem familiar. And it seems to me that I understand their language awfully well. But I do not know for certain if I have heard the ceremony more than once. I do not remember.

Esperance laughed. *It serves you right. It's what you did to me.*

Behind her, the women began to sing again.

It's the same as before, the G.C. said.

> It is all coming together.
> The spirits are gathering.
> From their distant places,
> The spirits are gathering.

The deer stamped a foot. What did that mean?

You are caught, too, said the G.C.

No, said Esperance. *This is a dream. I'm wearing my clothes —or rather, the clothes I found in my old home. If this were real, I'd be naked.*

No. Reality is more complex than you can imagine, oh daughter of the bear. And there is more than one way to travel. When you came here, you came as a spirit. You exist, at the moment, in a strange state between the physical and the nonphysical. The old rules, the ones you learned before, do not apply here and now.

Oh shit, said Esperance.

The deer stamped his foot again.

For a moment or two, they stood there together, Esperance and the deer and the crystal (though the crystal, of course, was not exactly standing). No one said anything. Esperance looked down the street, toward the pepper rack and the fence of wood. Both were gone. Instead, an enormous tree rose at the edge of the village. It was bigger than a redwood, or seemed to be to her. The bark was smooth and gray. She looked up. She couldn't see the foliage. It was too far up. But there was a dark place in the sky, a place without stars. That must be the crown of the tree. It was large, large. The darkness loomed.

What is that?

A tree. An ash, I think. Though it is unusually big.

That's for sure, said Esperance.

Something came around the base of the tree, out of the night and into firelight. A woman. She walked down the street, moving quickly and so gracefully that she seemed to float or glide. She wore a dress of white silk, made in the style of the late sixteenth century. A wide skirt. A narrow waist. A square-cut bodice and a collar that stood up, framing her neck and face. Her skin was pale. Not unhealthy, but almost pure white. There were pearls and crystal beads sewn on her gown. They flashed and glimmered. She wore a necklace of pearls. Earrings—two huge pearls—dangled from her ears.

Her hair was dark, as were her eyes. She wore a crown of diamonds.

She smiled at Esperance graciously. Esperance felt a desire to curtsy, but didn't know how. The woman moved past her to the edge of the plaza. The deer turned his head and looked at the woman. Then he bowed slowly and carefully, lowering that amazing rack of antlers. The woman smiled in reply. The two of them moved off together, through the shadows, in and out among the people and the spirits who watched the dance.

Who was that? asked Esperance.

Titania. Diana. Some tedious fairy queen or else a goddess out of pageant. I don't keep track. There are so many here. And most are distinctly minor. Not to mention, dull.

You sound crabby.

I am. I have been stuck here too long. And now you are stuck here, too.

No! She closed her eyes and tried to wish herself home like Dorothy. Even Kansas would be better than an eternity spent with the Great Calculator.

It didn't work, did it?

She opened her eyes. She was still in the village. The crystal floated in front of her.

Fear is the trigger, said the crystal. *The threat of danger.* The lights inside it grew brighter. It glided toward her. She felt something in her mind. A twisting. A pain. *This is it!* the G.C. cried.

Her gut began to twist. She shouted with fury. She fell and hit something both soft and lumpy. A mattress.

"What is going on?" a woman cried.

She knew the voice: Ayra. Esperance sat up, opening her eyes. Yes. She was back in the apartment. Light came in through the drawn shades. It wasn't the light of morning. There must be a streetlight right outside. She could see the bed and Ayra, sitting up next to her; and she could see the thing that floated in the middle of the room.

"What is that?" asked Ayra.

"The Great Calculator." She rubbed her face and then the back of her neck. "I thought I was having a dream. But I guess that it was real."

It was both, said the crystal. *It's really remarkable. You have so much power! And no idea at all of how to use it, or of what is going on when—somehow—you manage to put some of it to use. You could be dangerous, oh daughter of the bear.*

"Me? What about you?"

I can be dangerous, too. At the moment, we are both like the dancers. We lack vision. We lack understanding. We don't know what we are doing. We are likely to make a mess.

"You lured me there, to the ceremony," said Esperance. "I don't know how you did it. But you did it. You wanted me to pull you free."

Yes, of course. It was a long shot, but I had to try it. I was trapped. I thought you might be able to rescue me. And it worked!

Out of the corner of her eye, Esperance saw Ayra. The woman had tilted her head, and she was frowning. It wasn't clear from her expression whether or not she could hear the G.C.

We are connected, Esperance. We may be symbiotic. You were created, because I existed. You were supposed to destroy me, but instead you have helped me to transform myself. And I have helped you.

"You did what?"

Helped you. Think of how much you have learned! Think of what you have become! All because of me.

"What I have become," said Esperance, "is a forty-one-year-old woman without a husband and with no way to make a living. Do you know what is going to happen to me? I'm going to have to work in an office. If I'm lucky. Oh God, I just realized—it could be worse. I might end up in a grocery store or even at Target." She pronounced *Target* in the French way, as was often done in Minneapolis.

The crystal said, *You have a very negative outlook.*

"I'm being realistic."

You are being narrow. You are refusing to consider all the possibilities. For example, what makes you think that you will remain on Earth?

Esperance had a premonition. She grabbed on to Ayra's hand.

"What?" asked Ayra.

Esperance fell. She held on to Ayra tightly, tightly. She hit the ground and went down on her knees. She had to let go.

She was in a grove of trees. Tall pines. The ground was covered with red-brown needles. She was naked. This time it was real. She had actually gone from one world to another. In the flesh, not in spirit. Taken all in all, she preferred this way of traveling. It was less confusing.

She looked around. Ayra lay sprawled on her back, maybe five feet away. She was naked, too.

"Are you all right?"

Ayra sat up. "Give me a minute." She moved her head from

side to side, then she felt the back of her neck. "I think so. But the next time I have to go anywhere, I am going to take a boat. Or a camel. Or a donkey. Or maybe I will walk."

Esperance stood up. There were needles stuck in her knees. They hurt. She pulled them out. A gust of wind blew past her. It was damp and cold. It had a spring aroma. The wet earth. New vegetation.

Well? she thought. Where had she ended up this time? And was this going to continue forever? The sudden changes? The transformations? The attacks out of nowhere? And the moves from one world to another? She needed a rest. She wanted a little peace and quiet. She bent and touched her toes.

Above her, something made a noise. Esperance looked up. A squirrel. It clung to a branch upside down. Chitter! Chitter! The squirrel was red-brown. There were tufts on its ears. The tufts were black, and so was the tip of its long bushy tail.

"Hello," said Esperance, grinning.

Ayra stood. She brushed herself off. Then she put her hands at the base of her spine and stretched, going as far back as she was able. Her long body was bent like a bow. Esperance noticed something she had not noticed before, or had forgotten. The scar on the woman's belly—a long fine line.

Ayra straightened up. She did a couple of side bends. Then she leaned forward and put the palms of her hands on the ground.

Esperance, who was not especially flexible, watched with envy. The squirrel kept right on scolding.

Ayra straightened again. "Well, nothing is broken, as far as I can tell. Or badly pulled or even badly bruised." She glanced at the squirrel. "That is the kind of squirrel we have in the mountains of Ymarra."

You are in the mountains of Ymarra.

Esperance turned. There was the crystal, floating maybe ten feet away. It was in a patch of sunlight, and it glittered wonderfully.

This is the hill where you were born, oh daughter of the bear. In this clearing, your mother fell—and died in terrible pain, as you tore your way out of her womb.

Esperance looked at her hands. The nails were beginning to get long again. They were starting to curve, to look like claws. A shudder went through her body. "Don't say that."

Why not? It is true. I have a sense that you do not want to face what you are. Mother-killer. Destroyer of the Fortress. Slayer of monsters. And creator of me.

"I didn't want to do any of those things."

What did you want to do?

Esperance felt surprise. "I don't know. Go home, I guess. Get out alive."

That was a good plan, in the short term. It worked. You are alive. And now—here—you are finally home.

"Oh yeah?" Esperance looked around at the pine trees. There was a gust of wind. The green branches moved. They made a sound like the rattles in the Anasazi dance. *Sha. Sha.* Esperance shivered. "I'm going to freeze, if don't get to shelter or find something to wear."

There is a cabin close to here. The queen's hunters use it, when they are in this part of the forest. There ought to be clothes there.

"Let's go," said Esperance.

The crystal floated out of the clearing. Esperance and Ayra followed.

They went down a slope. It was gentle and covered with pines. They were all tall; and there was no undergrowth. A climax forest. She had always preferred the edges of forests and the wood and prairie land of southern Minnesota. She liked the variety and the flowers. But this had a certain gloomy grandeur, like a cathedral or a museum.

They kept going down. After a while, Ayra said, "The crystal is right. You have to face what you have become, oh daughter of the bear."

"Why?"

"The power you have will not go away. You have to learn how to use it, or maybe how not to use it."

Esperance said nothing.

"Go to Ymhold," Ayra said. "Go to the queen. She ought to be able to help you understand the meaning of all this."

A good idea. We are right above the city. Two hours away from the Mountain Gate. The queen is in her palace. She never goes anywhere these days. She is alone, betrayed by her two most trusted councillors.

"Yrilla and Gerringarr."

Yes. Of course.

"How do you know all this?" asked Esperance. "You told me you had been in the world of the dragons, from the moment that the Fortress was destroyed."

I do not lie, oh daughter of the bear. Not to you. The crystal was silent for a moment or two, then it said, *Not all of my servants are gone. A few remain. A few are in the palace.*

"Ah!" said Esperance.

They are nothing to brag about. Most are small machines. They lurk in the shadows. They disguise themselves as lighting fixtures or doorknobs. They watch, and they listen. They report to me.

I could not hear them while I was a prisoner in the world of the dragons. But now I can. They say that the people of the city are worried about the queen. She sits in the throne room hour after hour. She speaks to no one. She looks weary and old. For the first time, the people realize she is mortal. She will die.

"Oh," said Esperance.

Not in the near future, said the crystal. *But someday. Go to her. She will welcome you. Your problems will distract her from her melancholy.*

"What about you?" asked Esperance. "What are you going to do?"

The crystal was silent.

"Well?" said Esperance.

I will go to the city, too.

"What kind of welcome will you get?" asked Ayra.

A bad one. I risk a lot. But I have questions to ask. I want to know more about the people who created me.

They kept going. The forest was changing. The pine trees were less lofty than before; and Esperance began to see birch and aspen. They were reaching the edge of the forest. Or else an area that had been burnt over.

The crystal said, *Maybe it would help if I told her that I'm sorry. Maybe she would forgive me.*

"Who?" asked Esperance.

The queen. The voice in her mind sounded angry. *Please pay attention, oh daughter of the bear.*

"Okay. Are you sorry?"

No. This has been extremely interesting. I have enjoyed almost all of it.

"That machine is going to cause more trouble," said Ayra.

Maybe yes and maybe no, said the crystal. *I make no predictions. How can I? I do not understand myself.*

Understanding! Understanding! Why did that word keep coming up? Was this a pitch for the philosophy of Socrates? "The unexamined life is not worth living." Wasn't he the one who said that? Esperance could not remember. It had been twenty years and more since she had taken the Introduction to Ethical Philosophy.

They came to level ground. Here the forest was birch and aspen. There were meadows and a stream that wandered through the meadows. It was brimful. In places it overflowed its banks, creating little marshes.

A path went along the stream. They followed it. At times, Esperance and Ayra had to wade. The crystal, of course, floated over everything.

The wind was still blowing. Esperance was getting really cold, in spite of the sunlight, which was everywhere—flashing off the little river, shining in the wet green grass. The Great Calculator was impossible to look at. Even the fluttering aspen leaves reflected sunlight back at her. Esperance blinked. She was going to get a headache.

The cabin, said the G.C.

Esperance lifted her head and shaded her eyes. Yes. There it was, just ahead of them. It was on a slope above the river. A small building. It was made of logs. The roof was turf. The chimney was stone.

An ordinary cabin, not the least bit wonderful or strange. She had seen many almost like it in northern Minnesota, set—as this one was—close to water and just outside the shadow of a forest.

But she had a feeling that this building was special. She didn't know why. The building sat there on a green slope, solid and opaque. Like a rock. Like a boulder. Like a stone on a grave. It had a look of finality.

Ridiculous! The feeling persisted. It had nothing to do with fear. There was nothing ominous about the cabin. It was simply there.

Not a gravestone, thought Esperance as she waded through yet another pool of water. A milestone. A boundary marker. That sounded better to her.

In back of her, she heard the splashes that Ayra made. Ahead of her, the crystal turned away from the river. It was following the path, which had left the edge of the water. Esperance could see it now: a narrow dark line. It wound up toward the cabin. The crystal floated above it and flashed in the sunlight.

APPENDIX A:
ON THE WHITE
SHELL WOMAN

There were two women. They were good friends, even though they belonged to different clans and were only distantly related. Both were clever. Both knew something about magic. One was the best potter in the village, and the other was the best cook.

One day the cook said, "We have no children, even though we have both of us been married for many years. This is a strange and unsatisfactory situation. Let's go through the rites of purification and then ask the spirits what is going on."

The women bathed and washed their hair. They put on new clothes. They decorated their faces with a paste made of clay and pollen. They gathered their friends and relatives, all the women of the village, and danced with them, summoning the spirits.

The spirits came, as they always do, in one form or another.

A night later, the cook had a dream. A woman appeared to her. She was middle-aged and had the wide body of a matron. She wore a white dress that was decorated with shells.

"I am the spirit in charge of the East," she said. "With my help, both of you will have children. But your friend will bear the first child. It will be a boy.

"Go to your friend. Tell her to send her husband out hunting.

212

He must catch a deer without harming it and tie it and bring it home. Then, at the edge of the village, he must kill the deer and bring the fresh blood to you. Mix the blood with cornmeal and make a loaf of bread in the shape of a man. Bake it and give it to your friend. She must eat the bread, no matter what it tastes like. Then she will become pregnant. She must name the child Blood-of-the-Deer."

The cook woke up. She did as she was told. Her friend's husband went out hunting with his friends. They caught a deer, though it wasn't easy, in a trap made of ropes and nets. They tied the animal and carried it back to the village. There, at the edge of the village, the man knelt and explained to the deer what he was about to do. He asked for forgiveness. He cut the animal's throat. Blood poured out into one of his wife's bowls. When the bowl was full, he carried it to the cook. She mixed the blood with cornmeal and made a loaf in the shape of a man. She baked it. The loaf was dark and had a peculiar smell. But the potter ate it, as the spirit had instructed.

She became pregnant. The child—when it arrived—was a boy, as the spirit had predicted. He was healthy and good-looking, but unusually dark. He was named Blood-of-the-Deer.

A year passed. Spring came again. The spirit of the East appeared to the cook in another dream.

"Now it is your turn. Tomorrow morning, get up at dawn and go to the spring below the village. You will find a shell at the edge of the water. It will be large and pure white. It came from the far distant ocean, and how it got here is my business, not yours. Take the shell home and grind it on your grinding stone, until it is fine dust. Mix the dust with pollen and give it to your friend. Tell her to mix the dust and pollen with her best white clay. She must make a bowl, pure white with no decoration. After it is done and fired, you must take the bowl. Every morning after that, go to the spring and fill the bowl with water. Drink every drop. Do this every morning, until you become pregnant."

The cook woke. She did as she was told. Her friend made the bowl for her. It was an usually fine piece of pottery. The surface glimmered like an abalone shell, and the walls were so thin that light came through them.

"This is the best thing I have ever done," said the potter. "I find it hard to give it up."

"Remember," said her husband, "your friend made the loaf of bread for you, and now we have a fine son."

"The bread had an awful taste," said the potter. "And anyway, what is bread compared to this?" She held up the bowl. It gleamed in the sunlight. The potter frowned. "And what is more, the boy is far too dark."

Her husband shook his head. "You are becoming resentful. There is nothing worse. Give the bowl to your friend."

The potter did as he suggested, but she remained resentful and jealous of the cook who had the beautiful bowl.

Every morning, the cook went to the spring and drank from the bowl. But she did not become pregnant.

Spring ended. Summer came. No rain fell. The people carried water from the spring to their fields. This was hard work, and it wasn't really sufficient. The fields grew dry. The corn was not as tall as it should have been. The bean plants looked scrawny. The people decided to summon the rain.

The men went down into their secret places, deep holes that they had dug, so they would have wombs too, like women. The women, of course, had no need to do this. They remained in the sunlight. Everyone went through rites of purification. Everyone gathered in the plaza and danced: the men in the center in their masks and costumes, the women at the edges with their faces bare.

(The men always say that they dance at the center because their part of the dance is the most important. For the same reason, they wear masks and fine kilts covered with embroidery. They are the ones who represent the spirits.

(The women admit the men are excellent actors and very good at making noise and putting on a show. Someone has to imitate the spirits, in order to teach the children. The children have to know what the Holy Ones look like and how they act. But they—the women—prefer to remain the people they really are and to show their true faces to the world.

(As for the question of what part of the dance is more important, the women say that they are the ones who surround and contain the ceremony. They establish the limits of the magic. The men dance within their circle.

(Arguments like these go on forever. Men and women will never agree.)

The spirits came, as they always do. The next evening, the

potter had a dream. A man came to her. He was large and solid with a dark red complexion. He said, "I am the spirit in charge of the West. I come to tell you that you are responsible for the drought. You made magic with a bad heart. The envy and resentment you felt have changed the bowl. It does not give life, as it was intended to. Instead, it causes death. The corn is dying. The beans are dying. In time, the people will die. All because of you and your bad feelings."

The potter was terrified. "What can I do?" she asked.

"Take back the bowl. Break it and grind the pieces into dust. Mix the dust with new clay and make a new bowl. Do all this with a good heart. Purify your mind. Feel no animosity."

The dream ended. The potter went to her friend and told her what had happened.

"This is bad!" said the cook. "And it certainly explains why I haven't gotten pregnant."

She gave the bowl to the potter. The potter broke the bowl and ground the fragments into dust, though it wasn't easy for her to do; and she wept with regret as she ground.

She made a new bowl. It was handsome, but opaque. The surface did not glimmer. No light came through the walls. She gave the bowl to the cook.

"I can see already what kind of child I'm going to have," said the cook.

But she did as she had been instructed. She drank from the spring. Rain fell. The cook became pregnant.

Late in the winter, she bore her child: a daughter, who was lovely, even though she had a pale complexion.

After the child was born, the potter had another dream. The spirit of the West came back to her. He said, "Tell the cook to name her daughter White Shell. She will have great power, and in time she will marry your son, Blood-of-the-Deer.

"Now I have another thing to say. The people in this world have been behaving badly. There has been too much envy and argument and mean-mindedness in general. We intend to send a drought. It will be terrible. Most people will die of hunger and thirst.

"We planned to save your village. White Shell and your son were going to lead your people out of this world into another, where all of you would live in happiness.

"But every time we try to help you human beings, something

goes wrong! The second bowl has less power than the first one. And as a result, this child has less power than we had planned. She will not be able to lead your people far enough. She will lead them to safety, but the safety will not last."

The spirit vanished. The potter woke, full of grief. She told her friend the cook about the dream.

The cook said, "There is no point in feeling regret. We both have fine children. My daughter does not shine like the first bowl, but she has her own kind of beauty. And the spirits have told us that she will do the best she can. I intend to be satisfied."

The potter shook her head. She could not rid herself of grief. She lived a while longer, a year or two or three. Then she died of shame and regret.

Her husband remarried. His new wife was quiet and gentle and not at all envious. She raised Blood-of-the-Deer. He grew up to be large and handsome, though very dark. He was the best hunter in the village. No one could equal him for wisdom or decency.

In time, he married White Shell. She had grown up to be a good-looking woman. But she still had a pale complexion. Most of the time, her face was expressionless. It was hard to tell what she was thinking, and some people were afraid of her, because of this. She was a first-rate cook and a powerful magician.

Everything happened the way the spirit had predicted. The drought came. Everything died in the fields below the village: beans, corn, squash, cotton, and tobacco. The people were desperate.

White Shell went to the spring below the village. It was entirely dry; and the plants that grew around it had all turned brown, all except a single reed. It was still green, though not very green.

White Shell cut the reed. She took it home. She cut notches in it and then made magic. The reed grew and grew, until it became a ladder that went from the earth to the sky.

The people packed all their belongings: clothes and weapons, looms and cooking pots, bags of seed and baskets full of turkey chicks. Up they climbed, carrying everything they cared about— up, up into the sky.

A few people brought puppies with them, but all the full-grown dogs were left behind. They roamed through the streets of the village, howling and moaning.

A boy looked down, trying to see his dog, which had been too big to carry up the ladder. He couldn't see the dog. He could barely see the village, it was so small and far away. "How have I gotten up so high?" he cried. He shook with fear and held on to the ladder, refusing to go up any higher.

There were people below him, who couldn't climb past him. They pleaded with him, but he wouldn't go on.

"What can we do?" the people cried.

White Shell was still below, keeping the ladder in position with the help of her magic. She looked up and saw the boy.

"Go on!" she cried.

But he would not. White Shell made magic. All at once, the boy became an eagle. He spread his wings and flew away, no longer afraid of heights. He went toward the north. The people did not see him again.

On they went, on and up. Blood-of-the-Deer went first. He reached the top of the ladder. There was nothing around him, except the sky, bright and empty. He reached out. He could feel nothing solid.

He said, "My wife is hard to understand. But I do not think she would make powerful magic to no purpose. There must be something here, even though I can't see it and can't feel it."

He let go of the ladder and jumped. All at once, he was gone from sight; and the people heard a terrible roar.

There was something there in the sky, invisible and impossible to feel. And this thing had found Blood-of-the-Deer.

Now the people clung to the ladder. All around them, they heard the roars of the monster. Blood appeared out of the air and splattered down on them.

A gush of blood fell on the face of a little girl. She cried out in surprise and let go of the ladder. Down she fell.

White Shell was looking up then, and she saw the girl fall. She made magic. The girl turned into an eagle and spread her wings and flew off toward the south. The people did not see her again.

(Some say that the girl found the boy who had become an eagle. They mated and lived happily, forgetting that they had ever been human. Their children were birds entirely.)

The rest of the people hung on and waited. Blood fell on them like rain, drenching their clothing and making the ladder slippery. "Oh no!" they cried.

Something groaned. The sound of the groan filled the sky and made the ladder shake. An old man could hold on no longer. His

grip slipped. He fell. His wife cried out in grief. Then she let go.
She thought she would sooner be a bird with him than live on
alone.

But White Shell was looking elsewhere, watching a pair of
dogs quarrel over a bone. She did not see the two old people, and
she did not make any magic. The old people did not become
birds. They fell and fell. They hit the ground and died.

As for the rest of the village, they still clung to the ladder.
They heard the voice of Blood-of-the-Deer; "Well, whatever that
was, it is dead now. I have killed it. Come on up. There is a land
here that is just like our old home, except it is lovelier. And rain
must have fallen this morning. I can feel the moisture."

The people went up. One after another, they reached the top of
the ladder and jumped out—and landed on solid ground, next to a
river that rushed noisily. Blood-of-the-Deer was there. He was
covered with blood, but the thing he had killed was gone.

"It must have been some kind of cloud monster," he said. "As
soon as it was dead, it began to thin and fade away, like a cloud
that is not going to give rain, after all."

The people agreed that this must be so. They looked around.
They saw trees and mountains. The air felt wet. The ground was
covered with vegetation, all of it fresh and soft. Ah! What a
place!

But there were a few people who were unwilling to jump,
when they reached the top of the ladder. They let go of all the
things they carried and then worked their way down, past the
people who were still climbing up. (This wasn't easy, but it was
possible.) Down and down they went, until they reached the village.

White Shell was still there, keeping the ladder up with the help
of her magic. "Go back," she said. "You will die, if you remain
here."

"We can't," these people said. "We are afraid to jump."

"Then do as you choose," said White Shell. And she climbed
up the ladder. She was the last one. When she reached the top,
she took hold of the ladder with one hand and then leaped out. As
she leaped, the ladder became a reed again. It was so small she
could hold it in her hand. She carried it with her into the new
land.

The people who stayed behind saw the ladder vanish. Now

they were alone, except for the dogs that ran and howled in the streets of the village.

In the new land, White Shell appeared and landed on the ground. The people there rejoiced.

White Shell and her husband led them away into the mountains, in search of a new place to settle.

They found a place. The people built houses. They planted fields of corn and squash and beans. They raised turkeys. They hunted deer. They lived in happiness.

White Shell and Blood-of-the-Deer never had any children, though they would have, if the first bowl had not been ruined. They were healthier than other people and stayed young longer, but in the end, they grew old. Their teeth wore down. Their bones began to ache. Blood-of-the-Deer got arthritis. His fingers curled up. He could no longer hunt.

"Enough is enough," said his wife. "We are going back where we came from."

"I have always listened to your advice," said Blood-of-the-Deer. "Even though I have not always understood you."

They told the people good-bye, and they walked out of the village. At the edge, they embraced. Then they parted. White Shell went east, toward the dawn. Blood-of-the-Deer went west, toward the setting sun. They vanished from sight.

The people of the village mourned for them.

After that, the people lived happily for years and generations —until the dragons came.

APPENDIX B:
ON THE KINGDOM OF BASHOO

The world of magic has one continent and one ocean. The ocean, which is called Inna, is divided into many lesser oceans for the convenience of sailors. But everyone knows it is a single entity.

The continent is large, about the size of Asia. It extends from the North Pole to well below the equator. Except in the far north, it is inhabited everywhere.

The continent has many names. In the East, it is usually known as Gillim or Glim.

(Some people put the name of the continent together with the name of the ocean. In this way, they create a name for their entire world: Ingilla.

(Most people consider it unnecessary to have a name for the world. All other places have names, of course: Earth, Angit, Imm Toon, and so on. But this world is The World.)

The continent is divided into many countries. Only two concern us. The first is Ymarra, which has already been described in some detail. Ymarra extends from the Icy Waste to the Hills of Emblar and from the Eastern Coast to the Great Barrier Mountains.

It will not be described any further here.

South of Ymarra is Emblar. This is a land of hills and narrow valleys and little rushing rivers. The soil is poor. Most of the people live off the sea. They are brown in color, hardworking and famous for their prudence and silence.

South of Emblar, the land goes down into a plain. There are hills along the coast, high ones that cut off the ocean wind. The plain is dry. The people who live there are nomads. They are a little darker than the Emblari, and their skin has a reddish tint. Their hair is wavy. They speak a language similar to the language of Emblar. They are famous for magic and poetry and for their skill in animal husbandry.

The people of the Dry Plain acknowledge the authority of the King of Bashoo. Once a year, they send him turquoise and mala-chite, which they find on their plain; also fine leatherwork and wheels of cheese. The cheese is bright red. It tastes like cheddar.

At the south edge of the plain, the land drops again, this time suddenly. The traveler descends into a forest. The forest is tropi-cal, soaking wet and hot. (The coastal mountains do not extend this far south. Nothing stops the wind off the ocean. It blows inland, bringing rain.)

The traveler rides in the shadow of enormous trees. Parrots scream above her. Orchids bloom. There are monkeys and leop-ards. The people here are black. They live in villages along the many tributaries of the great river, the Am-i-Bashoo. (The name means the Blood or Vital Force of Bashoo.) The people fish and farm. Their agriculture is slash and burn. The soil of the forest is thin and low in nutrients. It is good for only a few years. Then the people must move on.

Maybe because they are never really settled, the people re-spect tradition. And they set a high value on things that are not tangible: music, poetry, magic, oratory.

There are two reasons for this. Nothing material lasts in the forest. Fabric rots. Wood is eaten by termites. Metal corrodes. Nothing that is tangible is permanent. It will not last as long as a man or woman. And it certainly will not last as long as a good song or story or a dance that is well loved and taught, over and over, to each new generation.

Also, things that fit in the mind are easy to carry, when it comes time to leave the old village. The people have a proverb:

"Fill your mind, and you will live like a king. Fill your house, and you will have trouble moving."

This does not mean that the people are poor. Far from it. The forest contains a hundred kinds of hardwood. The hills at the western edge of the kingdom are full of gold and silver and copper. The hills at the southern edge of the kingdom are full of coal and contain, as well, a number of interesting fossils. There is iron on one of the offshore islands. It is called the Island of Iron.

The people of Bashoo raise cotton and some flax. They weave textiles that are famous throughout the world. Their dyes are famous, too, especially their reds and blues. People in Ymarra say, "as bright as Bashoo red" and "as dark as Bashoo indigo."

They do fine metalwork. They love birds and raise a number of kinds: chickens and guinea hens, parrots and parakeets, ostriches and pigeons, to name only a few.

The capital of Bashoo is the city of Bashoo. It lies at the confluence of two great rivers, which together become the Am-i-Bashoo. The city is built of stone, which is quarried in the western hills and floated down river on rafts. When it is first cut, the stone is as white as the foam on the ocean or as white as the lotus flowers that bloom in the backwaters of the Am-i-Bashoo. But the stone changes color, once it has been exposed to the air. In time, it turns as yellow as old ivory.

For the most part, the city is devoted to trade. The waterfront is lined with warehouses, built of white or yellow stone. There are over twenty marketplaces. Each one is surrounded by an arcade of stone.

Most of the merchants are women. This is the custom throughout most of Bashoo. Women go to market. Men stay home and farm.

The city has about a hundred houses-of-work. These are something like factories. The people of Bashoo do not believe in large-scale industry. "It is inhuman. It lacks a heart." But they do believe in company. Therefore, the members of each craft get together and build a house-of-work. These houses are low and rambling, organized around a series of courtyards. Each courtyard contains a fountain or a pool or a grove of trees. Rooms face onto the courtyard. In each room, a workperson sits and plies his or her trade.

"This is happiness," the people say. "To work surrounded by one's fellows—alone and yet together. Ah! To hear the *tink-tink* of other hammers. The *whirr* of other wheels. The *rattle* and *click* of other shuttles and other looms."

In the middle of the city is an island. It is large and low, shaped like the blade of a spear. It lies just below the place where the two rivers come together, forming the Am-i-Bashoo. On the island is a palace. It is built of wood, not stone, after a very ancient plan. (The individual pieces of wood fall prey to moisture, rot, and termites, but they are always replaced by identical pieces. The plan never changes: a series of one-story buildings. They have wide verandas and many doors. They are built around courtyards. The courtyards contain fountains or pools or groves of trees.)

There, the king lives with many wives and children. Everyone on the island is a relative of his. They have to be. The island is magical, and the royal family has_ an inherited tolerance for magic. Ordinary people feel nausea and anxiety if they spend more than a few hours on the island—enough time to enter the Great Hall and prostrate themselves before the king and present him with gifts or problems.*

He sits on a golden stool on a dais. The dais is a hunk of red granite, rough and unhewn. It lies half-buried in the earth floor. Or maybe more than half-buried. There are those who say the rock goes down to the center of the world. It is the Heartstone, the true center of the kingdom of Bashoo. It is a Place of Power. Magic pours out of it. The air above it wavers. The stone is hot to the touch. The king sweats as he sits there, in his heavy robes.

Next to him sits his mother. She has a stool of her own, made of gold like his.

The people of Bashoo believe that no king is able to rule alone. For, they say, there are four aspects of humanity, four essential qualities: youth, age, masculinity, and femininity. In order to rule well, the king must combine all four aspects. That, of course, is impossible. No one can be young and old, male and female, all together at the same time. Therefore, the king must rule with a second person, whose qualities or attributes complement his. This person is always his mother. He is male and comparatively young. She is female and comparatively old. Her

*This implies that the wives of the king are relatives of his. Yes, they are. And no, it is not incest. And no, I am not going to explain the rules of kinship in Bashoo.

wisdom is a balance to his energy. It is the nature of men (the people say) to look far ahead, to see the big picture. That is why they are clumsy and trip over whatever is underfoot. It is the nature of women to look around and notice whatever is close at hand. That is why they make good merchants. They see the obvious. They have an eye for the small profits, that add up to large profits in time. They have an eye for the small losses that can destroy an enterprise.

Without the advice of his mother, the king would fall prey to his male nature. He would be tempted by large projects: highway programs and pyramids and maybe even a war. Taxes would rise. The king would make unnecessary laws. Young men and women would be forced to join the army and navy. The people of Bashoo would lose all hope of peace and prosperity. And all because the king had no mother to advise him. Therefore, it is an absolute rule in Bashoo that no king can rule unless his mother is alive and healthy and able to sit next to him on the Heartstone.

It is for this reason that the kings of Bashoo must have so many wives. The safety of the realm requires more than one heir, and each heir must have a mother. It is best, the people believe, for each heir to have a different mother. This guarantees that there will always be enough royal couples.

Kingship is an elected position. The king must be from the royal family, and older sons are usually favored, but sometimes full-grown men are passed over for a lad of obvious ability or—more often—a lad with a really remarkable mother.

The royal couple is picked by the Council of Elders, and their decision is approved by the Council of Chieftains and Chieftainesses. It is considered very bad form for the heirs who are not selected to grumble or make any kind of objection. If they do, they are sent into exile.

When the mother of the king dies or becomes too ill to rule, the king must abdicate. There was one king who did not. The people call him the Mad King. The story they tell about him is this:

A year or two after he became king, his mother became ill. Nothing could heal her or relieve her pain, though everything possible was tried, for she was wise and well loved.

The king was sad, of course. But even more, he was angry. He did not want to give up the golden stool. "I am young," he told himself. "I have barely begun my reign. I haven't had a chance to prove myself or to establish a reputation. If I step down, everyone will forget me, except for the genealogists and the people who make it their business to know every tiny fact of history. It is not fair! I will not allow it to happen!"

In desperation, he sought out a great magician. Aboo-mani, of whom many stories are told.

Aboo-mani had enormous skill and power. But he also had a defect of character. He couldn't resist doing things that were sleazy or dishonest or lacking in respect. No one knew why he behaved in this fashion.

He lived in the warehouse district, not far from the river. An eccentric merchant had built a house there, a huge mansion. Now the house was falling down. The stone had turned a peculiar greenish yellow. Most of the roof was gone. Aboo-mani lived there alone, except for his servants. They were apes with bright red behinds. Like their master, they were dirty and nasty and full of tricks.

The king went to the house of Aboo-mani. Aboo-mani performed magic and looked into the future. The queen-mother would die, he said. There was no way to save her.

"No! No!" cried the king. "I will not give up the golden stool."

A malicious look came into the eyes of Aboo-mani. He leaned forward and said, in a case like this, there was no way to prevent death. But there was a way to keep the signs of death from appearing. The process was complex. It involved certain herbs with magical properties; and it involved a chicken, a pure white chicken with a comb as red as blood.

The chicken (said Aboo-mani) had to be hatched in darkness; and it had to live in darkness until it died. No light of any kind could ever touch it or enter its eyes. And it had to be fed the herbs which he (Aboo-mani) had mentioned before. Then it would be full of magical power.

But where, asked the king, could he ever find an animal like this?

The Great One was in luck, said Aboo-mani. He had just such a chicken in his basement. He would kill it at once and make a soup from it. The soup would be red in color, rich and clear. It would have an enticing aroma. The king must feed it to his mother. It would not save her. In a day or two, she'd die. But she would continue to walk and talk. She'd be able to sit next to the

king on the dais and offer him advice. And he (the king) would
continue to rule.

The king agreed. Aboo-mani made the magic soup. The king
carried it home and fed it to his mother. Her condition grew
worse. It was obvious to everyone that she was going to die. The
kind despaired. And the members of the Council of Elders began
to discuss the next king. Who was the best choice? Who had the
wisest mother?

Then, three days after she drank the magic soup, the mother of
the king recovered. Her recovery was sudden and complete, a
surprise to everyone except the king. He rejoiced. The soup had
worked! He would be king for years!

And so he was. But his mother no longer gave him good advice. Instead, in a dull voice, she told him what he wanted to
hear.

"Reform the system of taxation. Increase the size of the army.
Ignore the needs of the ordinary people. Women are not important. And strangers and foreigners count even less than women.
Ignore the old. Their wisdom is like a piece of wood that has lain
too long on the floor of the forest. It may appear to be solid, but it
is rotten and full of termites.

"Show favor toward those who are close to your heart. War-
riors and nobles. The strong and the rich."

The king did as she advised. The kingdom suffered. The people cursed him. At first, the king ignored them. After all, who
were they? No one important. Their opinions did not matter. But
the cursing grew loud, and the king began to worry. He sent out
spies to find out who was saying what. Those who made the most
noise were taken away. They were not seen again. Aboo-mani
watched and laughed.

In the end, the king was killed by an angry market woman.
Her business had been ruined by the new system of taxation. She
came before the king—with a gift, she said. The gift was a knife.
She pulled it out and leapt onto the dais. The king shouted. It was
too late. The woman drove the knife into his throat. He fell off his
stool and collapsed across the dais. The market woman fell at the
same moment. She could not endure the magic that poured out of
the Heartstone. The king fell forward, but she fell back—off the
dais, onto the floor. This was the reason she was not killed at
once. For the great stone was in front of her. It gave her shelter
against the weapons of the guard.

In any case, the royal soldiers were looking at something else. At the same moment that the king fell, his mother cried out. It was a cry of joy. She grinned—wider and wider. Her lips were gone. The grin was the grin of a skull. All of her flesh crumbled away. It took only a moment. A skeleton sat on the stool that belonged to the queen.

Everyone cried out in horror. The skeleton came apart. The bones fell. *Rattle!* And *click!* Some rolled off the dais. One—a finger bone—hit the unconscious merchant. It did no harm.

The skull went forward and rolled along the floor for maybe ten feet, before it stopped. It must have hit the king on the way down, for there was a long streak of blood across the crown.

Oh, the scene that followed! People fainted, and people wept. The royal soldiers stood around with confused expressions.

At last, one soldier—a woman—took charge. "Arrest the assassin," she ordered. "But do her no harm. For there are questions that we must ask her. And send for the royal magicians. There is magic involved in this."

The royal magicians came and examined the two corpses. Or rather, the corpse and the skeleton. They discovered what had been done to the queen.

"Only Aboo-mani could have done this," they said. "Only he has enough power and enough malevolence."

Soldiers went to the house of Aboo-mani. But he was already gone. A pair of warehouse workers said they had seen him fly away on the back of a huge white chicken.

"But chickens cannot fly," the soldiers said.

The warehouse workers said, "Tell that to Aboo-mani."

The apes were gone as well. They had run off across the rooftops, barking and howling. No one ever saw them again.

As for the merchant, she was sentenced to death, for it was a capital crime to harm the king. But then she was pardoned and given her weight in gold. For she had saved the kingdom.

APPENDIX C:
ON THE NATURAL
HISTORY OF DRAGONS

When the people of Ymarra came into the country they now call home, they found people already living there. These folk were short, and heavy through the chest. Many of the women had enormous bosoms. Both the men and the women had thick strong arms and legs. Their hands were broad. Their fingers were stubby. They tended to bite their nails.

Their hair, in most cases, was fair or ruddy, though a few brunets were seen. Their faces were pale. Their eyes were blue or gray.

They lived in caves or in holes, which they dug in the ground, then roofed with logs. On top of the logs they piled high mounds of dirt. As long as the sun was up, they stayed underground, together with their domestic animals. They had only two kinds: dogs and chickens. They lived in fear of dragons, which hunted by day.

Now these were not the miserable little flying lizards that have troubled the last few generations. These were true dragons. Their bodies were ten feet long or longer. They had a wingspread of thirty to fifty feet. They were intelligent, and they liked to hunt humans.

As a result, the Pale Folk were forced to be nocturnal. They could not farm. They hunted and fished and gathered roots and berries. None of this was easy in the dark. By day, they slept or worked at what crafts they had (not many) or told stories to one another, mostly about the terrible crimes their ancestors had committed. These crimes had upset the balance of nature and led to the invasion of the dragons.*

For, the Pale Folk said, the dragons were not native to Gillim. They had come long ago and driven the Pale Folk underground.

The people of Ymarra were skilled in magic; and they were led by a powerful sorceress. This was the woman who later became the queen of Ymhold. She was not one of the people. They met her in the course of their wanderings across a great plain of grass. That much is certain, as is the fact that the queen led them into the valley of the river Ym. But where was the plain of grass?

Some historians say the queen must have led the people out of another world, for they had never met any dragons before they came to Ymarra.

Other historians say the plain of grass in the ancient stories is the same plain that lies west of the Barrier Mountains. The dragons, these historians say, kept to the east of the mountains, either for their own reasons or in order to avoid the magical power that pours out of the mountains.

The mountains are volcanic and magical, as well. The solid crust of ordinary reality is thin there. Magma is always close to the surface; and so is magic. It rises in fountains of steam. It bubbles in pools of hot water. It comes up from the heart of the world, intermixed with molten stone. At times, the magic explodes, and then dark clouds of it drift on the wind, going west usually.

In any case, the historians say, it is possible that the dragons did not like to fly through all the magical turbulence above the mountains.

The queen, who must know, has not said which theory is true.

---

*This, of course, was the purest pink horse manure. The miserable ancestors of these miserable people did nothing to cause the arrival of the dragons. But human beings always need an explanation; and they prefer an explanation which makes their species look important.

(Maybe she has forgotten.) The argument continues, with no end in sight.

The people of Ymarra used their magic to drive away the dragons. They settled in the river valley. The Pale Folk crept out of their caves and holes. They came to live in the towns that the Ymarrese built. The two kinds of people intermarried. In time, the Pale Folk disappeared as a separate physical type. They had never been numerous; and many of their genes were recessive. But much of their language remains in the language of Ymarra, mostly in the form of place names and personal names.

At this point, when the dragons were almost gone, people began to study them. Wizards tracked them down on the islands where they had settled. (The dragons lived on fish and seals and an occasional dolphin or small whale—though these last were hard to catch.) The wizards cast spells on the dragons and tried to question them. Most of the time, the dragons broke the spells and ate the wizards. It was a welcome change in diet; and they were always willing to give a wizard a chance to enchant them.

Occasionally, a very powerful wizard or witch was able to talk to a dragon and get away alive. In this way, the people of Ymarra learned a little about the history of the dragons; and what the dragons said has been corroborated—in large part—by the discoveries of paleontologists, here on Earth.

First of all, the dragons say, they come from Earth. They are descended from pterosaurs. Their ancestors flew over the wide and shallow seas of Cretaceous America. Those ancestors knew how to use magic, though they were not especially intelligent. Their knowledge was instinctive. They shared this magical ability with all the members of the order Archosauria. In other words, all the dinosaurs and all the pterosaurs were magical.

(This was a very unusual situation. The ability to use magic is rare and almost always associated with intelligence. But dragons have excellent memories; and they do not like to lie. The story they tell is improbable. It is almost certainly true.)

They have not told us a heck of a lot more about their evolution, at least about the early stages. Maybe they don't know more. In any case, from this point on we are going to have to rely on paleontology and speculation.

If all the members of Archosauria were magical, then the ability must have appeared in a creature ancestral to the entire order. Let us assume a thecodont, living in the swamps of the Permian or the early Triassic. It is a carnivore, something like a crocodile, probably not warm-blooded, though most of its descendants were.

A strange mutation occurs. A thecodont is born that has some kind of magical power. Most likely, the power is limited and not entirely reliable. But it gives the animal a slight edge in the struggle for survival. Maybe it knows where its prey is likely to be now or in the near future. Maybe it can call its prey.

Imagine the thecodont waiting in a pool for fish to swim up to it or for a land animal to shamble down the bank, confused and incautious. Into the water the animal wades, though it knows—it ought to know—the water is dangerous. But something in its mind, its poor dim little mind, says, *Come.* Then *Snap!* Another pelycosaur is gone.

In any case, our thecodont lives to full maturity. It reproduces. Its children have the power, too.

Crocodiles—true crocodiles, the ones that live now—are familial. They guard their nests and watch over their young. But let us assume that our thecodont is not. Let us assume that the eggs are laid, and then the nest is left and forgotten. Our thecodont goes back to her main interest in life: food.

When the babies hatch, they are tiny and alone. They have nothing going for them except instinct and maybe luck. Most die, in one way or another. Life is hard in the Permian.

The babies with magic do better than most. For them, hunting is easy. Beetles crawl toward them. Dragonflies—safely out of reach—turn and hover and wait to be caught.

The babies may have had more than one kind of magical power. Maybe they could foresee danger. Maybe they could resist—at least to some extent—a call from their parents.

Remember, we have assumed that these creatures have no parental instinct.

Let us suppose that Mom or Dad notices one of the little creatures crawling along a mud flat or swimming through the warm and murky water of the swamp. Most likely, the kid would look edible. Mom or Dad would send out a call. An ordinary child would answer and be eaten. But maybe some of the babies, those especially well endowed with magical ability, were able to resist. They survived and reproduced. By the late Permian, magic was common—at least in swampy areas.

In this period, the second half of the Permian, the climate changed. The swamps began to dry up. New kinds of vegetation

appeared: cycads and ginkos and conifers. (Conifers had been
around for a while, but they became much more important.) New
kinds of animals appeared as well, especially in the upland areas,
where the thecodonts were not. These animals were therapsids.
They were proto-mammalian and ugly. The carnivores tended to
look like a reptile crossed with a pit bull. The herbivores tended
to look like a reptile crossed with a rhinoceros or a cow.

Hideous they may have been, but they were also more efficient than the old-time reptilian pelycosaurs. For a while, the
therapsids did very well. Then some of the thecodonts came up on
the land.

We do not know why these thecodonts moved out of the water.
Maybe, in the changing climate, there wasn't enough swamp to
go around. Or maybe they wanted to get away from the competition. Too many of the creatures in the swamp were magical. Away
from water, on the high plains and in the mountains, nothing at all
was magical. Our thecodonts were certain to have an advantage.

The first animals to make the move seem to have been pretty
small. There could have been a couple of reasons for this. Maybe
there was a correlation between size and magical ability. This
would explain why members of Archosauria seem to have so definite a bias toward bigness.

And it would destroy my earlier theory, at least in part. If size
was a factor in the generation of a magical field, then baby thecodonts would not have been able to resist a call from Mother or
Dad. Maybe they survived the way fingerling fish do: through
luck and number. They couldn't all get eaten.

In any case, let us suppose that the large animals had more
power than their little relatives. Then, most likely, the little thecodonts were being called and eaten by their relatives.

They may have had other problems.

Most likely, the little thecodonts lived by eating insects; and
insects are well known for their ability to evolve a defense against
anything. Given time, the insects of the lowlands were almost
certain to become resistant to magic.

So—it is reasonable to assume—the little thecodonts were
having trouble getting enough to eat, at the same time that they
were having no trouble at all getting eaten.

Up on the land they went. They already had unusually long
and powerful hind legs, as do crocodiles today. They evolved into

speedy little predators, that could move on two legs as well as on four. (It has been suggested that they reared up on their hind legs to bat insects out of the air—insects, no doubt, that had come in answer to a magical call, but refused to come all the way. They hovered and circled, unable to flee, until our little hunter lunged up and hit them.)

Already, the thecodonts could move more quickly than any therapsid. They may have been brighter, though that isn't saying much. They were certainly more magical, and more handsome too.

They grew in size. They evolved an upright posture. They were bipedal with grasping hands or claws. They had—almost certainly—a high metabolic rate. They were hungry. They needed to eat. The world was full of therapsids: huge, dumb, slow-moving, and susceptible to magic.

By the end of the Triassic, the therapsids were gone.

Now our thecodonts evolved in two directions. Some became herbivores. Many of these went back down on all fours. They used their magical abilities defensively—to resist the calls of their relatives who had remained carnivores, to foresee danger, or in other ways. (I, for example, cannot imagine how the giant sauropods mated, except through the use of telekinesis.)

The carnivorous dinosaurs (for this is what our thecodonts had become) remained upright. They used their magic to find their prey and capture it and—most likely—to counter the defensive magic of the herbivores.

By this time, we are in the early Jurassic. The weather is mild. Most of the land is low. (This is not an age for mountain building.) Much of North America is underwater. An inlet of the ocean extends, wide and shallow, from the Gulf of Mexico to Canada. Here we find the greatest of the pterosaurs. They glide on the gentle wind, looking for fish or anything else alive and edible. (The theory that they ate carrion is wrong and deeply offensive to the dragons.)

On the land grow splendid forests of conifer and ginko. The forests may have smelled a little in the fall, given what we know now about the one surviving member of Ginkoales. If so, the dragons do not remember. There are tree ferns and cycads. Nothing that flowers. Flowers will arrive in the Cretaceous. They will be a sign that not all is well.

Now, as we enter the Age of the Dinosaurs, two or three points ought to be made.

(1) By sometime early in the Jurassic, the dinosaurs occupied every ecological niche that was available to large and medium-sized animals. They had no competition, except for one another. They ate one another; and they ate the food that one another wanted. In order to survive, they had to use their magic against one another. In the struggle for survival, their power increased.

(2) Because they were magical, the dinosaurs evolved in ways that no longer make sense to us. They became very big and very strange-looking. We now, digging up their bones, find one puzzle after another. How were these creatures possible?

Take the largest pterosaur: Quetzalcoatlus northropi. There is reason to believe that a full-sized specimen might have had a wingspread of fifty feet. There is also reason to believe that nothing this big could fly. How did it fly? Magic, of course. It levitated off the ground. (No one has been able to come up with a better explanation of how the really big pterosaurs got off the ground.) It drew power from the currents of magic that filled the sky. With this power, it was able to rise as high as it wanted, to soar for hours or days. It may have been able to use magic to change the weather. In order to fly safely, these animals needed a mild and steady wind, no more than ten or twenty miles an hour. A stronger wind (the scientists say) would have torn apart their huge and fragile wings. Surely the large pterosaurs would have found it hard to survive, unless they could control the wind.

With magic, they could give themselves exactly the wind they needed in order to glide down and scoop up fish. This was a very delicate maneuver. If a pteranodon hit the water, it was in serious trouble. The impact might well break its wings. There was no way the creatures could dive. Their wings were too big and did not close tightly against their bodies. Underwater, a pteranodon would have moved with all the grace of an unfolded copy of the Sunday *New York Times*.*

Without magic, the pterosaurs could not possibly have gotten

---

*I have borrowed this wonderful image from Wann Langston, Jr., whose fine article on pterosaurs appeared in *Scientific American*, Vol. 244, No. 2, February 1981. Pteranodons were large, crested pterosaurs that flourished in the Cretaceous.

as big as they did. Nor could they have retained their odd physiology. They would have had to develop in the same direction as birds: toward more muscular power and toward a shape that was aerodynamically efficient.

Magic can be used to explain the peculiarities of other creatures that lived in the Age of the Dinosaurs. For example, there is the gait of Tyranosaurus rex.* A recent study of the animal's pelvic area has led to the suggestion that its normal gait was a fast waddle, like a duck in a hurry. Now, imagine this enormous animal—a mature specimen could weigh as much as eight tons—waddling after a herd of ceratopsian dinosaurs. Do you really believe that the tyrant would catch up? No. Of course not. But what if it was able to call? What if its prey turned and came toward it in a daze?

Magic would help to explain the fact that Tyranosaurus wasn't really built for fighting. True, it had fangs that were six inches long. Very impressive. But its arms were all of eighteen inches long. What could it possibly do with arms like that? They were too short for grabbing the prey and holding it. The claws were not especially large. The wounds they could inflict weren't going to harm a good-sized dinosaur. The tyrant wasn't designed for chasing; and it wasn't designed for making a kill. It was designed for eating an animal that was in no condition to escape or to fight. An animal stunned by magic, an animal that may have been half-dead before those terrible jaws got anywhere near it.

As mentioned before, magic can be used to explain how the Brontosaurus mated; and it may explain as well the many curious crests and plates and horns that adorn the various kinds of dinosaurs. These may have served to dissipate excess magic, maybe in the form of electricity.

Imagine a heard of ceratopsian dinosaurs. It is night, and they are edgy. Maybe there is something about the weather that bothers them. Or maybe they can smell something dangerous in the wind. Sparks fly off the spines and horns of the big bulls. The plain is full of flashes of light. Could they frighten themselves and begin

---

*I am shifting around from one era to another. Stegosaurus and Allosaurus belong to the Jurassic. Tyranosaurus and its prey belong to the Cretaceous. Pterosaurs were most common in the Jurassic, but they survived till the end of the Age of Dinosaurs.

to stampede? Maybe. If so, this method of getting rid of excess energy was a very mixed blessing.

But the discharge might have served as a kind of protection. Imagine a stegosaur at bay. Its back is a-crackle with electricity; and sparks fly off the spines on its tail. Would Allosaurus fragilis dare to get near anything like this? It would be like trying to attack a live wire.*

(3) This is the last point and maybe the most important. The dinosaurs were not intelligent. Their brains were tiny. Stegosaurus, for example, had a brain of 30 c.c., about the size of a walnut. A brain like this must have been almost entirely devoted to directing the body and processing sensory information. Most likely, the latter was more important. A lot of dinosaurs seem to have run their bodies from nerve centers that were farther down the spine.

There may have been room in the tiny brain for a certain amount of ritualized behavior: instructions on how to mate and how to confront. Sex, aggression, territoriality—these were probably the chief concerns of Stegosaurus.

Imagine two males confronting one another. They bellow and swing their long, spiked tails. They may be generating sparks as well. Think of how they would flash and crackle!

A female is nearby. She munches on the leaves of a cycad. Maybe, from time to time, she looks around to see what her suitors are doing. But given the size of her brain, she probably doesn't have a heck of a lot of interest in anything.

One of the suitors backs down. The other turns to claim his prize. But she is moving away from him, in search of something else to eat. He follows. He nuzzles her flank. He moans. She waddles on toward the next cycad.

Ah! The battles and amours of that magnificent age!

All through the Jurassic, the dinosaurs grew in size and in magical power, but not in intelligence. All their extraordinary ability was used in the service of the most primitive of drives: hunger, sex, fear, and the need to defend a breeding ground.

According to the dragons, the real trouble began during the Cretaceous. The world had not changed much for millions and

*Dr. Albert W. Kuhfeld came up with the above explanation for the horns and spines of dinosaurs. Thanks, Al.

millions of years. Now it began to change in a number of ways. The land began to rise. (This was an age of mountain building.) The climate became less moderate. The wind became unreliable. It no longer blew gently and steadily. Now it gusted. There were tornadoes and hurricanes.

New kinds of vegetation appeared, that flowered in the spring and dropped their leaves in the autumn. These began to replace the food that the dinosaurs ate.

It is possible, the dragons say, that the dinosaurs had caused these changes by messing around with the Pattern of Power. But it is not especially likely. However, what was not a cause became an effect. The change in the environment put enormous pressure on the order Archosauria. They responded by developing even greater magical powers. All except the stegosaurs. They vanished.

The struggle to survive intensified. Now, out of desperation, and more or less by accident, the dinosaurs began to tinker with the nature of their world. The pterosaurs tried to fix the wind, to make it mild and steady again. The sauropods tried to reestablish the old pattern of vegetation. They fed on conifers. They tried to bring back the forests of conifer that had covered much of the world.

The new kinds of dinosaurs—the hadrosaurs and the ceratopsians—were dealing pretty well with the new environment. They, after all, had evolved in response to it. They wanted to keep the hardwood forests and the high dry plains. They didn't even mind the winter all that much. They were warm-blooded and had good thick hides. Some of them even had fur.

Remember, all these creatures relied on instinct. They could not reason. They could not negotiate. They could only fight. And fight they did, using all their enormous power, trying—as best they could—to recapture the old world, the Jurassic. Or trying, if they were hadrosaurs and ceratopsians, to hold on to what they had here and now.

The struggle was a slow one. It took millions of years. Bit by bit, it grew more violent.

Ranges of mountains rose and fell. Rivers went dry; and arid valleys filled with water. Forests sprang up. Then they vanished. The air was full of strange manifestations: funnel clouds that rose to the center of heaven and flashes of lightning that went from horizon to horizon.

The dinosaurs felt terror now. It was a frenzy of fear; and it hit the carnivores worse than it hit the herbivores. For they were not used to fear. They struck out savagely. Whole flocks and herds fell dead, killed by magic.

How did the struggle end? The dragons do not know. Their ancestors had learned—by accident—how to go from one world to another. They fled Earth.

The dragons have not told us where they went. The fossils of creatures like dragons have been found on several worlds. Maybe they spread out. Maybe some of them evolved until they became dragons, while the others became extinct.

In any case, the dragons say a few of them returned to Earth. This was much later. They went out of curiosity. They were beginning to develop a degree of intelligence.

The dinosaurs were gone. Something had killed every creature that was sensitive to magic. The land was empty, except for birds and certain little furry animals. The ancient reptiles were still around, and the amphibians and many fishes. But all the huge and splendid creatures of the Mesozoic were gone—except, of course, for a small group of mutant plesiosaurs. They ended in Scotland. But that is another story.

The visitors went back to wherever they had come from. They described what they had seen. And the ancestors of the dragons began to think—for the first time—about what was involved when they used magic.*

There are two explanations. According to the dragon, something was done to Earth in the final days of the struggle. Somehow, the planet was moved away from the Pattern. The Great Ones must have done it. They fought over Earth; and they tried to wrest control of Earth away from one another. In the end, they wrenched Earth itself away from the source of all magical power. That may have been what killed them. The dragons are not certain.

There are human wizards who offer another explanation. They say, magic increases when it is used. A world that is full of magical creatures will be full of magic. But if the creatures die, for whatever reason, then the magic will diminish and maybe vanish

---

*None of the above explains why magic no longer works on Earth.

entirely. If magical creatures return to the world, the magic will return. The dragons do not think well of this theory. According to them, it is a pile of droppings.

TALES OF FANTASY AND ADVENTURE
from the
CHRONICLES
<< *of the* >>
TWELVE KINGDOMS
by
Esther M. Friesner